The Theatre of Dreams

Rosie Travers

CROOKED CAT

Copyright © 2018 by Rosie Travers
Cover Photographer: Adobe Stock © Rosario Rizzo
Design: Soqoqo
Editor: Jeff Gardiner
All rights reserved.

No part of this book may be used or reproduced in any manner whatsoever without written permission of the author or Crooked Cat Books except for brief quotations used for promotion or in reviews. This is a work of fiction. Names, characters, and incidents are used fictitiously.

First Edition, Crooked Cat Books. 2018

Discover us online:
www.crookedcatbooks.com

Join us on facebook:
www.facebook.com/crookedcat

Tweet a photo of yourself holding
this book to **@crookedcatbooks**
and something nice will happen.

For Neil, Ellen and Zoe.

Acknowledgements

With thanks to all my friends who have supported me on my writing journey, but especially to my fellow scribblers, Ant, Grethe, Gill, Sally, Anne, Avril, Tania, Linda and Julie, and to dear Barbara, an inspirational teacher. To Carrie and Sandra who read very early drafts of this novel, and of course to my family, my star performers Ellen and Zoe, and my husband Neil – a man of great patience.

Also, a big thank you to the team at Crooked Cat for making my own personal dream come true.

About the Author

Rosie grew up in Southampton and loved escaping into a good book at very early age, devouring Enid Blyton as soon as she could read, and later anything she could lay her hands on after commencing her dream Saturday job in WH Smith. As a teenager she scribbled many short stories and novels, none of which she was ever brave enough to show anyone, before training to be a secretary and moving into the real world.

After several years juggling motherhood and a variety of jobs in local government, Rosie moved back out of the real world and into Southern California when her husband took up an overseas work assignment. With time on her hands, she started a blog about the perils of ex-pat life which rekindled that teenage desire to become a writer. On her return to the UK she took a creative writing course intending to turn her US adventures into a book, but instead re-discovered her talent for writing fiction. Another overseas posting to the Netherlands gave Rosie ample time to refine her craft, and following competition successes for flash-fiction and short stories, she decided to try writing a novel.

Rosie takes inspiration from the towns and landscape of her native south coast and enjoys writing heart-warming stories sprinkled with mystery, tragedy, comedy and a dash of romance.

The Theatre of Dreams

Prologue

Tara

I met the man who orchestrated my downfall in a Soho nightclub. He began his attack bearing a benign smile and two glasses of champagne. I wasn't a household name, so being recognised offstage was still a thrill and something of a novelty. It would never occur to me to ignore an approach from an admiring fan, not even when I was drowning my sorrows. I was a great believer in the old adage that it always paid to be nice to everyone you met on your way up the career ladder, as you never knew who you might encounter on the way down. I still had unfulfilled ambitions. He instantly endeared himself further by not just knowing my name, but listing several of my previous productions. His failure to mention my current musical extravaganza earned yet more Brownie points in his favour. It wasn't that I was ashamed of my role as a six foot avian puppet's tap-dancing sidekick, far from it, I was having a whale of a time, but the omission indicated he probably wasn't a family man with pre-school children. *Puffin the Pirate* was aimed predominantly at the under-fives.

Bea bellowed something into my ear about making a move, but Jamie, or at least I thought that was his name, suggested a spin on the dance floor instead.

Bea tugged at my arm but I shook her off. I had arrived on her doorstep a few days earlier with two suitcases and a tomato plant, the sum total of the personal possessions I'd salvaged from the breakdown of a four year relationship. I wasn't the first woman to be unseated by a nubile twenty-two year old. Hal Claydon wasn't the first forty-four year old theatre director to have a mid-life crisis. It was the fact that his crisis involved offering what I had thought was my guaranteed role in his next musical to the winner of a TV talent show that had been the deal-breaker. There was no loyalty in show business. Hal had broken my heart, while Georgie Gold and her pet Cockapoo had taken my place in his. It had been Bea's idea to hit the town, offering up a sparkling dress, matching clutch bag and six-inch stilettos like a modern-day fairy godmother. Now she was behaving like a party-pooper.

The night was still young and I was enjoying Jamie's attention. I waved Bea goodbye and took Jamie's offered hand.

'How could Hal Claydon prefer that bimbo Georgie Gold to a gorgeous woman like you?' Jamie shouted across the dance floor. 'There was no way she should have got the lead in *Rockabilly Rose*. You were made for that part. You must be feeling pretty disappointed right now.'

'You could say that,' I agreed, grateful to have found a sympathetic ear. Disappointed was the understatement of the year.

'Why don't we go somewhere quiet later then you can tell me all about it,' he suggested with a grin.

If the champagne had softened my defences, spirits from the mini-bar wiped out what little common sense I had left. I'd never had a one-night stand in my life. Waking up in an unfamiliar room beside a snoring stranger was not my idea of having a good time. It was mortifying enough that Jamie opened one bleary eye as I squeezed back into Bea's red mini-dress, intent on making a hasty exit; worse still that he reached for his wallet from the bedside table and insisted on handing me his business card. I thrust it into my borrowed bag without so much as a glance, determined to bin it at the first opportunity.

'Thanks for a great evening,' he murmured from the bed, 'we must do it again sometime.'

It was only much later that morning as I was preparing to head off to the theatre, desperately swigging coffee and hoping that my audience would be so busy stuffing themselves silly with pick'n'mix and popcorn buckets that they wouldn't notice if I missed a step or two, or probably several, during the two o'clock matinee performance, that I noticed Jamie's card amongst the detritus on Bea's dressing table.

It was such an innocuous looking card, plain back print, nothing flamboyant or fancy, yet it delivered the impact of a physical punch. *James Coulter, Entertainment Correspondent, Stargazer Media.* I hadn't just made the mistake of sleeping with a stranger, I'd had sex with a tabloid journalist. Through the thumping fug of my hangover, I realised it wasn't so much a question of what had I done, but what had I said. My fears were answered as I flipped the toxic rectangular reminder of my shame onto its reverse. Next to his mobile number, Jamie had scribbled my epitaph. *The cheque's in the post.*

Chapter One

Kitty

Kitty Keaton intended to be as formidable in death as she was in life. She was determined to defy mortality. Cheating had always come easily for Kitty; at the poker table, on her tax form, on at least two of her three husbands. The grim reaper was not going to get the better of her, or at least if not the grim reaper, then Robbie Mayhew. Right now, Kitty regarded them both in the same light.

'So that's the deal,' Robbie said, sitting back in the armchair and looking very smug. 'I don't think you'll get a better one.' He rested his hands on his belly. He was making Kitty's front room appear very small. The bungalow wasn't big enough for the both of them.

You're getting fat, Robbie, Kitty thought. Jez would never have let himself go like that. But Jez wasn't here. Robbie was a poor substitute.

'How's Lindy?' Kitty asked, ignoring the letter Robbie had placed on the coffee table in front of her. It was the second letter he'd bought to her in as many weeks.

'Lindy's fine. Enjoying the sunshine.' Robbie glanced at his watch. 'In fact, its five o'clock over there now, Kit. I expect she'll be having a G&T as we speak.'

Kitty glanced at the cocktail cabinet. She would have quite liked a G&T herself. 'I need to think it over,' she said. 'I can't make an instant decision.'

'Oh, come on now, you've had plenty of time to think about this.' Robbie prodded the letter with his forefinger, edging it towards her. 'We've been talking about this proposal from Coastline for months now. They won't hang around forever. Cut your losses and run. Sell the pavilion whilst you've got a buyer.'

'I don't feel ready yet,' Kitty said. She nestled further into her chair, and closed her eyes. Perhaps if she pretended to fall asleep Robbie would leave. Unfortunately he knew her too well. She recognised the increasing impatience in his voice.

'The council won't grant me another licence, if that's what you're hoping. They've made that perfectly clear. In any case, the residents of Hookes Bay don't want a nightclub anymore, Kit. The pavilion has had its day. They want this redevelopment.'

Did they really? Kitty wondered how many residents of Hookes Bay Robbie had canvassed. If the nightclub had had its day, it was entirely Robbie's fault. She had handed the management over to him and he had let her down. He'd let Jez down. The venue had become the archetypical den of iniquity. Robbie had turned a blind eye to the under-age drinking, the drug taking, the rowdy revellers loitering outside on a Friday and Saturday night. It was almost as if over the last few years he had been deliberately running the club into the ground. Kitty wasn't stupid.

Who were these Coastline Developments people who wanted to 'upgrade' the esplanade? Robbie's friends, that's who they were. Young Dominic from the junkyard had read through Coastline Developments' proposal word for word. She knew the name Grant Hastings. He'd been at school with Jez and Robbie; not one of their little gang, but he'd hovered in the background. He might well have started out as a taxi driver but he'd somehow worked his way up the property development ladder until he owned not just one, but several local building companies.

Kitty had no objection to the redevelopment of the old Carlisle Hotel site across the road from the pavilion. The Carlisle had been a derelict eyesore for many years. It wasn't even such a bad thing that Coastline wished to include a new pedestrian area and landscaping in their plans. However, that they wished their proposed new apartment block to have direct access to Hookes Bay's south-facing shingle beach, was an entirely different matter. The words *'over my dead body'* had never come to mind so readily.

It was not Kitty's problem that the pavilion stood in their way. Coastline should have done their homework. If they'd have talked to her, as opposed to Robbie, she would have told them straight away that the building was not for sale. They would have to do their landscaping around it. Coastline could build their apartment block, but the pavilion was staying put.

'Accept this offer and you can spend the rest of your days living in the lap of luxury,' Robbie had told her when the proposal from Coastline had first been mooted. 'It's perfect timing. Take the money and move into that brand new nursing home complex in Fareham. It's almost as if somebody up there is looking after you.'

Kitty knew nobody up there was looking after her. Robbie could spin any tale he liked but Kitty highly suspected if he secured this deal his friend Grant Hasting would reward him very generously. In addition, Robbie knew darn well that Kitty would never move into Fareham. She didn't need the money at this time in her life. The only person who'd profit from the sale of the pavilion would be Robbie Mayhew. Kitty had no-one else to leave her assets to.

Lack of foresight had never been an issue for Kitty who liked to retain control of every aspect of her life, and death. It was not a pleasant thought, but one which inevitably troubled most people her age. The trick was to plan, to leave a legacy – very difficult when your one son was long dead, and the only family you were left with was Robbie Mayhew.

'Look after Robbie for me,' Don had pleaded on his deathbed. 'The boy's not the brightest button in the box, but he means well.'

Deathbed promises were never a good idea.

'The pavilion is nothing but a drain on your resources,' Robbie sighed from the armchair. 'It's a white elephant, Kit. Without the club, it's not providing any income. You've still got all the expenses, your business rates, utility bills, insurance premiums, maintenance, security. An empty building is far more at risk from vandalism than one that is being used.'

'It was being used, until you kicked Mari Freeborn out,'

Kitty snorted.

'I told you, Mari went on her own accord. Anyway, the rent she was paying you on those rooms was negligible. You'd still probably get something for the fixtures and fittings if you sold up now.'

'I'm not selling.'

Robbie's patience had its limits. 'How many times do I have to spell it out? If this development goes ahead the Council get a whole new road-scheme out of Coastline. It's a major investment in Hookes Bay's future. The Council won't allow the pavilion to stand in the way. We'll be handed a compulsory purchase order, and then what? This is the best offer you're going to get.'

'What does Lindy think?' Kitty asked, not because she particularly valued Lindy's opinion but she because wanted to stall for time. She was quite fond of Lindy, even if she had married an idiot. There had been a time, long ago, when Kitty had thought that maybe Jez and Lindy might have got together. How different things might have turned out then. No point dwelling on what might have been. 'I'm not selling,' she said again.

Robbie sighed. 'I'll leave it with you.' He eased himself out of the chair, accepting defeat for today. 'Thanks for the tea. I'll see myself out.'

Kitty waited a good five minutes before reaching into the handbag by her feet and retrieving her mobile phone. She'd rarely used the device since Robbie had bought it for her. Lindy had left written instructions on a piece of paper.

She wouldn't renege on her promise to Don Mayhew. She had always looked after Robbie and she would continue to do so. After all, she'd made him the sole beneficiary of her will, hadn't she?

She could hold off selling to Coastline Developments for now but as things stood, Robbie was in a win-win situation. It wouldn't be too many months before the pavilion fell into his chubby hands, not if the latest prognosis from Dr Birtwhistle was to be believed. She had to have faith in the medical profession even if it was bad news. They usually knew what they were talking about. Robbie would probably sign on the dotted line before she was even in her grave. Hence the pressing need to defy death. To defy Robbie.

Dominic Flynn picked up after a couple of rings.

'Coastline have written again,' Kitty said. 'Robbie is urging me to accept their offer.'

'Don't you go signing anything, Kitty, my love,' Dominic said at once. Kitty found the Irish inflection in his voice irresistible. If only she were twenty years younger. No, not twenty, more like forty.

'He says the council will support Coastline's plans. They'll be calling for the pavilion to be demolished,' Kitty told him. 'I can't allow that, and I can only delay Robbie for so long. He can be very persuasive.'

'Don't let him threaten you. You should have called me earlier. I'd have been round like a shot.'

As much as Kitty liked the idea of Dominic Flynn rushing to her defence like a medieval champion, the only way he would ever stand a chance of beating Robbie was in a game of stealth, and even then the odds would be stacked against him.

Kitty had been a gambler all her life. There was no need to stop now. She took a deep breath. 'You remember what we were talking about the other day? I really don't think I've got much choice.'

'Oh Kitty, it's too risky a strategy. You don't know these people. You don't know what you're dealing with.'

It couldn't be any worse than burying three husbands. It couldn't be any worse than losing her only son. One final shuffle of the pack. She had to do it. She owed it to Jez.

Chapter Two

Tara

The Veggie Shack was one of my agent's favourite haunts. The restaurant was famous for a menu designed by a chef determined to use every item lingering in the back of his fridge. Anne Zachery hated waste. Food, like talent, was a precious commodity to be used wisely.

Over the years she had mastered a heartfelt, earnest look. It was the expression she adopted when you had missed out on a part, failed a call-back, or far worse, when a casting director didn't want to see you in the first place.

'Tara, are you even listening to me?'

'I'm sorry, Anne, what did you say?' My attention had momentarily drifted across the street to a florist. Perfect. After Anne had finished unveiling her plan to re-launch my career I would thank her with a flamboyant bouquet.

'I said, we all make mistakes. *To err is human*, after all.'

Anne was perfectly poised with one hand under her chin, one elbow rested on the table and one eyebrow raised just a millimetre higher than the other. 'Anyone can fall from grace, but it's how you fall that matters,' she said, 'especially in this business. Maintain a dignified silence and you can glide above the clouds of discord and return to terra firma once the winds have settled. Or you can spiral like an out of control rocket on course to crash land. You, Tara, have done the latter.'

'I'm very sorry about *Puffin the Pirate*,' I confessed.

'I think *Puffin* is the least of our worries.' Anne shifted position to slide the last of her pine kernels onto her fork with great dexterity. 'I've called up every contact in my address book. Right now, I can't get anyone to touch you with a proverbial barge-pole.'

I gave a sigh. With one notable, tragic childhood exception, I was having the worse few weeks of my life.

I had been summoned into *Puffin's* production office first thing on the Monday morning.

Gabriel Prettiman held up the copy of the *Sunday Stargazer* one of his underlings had thoughtfully bought to show him. 'I take it you have seen this so-called exclusive?' he'd said, turning to the relevant pages with great flourish. 'Just in case you haven't, let me enlighten you.

'*Panning for Gold.*' He visibly winced as he read out the headline. '*Actress Tara Wakely, 34, has launched a bitter attack on her love rival, TV talent show winner, Georgie Gold, 22, after being forced to move out of theatre director, Hal Claydon's dockside love-nest. Georgie has recently been cast as the lead in Claydon's new West End production, 'Rockabilly Rose', while Tara is currently appearing as Pally Sally in the stage version of Gabriel Prettiman's family favourite, 'Puffin the Pirate'. Our reporter, James Coulter, asked Tara, 35, what she thought of Georgie Gold's acting ability. "Like her boobs," Tara replied, "over inflated. Puffin has more talent in his left-wing, and he's a mere puppet".*'

I'd poured my heart out to Jamie, and in return he had transposed every detail into a hissing, spitting, vehement rant against national treasure Georgie Gold. In addition, he had been only too happy to divulge exactly how his 'under-cover' interview technique had worked. The double page spread was accompanied by the most hideous picture ever published. I hardly recognised myself as the clearly intoxicated bleached blonde clutching a cigarette in one hand and a cocktail glass in the other; breasts bursting out of a too tight red dress, the dark circles of both nipples clearly visible. *Puffin the Pirate's* faithful friend, *Pally Sally,* was no longer every child's favourite mad-cap auntie. She was an inebriated slut with a grudge.

My ignorance of Jamie's occupation did not appear to be an adequate defence. Gabriel Prettiman was at pains to point out that in nearly thirty years in show-business he had never once had to let an actor go. Bill Whittaker, who operated Puffin's left wing was a RADA trained puppeteer and ironically, Gabe's right-hand man. He'd taken my comment as a personal insult and was not prepared to have his award winning skills associated with articles in the gutter press. Gabriel and Bill were pioneers in the world of animatronics and *Puffin the Pirate* was just the latest in a whole string of balsa wood and papier-mâché creations that had brought pleasure to millions of children across the world.

'You do understand, don't you, Tara?' Gabriel had said, with a doleful shake of his shiny bald head. 'We just can't have this sort of publicity tarnishing *Puffin*'s reputation.'

As far as I could see *Puffin*'s reputation was still intact, it was mine that was in tatters. If anyone could smooth over *Puffin*'s ruffled feathers, I'd hoped Anne Zachery could. But she couldn't. Two weeks' pay in lieu of notice was the best deal she'd been able to negotiate.

'Tara, you're really not with us today, are you?'

It was a second rebuke in nearly as many minutes. 'I'm so sorry, Anne, you were saying?'

'You had the chance to redeem yourself and you didn't. Now this business over accepting payment from the *Sunday Stargazer* is all over the internet.'

I momentarily closed my eyes and took a deep breath. 'I wasn't thinking straight,' I muttered.

'No,' Anne agreed. 'Thinking straight is not one of your strengths, is it?' She pushed her finished plate to one side. 'I've been in this business for more years than I care to recall, but even I can't turn a tide like this, honey.' The look on her face had changed from one of regret to one of relief. 'It's time for a parting of the ways.'

I stared at her. 'You're dumping me? I thought you were here to rescue my career, not proclaim the end of it.'

'I believe the damage is beyond repair,' Anne said, swivelling in her seat to try and attract the attention of the waitress. 'Take a back seat, look for something behind the scenes. It's the only practical advice I can offer.'

'I don't want to work behind the scenes,' I protested. 'I'm a professional performer.'

'I suppose there might be cabaret openings overseas, Dubai or the UEA for example, but obviously that's not part of the industry I deal with.'

'Next you'll be suggesting I apply for a summer season working on a cruise ship.'

Sarcasm was wasted on Anne. A brief smile flitted across her taut, Botoxed features. 'The big vacation companies generally take kids straight out of performing arts school these days, so your age might be against you. But hey, it might be worth a try.'

I'd been dismissed by the headmistress. Arguing would be pointless. I offered to pay for my miserable salad of grapefruit pulp and micro leaves and Anne accepted my cash without any hesitation. All thoughts of bouquets, apart from one of barbed wire, were forgotten as I trudged to the nearest bus stop.

It was a long, lonely journey back to Spitalfields. Far too much time to reflect and contemplate. As I alighted at Liverpool Street Station I caught sight of a familiar shaven-headed figure in a charcoal grey suit strolling across the concourse.

Aaron was predictable to the extreme. I caught up with him outside The Tasty Pastry.

'Hey, sis, are you stalking me?' he asked, swinging around.

'I don't suppose you're still on your lunch hour? Can you spare me five minutes?'

'Just let me get a pie. You want anything?'

I'd just consumed a meal which contained less than 300 calories. Recent events had led to years of exemplary behaviour heading straight out of the window. 'Oh go on, then, but not a pie, a sausage roll, one with cheese, not sausage. And onion.'

We found an empty bench in a quiet corner of the station mall. I wanted to remain inconspicuous. Aaron was an exotic mix of North African and North London. He turned heads wherever he went.

'So,' he said, dusting flakes of pastry off his jacket. 'What have you done now?'

'My agent's just sacked me. She thinks I'm unemployable.'

'There's no hope that show you were in will take you back?' I shook my head. 'Hey don't cry. You'll get through this, sis.'

'I don't see how I can. I can't see a way out, Aaron. It's as if I've dug myself into this bottomless pit.' I was unable to stop the tears.

Aaron held up a hand. 'Stop,' he said. 'What's done is done. Come on. You're better than this.'

'No, I'm not,' I said miserably. I stared into my lap. Aaron had always been the voice of reason. We'd been thrust together as two anxious teenagers, arriving within days of each other at the same foster home. I'd approached the situation with typical teenage petulance, whereas Aaron had demonstrated a maturity way beyond his years, determined to make the most of a bad situation. We'd stuck together through thick and thin, friends for nearly twenty years.

He stole a covert glance at his watch. 'You're a talented performer. You'll get another job soon.'

'No I won't. Now I'm not just Tara Wakely, embittered ex-mistress of theatre director, Hal Claydon, infamous for her malicious outburst over his affair with the gorgeous Georgie Gold. I am now Tara Wakely, the mercenary bitch who steals money from babes and Eritrean orphans.'

'What?' Aaron paused mid-bite.

'The story is all over the internet. *Jilted actress shuns charity.* It's a complete lie. My agent knows that I do charity work on a regular basis, and that I care about Eritrean orphans, any orphans, in fact, very much, but she'd rather believe her assistant's side of the story than listen to me. A cheque arrived at the office from the *Sunday Stargazer*. Leiselotte said I couldn't possibly keep it as Georgie and Hal were donating the proceeds from their engagement photoshoot to Battersea Dogs Home.'

'Georgie and Hal are engaged? Christ, that's quick.'

'I know. Hal and I dated for six months before he let me even keep a toothbrush at his place. I felt I'd been stabbed in the back and when Leiselotte suggested I forward James

Coulter's money to Oxfam or some other worthy charity to restore my reputation, I snatched it off her and made some stupid comment about deserving every penny after what I'd just been through. Next thing I know my remarks are all over the internet.'

'That's a bit harsh. You were obviously upset.'

'I know. Leislelotte's never liked me. She once told me Anne only agreed to represent me as a personal favour to Doug Astley. You remember him? We were in that play together, and Doug was up for an *Evening Standard* Award and I was nominated for Spotlight's Best Newcomer. Leiselotte said Anne was so keen to stay on the right side of Doug she'd have signed his elderly grandmother to his books if he'd asked her to.'

'Whatever happened to Doug Astley?'

'Exactly. Faded into obscurity after he went off to the US chasing a part in some dreadful Sci-Fi series. I never heard from him again.'

'Oh Tara, you poor old thing.' Aaron scrunched the remains of his pie and its wrapper into a ball. 'Can't you issue a press release or something, saying how all this has been taken out of context?'

'Of course I could, but who'd listen? People's minds have already been made up. In any case, I don't want anything to do with the press, or get embroiled into some social media debate. I just want my life back.'

'I'm so sorry but I need to get back to the office.'

'I'll come with you,' I sighed, depositing my mock-sausage roll into the nearest bin.

I made a futile attempt to resist glancing at the newsstand as I accompanied Aaron back out onto the street. The nation's two leading gossip mags, *What's Hot* and *Let's Chat* occupied prominent positions on the counter-top. Both had chronicled Georgie Gold's rise to fame, and now that she was so *'blissfully in love with the new man in her life'*, she was only too happy to feature in whichever publication would have her, dragging my name in her wake. It was too much to hope that one day soon they would chew her up and spit her out.

Contain the venom, Tara. Aaron didn't need to say the words out loud, I could read his thoughts. We reached the revolving door of his office.

'Have faith, Tara,' he said. 'You'll soon find another job. Maybe you should look for something behind the scenes for a bit.'

'That's just what Anne Zachery said,' I told him. 'I've worked on stage since I was eighteen. I may not be a household name, or at least I wasn't until this all blew up in my face, but nobody could accuse me of not being consistent. I don't know how to do anything else.'

'Yes you do,' he said. He gave me a playful punch on the arm. 'You can do anything if you put your mind to it. How about stand-up comedy? You did that improv night a few years ago. You were brilliant.'

'I don't feel particularly funny right now.'

'Sorry. Look, if you need your CV re-hashed or a false ID, give me a call.'

'Actually, adopting a whole new personality doesn't seem like such a bad idea,' I remarked.

'I was joking,' Aaron said, giving me a hug. 'That's fraud, and the last thing you need is a criminal record. You'll bounce back. You always do. You've had it worse, remember? Something will turn up.'

How could it? Without an agent my chances of re-employment in any sort of theatrical production were non-existent. I had been cast overboard without a life-raft.

Or so I thought.

Chapter Three

'*My dear Miss Wakely, I hope you don't mind me writing, but I have a proposition to put to you.*'

I was losing count of the number of propositions I had received in the last few weeks. I'd changed my email address twice, deleted my Twitter account and suspended my LinkedIn and Facebook pages; actions which weren't particularly conducive to securing genuine offers of future employment. I had now resorted to an ancient pay-as-you-go-mobile Aaron had discovered in the depths of his man-drawer to protect myself from the omniscient presence of the internet. A slow news week had seen my notoriety rise. It appeared there was little else to talk about. *Rockabilly Rose* had opened in the West End and Georgie's back-story was filled with references to Hal Claydon's vindictive ex.

Two sacks of mail had arrived at Bea's flat courtesy of Anne Zachery.

'Bedtime reading,' Leiselotte had sneered as she offloaded the delivery.

To my immense gratitude Bea offered to act as my censor, shielding me from the most vicious hate-mail and only passing on the few letters of support, the majority of which appeared to have been written by inmates of various secure institutions and a couple of 'women of a certain age' who had found themselves unceremoniously exchanged for a newer model. We were all 'sisters' together, one wrote. They told similar tales of woe.

'*He ran off with his secretary.*' How unoriginal.
'*She's the same age as our daughter.*' Tell me about it.
'*She was at school with our daughter.*' Even worse.

The 'pro Tara' pile of correspondence was considerably

smaller than the anti.

'The nation appears to have taken Georgie Gold to their heart,' Bea remarked. 'You really do seem to have upset an awful lot of people.'

I hadn't upset Mrs Katherine Barker, of 35 Crabhook Avenue, Hookes Bay, Hampshire. Far from it. She thought I was the ideal candidate to help her out of a predicament.

'She's another crackpot,' Bea said, dismissing Mrs Barker's handwritten letter to the pile for burning.

I snatched the sheet of violet notepaper from her hands. 'Don't be so hasty.' Mrs Barker had written in fountain pen. Her words sloped and looped across the page, polite and deferential.

'For many years I taught youngsters the rudiments of music, dance and drama skills from my privately owned studio on the south coast. Ten years ago I took the sad decision to sell the business to a younger colleague. I have recently heard that she wishes to relinquish her interest in the Hookes Bay Academy of Music and Dance. So far she has not had any success in attracting a new buyer. There has been a performing arts school in Hookes Bay for nearly fifty years and it is a valuable community asset. I would hate to see it disappear. I am proposing to buy the business back in order to continue to provide the opportunity for local youngsters to fulfil their artistic and creative potential. However, now in my eighties and in failing health, I would need a competent, experienced individual to take over the running of the Academy on my behalf. I feel you could be the ideal candidate. I am prepared to offer a competitive salary which will include accommodation.'

'Why would anyone think you are the ideal candidate to run their dance school?' Bea asked. 'She's going to offer you up like a freak show to attract new customers for her own benefit.'

'No she's not, listen.' My eyes had already skipped to the bottom of Mrs Barker's letter. 'She goes on to say she's not interested in attracting adverse attention and she appreciates in my current circumstances that I may wish to work under an assumed name. Perfect. And she's done her research. She knows I have teaching experience.'

'I told you she was nuts. You call your efforts with Drama Queens teaching experience?'

Drama Queens was a small collaborative of actors who provided workshops for mainstream junior and secondary schools. I volunteered with them between jobs and enjoyed the work so much that with support from Hal I had been toying with idea of setting up a similar project of my own. I envisaged something a little grander than Drama Queens: a fully accredited stage school. I'd even started looking for permanent premises and developed a business plan, with Aaron's help.

James Coulter hadn't mentioned that in his salacious article. Or perhaps I hadn't mentioned it to him, but the information was readily available to anyone who bothered to Google me beyond the recent headlines.

In my mind Mrs Barker's proposition was worthy of consideration. This was a woman who had taken the trouble to find out more about me.

'I've nowhere to live and no income,' I pointed out. 'When I've had that so-called publicity guru David Henning phoning me up and offering to represent me because he thinks I'd be perfect for a D-list celebrity TV survival series, I don't think this is such a bad option.' I turned Mrs Barker's letter over in my hand again.

'You did not get a call from David Henning?' Bea looked appalled.

'Yes I did.' I assured her. 'And do you know what he said? He said I'd be the one they all love to hate. His wasn't the worst offer I've had, I can tell you.' I was about to reel off the list of other dubious opportunities that had come my way when we were interrupted by an unfamiliar chiming from my handbag.

'Did you steal that from a museum?' Bea asked, as I retrieved Aaron's phone.

I'd only given my number to a very few privileged contacts. I headed out into the hallway, still clutching Mrs Barker's letter.

My former foster mother Viv was in tears. 'Ray's just come back from the allotment in a right state,' she sobbed. 'One minute this stranger was complimenting him on his runner beans, the next he was asking if he thought your tragic childhood was to blame for your personality disorder.'

'My personality disorder? You are joking?' Both Aaron and I had stayed in touch with Viv and Ray over the years. They were the nearest thing to family I had.

'I wish I was,' Viv replied. 'Turns out he was from the local newspaper. He wanted to know where you were and if we'd be prepared to give him an exclusive interview. Ray saw him off with his shovel, but the man took a picture and now Ray's worried he's the one who's going to be on the front pages. Oh Tara, what a mess. What are we to do?'

'Oh Viv, I'm so sorry. That's outrageous.' I was incensed. Was there no escaping the media circus? The shadow of James Coulter lurked around every corner. The old adage of never being more than six feet away from a rat seemed to equally apply to undercover journalists.

'People here know Ray, they know he's not a violent man,' Viv continued, 'but where will it stop, Tara? Where will it end?'

It was a very good question. 'Look, Viv, I think I might go away for a while. If anyone pesters you again, you tell them I've gone abroad. I'm on retreat in Thailand. You don't know whereabouts, or when I'm coming back.'

'Oh, Tara. There's no need for that, is there?'

I unfurled the crumpled sheet of purple notepaper from my clenched fist. No, there was no need. If any journalists or publicity gurus were desperate enough to waste their money following a false trail out to the Far East in search of their story, then good luck to them. I said goodbye to Viv and punched Mrs Barker's number into the phone.

Chapter Four

My knowledge of the English seaside extended no further than childhood trips to Southend or Margate and more latterly snatched romantic weekend breaks with Hal in idyllic Cornish coves. According to the internet, Hookes Bay's one claim to fame was as the historic location of a Navy training base. There was no mention of it ever being a popular tourist destination.

At Mrs Barker's suggestion I caught a taxi from Fareham, the nearest mainline railway station. As soon as the taxi driver established I wasn't local, he insisted on providing a running commentary for the twenty minute cross-country journey to the coast. Fruit farms, he told me, had dominated the area before '*the military had come along.*'

The airstrip, built post-war, was now disused; the properties on the naval housing estate sold off to a housing association; the storage depot, which had been the mainstay of the Hookes Bay for the last fifty years, vacated and manned by a handful of civilians. According to my driver, the only redeeming feature in the area was the wetlands nature reserve.

'We've whole colonies of bar-tailed godwits and little ringed plovers,' he enthused. 'Come winter, you might be able to spot a lesser redpoll or even a razorbill.'

Would I still be in Hampshire come the winter? Based on my first impressions, it seemed highly improbable.

It was a relief to arrive in a main street surrounded by a small but familiar selection of shops and chain-takeaways. My ultimate destination was wedged between a supermarket and a building society.

'Here we are,' the taxi driver announced. 'The Sir Winnie. That'll be twenty-five pounds exactly please.'

If I'd had known the guided tour was an added extra I'd have asked him to shut up long ago. 'Do you take cards?' I asked.

'Cash only I'm afraid,' he said. 'Do you want me to wait while you use the ATM? There's one in the Co-op.'

'No I've got it, but I'll need a receipt.' Mrs Barker had promised to reimburse my travelling expenses.

I had done what I could to change my physical appearance since the Georgie Gold scandal, partly out of necessity and partly as a step in the cathartic process. The platinum blonde hair had gone; instead I sported a chocolate brown pixie cut. Bea declared I was unrecognisable. I had swapped the nondescript sweatpants and T-shirts I'd adopted 'post Georgie' for a smart black and white geometrical patterned shift dress, and carried my CV and portfolio in a large dusky pink Michael Korrs handbag.

So much for hoping to appear anonymous. I was completely over-dressed for Hookes Bay. Heads turned as I met my audience in the Sir Winston Churchill's jaded interior – a sparse midweek lunchtime clientele of pensioners, young professionals and a couple of builder types propping up the bar. One wore a garish orange fleece, complementing the pub's 1970s ambiance.

The barman offered me an encouraging smile. 'What can I get you, love?'

It was tempting to order a Campari. 'Just a soda water, please,' I replied. My eyes scanned the room for a sign of anyone who could possibly be Mrs Barker. She was sitting in a window seat. As purple as the notepaper she had written on.

She raised her hand in a greeting. 'Hello, dear,' she called. 'I'd have recognised you anywhere.'

How could she possibly recognise me? I looked nothing like the woman whose florid face had been splashed across the Sunday newspapers a few weeks previously. I didn't even look like the Tara Wakely in the photographs I had carefully selected for my portfolio. There was no opportunity to turn back.

'Take Kitty over another G&T while you're here,' the

barman said, pouring a second drink.

'Yes of course. Let me pay.' I reached for my purse until I remembered that the taxi driver had just taken the last of my cash.

'Don't worry,' the barman smiled. 'Kitty's already set up a tab.'

After fifteen years on stage my job interview with Mrs Barker was one of the most bizarre auditions of my life. Within seconds of our meeting I realised her cleverly crafted letter had been nothing but a trap.

'I like to call a spade a spade,' she began, 'so this is the role I want you to play.'

Her lines were very well rehearsed. 'I own Hookes Bay Pavilion,' she said, 'you've probably not heard of it, coming from London, but it's one of the very few genuine Art-Deco seaside pavilions left in the country. Its external appearance hasn't changed since it was built back in the 1920s, although it's taken a bit of a battering inside. My late husband, Lionel Keaton, bought the pavilion just after the War. Lionel was a theatre impresario, based in London. That's where we met. I was on the stage you see, just like you.'

Mrs Barker had taken the liberty of pre-ordering a round of the Sir Winston Churchill's finest sandwiches. 'I hope you don't mind but they do a fabulous mature cheddar and homemade pickle,' she said as the platter arrived at the table, briefly interrupting her opening lines. 'I've also got you a prawn in Marie Rose sauce, just in case. I know you youngsters have more sophisticated tastes. Prawn in Marie Rose was Jez's favourite. Jez – Jeremy – was my son.'

Before I could make any comment, she returned to her script.

'The pavilion was originally designed as a theatre. We kept things traditional at first, putting on a summer season variety show for the holiday makers, a pantomime at Christmas. Lion had this vision of bringing the Arts to the masses. We set up our own repertory company to perform the classics: Shakespeare, Noel Coward, Oscar Wilde, Chekhov. We were able to attract visiting ballet companies, touring operas, and musical recitals. I'll get young Dominic to show you later. I've kept a lot of our original handbills and programmes. In between I taught piano, dancing, acting. I even gave elocution lessons and deportment, when those things were still considered essential life skills.' She gave a chuckle and pushed the plate of sandwiches towards me. 'Go on, help yourself, love. I can't eat dairy. Or seafood.

'Then they took the railway away and the town died almost overnight. The Carlisle Hotel was very grand and prestigious in its day, but after it was converted into flats, others followed. We had to do something to keep the money coming in so we transformed the theatre into a ballroom. Then I lost Lionel to cirrhosis of the liver. Inevitable I suppose, the sort of business we were in. After that, it was just me and Jez. Lion and I had waited a long time for Jez to come along, and then he passes away with the boy not five years old.'

'I'm so sorry,' I murmured. I was at a complete loss to know where Mrs Barker's tale was going.

'Well, you do what you have to do to survive, don't you,' she continued, hardly pausing for breath. 'Lion had converted two of the old theatre rehearsal rooms into a dance studio so I kept on teaching. It was the swinging sixties and people lost interest in ballroom dancing, but that's when I met Don Mayhew. It was his idea to turn the pavilion into a private member's club. We installed a kitchen, employed a professional chef. He said he could get the bands down here to play and he was as good as his word. We had the top acts of the day. When the seventies came along, Don said we should reinvent the club as a discotheque. Cost me an arm and a leg it did, but it worked. We kept our heads above water.'

She gave a slight sniff. Her sense of timing was terrific. 'Jez was a talented musician. He could play the piano almost before he could walk, then he learnt the guitar. When Jez left school, Don gave him a bit of work at the club. Naturally they had a few arguments, the generation gap and everything. Jez would have squabbled with Lion if he'd still been alive. Still,' she sniffed again, 'Don went down with emphysema. He'd always been a forty a day man. He spent the last few years of his life as an invalid. I kept up the teaching during the day, but evenings Don wanted me at home looking after him. Jez had to take charge of the club, and Robbie of course. I mustn't forget to tell you about him.'

She pulled a handkerchief from her mauve clutch bag and dabbed at her eyes. 'Robbie is Don's son, from his first marriage. We came to rely on Robbie a lot. Jez had his own rock band, Urban Rebel they were called. It wasn't my taste in music but people told me they were good. There was talk of a record deal. They went off to London, were gone a couple of months. Then, just when it looked like Jez was about to hit the big time, well, we lost him. I lost my poor boy.'

Mrs Barker stopped to blow her nose.

'I'm so sorry,' I said, adopting a look and voice of concern. I could act just as well as she could.

'Thirty-four years ago.' Mrs Barker sighed. 'He'd have been fifty-seven this month. He's like James Dean, you see. Do you know how old James Dean would be now? Eighty-four. Can you imagine? You see you just can't, can you, because you always have that image, that picture in your head of a young man in a leather jacket. Well, that's how it is with Jez. You haven't touched the sandwiches, love. Go on, don't mind me.'

The bread was already starting to curl. I picked up a cheese and pickle and took a tentative nibble.

'So, back to the pavilion.' Mrs Barker re-composed herself. 'Robbie's been running the club for me ever since. I carried on teaching well into my seventies, always hoping I'd discover another Jez, or a girl I could recommend to the Royal Academy of Music or the English National Ballet. I had some successes but I started to find it all too much. Parents wanted examinations, certificates, end of term shows that were like Hollywood productions. I had an assistant by this time, Mari Freeborn. She was an old pupil of mine who'd taken her teaching exams, so I sold the business on to her and retired. I remarried, opted for a quiet life, moved into a bungalow. Hughie wanted to travel so we took a couple of big cruises each year, saw the world, toured Australia, Asia and America.'

It finally sounded as if she was running out of steam. 'I've outlived three husbands and my only son, but the one constant, the one certain thing in my life was always that pavilion, and now Robbie wants me to sell up. There's a big redevelopment being planned for the seafront and the pavilion is in the way. Last year, the council took away Robbie's licence and closed the club down. There had been too many complaints from local residents. Mari Freeborn had already moved out. The studio needed a few repairs but Robbie refused to get them done. The heating system broke down, the children had to dance in their coats. Since then the whole place has been boarded up. Why keep it? Robbie says.'

I made another sympathetic murmur. It sounded as if Mrs Barker would be well shot of her pavilion.

'I know Robbie's been planning this for some time,' she said with a sigh. 'He's in cahoots with the developers. If I don't sell, the pavilion comes to him anyway when I die. It'll just be a matter of time before the building is razed to the ground. I've no other family. The pavilion is all I have left of Jez, of Lion, and of Don. Call me a sentimental old fool, but I can't bear the thought that those memories will be erased, my family history destroyed, just to make way for a fancy flower bed and some crazy paving. I don't care if those people who buy those posh new apartments want to have an unobstructed view of the sea. Bugger them. Bugger them all. I can't allow my pavilion to be demolished. I want to see it restored. When I die I want to know that the Hookes Bay Pavilion is going to be resurrected as a centre for beauty, art and culture, just like it was in the old days, when Lion and I started out. That's the legacy I want to leave.'

Beauty, Art and Culture. In light of recent events, how could this deluded old lady possibly think I was the right person to help her out? Did she think I had made enough money out of selling my story to buy the pavilion from her and transform it? Was that her plan?

'Mrs Barker ...'

'Call me Kitty, dear, everybody else does.'

'Kitty, I can see how much this pavilion building must

mean to you, but I thought you wanted me to run your dance school?'

'Oh I do. I do want you to run my dance school.' Claw-like fingers reached out and clasped around mine. I'd never seen so many rings on such tiny gnarled hands. 'But by doing that, you see, you can save the pavilion.'

I tried to keep my voice calm and neutral. 'I don't want to be rude, Kitty, but I don't see how. I'm not prepared to lend my name to anything that is likely to get me back into the newspapers. I don't think that's what you need to preserve your pavilion. It won't help.'

The old lady shuffled on her seat. Her grasp tightened. 'I thought I'd made it clear in my letter. It's not publicity I want, Tara, dear. What I need is time.' She leaned closer. 'You see I've got cancer. The prognosis isn't good.' Once again her eyes filled with tears. 'Come. I want to show you.'

She looked up and caught the barman's eye. 'Mike, can you call the van now please?'

'Yes of course, Kitty, just give me two secs.'

'Help me, dear,' she said, struggling to rise out of the seat. I took her arm, she wasn't any weight. The skin on the hand that gripped mine was paper-thin and cold, despite the stuffy heat of the pub. She could barely lift her purple sandal-clad feet to walk. Seated, Mrs Barker's frailty had been well-disguised. Her face was made up; her hair, an immaculately coiffured luscious dark wig. Diamonds glittered on her ears. Her alert, beady eyes had deceived me.

By the time we had shuffled to the door of the pub a blue van adorned with the logo of Hookes Bay Good Neighbours Scheme was already pulling up outside.

'Where to now, your Highness?' the driver asked, opening the door with a bow. To my immense relief we were his only passengers.

The esplanade was flanked on one side by the beach, a scruffy bank of pebbles and shingle which fell sharply into the sea, and on the other by a handful of beach-themed shops and fast-food kiosks.

'Can you see it?' Kitty cooed, the faint tremor of excitement clearly detectable in her voice.

'You mean the island?' I asked. Across the slate grey water of the Solent, the Isle of Wight was impossible to miss.

'No, silly girl, the pavilion. Look, beyond the park, at the end of the esplanade.'

A low-rise white edifice sat isolated on the promenade, some distance from the central hub of Hookes Bay. A two-tier wedding cake, dumped on the seafront like an afterthought. Adjacent to the peculiar shaped building, jutting out across the shingle, barely reaching the low tide mark, were six rusty iron girders supporting the shortest pier I had ever seen.

Art, Beauty and Culture. Hookes Bay Pavilion certainly needed an injection of something.

'That's the old hotel site,' Kitty said, as we approached the half-demolished building on the other side of the esplanade. 'According to Robbie the road will divert inland and encircle the rear of the development. This area here will be pedestrianised. The council are very keen. There will be a café, some of those useless gift shops. You must know the sort of thing I mean.' I certainly did. Bea had an addiction to Yankee Candles. 'Go on, get out, take a closer look.'

I had expected the pavilion to be a traditional seaside theatre, with a domed roof, and ornate Victorian gilding. My knowledge of architecture was appalling. Art Deco, Kitty had said, the era of flapper girls and the Charleston, and here it was, a small but perfectly formed slice of smooth, stylish South Beach Miami, transposed to unfashionable Hookes Bay.

Garish graffiti decorated the walls and tattered fly-posters hung from the woodchip boards that protected the main entrance. Polystyrene food cartons, crushed beer cans and cigarette butts littered the marble steps. Pigeons and seagulls had colonised the flat roof and first floor balconies. The smell of decay was everywhere. I took my time walking around the building. At the rear, the entrance to the defunct pier was off limits behind an ugly chain-link fence.

I completed my circuit and returned to the front of the building where the imprint of a long-lost sign was etched onto the grubby concrete above the door like a tattoo: *The Pavilion*

Night Club and Cocktail Bar. No doubt the original would have been in flashing neon complete with florescent pink flamingos and swaying tropical palms. I could quite see how the landscape of Hookes Bay might be improved by the removal of the derelict pier, but the pavilion had already captured my imagination.

I took one last look before clambering back into the van, and was almost blinded by the glare of late spring sunshine glinting like diamonds in the glass of the pavilion's curved atrium. Could this place really be transformed into Kitty's vision? There was no denying in that moment the shining pavilion shared its owner's aura of vintage grandeur.

'So,' Kitty said, the look of excited anticipation evident on her face. 'What do you think? Beautiful isn't it?'

'A little incongruous, but it's certainly got something,' I admitted.

'It certainly has.' She nodded her approval. 'So, will you do it or not? Will you come to Hookes Bay and run my dance school?'

I didn't even hesitate before I answered.

'Good girl,' she said, clutching my hand across the peeling faux leather of the van's seats. 'The minute I saw you, I knew.'

Chapter Five

Kitty

She couldn't help but feel smug. Tara Wakely really was the perfect woman for the job; attractive, congenial and highly gullible. She was desperate to put the humiliation of London behind her. Kitty knew all about scandals. She easily recognised the symptoms of shame and guilt.

Kitty had remained evasive and told her only what she needed to know. She'd seen the girl baulk at her first sight of 35 Crabhook Lane, but it was a familiar reaction. Hughie had chosen to repaint the external walls of the bungalow in memory of their many happy Mediterranean holidays, and although terracotta had been the original aim, Kitty had assured him the vivid coral would do. She wasn't going to redecorate now.

Tara had briefly raised the subject of Kitty's medical condition, but Kitty had been quick to assure her that her stepson's wife and Penny, the home help she already employed, took care of most of her needs.

'That's not what you're here for, dear,' she said.

The bungalow's second bedroom had already been cleared in anticipation of Tara's arrival. Penny's son, Callum, had worked wonders with a paintbrush and the furniture had been re-arranged for a more spacious look. The en suite was tight, but afforded the privacy Kitty knew modern young girls desired. Hughie had insisted separate bathrooms were the key to a happy marriage. Kitty was of the opinion separate bank accounts helped too.

Tara was only too happy to agree to a new name.

'Unfortunate though it was,' Kitty remarked, 'if it hadn't

have been for all that trouble we wouldn't have found each other. But, as I've already said, we definitely don't want the wrong sort of attention. You're here to do a job. I like the disguise, although I'd have recognised you anywhere. Keep your hair dark, it suits you better. What would you like to be called?'

They had agreed on the surname Paige, both being fans of Elaine.

'I could use my mother's name,' Tara had suggested. 'Nicki Paige?'

'No, not your mother's name. How about Alice?'

Alice Paige it was to be. Jez would have liked that, Kitty thought, although he would have liked the name Tara too. Alice's salary was discussed. Kitty intended to be generous. She took a great deal of pleasure in spending Robbie's inheritance. It was agreed that Tara would return to Hookes Bay the following week. Almost as an after-thought she asked Kitty if everything was legal. Kitty pretended to look affronted before ushering her out of the front porch.

She felt more alive, more animated than she had for some time despite the physical exhaustion of the outing to the pub. It was a shame the Sir Winnie was the best Hookes Bay had to offer. The yacht club was restricted to members only, and there was no way she was conducting her business at Pebbles, the café on the seafront, not with Terri Cawle eavesdropping on every conversation. No doubt Hookes Bay had seemed a very dull place after London, but the pavilion had worked its magic.

Kitty couldn't wait to see Robbie's face when she told him. But not yet. The wait had to be savoured. She picked up the latest proposal from Coastline Developments and shoved it into the nearest drawer. Robbie had called around again the previous evening. Coastline had upped their offer by another ten thousand pounds. Robbie had told her she was a fool to even think about refusing. She settled into her favourite wicker chair. Kitty was looking forward to having Alice for company and some semblance of sensible conversation, which was impossible with Robbie when Lindy wasn't around. Mind you, when Lindy did return, Kitty would have to keep Tara, or rather Alice, well out of the way. Lindy wasn't always quite as dumb as she looked.

Chapter Six

Tara

Kitty met me on the doorstep of her salmon pink palace wearing a gaudy bright sunflower print dress. She fussed like a twittering canary as she showed me to my room.

When Kitty had vacated the family home she had shared with her second husband, gangster Don, she had obviously not fully embraced the concept of downsizing. Every room was crammed with furniture and ornaments, with barely an inch of floor space or surface area left uncovered. Her criticism of home décor shops seemed somewhat hypocritical, considering she could easily have stocked a retro one of her own.

The front garden had been gravelled, presumably for ease of maintenance, whilst the concrete slab patio outside the back door led to an area of lawn. The borders were sparsely planted. The chaos inside had not extended out.

'Robbie sends someone round to cut the grass every now and then,' Kitty explained. 'Hughie liked to potter, but Robbie took most of the plants out. He said it would be easier to look after.'

Tucked away behind a wooden trellis I spotted a large shed and a greenhouse. If I'd had noticed it on the day of my interview, I'd have bought my tomato plant with me. I'd rescued it from Hal's balcony only to leave it at the mercy of Bea's windowsill. Sadly, I didn't rate its chances of survival.

'Does Robbie live nearby?' I asked. Having already been painted as the villain of the piece, I wasn't keen to run into Kitty's stepson anytime soon.

'They've got a house in Broken Lane,' Kitty replied. 'Great big place. They've also got a villa in Lanzarote. Lindy spends a lot of time there.'

'Oh that must be nice.'

'I've no idea if it's nice,' Kitty retorted. 'I've never been invited out to join them.'

This seemed like another black mark against Robbie. 'Do Robbie and his wife have any children?' I enquired. I'd noticed several photos in the living room but hadn't had a chance to study them in any great detail. I certainly couldn't recall seeing pictures of any smiling grandchildren.

Kitty shook her head. 'No. It never happened.'

After we'd had a cup of tea in the conservatory she suggested I might want to stock up on some groceries.

'There's a Sainsbury's behind the Health Centre,' she told me. 'It's only ten minutes away.'

A quick search of Kitty's numerous kitchen cupboards before setting out confirmed my suspicions that she didn't consume solid food. She was dozing when I returned an hour later.

She had already told me to help myself to her computer. She had a dated console tucked into her box room, something Robbie had sorted out for her, she explained somewhat begrudgingly. A post-it note was stuck to the screen with KITTYK written across it in bold black letters which I took to be her password. No Wi-Fi signal had popped up on my laptop, which wasn't necessarily such a bad thing. It was a lot easier to resist the temptations of the internet when a PC took fifteen minutes to warm up.

It wasn't a great surprise when I finally sat down to conduct some research to discover Kitty's browsing history consisted of an extensive list of online gossip pages charting the entire Hal Claydon and Georgie Gold affair, together with, I noted with some surprise, a couple of very dubious websites usually the domain of teenage boys. Was this Robbie's doing? I dismissed the idea immediately. Although I disliked Robbie more with each passing minute, he hardly sounded like the kind of man who would use his elderly mother's antiquated computer to look at softcore porn. More likely this was the work of the 'young Dominic' whose name Kitty had dropped into conversation several times and I assumed was another regular visitor.

For our first supper together I opened up a packet of the fresh gourmet soup, ignoring Kitty's protests that I wasn't there to look after her. At seven-thirty Kitty announced she was ready for bed, which seemed ridiculously early for a woman who had spent her entire career being nocturnal.

I spent another hour or so on the computer, half-watched the TV and then slipped under my brand new floral duvet just two hours after Kitty, eager for a good night's sleep before my job really began.

Kitty had arranged for me to see her former assistant, Mari Freeborn, at ten the following morning. Kitty's initial letter had intimated that she planned to take ownership of the dance school herself. However, before I set off to see Mari she made it clear her name was to be kept out of any official transaction. The dance school was to belong to Alice Paige.

Mari lived a five minute walk from Kitty's bungalow. She opened her door at the second ring of the bell, struggling to restrain a large dog which took no notice of her commands to either sit down or be quiet.

'So sorry,' she said, after she had thrust the animal into the kitchen and slammed the door. 'I'm not sure what's got into him today. Come into the sitting room.'

Mari had the poise and grace befitting a former professional ballerina. She was in her mid-forties with the figure of a twenty year old and a mass of auburn curls. I followed her into a room littered with the paraphernalia of teenagers, cast off trainers, phone chargers, and abandoned mugs.

'You remind me of someone,' Mari said, inviting me to sit down. 'Have we met before?'

'I don't think so,' I said, with a very assertive shake of my head. Kitty had said my disguise was impregnable, yet both she and now Mari claimed some sort of familiarity.

Maintaining a slightly puzzled look she apologised for the mess. 'I've not had time to have a clear up this morning, although to be honest, it's such a thankless task. So, you're interested in buying my dance school?'

'Yes. Kitty's told me the price you would like for the business and I am very happy with those terms. I'd like to take the classes over straight away.'

Mari looked surprised. 'My, you're keen. I don't have a problem with a swift takeover. To be honest the summer term is always the worse. The parents always expect a show. To quit now and not have to deal with any of that would be heaven for me, but it would be a baptism by fire for you. Are you sure you could cope?'

After what I'd had to cope with over the last few weeks I was fairly confident organising an end of term children's dance show would be no problem. Mari asked where I'd completed my training.

Kitty had invented a very plausible history. 'I won a scholarship to the Boston Conservatoire at the age of sixteen,' I said. 'I've worked all over the world. Kitty can vouch for my credentials.'

'Oh, I'm not concerned about your credentials,' Mari assured me, 'although some of the parents might be. To be honest, I'm just glad to have some time off so I can finally get my bunions treated. How is Kitty by the way?'

'Frail.'

'Poor old dear. Sounds like you've come along at just the right time. She'll be pleased to know her beloved Academy is in safe hands. To be honest she looked devastated when I told her I intended to quit.'

'You're not really quitting because of your bunions?'

Mari laughed. 'Trust me, if it was just my bunions I'd have probably carried on, especially after seeing Kitty look so upset. I've got eighteen-year-old twin boys, off to university in September. I've been tied up every weekend since I don't know when with classes on Saturday from eight-thirty in the morning until six in the evening. I do four after-school clubs a week as well as baby-ballet daytime classes. We've got a yacht sat in the marina and with the boys off our hands, John, my other half, says this should be our time. He's no great fan of Kitty's, but as you probably know, she's had a tough life. She established her academy all those years ago, built it up from nothing and she was the best teacher ever. I have very happy memories of her lessons in the pavilion. Have you seen the studio? It's a fantastic space. Things were never the same after I had to move the classes to the community centre.'

'You moved out because of Robbie?'

'Basically, yes. He was making things very awkward for me, always asking for extra contributions to cover cleaning costs, security and the like, expenses incurred by his club, not my dance studio. In the end I decided I didn't want the hassle. The community centre was the only alternative if I wanted to stay in Hookes Bay. There are obvious downsides. The Parish Council have a container in the car-park but you're fighting for storage space. I keep my portable barre there, and spare props and costumes, but all the other paraphernalia I carry around in the back of my car.'

Kitty's plan for me to take over the dance school had several weak points, but I had found its first major flaw. I didn't have a driving licence, let alone a car.

Mari must have seen my look of dismay. 'Oh dear. You don't have your own transport? Realistically you'd only need an iPod and a couple of speakers, and you could do all the admin on a laptop. I'm sure you could make more room in the container if you tried. The Taekwondo Club have far more than their fair share of space.'

From the kitchen the dog began a series of pitiful whines. Mari apologised.

'I'm going to have to take him out. Look, I've got a toddler dance class tomorrow afternoon, why don't you come and watch? Maybe you should take a look at the facilities before you commit, just so you know what you are letting yourself in for?'

I was already committed, but too much haste would arouse too much curiosity. Nobody bought a business without seeing it first, or checking the accounts. I had to immerse myself into the character.

'Sounds like a good idea,' I told Mari. 'And maybe a quick look at your financial records too?'

'Of course.' She looked quite relieved. 'I'll have everything ready for you tomorrow.'

Chapter Seven

When I returned to the bungalow, Kitty was not alone. As I stepped through the ornate wooden front door into the hallway I heard the murmur of voices from the conservatory, a man's laughter. Was she entertaining Robbie Mayhew?

I'd already established that Kitty was a little hard of hearing, so I tiptoed through to the kitchen.

Kitty's visitor was talking in a soft Irish bur, with his back towards me, slightly scruffy dark brown hair just visible above the back of the wicker chair. Long legs encased in black jeans stretched out across the tiled floor, converse trainers. Certainly younger than Robbie. Perhaps this was 'young' Dominic, although from the depth of his voice he was hardly adolescent. Kitty was behaving very coquettishly, smiling enigmatically, giggling at his every word.

I cleared my throat and she looked up.

'Oh Alice, come and meet Dominic. Dominic, this is my good friend Alice Paige. Alice is the new owner of Hookes Bay Academy of Music and Dance.'

Dominic sprang out of his chair as if he had been stung. 'This is Alice?'

'Alice Paige,' I confirmed and held out my hand. He took it very cautiously. He was in his mid-to-late-thirties, six feet tall. His handsome face was a mixture of confusion and shock.

'Here, have my seat.' He stepped sideways. There were only two chairs in the conservatory and a threadbare leather pouffe, currently home to Kitty's purple slippered feet. 'I'm just off anyway.'

'Oh don't rush,' Kitty protested with a pout. 'I wanted you to show Alice around the pavilion.'

'I'm a bit pushed for time to be honest, Kitty. As always, your hospitality has kept me from my work.'

'What do you do?' I enquired. I wanted to know more about Dominic. He certainly seemed to have captivated Kitty into submission and for some reason I felt wary. I knew all about con-men who swindled vulnerable old ladies out of their life-long savings. It was bad enough that Kitty had Robbie to deal with, I didn't want anyone else taking advantage of her. Slick wheeler-dealer-types played on their good-looks, and when it came to good-looks, there was no denying Dominic had been dealt a very good hand. It was hard to draw myself away from his well-defined cheek bones and baby blue eyes.

'Dominic's into architectural reclamation,' Kitty informed me. 'He runs his own salvage business.'

Why wasn't I surprised? Presumably Dominic had those baby blue eyes firmly fixed on stripping the pavilion of the few, if any, period features it had left. He had probably already picked out its most valuable assets, earmarked all the chandeliers and architraves to sell on at vast profit. Poor Kitty, surrounded by vultures, even if this was a very handsome one. I felt my hackles rise.

'Kitty's description of my business is flattering but a little grand,' Dominic said, instantly confirming my suspicion that he was nothing but a con-man. 'I run a junk yard on the marina.'

'I want Dominic to take you on a tour,' Kitty said. 'He's very knowledgeable about the pavilion's history.'

'I'm more than happy to show you around,' Dominic said with a slight hesitation. 'But not today.'

'How about tomorrow?' Kitty suggested.

'I'm meeting Mari at the community centre at two tomorrow afternoon,' I told her.

'After that then,' Kitty said decisively. 'I'm sure you can spare half an hour, Dominic.'

He sighed. 'Sure.' His smile was brilliant, if somewhat forced. 'Of course I can. I can fit you in at four?'

I nodded. We shook hands and he kissed Kitty on the cheek.

'See you soon, Kit, my love. And take care.' He gave me what seemed suspiciously like a warning glance. 'I'll see myself out.'

Did he see me as a rival, vying for Kitty's patronage? I was intrigued and wanted to know more, but Kitty was keen to get back to business as soon as he was out of the door.

'So,' Kitty said, once we were alone. 'Mari was happy with everything?'

'I think she was surprised at the haste,' I replied.

'At least it's done,' Kitty said. 'Don't look so weary, girl. That's only act one, scene one complete. Don't tell me you are running out of oomph already?'

Over a light salad lunch, little more than a couple of lettuce leaves and a tomato, I asked Kitty about her stage career. The decades melted away as she painted a picture of her life as an actress in austere post-war London before coming to Hookes Bay.

'When Lionel bought me here,' she said, 'it was the first time I'd been to the seaside. Despite the damage the Luftwaffe had caused, Hookes Bay was an attractive place. Do you know what struck me most? The colours. London was so dull, nothing but bombsites and brick dust. Here, you had the all those fields, and then the beach with those cheerful striped deck chairs, and the awnings on the big hotels along the front. The Carlisle was magnificent then, and there were others: The Osborne Towers, The Royal Lyon.

'Off Broken Lane, where Robbie lives now, we had one of the first ever holiday camps. In truth it had been a cadet training base before the war so someone told me, attached to the military, but some entrepreneur saw the potential in revamping it. It was there until the 1970s. I suppose that's when everyone started going on package holidays.'

I found it hard to picture sleepy Hookes Bay as a bustling resort, just as I found it hard to picture the shrunken old lady in front of me as a boisterous teenager, treading the boards in variety shows and reviews.

'Dominic's got my old picture albums. Ask him to show you,' Kitty said.

I wondered why Dominic had been entrusted with Kitty's personal effects, but I said nothing. While she dozed I returned to the computer and sent Viv an email; without giving away too many details I told her I was enjoying Thailand. *'Although facilities are a bit basic,'* I wrote, which, as I found out when I tried to take a shower in my bijou en suite later that evening, wasn't a complete lie.

Hookes Bay Community Centre shared the same utilitarian and functional design as the houses on the surrounding former military estate. A notice board outside the pre-fabricated pink pebbledash building listed at least a dozen clubs and societies who frequented the premises. Multi-functional facilities were definitely not ideal for any sort of performing arts teaching, yet all over the country, clubs operated out of facilities like this. Any enterprise had to turn over a good profit to warrant its own purpose-built studio.

My lack of a driving licence was just the first in a long line of inadequacies that became apparent as I watched Mari taking her toddler ballet class. My experience with Drama Queens had taught me how to keep a class of bolshie inner city teenagers amused with a modernist twist on Shakespeare, but I didn't know anything about placating toddlers, or teaching classical ballet to the middle-class prepubescent tweenies who were the mainstay of Mari's classes. I might just be able to convince a group of three year olds that I was a trained dance teacher but I couldn't possibly instruct the older children who would have long surpassed my basic level of knowledge.

The lesson ended with a curtsey and a chorus of 'Thank you, Miss Mari.'

'As you can see, it's hardly the most salubrious venue, is it?' Mari said as she began to gather up the selection of tiaras and wands she had been using as props, and which were now scattered around the room. 'It's a bit of a come-down from the Royal Opera House, I can tell you. I take it you are familiar with the RAD syllabus we currently follow? I just had a thought, you being trained in America and all that?'

Did three year olds need to follow a syllabus? Kitty had seriously over-estimated my technical abilities if she thought for one minute I could claim to be the same calibre of teacher as Mari. A flash of inspiration. Kitty hadn't been a ballerina, she'd been a variety act. If I was to stand any chance of not screwing up completely, I had to stick with what I knew best.

'My personal ambition is diversity,' I told Mari. 'I want my pupils to have the space for individual expression. Ballet is a very restrictive discipline and I want to encourage creativity and freedom. I'd like to open up the academy to a much broader spectrum of participation. I don't just want white middle-class kids in tutus, I'd like to teach all-round performance skills, everything from classical dance to hip-hop.'

Mari's eyes nearly popped out of her head. 'Hip-hop in Hookes Bay?'

Anyone would have thought I'd suggested opening up a brothel. I immediately became defensive. 'Why not? I've seen those teenagers hanging around outside the amusement arcade. Why not reach out and pull them in?'

'Does Kitty know your plans?' Mari asked cautiously.

I was thinking on my feet. I didn't know I had a plan until thirty seconds ago. 'My ideas are still very much in their infancy,' I said. 'But long term, I would definitely like to expand what's on offer.'

Mari regarded me sceptically. 'How about you shadow my classes for a few weeks to become familiar with my existing methods and pupils before making any decisions? If you do still want to proceed with making the purchase, perhaps you should just concentrate on the summer show and not think about diversifying before the autumn? Hookes Bay is a bit of a traditional sort of place. People aren't always receptive to change.'

Kitty had stressed that it was imperative to keep on the right side of Mari. I could learn to teach ballet. I could study YouTube, watch DVDs, probably take a crash course. I had to remember I was simply playing a part. I needed to stick to the script. And learn to drive.

'I don't suppose you know a driving instructor?' I asked, changing the subject.

'I'll email you the details of the guy who taught the boys,' she promised. 'If he can teach them, he can teach anybody.'

Chapter Eight

With half an hour to kill before my rendezvous with Dominic, I headed back to the bungalow. I felt protective of Kitty. Dominic needed to know I was a force to be reckoned with, which called for a change of outfit. Leggings and a T-shirt would impress no-one.

I'd only brought the minimum of clothes to Hookes Bay beside the dance teacher attire required for the job. I opted for the one pair of heels I had with me, designer ripped jeans, a plain white T and my favourite leather jacket. I applied a good dose of make-up and wore my aviator Ray-Bans on my head. Subconsciously I hoped to create an attractive, intriguing 'continental' look.

Dominic barely gave me or my outfit a second glance. He kept me waiting a good ten minutes, an act of deliberate rudeness no doubt intended to remind me how far down his to-do list our meeting was, turning up in a pair of filthy non-designer ripped jeans, complete with a baggy sweatshirt of a non-descript colour. He alighted from an ancient rusty red pick-up truck, shaking what was either a very bad dose of dandruff or plaster dust out of his hair.

'Ready for your history lesson?' he asked, holding up a set of keys. 'We have to start at the tradesman's entrance. This way.'

I followed him to the old stage door at the rear of the building. It was quite apparent that over the years a great deal of re-configuring had taken place inside the pavilion. It bore no resemblance to any theatre I'd ever performed in. I followed Dominic through a maze of passageways created by stud partitioning. At the end of a long dank corridor a heavy swing door opened out into a welcome blast of dazzling natural daylight.

We stood on a sticky moth-eaten red carpet in the grand foyer beneath the full height glass atrium. A sleek brass and marble staircase swirled in a spiral to the second floor. It was so unexpected it took my breath away.

'We'll avoid the black hole in there,' Dominic said giving a cursory nod towards a second set of black painted swing doors. 'That leads to the nightclub. Let's start at the top and work down, in every sense of the word.' He took the stairs two at a time, while I followed at a slower pace, marvelling at the splendour of what was left of the pavilion's original interior. The snaking staircase was beautiful, a work of art in itself. An opulent chandelier hung from the ceiling, comprised of layers of shimmering shards of iridescent opaque glass. Reflections flashed across the staircase like dancing sunbeams.

'Is that genuine?' I asked as Dominic bounded ahead.

'I believe so. If not, then it's a very good reproduction. From what I understand from Kitty, Robbie rarely ventured up here. This was her domain. If he knew its true worth I'm pretty sure he'd have ripped it out and sold it long ago.'

It was hardly the sentiment I expected to hear from a man with designs on grabbing the chandelier for himself. Was Dominic's interest in the pavilion altruistic after all?

He paused at the top of the stairs. 'What are you waiting for?'

I wasn't sure. I wanted to savour the atmosphere. The magnetism was overwhelming. *I belonged here.*

'Don't you want to see your studio?' He leaned over the balustrade, the streaming sunlight highlighting the copper tones in his hair. In that moment Dominic made a very appealing addition to the vista. It was a shame his tetchy personality didn't complement the atmosphere.

My studio? *If only.* It was probably just a slip of the tongue, or I'd misheard during my momentary lapse into rapture. I continued slowly up the staircase.

The studio was exactly as Mari Freeborn had described it, the perfect teaching space and at least twice the size of the hall at the community centre. An entire wall of windows overlooked the sea. Even when I'd been discussing my stage school idea with Hal, I hadn't envisaged operating out of a facility like this. I immediately took off my shoes so that I could feel the sprung floor beneath my feet. What was it? Premium maple?

'Impressed?' Dominic asked, a look of amusement on his face. His smile changed his whole demeanour.

'Very. Makes the Community Centre look like a very shabby affair.'

In one corner an upright piano sat under a dust sheet. I lifted the lid and ran my hands across a couple of the keys. Miraculously it sounded as if it was still in tune.

'Can you play?' Dominic enquired.

'Not really. I'm a singer, not a musician.'

This seemed to surprise him even more. 'A singer?'

Alice Paige didn't sing; she was a dance teacher. 'It's just a hobby,' I said realising my mistake. I closed the lid.

'That's a shame,' he said, opening up a cupboard at the rear of the room. The shelves were lined with plastic crates and boxes. He reached in and pulled out a tambourine, giving it a mischievous rattle as he handed it over. 'See here, musical instruments by the score. It must all be Kitty's, I suppose. There's all sorts. Cymbals, triangles, and what are these things called?'

'Maracas.' I took one from him and gave it a shake to demonstrate. Kitty had enough instruments to start her own orchestra. There were music stands, boxes of sheet music, even a basic sound system. It was as if the Hookes Bay Academy of Music and Dance was waiting in limbo for its resurrection.

I turned my attention back to the studio where evidence of the last class remained: a pair of abandoned ballet shoes, a child's pink cardigan, and a plastic drinking flask, all swept into a dusty corner

'This is such an amazing space.'

'Isn't it just,' Dominic agreed, closing the door on the music store. 'And it's all just sitting here, lying dormant.'

He was echoing my very thoughts. If only I had a magic

wand, I could be the one to wake it up. I could barely contain the stem of ideas spontaneously popping into my head.

'You've gone very quiet.' Dominic said, looking perplexed. 'Am I boring you?'

'On the contrary,' I assured him. 'I'm finding this fascinating.'

'You are?'

'Yes.' I nodded emphatically. 'I can't believe this place has been allowed to sit empty. It's such a waste. Can I see more?'

'I've only got a few minutes.'

I wanted to point out that was his fault, not mine, but he was already making his way out of the studio. I followed him back onto the landing for a quick peek into a small office plus two spacious changing rooms, both with ample lockers and clothes rails.

'That's it for up here,' he said, jangling the keys in his pocket. 'Apart from the roof terrace.'

'There's a roof terrace?'

'It's typical of the design.'

'Could you show me? Please?'

He raised his eyes to the ceiling and sighed. Through another door and then up a precarious industrial metal staircase and we were on the flat roof. I could see the entire length of Hookes Bay.

'I feel like I'm standing on the bow of a ship,' I remarked.

'That's the impression you're supposed to get.' Dominic replied. 'The pavilion's architect, Eric Milner, was commission by Conrad Carlisle to design one of the very first themed hotel and entertainment complexes in the country. Carlisle's family were hoteliers in Atlantic City, America. He originally had big plans for little old Hookes Bay. He wanted his guests to imagine they were travelling on the great ocean liners they could see from their hotel balconies, heading off out into the English Channel. Milner designed a lido as well as the pavilion, and I believe there were plans for a casino but Carlisle ran out of cash. War was about to break-out. If you come over here, you can see where the lido used to be. It's now a skate-park.' I turned my gaze away from the water and

49

followed him across to the landward-facing side of the roof, disturbing more pigeons. Between the half-demolished former hotel and its neighbours, I could just glimpse the concrete ramps of Hookes Bay skate-park. 'That's about to get the chop too, so I understand,' Dominic continued. 'I'm sure Kitty will have already told you that her first husband, Lionel Keaton, bought the pavilion from the Carlisle family just after the war. The pier and the theatre had been badly damaged in an air-raid and the Carlisles didn't want the expense of the repairs. Keaton's idea of repairing the pier was to demolish the damaged end, and having saved money there, he concentrated on building up his seaside entertainment business. He and Kitty put on the most elaborate productions. They were way ahead of their time.'

Dominic really didn't sound like a man intent on grabbing a slice of the pavilion's history for himself. I wanted to prolong our time together to find out more about him.

'Kitty mentioned you had some old programmes and photographs?' I said. 'Could I see them at some point?'

Again that perplexed look. 'Sure.'

I took another look seaward. Down below, the fenced off pier was an ugly intrusion on the landscape.

'It's a shame nothing has been done about that pier,' I remarked.

'The whole thing should have been demolished years ago, after Jez's accident,' Dominic replied.

'I'm sorry?'

'Jez Keaton, Kitty's son. She has told you, hasn't she, about Jez?'

I shook my head. 'Only in passing. I wasn't sure what had happened to him. He had an accident?'

Dominic's puzzled look remained. 'He fell off the pier, drowned. He was only twenty-three, twenty-four. They'd been having some sort of private party at the club. I don't know the details of what happened, but I believe it was all investigated by the police at the time. I'm surprised she hasn't mentioned it.'

'Presumably it's all too upsetting for her.' I was ashamed of the mock sympathy I'd expressed that afternoon in the Sir Winnie. 'Poor Kitty. I had no idea.'

Somewhat reluctantly I followed him back to the doorway that led to the metal ladder. The rungs were trickier to negotiate going down, especially in my impractical heels. Halfway down the steps I missed my footing. Dominic grabbed my arm.

'Hey, careful,' he said. At that moment, our eyes locked. It was as if a switch had been flicked on somewhere in my head, or in my heart. I'd always told myself I didn't believe any of that corny nonsense about chemical reactions, or the alignment of stars, but there it was, like a lightning bolt, that moment I'd felt in the foyer all over again, only this time I wasn't dazzled by the building... It was Dominic.

His clutch was firm and steady. 'Kitty would never forgive me if anything happened to you,' he said, his voice a little hoarse but his face inscrutable. Had he felt that lightning bolt too? It appeared not. He released my arm.

Still slightly shaken but determined to stall him, I asked to see the nightclub. I really didn't want the tour to end.

'I have to go,' he replied.

'Just a quick peek?'

'You'll be very disappointed.'

'Please?'

He gave in. I immediately understood his reticence. If everything upstairs and in the atrium was the epitome of classical good taste, the nightclub was the antithesis.

'I can see why you described it as a hole.' I remarked. 'It's poky. After being upstairs I imagined this space would be a lot bigger.'

'Oh, it once was.' Dominic hammered a fist on the vermillion wall behind the DJ booth. 'Robbie must have had shares in plasterboard. Behind here is the rest of the original ballroom. He halved the size of the place at some point in time, presumably to reduce his running costs.'

'Can we get behind there and have a look?'

'Not today. In any case, there really isn't anything to see. What's beyond the kitchen has been left to rot for the last twenty years or so. You'd need an awful lot of vision to imagine it in its full glory.'

'I can do vision,' I said with a brilliant smile. 'What are you doing tomorrow?'

'Working.'

'The day after?'

For a few brief moments in the studio and on the roof it was as if I'd seen a different person altogether. I hadn't been able to stop Dominic talking. Yet now his truculence had returned and he appeared determined to keep me at arm's length.

'Look, Alice, I appreciate the efforts you are making to play your part, but just because we're in this together, it doesn't mean we have to be the best of mates.'

'We're in this together?' I queried. I was quite sure Dominic was not a fellow-thespian. 'What do you mean?'

He frowned at me. 'Kitty has explained why you're here?'

'Well yes, or rather no. So far all I know is that she wants me to take over Mari Freeborn's dance school. I was under the impression that doing that would somehow help save the pavilion.'

Dominic sighed. 'Yes, ultimately, but as I understood it, you're also here to be a distraction.'

'What do you mean?'

'I take it you haven't met Robbie yet?'

'No. All Kitty told me was that I was buying her some more time.'

'Ah, so that's what she said.' Dominic gave a wry smile. 'Well, it's not Kitty you're buying the extra time for, Alice. It's me.'

Just as it seemed he was about to say more, we were interrupted by an irritating Irish jig. He reached swiftly into his pocket for his phone. 'Sorry, that's my call to go.'

I followed him back outside. I felt cross and irritated. Not just with him, but with Kitty. As I walked back to Crabhook Lane I attempted to make sense of what I'd learned. Why did Dominic need the extra time? Was he trying to scrape together the finances to buy the pavilion himself? He certainly didn't look as if he had the odd million going spare, which I assumed would be necessary to outbid a property developer.

I liked the idea that Dominic and I were united in the aim of defeating the common enemy, but he had clearly implied that Kitty had brought me onto the scene to distract her stepson. I couldn't see how Alice Paige, unimposing dance teacher, was supposed to tempt Robbie away from any thoughts of selling the pavilion. Did she want me to seduce him so that he'd become side-tracked and change his mind about pursuing the deal? Had she seen the pictures in the *Sunday Stargazer* and assumed that I would be happy to prostitute myself to save her pavilion? The idea was not just ludicrous, it was appalling. In any case, surely I would have been more of a distraction if I'd been allowed to be myself, to be Tara Wakely, the drunken actress falling out of her skimpy red dress, than mild-mannered Alice Page?

Kitty was asleep when I returned to the bungalow. She was slumped in her armchair, wig askew, snoring softly, a tiny brown sparrow in beige slacks and a cardigan. The brightly coloured clothes were part of the stage show, strictly kept for when she had an audience. Kitty hadn't divulged the exact nature of her illness to me and I hadn't pried. Initially, I'd decided if she wanted me to know she would have told me, although now I sensed there might be an awful lot of things Kitty wasn't being strictly honest about.

Chapter Nine

By the time Kitty awoke, disorientated and unsure what I was doing in her bungalow, I dismissed the whole seduction scenario as a figment of my over-fertile imagination. There was no way a woman who struggled to unbutton her own cardigan could come up with something that devious. Instead, once I'd reminded her who I was – '*Yes, of course you're Alice, silly me*' – Kitty wanted to know what I thought of the pavilion's studio.

'I think it's fantastic,' I told her.

'Better than that awful community centre?' she remarked.

'One hundred percent better,' I agreed.

'Good, I'm glad you liked it.' She fixed a smug enigmatic smile on her face as if she was nursing some great secret.

I spent the next couple of days learning my lines and brushing up my teaching skills at Hookes Bay Academy of Music and Dance. Mari seemed reluctant to finalise the finer details of the purchase. I understood why she felt protective of her business; but I was determined to prove I was perfectly capable of taking over from her. Every time we met she seemed to want to put me through some sort of test.

'How do you feel about dance wear and clothing sales?' she asked. 'I've got some surplus stock. It can be quite a lucrative sideline. And there's the church fete in August. They always ask for a spot of country dancing. Some of the younger pupils are always happy to do it. You might need to start planning that now.'

Mari also entered pupils for exams. 'The girls have to go into Fareham to the Leisure Centre. The examiner usually gives us a couple of options on dates so you'll need to liaise for the most convenient times.'

It was hard to imagine Kitty ever functioning at this level.

On Fridays after-school classes began at four and Mari was still teaching at nine, without a break. She introduced me to all her pupils as the new 'Principal'. That wasn't the only thing I decided I needed to change. Despite implying she was glad to be relinquished of the task of organising the summer show, Mari seemed keen to have an input into my plans.

'We usually focus on a show centred around a traditional musical or adapt a well-known book,' she said. 'What's your current thinking?'

'I think I'd like to celebrate individual expression,' I said, sprouting the first idea that came into my head. 'I'll ask the girls to each choreograph a piece to showcase their talents.'

'Yes, but don't you want the show to have an underlying cohesive theme?' Mari persisted.

'I'd like to introduce something more innovative.'

She was unconvinced. 'I'm really not sure my pupils are ready for that,' she said, not unkindly. 'Alice, please don't think I'm being rude, but you have done this before, haven't you?'

'Yes, of course.' I nearly snapped her head off. 'I am a professional performer with many years' experience in the West End.'

'But you're not, are you?' Mari said, her voice still gentle. 'I'm sorry, Alice. I've Googled you. I can't find records of any West End productions you've been in.'

How could I have slipped up so easily? 'I've been working abroad,' I mumbled, 'you might not have been searching in the right places.'

'Look, I know Kitty is very keen for you to take over the Academy, and I think I know why, but I've built up a reputation here in Hookes Bay. My pupils are very precious to me. Some of my parents might start looking into your background a little deeper. You might need to prove you've got the relevant DBS and first aid qualifications, if nothing else.'

Aaron had warned me about producing certificates in a false name. *Just pretend you've lost them in a house move,* he'd suggested when I'd discussed Kitty's proposition with him. I liked Mari. I didn't want to deceive her. I had the distinct impression she was an innocent pawn in Kitty's game.

'I am willing to sell the business to you, Alice,' Mari continued, before I could say anything in my defence. 'But maybe I should just hang around a bit longer, help you out until you get established, especially with some of the older girls. That way everything remains above board. To be honest, I'm not that keen to spend too much time out on the boat with John. It's the après-sailing I prefer.'

Mari's kindness was very humbling and I didn't deserve it. 'Thank you,' I muttered.

'That's settled then,' she said with a smile. 'It must be a bit lonely for you, living at Kitty's, not knowing anybody. Why don't you come for Sunday dinner this week? Meet John and the boys?'

It was the first social invitation I'd received in over a month. I just about managed to bite back my tears.

On Saturdays Mari started at eight thirty and worked until six. I felt much more at home with the tap and jazz dance lessons, but by the end of the day I was physically and mentally shattered. When I arrived back at Crabhook Lane a mobility scooter was parked on the drive. Kitty was entertaining again; this time her guest was a dapper elderly gentleman in a three-piece suit and bow tie. Cyril was a Saturday evening regular.

'Kit and I always enjoy our fish and chips together,' he informed me. 'I hope you are going to join us. I've taken the liberty of ordering a couple of extra fish cakes.'

I was famished and gratefully accepted the offer. Kitty and Cyril sat at either end of the large dining table, as if carrying on some grand country house tradition of formal dining.

'Kitty's told me all about you,' Cyril said with a wink, as I sat down. 'You must find Hookes Bay a little quiet after all that globetrotting.'

Kitty had told him about Alice. Not me.

'I like quiet,' I said, which wasn't a total lie, especially when I thought about the alternative, returning to London and facing the flak of the gutter press and the cold shoulder of the theatrical world.

'I was telling Kitty about the Local History Society meeting on Thursday,' Cyril said, covering his chips with lashings of ketchup. 'I promised her a full report.'

'Oh? Was it fun?' I prepared to close my ears and concentrate on the fish and chips.

'It was very good.' Another wink, this time directed at Kitty. 'That young lad of yours did well, Kit, love. He's very passionate about the pavilion, isn't he? There are enough of us old stalwarts to help him out. You should come along to our next meeting, Alice, we're going to form a conservation committee.'

Cyril had to be talking about Dominic. Things were looking up – a second social invitation in twenty-four hours, and, even better, another opportunity to see Dominic. Following our encounter at the pavilion I had been hoping to contrive another meeting.

'How many people go to these local history things?' I asked.

'Depends.' Cyril replied. 'If Tom Whybrow is on his usual hobby horse, very few.' I decided the wink was a facial tic.

'Tom did get that signal box preserved,' Kitty chuckled.

'True, but we've heard it all before. The Borough Council don't have the money to spend extending the nature trail. We had the Parks and Countryside people out to speak back in the autumn and they said no more funds were available. If Tom wants a path to go all the way from his precious signal box to the sidings then he's going to have to clear the rest of the railway cutting himself.'

'Did the community support the signal box preservation?' I enquired. If the residents of Hookes Bay had restored an old station signal box, surely they would rally around a campaign to save the pavilion?

Cyril smiled. 'Hookes Bay signal box is Tom Whybrow's pet project. He's the local history society chairman. He managed to get the box preserved and a nature trail to the site of the old town station, which is now buried beneath

Sainsbury's car-park. In theory, the trail could go all the way to Fareham. On the other hand, there's another faction of supporters who would like to see a path created in the opposite direction, along the old branch line to the Titan military base.'

'That would never get the go ahead,' Kitty said, looking up. 'When they sell off Titan the land will go for housing. They don't want a nature trail there.'

'You don't believe those rumours, do you?' Cyril laughed.

'Why not?' Kitty asked. 'Hastings' plans for the Carlisle site are just the first step. Once he's got his permission for that, Titan will be next on his list, you see.'

'The MOD won't give up Titan for years yet,' Cyril said. 'They can't. There's far too much toxic waste in that soil for it to be used for housing. We'll all be long gone before it's safe to build on.'

'What did they used to do there?' I asked. Despite my tiredness I was enjoying the old couple's banter.

'Best not to ask.' Cyril replied with another wink.

Kitty put her hand to her mouth. 'Chemical weapons,' she hissed. 'Top secret it was.'

'Not so top secret if you both knew about it,' I pointed out.

'They couldn't keep it secret,' Cyril replied. 'Everyone who worked there glowed in the dark. You could spot them a mile off.'

'Lindy's father was the commander there for years,' Kitty grunted. 'He certainly didn't glow.'

'Have you met Belinda yet, Alice?' Cyril asked.

I shook my head. Kitty appeared to be in no hurry to introduce me to either her stepson or daughter-in-law. Another reason to discount the seduction theory. Surely if she wanted me to distract Robbie I would have met him by now.

'She's still in Lanzarote,' Kitty informed Cyril, 'doing one of those of workshops of hers.'

'What sort of workshop is she attending?' I asked intrigued.

'She's not attending one, she runs them,' Kitty replied. 'Poetry. That's why they bought the house in Lanzarote. People pay to go out there to read poetry to each other. Sounds daft to me.'

'I've heard the landscape out there is very impressive,' Cyril remarked. 'It probably provides a great source of inspiration.'

I'd already formed my own impression of Robbie's wife, and a woman who ran poetry workshops was far removed from the vacuous trophy wife I'd imagined. There was a photo on Kitty's mantelpiece of a middle-aged couple holding hands on a beach. He was balding, with a slight paunch, Hawaiian shirt and chino shorts. She, slighter taller, sleek in a coral sundress, with ash-blonde shoulder-length hair.

'It's just pandering to rich people with nothing better to do,' Kitty grumbled.

'You don't begrudge her, do you?' Cyril asked. 'It sounds like quite a lucrative business.'

'So does Lindy write poetry herself?' I asked. 'Has she ever had anything published?'

'I don't think she's that good,' Kitty said, her fish and chips finished. She dabbed at her mouth with a tissue. 'Robbie indulges her, that's all, and if he can make some profit on the side, all well and good. That's all he really cares about, the money.' She couldn't hide her bitterness. 'They're on the internet. Posy Mountain or something they're called. Look them up. Maybe it'll tell you what she's written. She's never shown me any books.'

'Don't be so harsh,' Cyril chided. 'Ignore Kitty, Alice. Lindy regularly has her poems featured in literary magazines. She also writes the occasional column for the South Coast Gazette.'

Alarm bells started to ring. 'A newspaper column? You mean she's a journalist?' Why hadn't Kitty thought to mention this before?

'Oh no, she writes reviews, books, films, theatre, that kind of thing,' Cyril said, wiping the last dregs of ketchup from his plate with a soggy chip.

Alarm bells and a red flag. No wonder Kitty was avoiding my eye. An amateur journalist was bad enough, but a theatre critic was positively dangerous.

Chapter Ten

Hoping for my first lie-in of the week, I was disturbed at six thirty the following morning by a series of wails from Kitty's room. Kitty had insisted I wasn't in Hookes Bay to look after her. She was a proud woman who treasured her independence and privacy. Did I ignore the crying, or cross the hallway to her room and see what was wrong? What if she had fallen out of bed? A gentle, enquiring tap was surely the very least I could do.

'Kitty? Is everything all right?'

I gently pushed the door ajar. Kitty's room was a shrine to her favourite colour. Walls, carpet, curtains, bed covers, all purple. A large white dressing table dominated the room, covered with photographs, perfume bottles and toiletries. Kitty's various wigs were displayed on a row of mannequins.

She lay lost in the middle of her bed, shrivelled and shrunken, sparse tufts of white hair framing her head.

'Shush, what's up?' I perched on the edge of the bed and reached across for her hand. She had tears on her cheeks.

'Oh no, oh no.' She sounded as if she was in some sort of physical pain. 'I must have been dreaming. Jez was here, clear as day.'

A picture of a schoolboy in a red jumper had pride of place on the bedside table. He was perhaps ten or eleven, dark-haired, brown-eyed, cheeky grin.

'Is this Jez?' I asked.

She nodded. 'He was on the pier.'

Oh yes, the pier. Poor Kitty. No wonder she had nightmares.

'You should try and get back to sleep,' I soothed. Now was not the time to start quizzing her about her son.

'Stay with me.'

'Yes, yes, of course I will.'

To my relief she closed her eyes and her breathing regulated. After another ten minutes it felt safe to leave the room. She didn't wake again until nine, and when she did finally emerge, fully dressed and made up, she didn't mention the incident.

'You look very smart,' I said, feeling considerably dowdy in my grey running gear. It was a beautiful sunny morning and I intended to explore more of Hookes Bay before heading over to Mari's for lunch.

'It's Sunday,' she replied. 'Sunday best as always, duck.'

I suddenly felt guilty that I was leaving her on her own. 'What's your normal Sunday routine?' I asked, hoping she had some sort of social activity to keep her occupied in my absence. 'Do you see friends, family, church?'

She gave a derisive snort. 'Church? Me?' Then she cackled. 'Oh, don't you fret about me if you've got something else planned, I've got plenty to keep me busy.'

'Are you sure? Mari has invited me for dinner.'

'Of course I'm sure.' She replied. 'How do you think I've managed without you for the last thirty odd years?'

The air was already warm as I set off for a jog along the seafront. Beyond the pavilion, the beach petered out into an unkempt strip of rocks and stones, clearly inaccessible. I skirted back into town and took a quick detour towards the yacht club.

The white weatherboard clubhouse sat at the water's edge, beside a small grassy area for the storage of dinghies and canoes. The main road circled behind the clubhouse and led to a small working marina. It was low tide and most of the yachts were mud-bound. On shore, commercial units offered an array of marine related services. It all looked very new apart from one dilapidated wooden boatshed which was home to Hookes Bay Architectural Salvage & Reclamation Yard. Through padlocked gates I could see stacks of paving stones, slates and tiles amongst garden statues, chimney pots and Butler sinks by the dozen, but unfortunately, to my disappointment, there was no sign of the proprietor.

Dominic Flynn had occupied my thoughts a lot over the last week. I was still keen to look at Kitty's old photographs, and now that I knew where to find him, it would be easy enough to pop along on a free morning during the week.

Mari had identical twin boys, George and Marcus, strapping youths with the physique of rugby players. John was in the garage when I arrived, half hidden amongst the sailing paraphernalia.

'I'm just having a clear out,' he explained, handing Mari a child's wetsuit. 'Why are we keeping this, dear? And what about that old bike of yours? Can I take it to a car boot sale?'

Mari clutched the wetsuit as if it was of great sentimental value. 'I can't believe the boys were ever this small,' she said wistfully. 'But yes, one for the car boot, and the bike, unless you want it, Alice? It might give you a bit of freedom getting around? It's got a big basket, cumbersome but very useful.'

I accepted her offer gratefully and John promised to give the bike a quick clean.

We retreated to the kitchen where Mari was putting the finishing touches to the dinner.

'Kitty had a friend around last night,' I said. 'Cyril. Do you know him?'

'For a time I thought she had him lined up as husband number four,' Mari laughed. 'Bless him. He's a lamb. Devoted to her, he is.'

'Kitty seems to be able to charm anyone and everyone,' I remarked. 'Tell me about the husbands. Kitty's life story fascinates me.'

'I think it fascinates everyone,' Mari replied. 'She's a remarkable woman. Hughie was the only one of the husbands I knew. When I was a girl having lessons she was married to Don, but he was more or less housebound. By all accounts he was a bit of a rough diamond. Hughie must have been an absolute poppet in comparison. They'd known each other for years. He used to work as her pianist. I always thought he was gay to be honest, but I suppose by the time they got married they were looking for companionship more than anything else.'

'So if you had lessons with Kitty when you were younger you must have known her son, Jez?'

It was almost as if Mari had been waiting for me to ask the question. She poured two generous glasses of wine. 'Here, have one of these,' she said. 'Everyone in Hookes Bay knew Jez. He almost lived at the pavilion. He was probably my first crush. My friends and I swooned if he so much as glanced in our direction, and he always humoured us. *Hi girls, how's it going? How's the dancing*? That's what he was like, a big charmer. He was a really popular guy. On a Saturday the whole band would be there, rehearsing downstairs in the club.'

I hesitated slightly. 'What exactly happened to him? I understand he had an accident on the pier?'

'You don't know the story?' I shook my head. Mari took a sip of her wine. 'To be honest the details of what happened have always been a bit vague. He had thrown a party at the club. The others had all left and he was there on his own. The police reckoned he'd consumed some sort of lethal cocktail of drink and drugs, taken a walk to get some air and somehow tripped and slipped into the water. Tragic.' Mari sighed. 'I'm sorry.'

I wasn't entirely sure why she felt the need to apologise to me but I echoed her sympathetic sentiments with a 'poor Kitty'.

'I know. It must have been awful for her. They never found his body.'

'I take it they sent out search parties?'

'Of course they did. Back in those days Titan was fully operational and the military were called in but they never found anything. They employed Navy divers, scoured the coast. I think some clothing was retrieved from the mudflats but it wasn't his. There were a lot of salacious rumours, a little place like this gossip soon starts flying around. I mean, without a body, there's always going to be speculation.'

'You mean people didn't believe he'd drowned?'

Mari nodded. 'Awful isn't it? Some people said it wasn't an accident. They talked about suicide, then that he'd done a runner, and faked his own death. The whole thing was ridiculous. I believe the police even arrested a man busking outside Portsmouth Harbour station because a passer-by swore blind it was Jez. Jez had just got a recording contract, why would he fake his own suicide?' Mari reached out and patted my arm, 'Jez wasn't like that.' She smiled. 'He loved life.'

'But nobody saw him actually go into the water?'

She looked surprised at my question. 'No. As I said, he was there on his own.'

'And his band were good?'

'Oh yes,' Mari confirmed. 'It was no surprise they were picked up by a London record company.'

'Was Robbie in the band?'

Mari nearly choked on her wine. 'No. Robbie isn't musical.'

'Did you ever see the band play?' I asked.

'Only a couple of times. I can remember them doing a summer carnival. The annual Hookes Bay Regatta was a big thing back in those days, you know, besides the sailing events there was always a procession with majorettes and decorated floats. Then in the evening, on the recreation ground behind the church they'd have a barbecue and a firework display. Jez had a cracking voice, could send shivers down your spine. Mind you, as I said, I was only twelve or thirteen. It's a very impressionable age. They had this one song, you know, like an anthem. I can remember the opening line even now. *Lulu my love, you're my dirty little secret.*'

'Lulu?'

'Yes, you know, like the Scottish singer.' Mari laughed and ruffled her curls. 'We share the same hair colour. I took a lot of stick at school and I liked to think maybe Jez had a secret crush on her, and liked the ginger look.'

As much as I was admirer of Lulu as a performer, I wasn't convinced a young man in his twenties would have dedicated a song to her. Not wanting to cast doubt onto Mari's aspirations, I decided to change the subject. 'What about the other guys in the band? Were they all locals?'

'Yes. The guitarist Woody was Jez's best friend. As for the

Bonetti brothers, their family own the Italian restaurant, La Scala, on the corner of the high street, have done for years. Paolo still works there. You should pop in and say hello.'

I was immediately on my guard. Did Mari know who I really was? She'd certainly sussed I wasn't an authentic dance teacher, that was for sure. On the other hand she didn't look like an avid reader of the *Sunday Stargazer* or its contemporaries. Sometimes headlines were hard to avoid. *Let's Chat* always had the prime spot next to the supermarket checkout. Was the restaurateur a Tara Wakely fan? It was a horrid thought which made me immediately defensive.

'Why would I do that? He doesn't know me.'

Mari coloured and took a hurried gulp of her wine. 'No, no, of course not, but you're new in town, it's a good place to eat.'

She looked decidedly relieved as the twins burst into the kitchen demanding to be fed.

Chapter Eleven

Kitty

Kitty was feeling remarkably pleased with herself. Alice was attacking her role with great gusto; she had agreed to spend two weeks shadowing Mari's lessons, demonstrating an old-fashioned work ethic which Kitty admired, although it wasn't necessary at all. Kitty had every faith that Alice was perfectly capable of running the Hookes Bay Academy of Music and Dance. After all it wasn't as if she had to do it long term, but if the girl wanted to immerse herself in the part, so be it. She was growing quite fond of Alice. She had soothed her during her nightmare, held her hand. How long since it felt as if someone actually, genuinely cared? Robbie certainly didn't have the bedside manner, and Lindy, for all her show of devotion, could be a bit of a cold fish.

Kitty hadn't realised how lonely she'd got living by herself in the bungalow. Thank goodness Hughie had ignored her all those years ago when she'd insisted she wanted to stay at Balmoral Heights, the house she had bought with Don. Hughie had refused to take no for an answer. He had pointed out all the merits of moving to something modern and smaller; a heating system that worked, hot water literally on tap, windows that didn't rattle in the breeze. The double glazing had been the Holy Grail. Hughie had seen the PVC frames and made the agent an offer on the spot.

Instead of that huge garden with its shrubs and hedges that always needed trimming, trees that needed pruning, leaves that needed gathering, just a simple lawn and small area for growing vegetables.

'So easy to maintain,' Hughie had beamed. 'And still room

for my greenhouse.'

Kitty had saved as much as she could from the Heights, but there was only so much room in the bungalow. The worst bit had been clearing out Jez's room, untouched for all those years. What to do with the single bed with its beige candlewick bedspread? She'd made the bed, of course, washed the sheets regularly over the years, just in case.

The bedside table and matching chest of drawers full of Jez's clothes, his private belongings, it all had to go. The notebooks she'd found crammed into the shelves of the vast oak wardrobe. She'd never known her son had been such a prolific song-writer. How could she not have known? Music and lyrics had flowed across the pages.

And then that awful thought. What if he did come home? What if he did suddenly return to the Heights and she wasn't there? The people who'd bought it had converted the house into flats. That vast garden was now a car-park.

'Look, if you really can't bear to part with this stuff,' Lindy had said, 'why not hire a storage unit? There's a new place off the Fareham Road. You can rent a small storeroom, keep it safe.'

The storeroom.

'Do you employ somebody to go in and keep that place tidy for you?' Dominic had asked when he had returned from collecting the crates of old theatre programmes. 'I've never seen such a clean organised storage unit.'

She and Hughie had left it in chaos, boxes and cases all over place.

Alice told Kitty she wanted to spend the day exploring on her new bicycle. She left a flask of soup on the table beside Kitty's wicker chair. Kitty insisted there was no need. She had a month's worth of microwave meals labelled Monday to Friday stacked in the freezer. Lindy ordered them for her.

Kitty's ears suddenly pricked up. Her hearing was letting her down a lot lately, but she was pretty sure she had just heard the latch on the side-gate.

'Kitty, are you home?'

Mari poked her head into the conservatory. Most of Kitty's regular visitors knew where to find her.

'Hello Kit. Can I come in?'

'Of course you can come in,' Kitty said. 'If you want tea you'll have to make it yourself.'

'I'm more than happy to,' Mari said. 'Would you like one too?'

Kitty never turned down tea. It was the only thing that kept her going on bad days. Kitty's taste buds were pickled in nicotine long ago, but tea... The act of taking tea was not something she was prepared to relinquish, even if she could no longer taste the difference between a Twinings Finest and a Tesco value. No mugs for her – a tea-cup and a saucer every time. Luckily Mari knew that. She returned from the kitchen with a tray and a plate of biscuits.

'I picked these up on the way here,' she said. 'Ginger snaps.'

Mari Freeborn was a beanpole who hadn't eaten a biscuit in her life, but Kitty had never been able to resist a ginger snap.

As Kitty took her time taking dainty sips of tea and chewing on morsels of ginger biscuit, Mari talked about John's planned sailing excursion to the Channel Islands, about George's A level revision, and Marcus' last cricket match, everything in fact, apart from the subject Kitty guessed she had come to speak about. Kitty was more than happy to keep Mari talking trivialities.

Kitty could feel her eyelids drooping as Mari continued with a tirade about dog muck in the park. Kitty didn't like dog muck more than anyone else but she was never going to walk in the park again. In any case, didn't Mari have a dog? A great big boisterous thing that left clumps of hair everywhere. Did Mari pick up every single splodge of turd? Kitty highly doubted it. Still at least Mari's dog was a proper dog, not like that little scrap Belinda carried about in her handbag. Did Robbie know how stupid he looked taking that thing for a walk?

Mari lamented the closing of the Nat West. There were no banks left in Hookes Bay now. That didn't bother Kitty; she'd always kept her money in the Post Office. Lionel had always insisted under the mattress was the safest place, but not with Robbie around. As for the sob story about broken domestic appliances, Kitty had no sympathy. Had Mari forgotten Kitty had grown up in an era when nobody even had a washing machine? People today were obsessed with cleanliness. Penny was exactly the same, insisting Kitty was bathed or showered at least once a week. It wasn't as if she went anywhere to get dirty.

The bedding was changed every Wednesday. Kitty could remember sleeping in the same bedding for weeks on end. She could also remember sleeping in a different bed every other night of the week. The thought made her chuckle, which turned into a splutter.

'All right, Kitty?'

'Yes of course.' Now what was Mari saying? She had taken the tea tray back to the kitchen, washed the cups even though there was no need.

'Kitty, about Alice.'

Ah, so here it comes, Kitty thought. She gave Mari one of her special smiles, a look of indignant innocence she had perfected many years ago. 'Yes? What about her?'

'Well,' Mari said hesitantly, 'is she who I think she is? And if so, how did you find her and convince her to come to Hookes Bay?'

Chapter Twelve

Tara

My foster parents had been keen cyclists. Ray had a campervan. He'd load the bikes onto the back and we'd head out to the countryside, a totally alien environment to a city kid like me. Hookes Bay had re-awoken those memories. I followed the road that ran around edge of the military compound and ended up at the nature reserve. Flocks of sea birds roosted on the distant mudflats. It was a solitary, tranquil spot, the silence only broken by a middle-aged couple having some sort of domestic argument at one of the observation posts, and a fierce-looking Staffie, charging towards me through the brambles.

I took a welcome break at a garden centre. Horticulture had been another of Viv and Ray's pet hobbies, hence my obsession with saving the feeble excuse for a tomato plant I'd cultivated on Hal's balcony. It was a reminder of happier times. Kitty's bare patch of garden certainly needed brightening up and the nursery had plants by the score.

Ten minutes later, complete with the purchase of a colourful planter for Kitty, and three tomato plants for me, all balanced precariously in the bike's basket, I gave up on further exploration and decided to head straight back into town. Not entirely sure of the way I followed a road signposted Reading Room Lane. The reading room turned out to be a quaint red brick chapel, sat in its own little patch of overgrown garden, while the road twisted and dipped across farmland until coming to an abrupt end behind the marina.

To my delight a red truck was parked outside the gates to the salvage yard. Even more delightful was the sight of

Dominic Flynn in shorts and T-shirt, heaving a large statue of a Great Dane out of the trailer.

'Hi, Dominic.'

He looked up. 'Oh. It's you.' It wasn't exactly the welcome I'd have hoped for. He continued to manoeuvre the statue into his yard.

'Do you need a hand?'

'No, I'm fine, thank you.'

I could see that he was perfectly capable; muscles rippled on his tanned arms as the Great Dane reached its resting place beside a pair of cherubs.

'I don't suppose now is a good time to have a look through some of those old programmes and photos you mentioned?' I asked, following him into the yard.

Dominic seemed to hesitate, then gave a shrug. 'Sure. Come in.'

The interior of the warehouse appeared to contain the same jumble of artefacts as the outside.

'You've got quite a collection here,' I remarked.

'It's how I earn my living,' he replied.

I was determined not to be put off by his rudeness. 'Where do you get it all from?'

Now he looked bored. 'I buy it. You want to see the old programmes? I've got the box in my office. It's this way.'

Dominic's green T-shirt did something wonderful to the colour of his hair, his eyes and his skin. Most of the men I worked with had tans that came from the spraying booth. Dominic Flynn was a man who spent a lot of time outdoors. His earthy ruggedness was doing something very strange to my insides.

At the rear of the boatshed was an untidy office. He lifted a plastic crate from the floor and placed it on his desk.

'This all relates to the theatre. I've also got some old ciné footage on my laptop.'

'Oh, I'd like to see that.' I said immediately.

'It's a bit grainy.'

'I'd still like to look at it though, if you don't mind.'

'Really?'

'Why do you doubt me?'

He didn't answer but cleared some of the clutter from his desk. 'I'll set it up for you. Then I'll have to leave you to it, because I've got work to do. It only lasts a couple of minutes but you'll get the gist.'

I smiled ever-so-sweetly at him. 'Thank you.'

The black and white footage was probably from the early 1950s. I recognised Kitty instantly. She and a suave dark-haired man who I could only conclude from the way they kept touching each other was Lionel Keaton, were conducting some sort of backstage tour for the film-maker. Kitty was dressed in a kimono, smoking a cigarette whilst Lionel, not dissimilar in looks to Kitty's fish and chip friend Cyril, was in a formal suit. They made an incongruous couple, at least a foot separating them in height and twenty years in age.

When the tour was complete, the image switched to Kitty on the stage in a sailor suit taking a salute, before jumping again to another scene of her in the middle of a line of dancing girls waving feathers and wearing very little.

Despite his protestation that he had work to do Dominic loitered outside the doorway with his back to me, rooting through a box of door handles.

'I hadn't realised Lionel was so much older than her,' I called out. My comment elicited no response. 'They must have caused quite a stir.'

A phone vibrated on the desk. A message notification popped up.

Danni: 'Are we meeting up or not?'

I put the laptop to one side and turned my attention to the box of programmes. Seconds later another message.

Hobo: 'Just come across a farm plough. Bit rusty. Interested?'

The plastic crate was piled high with old theatre programmes. I lifted a handful onto the desk, deliberately hiding the phone. Whoever Danni was she could wait and nobody, not even Dominic, would be interested in an old plough. I was saving him from himself.

At the bottom of the crate there were a couple of

photograph albums.

'Are these Kitty's personal pictures?' I shouted.

Again nothing. I got up. Dominic had headphones in.

'Anywhere round here I can get a coffee?' I asked standing in front of him. 'There's a lot of stuff to look through.'

He momentarily removed an earpiece. 'The chandlery. Get me one too whilst you're there. White no sugar.'

'How about a please?' I suggested, but it was too late. He had plugged himself back in.

The first photograph album contained a portfolio of publicity shots from various stages of Kitty's extensive career. There were pictures of her alone on stage, in others she posed with various groups of fellow dancers and musicians.

I deliberately left Dominic's coffee on the corner of the desk. Eventually he joined me. 'Is this Don Mayhew?' I asked, pointing to a picture of Kitty with her arm around a hefty gangster-type: teddy boy quiff and long dark sideburns.

He nodded. 'She hasn't always been the best judge of character, has she?'

I wasn't sure what he was implying so I ignored him. 'So how come you've been entrusted with all this stuff?' I asked, leaning back in his vintage tan leather swivel chair, a final attempt to engage him in some sort of civilised conversation.

'It's research,' he replied.

'Is that what I'm buying you the extra time for? Are you writing a book?'

'And how would that help?'

'What is it then? Do you want to buy the pavilion yourself?'

'I wish. If only it was that easy.'

'What then? Aren't there organisations set up to save valuable old buildings like the pavilion? Why is Kitty resorting to subterfuge, or whatever this scenario is?'

'Yes, you're right, there are organisations set up to preserve old buildings like the pavilion.'

'So, why aren't they involved?' I asked.

'They are,' he sighed. 'That's why you're here, why you need to take over Mari's dance school, and why you need to distract Robbie from his negotiations with Coastline

Developments.'

Not the seduction plan again. I pushed the photograph album away. 'I need to know what's going on here, Dominic,' I said. 'Seriously, if I'm to do this properly I need to know what's expected of me.'

He appeared to relent. With his coffee cupped in his hands he took a perch on the edge of the desk.

'Okay. Six months or so ago I got wind of the plans for the Carlisle site. I contacted Kitty to warn her. I'd already ascertained that the pavilion wasn't a listed building so there was nothing to protect it. It wasn't even on the Borough Council's list of buildings at risk, which was criminal. It took some persuading to convince Kitty that the pavilion needed protecting. She assumed Robbie would get his licence back and the nightclub would eventually re-open. She thought Robbie loved the building as much as she did and would look after it when she'd gone. It didn't occur to her that he would ever consider selling out to someone like Coastline, and that the pavilion could end up being demolished.

'Anyone can apply for a building to be listed. You don't need to be the owner, or have a vested interest, but the application process is very lengthy. You have to provide reports, photographs, evidence of the building's significance within the local community, not just its architectural merits.

'I went ahead and put the application in. It took a couple of months to compile everything I needed and it will take Historic England up to four months to make a recommendation to the Secretary of State who has the final decision.'

'So that's why you need the time? To wait for their verdict?'

'We can't afford to wait for their verdict. Buildings pending a contentious listing have a habit of vanishing overnight. Back in the 1980s The Firestone Tyre Factory in Brentford was demolished by its owners over a bank holiday weekend because they didn't want it listed. They wanted to sell off the land. The crux is the pavilion isn't going to be safe until it's out of Robbie's hands.'

'So why don't you buy it instead?'

'Trust me, if I could, I would.'

'Kitty doesn't need the money. Why doesn't she sell the pavilion to you for a nominal sum to guarantee its safety?'

'Oh I've already tried that one,' Dominic smiled. When he smiled his whole face transformed, as if there was another Dominic waiting to escape from behind his gruff antagonistic exterior. 'It's not just the expense of buying the building which is prohibitive, it's the cost of restoring it. In addition, Kitty has a great sense of misplaced loyalty to Robbie and his wife. I suppose without Don Mayhew's support back in the 1960s, the place would have probably closed down. I don't think Belinda Mayhew knows what planet she's on, let alone what the pavilion is worth, but Robbie does, and Coastline are making Kitty a very good offer.'

'So the solution is?' I was intrigued to learn the thinking behind Kitty's convoluted conspiracy, and I was enjoying listening to Dominic's melodic Irish voice.

'Originally I considered applying for an ACV, an Asset of Community Value. It's a relatively new piece of legislation allowing members of the community to preserve vital amenities and unique local landmarks, such as corner shops, sports facilities and even pubs.'

'That sounds perfect.'

'It's not. Persuading this borough council to approve the ACV designation would be impossible. Coastline Developments are planning to landscape the entire seafront. A few months' back there was a huge problem with joyriders, teenagers racing each other along the esplanade. They would congregate by the pavilion and see who reached the yacht club first. Coastline have promised to create a whole new pedestrian area and rejuvenate the Prince Albert Park. The main road will divert behind the new apartments, creating natural speed-calming measures. The development will bring in new businesses and retail opportunities. It's a major investment and if the pavilion has to make way for it, I don't think too many councillors will object. Apart from anything else, half of the men sitting on the borough council wouldn't recognise the significance of saving a slice of our cultural heritage if it slapped them in the face. There's only one thing these people care about and it's the money in their pockets. I imagine if this development gets the go ahead, lots of those councillors will receive a nice little bonus courtesy of Coastline Developments.'

'But that's corruption.' I was indignant.

'Of course is it, but that's how local government works.'

'Surely the development could go ahead without demolishing the pavilion?'

'Of course it could, but Grant Hastings, the man behind Coastline Developments, has already delayed submitting his plans while he waits on this deal. He's currently losing money because all he has at the moment is a derelict building site. He's pinned all his hopes on getting the pavilion. With the extra land, not only can he build several more apartments, but the majority of them will have interrupted sea views and direct access to the waterfront. You're not just looking at an increase in profits of a few hundred thousand, you're looking at millions.'

'And so?'

'And so I'm negotiating with an organisation called the Modernist Preservation Trust to fund a buy-out. I've managed to lure one of the directors, Sam MacDonald, down to Hookes Bay next week to view the pavilion. The problem is the MPT have stringent regulations regarding the projects they take on, which we don't currently fulfil, and which is why you're here.'

'Oh?' At last a proper explanation.

'The MPT want hard evidence of community support for the restoration project. Not easy when half the residents of Hookes Bay were calling for the nightclub to close down twelve months ago. Fortunately I've managed to convince a few members of the local history society to form a conservation society. And secondly, they also insist any facility they purchase is run as a viable commercial enterprise. I can happily announce that the newly appointed principal of the Hookes Bay Academy of Music and Dance will be running her business from the premises.'

'I'm moving the dance school into the pavilion?' I could hardly contain my excitement. A whole stream of endless possibilities were suddenly within my grasp. Hookes Bay Academy was not quite on the same scale as the stage school I had envisaged with Hal in London, but it was a small step in the right direction. The bottom rung of the ladder, and I couldn't have hoped for better surroundings. My joy was short-lived.

'Only in theory, yes,' Dominic said. 'I mean, if the MPT do go ahead then obviously a genuine teacher would need to be found. You're just playing the part for now, aren't you? But we need to watch out. Grant Hastings is not a man to be messed with. The most important thing here is that he doesn't get wind of any of these ideas. If words gets out he's not the only person interested in buying the pavilion, there's every likelihood the building could go up in smoke one weekend when nobody is looking, just like the Firestone building. I wouldn't put anything past him. He's a thoroughly nasty piece of work.'

I tried to mask my disappointment with what seemed like a sensible question. 'You've had dealings with him before?'

Dominic threw his coffee cup into the wastepaper basket by the door. 'You could say that,' he said, standing up with a stretch. 'He's my father-in-law.

Chapter Thirteen

Two blows in as many sentences. Not only was I not considered a genuine contender to be the new proprietor of the Hookes Bay Academy of Music and Dance, but Dominic Flynn had a wife.

Why was I so surprised? Mari Freeborn had done nothing but question my teaching abilities since I had arrived in Hookes Bay, and as for Dominic, he was handsome, if not exactly charming, so it was perfectly logical that some female had snapped him up along ago. No wonder he had got wind of Coastline's plans for Hookes Bay, it was probably pillow talk.

I fixed a weak smile on my face. 'Isn't that some sort of conflict of interest?'

The phone beneath the pile of paperwork began its Irish jig again. I directed the brunt of my disappointment into a disapproving glare at the untimely interruption. How could he put up with such an infuriating ring-tone?

'Talk of the devil,' Dominic said with an apologetic shrug. He shifted through the strategically placed programmes to retrieve the phone. It took a second impatient ring before he located it, answering the call with a cheerful 'Danni' as he headed out into the warehouse, well out of earshot.

I returned the programmes to the crate with far less enthusiasm than I had removed them and watched from the office doorway as Dominic paced around the far corners of the warehouse, deep in animated conversation. I heard laughter.

'Sorry,' he said, when he eventually returned to the office. 'I need to head out.'

An immediate picture of some romantic lunch at the yacht club sprang to mind. 'Sure. I'm done here too,' I said. 'It's too much to absorb in one go.'

'You don't need to leave on my account,' he said at once.

'I've a mate who's dropping some gear off in half an hour or so. He'll mind the office while I'm gone so it would help me out anyway if you stayed on until he arrives. I'm already running late and Mrs Flynn doesn't like to be kept waiting.'

I consoled myself with the knowledge that I certainly wouldn't want to be married to a man who referred to his wife as *Mrs Flynn*. Nor did he make any effort to smarten himself up before heading off for his lunch, not even pausing to wash his hands. Maybe they weren't meeting at the yacht club, maybe he was treating his wife to a greasy pasty at Pebbles, the café on the esplanade, or a curly sandwich at the Sir Winnie. I sincerely hoped so.

I wandered around the warehouse, browsing amongst the eclectic mix of fixtures and fittings. Not for the first time I regretted ever responding to Kitty's begging letter. I felt humiliated all over again. There had never been a plan for me to run Kitty's dance school. I was simply a means to an end. If and when the pavilion was preserved, a new dance teacher would be installed. Did Dominic and Kitty really believe they could continue plotting behind Coastline Developments' back? The whole idea was ridiculous.

Dominic had been gone barely ten minutes when a van pulled up outside, and a bearded man in his mid-forties, clad in a pair of dirty blue overalls clambered out of the cab and began to offload a set of antiquated agricultural implements. So much for my attempts to prevent Dominic investing in any more old junk.

'You minding shop?' the man called, as I headed out to greet him.

'Just until you came.'

He looked up from his task with a smile. 'Dom's a dark horse. He's been keeping you a bit of a secret. What's your name then? Haven't seen you around here before, have I?'

'My name is Alice,' I retorted in an attempt to quash any ideas that might have otherwise popped into his head. This man certainly looked like he could easily be a *Sunday Stargazer* reader. 'Alice Paige.'

'Not local, are you?'

I shook my head. 'No, I'm not.' The man's scrutiny was discerning. I wedged the door open whilst he moved his filthy pieces of equipment into the warehouse. 'I'll be off then, now that you're here.'

'Okay, suit yourself. I'm Paul by the way, but everyone calls me Hobo.' He held out a large grubby calloused hand. 'I expect Dom's mentioned me.'

I could hardly confess to snooping on Dominic's texts. 'No, he hasn't, I'm afraid.' I gingerly accepted the outstretched hand and nearly lost my fingers in the process.

Back at the bungalow Kitty made no comment about her gift of the plant pot which I placed in the direct line of vision from the favourite chair. That evening, I phoned Mari Freeborn and asked if I could call round to complete the paperwork for the purchase of the dance school.

Mari was home alone. There was no sign of John, the dog or the boys. In exchange for my cash Mari signed a contract downloaded from a dubious online solicitor, transferring the ownership of the Hookes Bay Academy of Music and Dance to the name of A Roberts.

Kitty dismissed legalities as trivialities, but as Aaron pointed out, I couldn't complete a binding contract under a false name. Kitty had given me the money to pay for the purchase of Mari's dance school before I'd even arrived in Hookes Bay, but I didn't use her money. I used my own, or rather I used the *Sunday Stargazer*'s. Aaron was more than happy to set up a new bank account in our joint names, and to appease any of Mari's families who were concerned enough to look me up on the internet, Alice Paige now had her own blog which included the briefest of details of her fictitious career and some very blurry pictures of her alter-ago Tara Wakely. I was treading a very fine line; apart from the obvious overtones of fraud, the last thing I wanted was anybody making a connection to my past. Georgie Gold was still making the headlines in London.

In exchange for my cash I inherited the school's name, Mari's equipment, props and costumes in the storage container, and her existing client base. The Hookes Bay

Academy of Music and Dance was now mine, not Kitty's, although officially, it belonged to Aaron. What was most important, however, was that I couldn't be dismissed the minute the Modernist Preservation Trust took over the pavilion. In addition, I now had my own business, ensuring I'd never have to return to the London theatre scene again, completely eliminating the risk of bumping into Hal or Georgie at an opening night party or an awards ceremony. I could hide myself away on the south coast for as long as I wanted. I really could wave my magic wand and put the life back into Hookes Bay Pavilion.

Don't let people use you, Aaron warned. I wasn't going to. Kitty Keaton was the queen of self-preservation, resilient and resourceful. I hadn't known her long, but she had already taught me a great deal.

I had my first driving lesson at eleven o'clock the next morning. I decamped to Pebbles on the seafront first thing with my laptop, anxious to be out of the bungalow. The café was advertising a newly installed high-speed Wi-Fi service which for the price of a croissant and a coffee seemed like a very good deal.

Despite telling myself I needed to prioritise with a crash course on the Highway Code, the first name I typed into Google was Dominic's. There were several hundred thousand search results. However, re-defining the search to *Dominic Flynn Hookes Bay* hit the jackpot and I was directed to the website of Hookes Bay Architectural Reclamation and Salvage where I learned that Dominic was a fully qualified architect with a specific interest in conservation and restoration projects. Further research revealed that Dominic and Danielle Flynn were joint partners in a chartered architect's practice, Flynn Design Consultancy, with an office in Old Portsmouth. One click on the FDC website and I uncovered a photograph of the happy couple, Dominic barely recognisable in a shirt and tie with a short back and sides haircut and rimless spectacles; Danielle, an attractive, brunette in silk blouse and a caramel skirt suit.

I was pretty certain that Dominic's concern for the pavilion's preservation was genuine. Although there was nothing on the website that gave any indication that he was not still an active partner in FDC, judging by the length and cut of his hair, the photograph was several months, if not years old. If he was still practicing as an architect, why was he running a junkyard?

He doesn't even like you. The voice of reason, the party-pooper. *He's still seeing his wife because he was meeting her for lunch...*

A lunch for which he couldn't even be bothered to change out of his filthy clothes. I suspected Mrs Flynn, immaculately turned out in her satin caramel-crème business suit, would have loved that. It was poor consolation but I cherished the thought.

I returned to the page on driving theory and wondered whether the driving instructor would mind that I didn't even have a provisional licence.

'So Alice,' Phil Kendrick said, after he'd elicited the promise the provisional licence would be produced on the second lesson. 'What brings you to Hookes Bay?' We had retreated to the skate park car park for some off-road tuition.

'Work,' I replied. 'I'm a dance teacher.'

'Oh, I see. That's how you know Mari Freeborn and Kitty Keaton, I suppose.' He had picked me up from Kitty's bungalow. 'You're staying with Kitty?'

'It's just a temporary arrangement. You know Kitty well?'

'We go way back,' he replied. He was a tall man, mid-sixties, with a very placid, calm demeanour, undoubtedly a necessity of the job. 'I met her thirty odd years ago. I'm ex-police.'

Why had I ever thought learning to drive was a good idea?

'You might want to adjust the seat height a bit,' Phil glanced sideways. 'That lever there.'

'Yes, thank you.' I tried to compose myself. I needed to divert Phil Kendrick's attention quite firmly away from any further questions about myself. An interrogation from a police officer was the last thing I needed. 'So have you always been based in Hookes Bay?' I enquired.

'Yes, back in the day when we had a station right here in the town centre. Now, of course, it's all moved to Fareham.'

'I suppose Hookes Bay is hardly the crime capital of the south coast is it?'

'You'd be surprised,' Phil replied. 'Where are you from? Do you want to switch on the ignition? Foot on the clutch. That pedal there, love.'

'London.'

'Oh yes, well I suppose this would seem like a sleepy little place. Of course we've had our moments. If you know Kitty, you'll know all about the Pavilion Club. That's kept us on our toes over the years.'

'I heard Robbie let the place fall into disrepute.'

'You could say that. I'm thinking more about young Jez. You know that story, I take it?'

'Not exactly. Were you involved in the investigations into his disappearance?'

'To begin with yes, before it was handed over to the CID.'

'It must have been so hard for Kitty, not knowing what exactly happened.'

'Absolutely,' Phil agreed. 'People need closure, to say their goodbyes. Unfortunately, I suspect Jez's disappearance will always remain one of those unsolved mysteries. Shall we just run through the gears? Let's try first, then second.'

'It seems odd that his body was never found. Surely it would have washed up somewhere along the coast eventually?'

'Not always,' Phil sighed. 'The night Jez went missing we had spring tides. Usually you can work out the pattern of currents and know where a body will end up after it's gone into the water, but spring tides can create anomalies. The Solent's a busy shipping channel and once something gets caught on a motor or a propeller, that's pretty much it I'm afraid. He could have ended up anywhere. And in several pieces.'

'Oh God, that's awful.' Something crunched horribly in the

car's engine.

'That's reverse, love. Try again. As you've probably noticed, what's left of the pier only sits above the water at high tide, so we were able to deduce roughly what time he'd fallen in. He had to be right at the end of the pier in order to hit the water with the outgoing tide.'

'What an earth was he doing wandering about on the pier in the dead of night?' I asked, wincing as the gears crunched again.

Phil seemed unflappable. 'We'll never know, will we? My heart went out to poor Kit. A postmortem might have helped. I know the truth is sometimes hard to accept, but she put that boy on a pedestal. If we had the body at least we might have been able to run some forensic tests to work out what happened. Personally, I suspect he'd taken something hallucinogenic. Poor lad thought he could fly and jumped off. Why his so called friends left him on his own in such a state I don't know, but they did. They were all a bit cagey, but what could we do? There was no evidence of drugs in the club, we conducted a thorough search, but you'd have thought one of them, especially Robbie Mayhew, might have stayed behind to keep an eye on him.'

'Robbie was with him?'

'Yes, they all were there, the band. They'd been celebrating this record contract or whatever it was. They'd all be drinking, that was for sure. Right. Let's try moving away. Put it into first, handbrake off. Are you a relative of Kitty's, did you say?'

I was about to shake my head when it occurred to me that some sort of relationship might help explain why I had suddenly turned up in Hookes Bay and taken over Mari's dance school. A stronger association to Kitty lessened the ties to my London life. 'It's very distant,' I told him. 'We've only recently become acquainted, to be honest.'

He nodded. 'Oh I see.' I sensed a slight change in his manner. 'Right then, let's concentrate on the driving, shall we? Foot on the accelerator, gently off the clutch. That's it. We're away, into second.'

The car lurched forward. Phil continued to issue

instructions without any further small-talk as I made several faltering circuits of the skate-park. Every now and then I caught his eye. It was rather disconcerting. I sensed my driving ability wasn't the only thing under scrutiny.

Chapter Fourteen

Kitty

Belinda was back. She and Robbie called round on Saturday morning when Alice was at the community centre with Mari. Kitty thought she looked even more pale and gaunt than usual, as opposed to a woman who had been sunning herself in the Canaries for the last three weeks.

'Has someone bought you a present?' Lindy asked, nodding at the pot of geraniums Alice had left in full-view on the patio. 'Don't they know you don't like flowers?'

'I thought the place could do with a bit of brightening up,' Kitty replied, remembering to her horror that Alice had also pegged out an entire line of washing that morning before she'd left for work. Kitty took pride in her floral-patterned M&S full briefs, but there was no way she could convince anybody that Alice's satin bras and lace thongs were hers. As much as she wanted Robbie to know about Alice, she wanted to defer the meeting until it became an absolute necessity. Fortunately the washing line was partially obscured by Hughie's greenhouse.

'Had any more thoughts about that offer I was talking about?' Robbie said, settling into the wicker chair whilst Lindy perched on the windowsill, her back, thankfully, to the garden.

'I've not been feeling too good this week,' Kitty said. 'Haven't had a chance to study the latest proposal. I did think I should perhaps get some independent legal advice.'

'I told you there's no need for that,' Robbie said, barely able to keep the frustration out of his voice. 'This is the best deal we could hope for and it's all perfectly legal. Any lawyer would tell you that.'

'But I'd like to make sure.'

'I trust Grant Hastings completely,' Robbie said, as if this endorsement was enough. 'There's no need for you to be paying out money for a solicitor to tell you the blindingly obvious.'

'Coastline are a very reputable company, Mum,' Lindy said from the windowsill. 'But if you need that extra assurance, I'm sure we could get someone to look over the paperwork for you.'

Kitty liked it when Belinda called her 'Mum'. At some point over the years she had just slipped into the habit. Kitty would have loved a daughter of her own, in fact when she'd got pregnant with Don Mayhew's baby she'd hoped for a girl, but the baby had been stillborn. In those days they took the body away without so much as letting you have a cuddle. No time to say goodbye, no goodnight kiss for Kitty's own little Alice. A nightmare. And after that, no more.

'We're just wasting time,' Robbie huffed. 'The place has been empty for nearly a year.' The tea cup clanged back into its saucer, the usual signal it was time to go. They'd barely been in the house twenty minutes. Still, that was probably just as well.

'I'll pop by later in the week,' Lindy said. 'We know it's a big thing for you, Mum, selling off the pavilion.'

Kitty sensed some sort of warning shot being issued in Robbie's direction. Robbie didn't seem to notice. It was good of Lindy to defend her, but really, right now, she just needed them to get out of the house before either of them caught sight of Alice's underwear.

Lindy gathered up the tea cups and took them into the kitchen. 'I'll make you a tomato soup before I leave,' she said.

Soup, soup, soup. Kitty was fed up of soup. She was fed up of everything really, apart from Alice and Dominic Flynn.

'Doesn't look like you've got any tomato left,' Lindy called after a few minutes. 'There's some butternut squash. Would you like that?'

Butternut squash. That had to be one of Alice's purchases. Kitty had never tasted butternut squash soup in her life and she didn't want to.

'That would be lovely, Lindy dear,' she called.

'Gawd, Penny's going a bit upmarket, isn't she?' Robbie remarked. 'Has she been shopping in that new Waitrose?' He put on a ridiculous accent. 'I say, butternut squash, tally-ho, eh. By the way I saw that little toe-rag of hers hanging around outside the amusement arcade this morning, looked like he was about to mug someone.'

'Are you talking about Callum?' Lindy called from the kitchen. 'He must be such a worry for her.'

Every Monday morning Penny recounted another edition of *what Callum did next* regarding her son's weekend exploits. Kitty wasn't going to give Robbie and Lindy the pleasure of knowing just how much Penny did worry. Been there, done that, thought Kitty. The last thing you want is people agreeing with you that your son is a bad lot. You want to believe.

'Oh, I didn't tell you. I bumped into Cyril Flemming in the Co-op,' Lindy continued from the kitchen. 'He says Mari Freeborn has found a buyer for her dance school. That's good news.'

At least Cyril could be relied upon to be totally unreliable. The soul of indiscretion. 'So I hear,' Kitty replied. 'I believe she has great ambitions for the Hookes Bay Academy of Music and Dance.'

'She does?' Robbie sounded surprised.

'According to Mari, she wants to take it up a gear,' Kitty continued. She felt quite pleased with herself. *Up a gear*. That was a good phrase. It sounded like something Jez would have said. 'She has plans for a major expansion, wants to raise the school's profile. She's even mentioned that she might be looking for new premises. Personally I don't see why she can't move back into the pavilion. I've a good mind to suggest it.'

'The pavilion?' Robbie stared at her. 'You can't be serious?'

'Why not?' Kitty said, enjoying the look of horror on Robbie's face. 'It's still my building, remember. You keep saying it shouldn't be sat there empty.'

Robbie's mouth dropped. 'Now, Kit, you listen to me. It's taken me months to get you this deal with Hastings.'

Lindy dug her husband in the ribs to silence him. 'There

you go, Mum,' she said, tipping the warm soup into a china bowl. 'It's a lovely idea but remember the state Mari left that studio in. You'd have to have a fair bit of work done. It hardly seems worth it.'

'You mean it's hardly worth it because I'm about to pop my clogs and the minute I'm gone Robbie will sell out to Grant Hastings anyway?' Kitty gave the soup a distasteful look. 'I'm feeling fitter than I have for weeks. I might surprise you all yet.'

Chapter Fifteen

Tara

During a break between classes, I noticed a parent loitering outside the hall, reluctant to come in.

'Excuse me, Mari, I think one of the mums wants a word,' I said.

Mari looked up, irritated. 'It's Beth Hobart again. Just tell her we're full.'

'But we're not.' I protested. If Beth Hobart wanted her child to learn to dance we should have been pulling her into the room with open arms, not sending her away. The woman looked quite frazzled. A young boy, no more than three or four, was half hiding behind her legs.

'How can I help?' I asked.

'Are you the new teacher?'

'Yes. I'm Alice Paige.' I smiled at the boy. He had Down's syndrome. I crouched down beside him. 'And who are you?'

'This is Ethan,' his mother said. '*She,*' she glared at Mari, 'wouldn't take him. Will you?'

'I don't see why not,' I replied. 'Although this next class isn't suitable. I have a class for toddlers on Wednesday afternoon.'

'That's pre-school ballet, remember,' Mari called out.

'How old are you. Ethan?'

'He's four.'

'Do you want to learn to dance?'

'He loves anything musical,' Beth informed me. 'I'll happily stay with him, I wouldn't expect you to take him unaccompanied.' The boy grinned and began to hum and hop, tangling himself around his mother.

'Ideally, I would like to introduce a music and movement class for pre-schoolers into my new timetable,' I said. I had no shortage of resources amongst Kitty's instruments in the pavilion, and there had been a percussion scene in *Puffin the Pirate* that was perfect for adapting into an entire term's worth of lesson plans. 'Unfortunately at the moment I'm limited to time and space. Let's try him out in the ballet class, and if that doesn't work, hopefully, maybe with a bit of juggling I might be able to offer something more suitable next term.'

Beth Hobart looked so grateful I thought she was about to hug me. 'Thank you,' she said. 'We'll be here next Wednesday, won't we Ethan?'

He grinned again and lisped a 'yes please,' at me.

'I hope you know what you're letting yourself in for,' Mari said after they'd gone.

'Well, if it doesn't work out, at least I'll have tried,' I replied. Her blank dismissal of Ethan irked. 'In any case, I would like to offer some additional classes. Why not a music class? I've got more than enough time.'

'You've got the time but try finding a venue with a free time slot. You've seen how tight it is here,' Mari said. 'The minute we leave tonight the Venture Scouts are coming in. Ask Bunny Mitchell, next time you see her. She'll tell you.'

Bunny Mitchell was the very officious parish clerk who operated out of the small community centre office. Sadly she confirmed Mari's theory.

'We're fully booked,' she told me, studying her diary. 'Mornings are out because of the pre-school and I don't have a single afternoon slot I'm afraid, although I suppose if short mat bowls could be persuaded to move forward half an hour I might be able to squeeze you in at three thirty on a Monday.'

'Three thirty is no good,' I told her. 'It would be right on the school run, impossible for parents with older children. I need to finish by three at the latest.'

'I can't help you dear, sorry,' Bunny closed her diary. 'You could always try the church hall. I take my Zumba classes there.'

'There's a Zumba class in Hookes Bay?'

She nodded. 'Monday at eleven. Why don't you try it out?'

I was missing my regular gym sessions so I promised to see her there. I could check out the facilities at the church hall at the same time.

Cyril was at Kitty's again on Saturday evening. He admired my plant pot. 'Have you been out to Craven Farm nursery, Alice?'

'Yes, that's where I picked up the planter.'

'They've got a big sale on tomorrow. Buy one get one free. I read it in the parish newsletter. You should go and take another look.'

I did need a bag of compost for my tomatoes but shopping at garden centres and Zumba dancing with pensioners wasn't quite the social life I'd envisaged for myself at the tender age of thirty-three. Not for the first time since I'd left London I felt a huge aching loneliness. I couldn't wait to escape to my bedroom. Theatrical friends had defected to Hal at the first whiff of a scandal, but the people who knew me well had remained loyal. I texted Bea.

How's things? Got time for a chat?

Sorry. Just off to Lorenzo's. How's Thailand? BTW another sack load of mail arrived from AZ. What do you want me to do with it?

When would the Tara Wakely versus Georgie Gold contest become old news?

Bin it, I replied and consigned myself to another early night.

Sunday morning dawned bright and beautiful, perfect cycling weather and the ideal opportunity to continue my exploration of Hookes Bay, via the garden centre.

Just as I was wobbling back out into the road following the rather rash purchase of two trays of bedding plants, a familiar rusty red pick-up truck pulled up beside me. Dominic Flynn leaned out of the window.

'That doesn't look very safe. Would you like a lift? Your bike will easily fit into the back.' There wasn't a hint of sarcasm in his voice. I accepted his offer gratefully. Dominic appeared to be in an unusually congenial mood.

'What are you doing out this way?' I asked, after my bike and the plants were carefully stowed into his trailer.

'I live here,' he replied. 'I'm at the caravan park. It's just a temporary thing.'

'Oh I see.' I glanced at the hands clutching the steering wheel. No ring. Not even the tell-tale mark of there ever having been one.

'It's a very upmarket caravan park,' Dominic continued. 'I have a luxurious mobile home with gas, electricity, a flushing toilet, my own shower, and a view over the nature reserve.'

'Sounds more sophisticated that Kitty's bungalow.'

'It probably is.'

If Dominic was living in a mobile home then it was highly unlikely all was well in his marriage. I decided to be brave. 'I did wonder, when you said about Grant Hastings being your father-in-law, how that might not be good for a harmonious family relationship.'

'A harmonious family relationship?' Dominic laughed. 'I don't think I've ever had one of those with Grant Hastings, and as for Danni, well things have been less than harmonious for some time. We're currently living apart.'

Little rays of sunshine leapt into my heart, but I tried to keep my voice neutral. 'You and your wife are separated?'

He kept his eyes firmly on the road ahead as we negotiated the many bends in Reading Room Lane. 'Danni has just commenced divorced proceedings but things are complicated by the fact that we run a design consultancy together. Between them, Danni and her father seem determined to ruin me, financially. The junkyard was originally just a sideline, but right now it's my only source of income. Basically, my life is in a mess. So, if I seem a bit rude, or a bit off, sometimes, it's because I've got all this other crap going on.'

If this was some sort of apology, I was happy to accept it. I was glad he had opened up and told me the truth, but I sensed he might appreciate a change of subject. 'Have you heard any more news from the preservation trust?' I enquired. 'You mentioned someone was coming down to Hookes Bay?'

'Next week,' he confirmed. 'I just hope I can pull it off. I'm meeting with the newly-formed conservation society beforehand just to make sure we've got all our facts correct.'

'Do you want me to be there? I mean, if I'm supposed to be moving into the pavilion, it might give you some more ammunition.'

'There's no need. Your moving into the pavilion is just a ruse and we can't employ too much deceit with the MPT. It's best you keep out of it.'

Having been warmed by his apology, I was now hurt by his off-hand rebuff. It was very tempting to tell him that I had no intention of keeping out of it now that I was the legal owner of the Hookes Bay Academy of Music and Dance, but I held off. It was best for now to stick to the role I'd been assigned.

We spent the rest of the journey in silence until the boatshed hove into view.

'Would you like me to drop you off at Kitty's?' he asked.

'No, the yard is fine. I can push the bike home from here.' I immediately regretted sounding ungrateful and unnecessarily prickly.

'Okay, if you're sure.' We pulled up outside the gate and he lifted my bike and plants out of the van. 'Look, I didn't mean to sound like I don't appreciate your help.'

'I know, it's what you said the other day. You have your part to play and I have mine. I take over Mari's, pretend I want to move back into the pavilion while at the same time seducing Robbie Mayhew.'

'Who said anything about seducing Robbie Mayhew?' Dominic looked aghast.

'You did. Okay, you said distract him. When we first met you said that was what Kitty had hired me to do. She wants me to take his mind off the fact that he needs to sell the pavilion to Grant Hastings just long enough for you to sort out this deal with the preservation trust.'

'I didn't mean you had to seduce him. God no.' Dominic ran his hand through his unruly dark hair. The result made him look even more attractive than ever. It was impossible to imagine him ever wearing a suit and working in an office.

'Christ, you really don't know do you? She hasn't told you, has she?'

'Told me what?' I asked.

'Come in,' he said, unlocking the gate. 'I need to show you something.'

I followed him to the office. He retrieved one of the photo albums from the crate of programmes.

'You didn't look at this the other day, did you?' he asked.

'No, not that one. I only looked through the one with all the pictures of Kitty.'

'This is what you need to see.' He flicked through the pages. It was an album of family snap-shots, Kitty, Lionel, but mostly the object of their affections, Jez. There were pictures of a totally over-indulged chubby, gurgling baby Jez, of school boy Jez on a carousel at a fair, Jez strumming a guitar, Jez with Don Mayhew, Jez posing on Hookes Bay pier with another pre-teen of maybe eleven or twelve, presumably his stepbrother Robbie.

Teenage Jez had a mop of shoulder length dark hair, his cheeky school boy grin transposed to something arrogant, sardonic and cocky. As the photographs morphed into colour, the haircut changed, the clothes became more radical, Doc Martens, a trademark leather jacket. The quality of the pictures was poor but there was no denying the grown-up Jez was an attractive young man.

'He must have had the entire female population of Hookes Bay swooning at his feet,' I remarked, halting Dominic's page turning to study a photograph of Urban Rebel; four brooding young men poised with their instruments outside the stage door of the pavilion.

'Not just Hookes Bay, as I understand it,' Dominic replied.

'Such a wasted life,' I said. 'All that potential never realised. Who knew what he might have achieved or what he would have become? The first time I met her, Kitty compared Jez to James Dean. Forever young. With that leather jacket, and those looks, you can see the physical resemblance too.'

'Can you?' Dominic didn't sound convinced. He turned the page. The last photo in the album was a single headshot of Jez.

It was the clearest picture in the book, bearing none of the grainy hallmarks of its predecessors. 'I believe this was a professional publicity shot,' Dominic said over my shoulder. 'Kitty said he had it taken the week he got back from London, just before he fell off the pier. Anyone else he reminds you of?'

I stared at the photograph, the deliberately untidy hair, those 'come hither' brown eyes, the wide generous mouth with its slightly crooked smile, and the penny dropped.

I looked up at Dominic's expectant expression.

'Well, yes,' I said. 'I suppose he looks a bit like me.'

Chapter Sixteen

'Now do you understand what I meant when I said you were here to distract Robbie Mayhew?' Dominic asked. 'You're here because she wants people to think that you're Jez's daughter.'

'But that's preposterous.' Even as the words came out of my mouth I knew it wasn't preposterous at all. It was exactly what Kitty had in mind.

'Think about it,' Dominic said, taking a step back to lean against a metal filing cabinet, tanned arms folded across his chest. 'Kitty hasn't mentioned the London tour? Has she not told you about Jez's great excitement when he came back to Hookes Bay? He told her he'd met someone in London who was going to change his life.'

'No. I mean, yes, she mentioned that the band had been playing in London for a couple of months. Surely if he met someone who was going to change his life he meant it was somebody influential in the music industry? Someone involved in this record deal or whatever.'

'Kitty is convinced he met a woman. According to her, the things he said, how he behaved, all implied he'd fallen madly in love.'

I closed the photograph album, leaned back in the office chair. 'But …'

'But what? It's the perfect story isn't it? Thirty three years later you turn up, with just more than a little of a family resemblance, she takes you under her wing, you take over from Mari.'

Snippets of conversations fell into place. 'Oh God,' I groaned. 'Mari already suspects.'

Mari's exclamation at our initial meeting that she thought

we had met before had nothing to do with recognising me from a gossip magazine. Her hurriedly retracted suggestion that I should visit the Italian chef to say hello was not because he was a Tara Wakely fan, but because he was one of Jez's old friends. If Mari had been hoodwinked, others would be too. Dominic looked quite smug.

'Why didn't you tell me before?' I demanded.

'I assumed you knew.'

'Of course I didn't know. You think I would have wittingly embroiled myself in something like this?'

He gave a nonchalant shrug. 'I've got no idea what you would wittingly embroil yourself in, Alice.' The use of my name was a deliberate reminder that I had already committed to playing a part in Kitty's games.

'Posing as a dead-man's daughter is a different scenario completely,' I protested. 'I was happy to help her out, to run the dance school, but this is a whole new level of deceit. Not only that, but it will never stand up to any scrutiny. What is she thinking of?' And what had I been thinking of, to invest in Mari's dance school with my own money on a rash impulsive whim? How could I extricate myself now?

'Kitty has a very vivid imagination,' Dominic said. He nodded at the pile of programmes on his desk. 'She used to write and direct all their shows, remember? She'll have plotted it all out. She'll have something planned to cover your tracks I'm sure.'

'Well, that definitely puts an end to the driving lessons.'

He cocked his head on one side. 'Driving lessons?'

'Yes. I want to learn to drive. Can you believe it? I booked a driving lesson with an ex-policeman, and not just any ex-policeman, but one who worked on Jez's case. I told him I was some sort of Keaton relative just to explain what I was doing in Hookes Bay.'

'Kitty would be proud of you. It's all going to plan, isn't it? Rumours will abound in a little place like this.'

So much for my aim of deflecting attention. 'But Robbie is never going to believe I'm Jez's daughter is he?' I argued, still horrified at the idea, despite Dominic's placid reassurances.

'And even if he suspects, he'd immediately want proof, a DNA test or something.'

Dominic seemed amused by my distress. 'You think things would ever get that far? All Kitty has to do is string him along for a while, let him suspect, let him have his doubts. Jez only has one living relative left, his mother. It's her DNA Robbie would need for a test. Do you think for one minute she'd agreed to it? The fact is if Jez did have a daughter, she would be the rightful heir to the pavilion.'

'Sounds like you and Kitty have been concocting this crazy idea together. It's almost Dickensian in origin. Little orphan Alice arriving at the home of her long-lost grandmother.'

'I've never read a Dickens novel in my life,' Dominic replied. 'Just think about the implications, though. What if Kitty decided to change her will and leave the pavilion to young Alice? Where would that leave Robbie?'

'Pretty pissed off I would imagine.'

'So he needs to keep his stepmother sweet, doesn't he? If Robbie thinks there's the slightest chance he might be disinherited, he'll do exactly what his stepmother says, which is he'll stop talking to Coastline now, and agree to wait. That's why you're buying us the extra time. Meanwhile, I keep working behind the scenes to convince the Modernist Preservation Trust to come up with an alternative deal.'

I shook my head. 'It will never work.' And I would definitely never work again after this debacle.

'It's all we've got.' Dominic said.

'It's far too risky.'

'As far as Kitty sees it she's got nothing to lose.'

'But I have! What happens if Kitty dies before you get the preservation trust on board? Where does that leave me?'

I would be exposed as a fraud in a town where I had just purchased a business and started to make a few friends. I couldn't go through another hate campaign. I really would be ruined and this time no amount of fictional detoxing in Thailand would save me. 'This ridiculous charade has to end,' I said. 'You may not think much of me, Dominic, but I do have some scruples.'

'I never implied that you didn't. I can't take the moral high ground. I went along with Kitty's plans. The pavilion is a building of great architectural and cultural merit and it deserves to be preserved, by whatever means that takes.'

'So your interest in all this isn't just about getting revenge on your father-in-law?'

'No, of course not.'

Did I believe him? Dominic's passion for the pavilion had been quite evident when he'd give me the tour, but what was at its root?

'I have a first class honours degree in building conservation,' he said, as if he could see exactly what I was thinking. 'I firmly believe we have a duty to protect the past. Surely you can see what a vital role you have to play in the pavilion's restoration?'

'I don't mind playing a part, but I have been totally miscast in this particular role,' I remarked. 'Seriously, what about your father-in-law? How will he react if Robbie backs out now? How long will he be prepared to wait? You've already said you're worried about the pavilion going up in smoke when no-one is looking. Isn't this just lighting the touch paper?'

'Oh, don't worry, I've put a night watchman on the pavilion.'

'You employ a security guard?'

'My mate Hobo lives on the esplanade, next to the Fishing Tackle shop. He's keeping an eye on the place for me. Oh, that reminds me, he says thank you by the way.'

'Thank you? What for?' I'd shaken the man's hand and held a door open for him whilst he'd unloaded his agricultural equipment. It was hardly a grand gesture.

'For agreeing to let Ethan have a try out in your lessons.'

'Ethan Hobart? The little boy with Downs Syndrome?'

Dominic's face softened. 'Yes, he's Paul's son. He's a great little chap.'

I immediately recalled Ethan's gorgeous wide-eyed smile, and his mother's relief when I had agreed to accept him into a class. Wasn't giving opportunities to children like Ethan one of the very reasons I was so keen to put my own stamp on Mari's dance school? I sighed. 'Look, I need to go away and have a serious think.'

'I understand.' Dominic hesitated. 'Let me at least give you a lift back to the bungalow.'

'There's no need.'

'Please. Business is pretty quiet. I can shut up shop for half an hour.'

He was attempting to be conciliatory. I relented. 'Actually, it would be a help.' I paused. 'How well do you know Ethan? Have you seen how he responds to music?'

Dominic nodded. 'Sometimes he has these terrible tantrums but music really calms him down, anything from "Wheels on the Bus" to Beethoven.'

'Could we stop by the pavilion? I could pick up some instruments from the storeroom. It might be useful to have something on standby for him.'

Dominic flashed me one of his brilliant, face transforming smiles. 'Of course. I can just see Ethan rampaging around the community centre bashing out a tune on one of Kitty's tambourines.'

So could I. I returned his smile. I really did have lots to think about.

Dominic's phone rang just as we entered the pavilion, not the irritating Irish jig of before, but a melodic acoustic guitar.

'You go on up,' he said, 'I'll join you in a sec.'

Back inside it was impossible not to be awestruck all over again by the faded magnificence of the grand atrium and that staircase. I could almost hear the echoes of the past as I headed up to the first floor; applause from the auditorium as Kitty took her bows on the stage, children tap dancing in the studio above, the thumping bass from the nightclub. With the building restored and revamped, an entirely new spectrum of opportunities could be unleashed. The potential was enormous. I could have my own space to do exactly what I wanted, to teach who I wanted, where and when I wanted. My stage school idea really could happen here. After all, I'd already made the financial commitment.

More to the point, what was the alternative? If I didn't stay in Hookes Bay, where did I go? I couldn't even begin to contemplate the consequences of an undignified and hasty return to London.

Was it a criminal offence to deliberately mislead? Kitty hadn't actually told anybody I was her long-lost granddaughter. She was relying on subtle clues that could be taken, or ignored. I might look like Jez Keaton. I might be about the right age to have been conceived during his London tour, but it was all supposition. I had never proclaimed myself to be anybody other than Alice Paige, the dance teacher without a history. I had created an online persona to appease Mari's parents, but surely I could be excused a little lie like that. Professional actors often used multiple identities to protect their privacy. That was all I was doing, surely?

'You've got what you wanted?' Dominic asked, joining me in the studio.

No. I'd been too busy wrestling with my conscience. I grabbed a box of instruments from the store room.

'You've changed your ring-tone,' I remarked. 'Did the fiddle finally get on your nerves?'

'Oh I save that for Danni,' he replied, straight-faced. 'Just to remind me how annoying she really is. Here, let me carry that box for you. Ethan's going to love playing with these.'

I followed him down the stairs, picturing Ethan's toothy grin. What harm could I possibly do by simply continuing in my designated role? I wasn't hurting anyone. It was suddenly very easy to defend my complicity.

Look at this beautiful pavilion I have saved from destruction. Look at all the opportunities now available in Hookes Bay. Beauty, Art and Culture returned after all these years.

Kitty's dream, Dominic's dream, my dream. All one and the same thing, and all totally within my grasp.

Chapter Seventeen

Back at the bungalow, making polite conversation with Kitty did not rank highly on my agenda. If she detected a change in my manner she didn't mention it. She sat wrapped in her kimono in her favourite wicker chair, like a faded leading lady learning her lines between scenes.

'I'm off to Cyril's for a birthday party,' she told me. 'One of his house-mates is celebrating his 90th.'

'House-mates?'

'He lives in sheltered accommodation. It's just like university halls, he tells me. Not that I'd know. I never went to university, but Cyril did.'

'I didn't know they had universities back in Tudor times.'

'You're a funny girl. Cyril's an educated man. He worked as a barrister at the Old Bailey. Still practices a bit of law.'

Kitty might well need legal representation if her daft plot was uncovered. Did she have any idea how close she was sailing to the wind? I spent the rest of the afternoon in the garden. I'd learned from Mari that Hughie had died less than eighteen months previously, and the bungalow was still filled with his memories. Souvenirs from those world cruises cluttered the box room. There was a whole area behind the greenhouse that could possibly have been a vegetable patch at some point in the past. A wooden bench was tucked behind the shed, as if Hughie had created a little sanctuary for himself where he could potter in peace. I could almost smell the lingering aroma of pipe tobacco. I cleared a jungle of bindweed and pulled up brambles; physical tasks which left me far too exhausted to spend a sleepless night debating my moral dilemma.

When the home help, Penny, arrived on Monday morning she was accompanied by a lanky teenager, who she introduced as her son, Callum.

'No school today?' I enquired as Callum shuffled into the bungalow behind his mother.

'No.' Penny glared at her son. 'He's on suspension, and I can't trust him at home on his own.'

'The boy can help Alice in the garden,' Kitty suggested. 'She's taken it into her head I like flowers.'

Penny raised an eyebrow. 'Do you like gardening, Alice?'

'Yes, I do. My foster parents owned an allotment, grew all their own vegetables. Kitty's patch just seemed a bit bare.'

'Didn't know you were fostered,' Kitty muttered. She looked a little put out, as if I should have told her. Not that we'd ever spoken about my childhood. In fact she'd shown remarkably little interest in my past, our conversations predominantly revolving around the pavilion, and reminiscences of her stage career.

'It was just for a couple of years, as a teenager,' I told her. 'It was actually my foster mother who inspired my love of musicals. We used to sit down together every Sunday afternoon watching those old Hollywood blockbusters.' Viv had done more than inspire me, she had positively encouraged my theatrical talents by ensuring that I continued to attend the North London drama club my mother had sent me to almost as soon as I could walk. Viv was a great believer in creating as much stability and continuity as possible in the lives of those children she took under her wing. Whilst Ray had ferried Aaron off to his computer hackers club every Saturday morning, Viv had driven me forty miles and back to London. She'd been in the audience at my first professional performance, but thankfully, not the last.

I glanced at Callum, hiding beneath his hoodie. 'It would be a help if you could dig over that patch of soil I've marked out behind the greenhouse,' I told him. 'I want to try out this Zumba class at the church hall at eleven. If the soil is prepared I'll do the planting when I get back.'

When I arrived at the church hall, I discovered to my horror that I was the youngest person present by a good twenty years. Worse was to come when I realised exactly what Bunny Mitchell had meant when she said she took a Zumba class. She wasn't a fellow participant, she was the teacher.

'Is she qualified?' I whispered to the woman warming up next to me.

'I doubt it,' the woman replied. She was about sixty, elegant and attractive with a sleek silver bob. 'I believe she once ran one of those Women's Leagues of Health and Beauty things, you know, back in the 1950s. Still, it's the best we've got.'

I made my own extensions to several of the exercises, determined to get the most of out of the class. Some of the more agile ladies followed my lead. I hadn't meant to undermine Bunny's teaching but I sensed a distinct air of hostility when I asked afterwards who I had to see regarding the hire of the room.

There was talk of decamping to Pebbles for coffee, which I politely refused. I was keen to get back to Kitty's to see what mess Callum had made of the garden. My new friend introduced herself as Barbara and offered to accompany me to the vicarage where the vicar's wife held the diary for room bookings.

'You're staying with Kitty Keaton aren't you?' she said.

I nodded. 'Am I notorious already?'

'There are no secrets in Hookes Bay. My husband, Phil, gave you a driving lesson last week.'

'Oh.' I felt myself blush.

She laughed. 'He's looking forward to your next session. It must be nice for Kitty to have some young company. Is it right you're planning to expand Mari Freeborn's dance school?'

'I'd like to, but first I need to find some alternative space.'

'Well, let's hope Jane Forster can find you a slot. I have the same problem. I run Hookes Bay Amateur Dramatics Club. We have to have extra rehearsals in my front room when we're putting on a big production. Maybe we ought to recruit you. We could do with someone with choreography experience. I've always fancied putting on some sort of grand musical. Why don't you think about joining us?'

As she deposited me at the vicarage door, Barbara insisted on giving me her phone number. It seemed a shame to rebuke her offer of friendship, especially when she could be a valuable ally. Surely an Am-Dram Club would lend their support to the pavilion's restoration?

By the time I returned to Crabhook Lane after a short and fruitless conversation with the vicar's wife, Penny and Callum had left but the bed I had outlined in the garden was turned over and cleared of weeds. I was impressed. I'd been nothing but an innocent bystander to Viv and Ray's gardening exploits, but I'd seen the benefits. Gardening was therapeutic, creating order out of chaos. I wondered what had become of the plants I'd left behind on the terrace of Hal's loft apartment. Was Georgie looking after things for me, or had Cockapoo already ruined my handiwork?

Hal hadn't featured in my thoughts of late. I found myself comparing him to Dominic who was younger, sleeker, and much less self-obsessed. Dominic seemed unaware of his effect on the opposite sex, or at least on me, whereas Hal was all charm, and very good at using his influence in the theatrical playing field to its full advantage. I thought Hal was the love of my life, but his cruel rejection had led me here to Hookes Bay. New doors had opened up, new opportunities. Had Georgie Gold actually done me a favour?

As my thoughts drifted back to Dominic, it occurred to me I'd never given him my phone number, an oversight I immediately rectified when I returned indoors by looking up the details of the reclamation yard website on the computer Callum had conveniently left running, and leaving a message on Dominic's voicemail. Now he had no excuses. Surely after the revelations of the previous day we had unfinished business to discuss?

With Tuesday free from teaching, I planned to spend the day perfecting my ideas for the summer showcase, determined to have something cast in stone before Mari could talk me out of it. The community centre was not the most appropriate venue for putting on a performance in front of an audience; the church hall even smaller. The pavilion, of course, would have been the perfect venue. *Dream on, Tara.*

Penny was back, minus Callum.

'Has he returned to school already?' I asked.

'No, there's a club in Fareham for exclusions. He's got a session there this morning. Kitty needs a bath so I think he was quite happy to keep out of the way.'

I was also quite happy to keep out of the way. I returned to Pebbles, where instead of drafting a plan for the summer showcase I found myself jotting down a list of activities that could utilise a revamped pavilion and form the basis of the Tara Wakely School of the Performing Arts. In order to be financially viable, the building had to offer a great deal more than children's dance classes. I had to think big. Drama and music were an integral part of the pavilion's heritage, but there was so much more that could happen in such a diverse space. Keeping a live music venue, although not a nightclub, was paramount, as was the need to make the facilities accessible to all sections of the community.

Once again I thought of Ethan. For the first time since I'd arrived in Hookes Bay I realised I was actually looking forward to taking over Mari's lessons. There was no subterfuge involved in teaching Ethan, no pretending to be the dance instructor it was becoming more apparent with every class that I wasn't. This was me – Tara Wakely. This was what I was good at: encouraging, mentoring, and providing opportunities. I was determined to make Ethan's session a success. Not only that, but offering to teach Ethan had put me in Dominic Flynn's good books, a place I was determined to stay.

Chapter Eighteen

Kitty

'Not much in there this month,' Maureen Batty said, placing a copy of the parish magazine on the side table. Kitty noted it was the same edition Maureen had delivered last week. Someone should let Bunny Mitchell know that Maureen needed to be relieved from her distribution duties. There were streets in Hookes Bay that received two copies of the local newsletter in as many weeks, whereas others went for months without ever receiving a single edition. Lindy never seemed to know what was going on, although that could just be Lindy.

No sooner was Maureen out of the gate when Kitty received another visitor. She had never been so popular. She hadn't seen Phil Kendrick for years. He used to drop in quite regularly in the old days to keep her updated. For one awful moment she thought, at last, after all these years some news, but then she realised he was out of uniform. Phil wore his uniform like a badge of honour. He would never have conducted an official task in plain clothes. This was a social call.

Her mind had slipped. How could she have forgotten? Some people, like Maureen Batty, embraced their memory loss. It let them off the hook, alleviated the responsibility. Kitty dreaded every missing minute. This wasn't about Jez, this was about Alice and the driving lessons. If only Alice had spoken to Kitty before engaging a driving instructor. Phil Kendrick was the last person Kitty wanted snooping around.

'Mind if I come in for a few mins?' Phil said.

He already had one foot in the conservatory. She could hardly say no. 'Make yourself at home, Phil,' she said, although he already had.

He eased himself into the wicker arm chair, glanced around the room. Policemen were trained to search for clues. 'Nice girl, your young protégé,' he said. 'Has a definite look of young Jez about her. Be about the right age too.'

'Umm.' Kitty wondered how best to react. Ambiguity seemed the best way forward. A vague, could-be, possibly, maybe, had kept Mari happy. 'I saw the resemblance too, when I first met her.'

'And how did you meet her?'

'It was just a question of putting some feelers out.' She liked that term. Another phrase that Jez might have coined. 'It wasn't that difficult.'

'I see. And she's now taken over Mari Freeborn's dance school? That was your idea I presume?'

Kitty nodded. 'Alice is the perfect solution to Mari's predicament. She was desperate to find a suitable buyer.'

'You have checked her out, I take it?' Phil leaned forward with an earnest look on his face. 'Made sure she's genuine? I'd hate anyone to take advantage of you, Kit. I can run some background searches if you like.'

'No! I mean, no, that's not necessary, Phil. Thank you.' Kitty hurriedly tried to regain her composure. 'Alice has the perfect credentials for running the Hookes Bay Academy of Music and Dance.'

'You know that's not what I meant.'

Why should she have to justify herself to Phil Kendrick? When had anybody ever taken this much interest in her houseguests before? Not that Kitty had hosted a great many visitors over the years. A few waifs and strays had come and gone, like Lindy for instance, after the Commander's stroke. Nobody had given her the third degree then. They'd all said then she was doing the right thing, offering up her home to the poor girl, but of course they'd still been living in Balmoral Heights then, and it had been Robbie's idea to invite Lindy to stay. Kitty had ample space. Here, she and Alice were living on top of each other.

She closed her eyes and willed Phil to leave. What had got into him? Phil Kendrick wasn't known for his powers of perception. After all, he'd never been able to fathom out which of the Bonetti boys had pushed Jez off the pier.

Chapter Nineteen

Tara

Kitty was agitated and spitting like a cat. 'Where have you been?'

'I had some research to do.'

'You've been out all day.'

'I went to Pebbles for the Wi-Fi.'

'What's wrong with my computer here?'

'It's too slow.' It was also infected with inappropriate soft porn pop-ups.

She gave a disgruntled snort. 'Cyril phoned earlier. It's the first meeting of the newly formed conservation committee tonight.'

'Tonight?'

'Yes. You need to go. They're meeting at Cyril's place, Wheatsheaf Court. Seven o'clock.'

'Thanks.'

'What are you doing now?'

'I thought I'd carry on in the garden for a bit.'

'Looks like rain. Come and have a cuppa with me. We need to talk strategy.'

'Do we?'

'Yes.' Kitty pursed her lips. 'We have to impress this preservation trust Dominic's persuaded to come and view the pavilion. You need to know what part I want you to play.'

If Kitty was about to confess to the whole *Jez Keaton is your father scenario* I didn't want to hear it. The less I knew about her crazy scheme the better.

'Oh, I know exactly what part you want me to play.' I couldn't keep the bitterness from my voice. 'I'm to pretend I want to move Mari's school back into the pavilion. That's my role, isn't it?'

She looked so put out I immediately felt mean for spoiling her game.

'Oh. Who told you that?'

'Dominic Flynn. I bumped into him on Sunday.'

She looked even more peeved. 'Oh.' She shuffled position in her chair. 'But you'll do it, won't you?'

'Yes, of course.' A thought suddenly occurred to me. 'Did you ask Mari to move back into the pavilion before you engaged me?'

'No.' Kitty replied far too quickly. She pouted. 'I thought you were making me that cuppa?'

Knowing I was going to be seeing Dominic again I chose my evening's outfit with great care. The continental look hadn't made much impression on him the first time round. I opted for casual faded jeans and a simple sweatshirt. Unfortunately, the heavens opened as I made way through the centre of town to Cyril's sheltered housing complex. No need to worry about being casual enough, I arrived drenched and bedraggled.

Gaining entry to Wheatsheaf Court wasn't easy either. I rang every single resident's bell on the panel outside the communal entrance before a whiskery gentleman in tweeds finally came to my rescue.

'What do you want, laddie?' he demanded, releasing the catch on the main door.

'Cyril,' I gasped. I ran my hand through my hair. 'He's expecting me. I'm Alice Paige.'

'Oh, you're Alice,' Whiskers grunted. 'Sorry. Easy mistake. We're in here.'

I followed him to a large lounge area at the rear of the sheltered housing complex. Several wingback armchairs had been pushed to one side and half a dozen or so elderly people sat around two trestle tables in the middle of the room. Dominic was fiddling with his laptop.

I was relieved to see Cyril. He beckoned me over. Dominic

looked up, nonplussed. 'Alice? What are you doing here?'

'I hope you don't mind,' Cyril answered, 'but I thought Alice might be interested in hearing what our newly formed Pavilion Conservation Society have to say.'

'Of course.' Dominic hid his irritation well. 'Is that everyone now do you think?'

A woman in a pink velour tracksuit patted the empty chair beside her. She had badly dyed carrot-coloured curls which clashed horribly with her outfit. 'Come and sit here, Alice,' she insisted. 'I've got something to show you later.'

It was slightly disconcerting to be in a room full of strangers who all seemed to know me intimately.

'Shush, Maureen,' the woman on the other side of her hissed. 'We want to hear what Mr Flynn has to say.'

Judging by the number of hearing aids on display I was surprised if any of them would hear what Dominic was about to say. Was this really the best support he could muster?

'Tom, do you want to start?' Dominic asked the grey-haired gentleman on his right. 'Why don't you give us a quick rehearsal of your presentation to Sam MacDonald tomorrow?'

Tom, who looked as if he had stepped straight off the golf-course, pulled a pair of reading glasses from his trouser pocket. 'Thanks, Dominic. I thought I'd begin with a brief outline of Hookes Bay's history and our relationship with the military.'

'Is that entirely relevant?' Whiskers interrupted.

'I think so,' Tom replied, 'because without the military's intervention in Hookes Bay, and the arrival of Conrad Carlisle, we'd still all be living on a feudal estate run by the Pepperthorne family.' He looked to Dominic for reassurance.

'I think it would be relevant if it's kept quite brief,' Dominic agreed. 'Concentrate on the salient points.'

'And don't mention that bloody signal-box,' Cyril twittered. The carrot-top next to me stifled a giggle.

Tom cleared this throat. His face was nearly as pink as his Pringle sweater. 'Right, well, ladies and gents, as most of you know, the Royal Navy used parts of Hookes Bay for training exercises from about 1900 onwards, creating a cadet camp at

Broken Marsh. During the First World War they requisitioned some more land from the Pepperthorne estate for a major shore-based training camp, HMS Titan. A handful of American troops were stationed at Titan towards the end of 1918, and for that, we all have to be very grateful, because a certain Conrad Carlisle, the son of an American hotelier who was billeted at the camp, fell in love with one of Raymond Pepperthorne's four daughters.'

Dominic turned his laptop to the audience to reveal a sepia wedding photograph of a very happy young couple posing in front of the chapel in Reading Room Lane. My imagination was captured already. I only hoped Sam MacDonald was an old Scottish romantic. He couldn't fail to be impressed. I caught Dominic's eye. He returned my look with a raised eyebrow.

Tom continued. 'With its unspoilt south-facing beach, ready access from the mainland thanks to a railway line already in operation to transport military supplies, Conrad Carlisle immediately saw the potential in creating a purpose-built resort in Hookes Bay. Within a year of his marriage to Cynthia Pepperthorne, Carlisle had engaged architect Eric Milner, and construction on the Carlisle Hotel complex began.'

All eyes switched to Dominic's laptop again to view a rare colour shot of the newly-built Carlisle Hotel in all its splendour, the lido filled with happy holiday-makers, and the resplendent pavilion. A long thin pier stretched out into the sea. Dominic gave Tom a nod of encouragement to continue.

'Due to the heavy Navy presence in the area the town suffered greatly during the Second World War. Several air-raids by the German Luftwaffe over nearby Portsmouth almost decimated Hookes Bay into oblivion.' Another shot, this time of a beleaguered Carlisle, one wing entirely missing, a crater on the esplanade directly outside the pavilion's entrance, and the pier in ruins. 'So, in 1946 along came theatre impresario Lionel Keaton anxious to extend his empire. The Carlisles welcomed him with open arms, eager to rid themselves of the damaged pier and pavilion. Keaton bought both amenities for little more than the modern-day equivalent of pennies.'

Another picture flashed up on screen; a shot of Kitty and Lionel on the steps of the pavilion.

'For nearly twenty years or so post-war Hookes Bay flourished. The Navy financed a house-building programme on the old Pepperthorne estate, not just to accommodate their own personnel but to soak up overspill from bomb-damaged Portsmouth. Eddie Munting bought up the old cadet camp near Broken Marsh and transformed it into a one of the south's first holiday villages. People needed cheering up so they came to the seaside. Keaton's theatre of dreams flourished.'

'Excuse me,' I interrupted, quite captivated by Tom's history lesson. 'Was that what the pavilion was called, The Theatre of Dreams?'

'Not officially, but that's what I call it,' Tom said with an indulgent smile. 'Post-war people didn't have the money to splash out on trips up to London and the West End, but Keaton bought that experience to them here.'

'He was a man of great vision,' Cyril remarked.

'Exactly,' Tom said, 'which is why his memory needs to be preserved. Sadly, when the Hookes Bay branch line was axed, the holiday makers stopped coming. Audiences dwindled. Necessity is the mother of invention. Lionel Keaton ripped out the old auditorium to create a ballroom. It was the first of several transformations. Don Mayhew, who ran the Sputnik Club in Portsmouth, amongst other rather dubious activities, took over during the late 1960s and created an intimate supper club and live music venue, being able to attract some relatively big names.'

Dominic had managed to acquire a picture of what looked suspiciously like a young Cilla Black on stage with Kitty concealed in the wings.

'The nightclub continued to run successfully for many years before it finally closed its doors for the last time just twelve months ago,' Tom finished. 'Since then, the building has sat empty. Hookes Bay Pavilion is not just unique, it's played an integral part of our town's history. We can't afford to lose it from our seafront.'

'Well done, Tom,' Dominic said. 'You've covered

everything perfectly. I'm going to take Sam on a tour of the pavilion first thing, then we'll head to the yacht club for lunch at twelve thirty.'

'Talking of refreshments,' Cyril piped up. 'Weren't you supposed to be making tea, Maureen?'

Carrot-top bobbed to attention. 'Silly me, yes of course.' She prodded me in the ribs with a bony finger. 'Come on, missy, give me a hand.'

I accompanied her to a small side kitchen off the lounge where an industrial-sized urn was already bubbling away. Maureen made a big fuss of swinging open cupboard doors hunting for cups and saucers while I managed to locate a teapot and a coffee jug.

'This is for you,' she said, offering up a bulky Sainsbury's carrier bag just as I had loaded everything onto a tray.

'What is it?'

'It's my scrapbook. My nephew was Kitty's boy's best friend. They were in that band together. I kept everything – all the clippings from the paper whenever he was in them, pictures. I thought you might want to have a look. Kitty said she always knew he'd got some girl into trouble. Found you just in time, didn't she?'

'Did she?' I replied doubtfully.

'Go on,' Maureen urged, thrusting the package into my hands. 'Take it away with you, have a good look through. And don't you go listening to any of those old rumours. Derek said they weren't taking drugs. None of them were. Why would they risk it when they'd just got that record deal? Doesn't make sense at all.'

I wasn't sure how to respond. Say too much, and I would only be adding fuel to Maureen's misconception that I was Kitty's granddaughter. Say nothing, and it would seem ungrateful. 'Thank you, Maureen. And where is your nephew, Derek, now? Is he still in Hookes Bay?'

'Derek had his own troubles over the years. Last time I saw him was at my sister's funeral, two… three years ago. He was based in Portsmouth then, at St Nick's, the homeless shelter.' She beamed at me. 'You want me to carry that tray?'

'No, thanks,' I tucked the Sainsbury's bag under my arm. 'I think can manage.'

Back in the main lounge we arrived just as Dominic was running through a slide show of computer generated 3-D projections of the pavilion.

'What stands in our favour is that despite the alterations to the interior of the pavilion, the exterior remains exactly as it was designed in 1922. Had it befallen the same fate as the old Carlisle Hotel, modified and extended numerous times over the years, we wouldn't be in this fortunate position. The pavilion remains one of the finest, albeit one of the smallest, examples of Milner's work. I've made a rough calculation of the length of time, and of course the costs, involved in restoring the building's exterior. The interior would be subject to debate, depending upon the proposed usage of the facilities.'

Whiskers grunted. 'And what are the proposed uses?' he asked. 'I think we all support the idea of saving the pavilion in principle but the last thing we want restored is that rogue Mayhew's nightclub.'

There was a general murmur of agreement.

'Well, fortunately for us, Mr Mitchell,' Dominic said. 'That's where Alice comes in.'

So Dominic did need me after all. I couldn't stifle a smug grin of *I told you so* as I handed him a coffee.

Before I could speak, he continued to address the room. 'As you know, Kitty Keaton established singing and dancing lessons in the pavilion for local youngsters way back in the fifties. That tradition continued right up until last year, when Mari Freeborn, Kitty's successor, relocated to the community centre. Alice here has plans to expand her dance school and would be one of the first community groups leasing space in the newly restored pavilion.'

'So is that the plan then? It becomes another community centre?' Cyril queried.

'What about the existing community centre?' Whiskers asked. 'The facilities there are perfectly adequate.'

'I don't envisage the pavilion would be in direct

competition with the community centre, Mr Mitchell,' Dominic said. 'The exact details of the pavilion's future use have yet to be thrashed out.'

I was determined to have my say. 'Perhaps I could just speak for a few minutes?'

Dominic looked agitated before caving in with a somewhat sarcastic invitation. 'Take the stage, Alice.'

I regarded my audience, took a deep breath, leaned forward, fixed a heartfelt earnest look on my face that would have made Anne Zachery proud, and began.

'I believe it is imperative that the pavilion's future use remains firmly centred on its traditional role as an entertainment venue, although, not, I hasten to add, a nightclub. My idea would be to create a Creative and Performing Arts Hub. There's nothing else like it on this part of the coast. It would be a unique, open-access facility for the entire community, and fitting tribute to the innovative and inspirational legacy left by Lionel and Kitty Keaton.'

All eyes were upon me. I took another deep breath, relishing the opportunity to unveil my ideas. 'My plan would be to encompass a whole range of activities for children and young people, covering disciplines as diverse as hip-hop and garage music, all alongside the traditional ballet, tap and modern classes that already exist in my dance school. I would like to establish a choir, perhaps even a youth jazz orchestra. The Hub would also provide a base for local musicians and music tutors; we could offer rehearsal rooms, maybe even a recording studio. Opening up the original auditorium space would create a venue suitable for hosting concerts and recitals, we could put on plays, shows and even films.

'It's not just the younger generation who could benefit from an arts hub,' I continued, winking at Cyril. 'Hookes Bay's more mature population would also be catered for, with a nostalgic tea dance or a big band performance. In addition, I've researched the current opportunities within Hookes Bay and see that resources for children with special needs, or adults with learning difficulties and restricted mobility, are very limited. How about dance therapy and remedial music sessions?

'We could include a gallery, maybe permanent exhibition space to display all those old photographs and mementoes of Hookes Bay's prestigious history. I'd also like to see the incorporation of catering facilities, a café bar with that idyllic view over the seafront. I propose we establish a consultation committee. If you have an idea, we could put it to the vote, see what people here in Hookes Bay want from their Community Arts Hub. This building would be ours... yours, to take ownership of, run by the people of Hookes Bay, for the people of Hookes Bay. If you open up your mind, the possibilities are endless.'

I met a stunned silence. Perhaps they didn't like it. Perhaps, as Mari had predicted, Hookes Bay just wasn't ready for change, for hip-hop, or sparkle and sequins...

It was Cyril who responded first. 'Oh my, Alice, what a brilliant idea,' he beamed.

Maureen clapped her hands with glee. 'What about a pantomime?' she asked. 'Could we have a Christmas pantomime, Alice?'

'Quite possibly,' I replied, although a pantomime wasn't quite the cutting edge entertainment I had in mind. However, it was important to keep all members of the conservation society on my side.

'Oh no, you won't,' Cyril chuckled.

'Oh yes, we will,' Maureen retorted with another clap. 'Oh, this is so exciting. Kitty will be so pleased.'

'Who knew?' I thought I heard Dominic murmur under his breath although his face was inscrutable. 'Well, thank you for that, Alice. You've certainly given us lots to think about.'

'Hear, hear,' Tom said. 'I hadn't even considered what we'd actually use the pavilion for, once we'd restored it.'

'No,' Dominic admitted. 'And neither had I in any great detail, although I am fully aware of the Modernist Preservation Trust's requirement for commercial viability.'

'Then this young lady needs to join us for lunch on Thursday and state her case,' Tom said at once.

'I agree with Tom,' Cyril said. 'Emphatically. Looks like

Alice could be our trump card.'

Whiskers grunted. 'Ah, but do we want a Community Arts Hub in Hookes Bay?' He had a way of making the words *Community* Arts *Hub* sound like a bad smell. 'We certainly don't want to encourage anything that attracts a crowd of young ruffians loitering outside. We've got enough problems with that by the amusement arcade.'

'Well hopefully, the youngsters will want to loiter inside the pavilion, not out,' I smiled.

'Now listen here, Mitch,' Cyril took charge. 'Haven't you been listening at all? If we don't come up with a plausible plan for utilising the pavilion, then young Dominic doesn't stand a chance of convincing this preservation trust to fund the restoration project. If you've got a better idea than the one Alice has just come up with, then I'm happy to hear it.'

'You'd have to put any ideas to the parish council,' Whiskers protested.

Dominic held up his hand. 'Right now, we don't want any of this getting beyond these four walls, and that includes the parish council. That's why we are meeting here, remember, Mitch.'

Cyril winked and tapped the side of his nose. 'Your secrets are safe in Wheatsheaf Court, 007.'

Dominic gave the old man a very patient smile. 'Seriously, confidentiality is vital. Just remember, Kevin Galliard sits on the parish council and he's Grant Hastings' right-hand man. If Coastline Developments get wind of any of this, we could risk losing that pavilion forever.'

Maureen sprang out of her chair, and gave Dominic a salute in a bid to outdo Cyril. 'Ay, Ay Captain. Understood, sir, understood.'

The old biddy next to her attempted to do the same and ended up sending her cup of coffee flying. It seemed a good time to bring the meeting to an end.

Chapter Twenty

'That was a job well done,' Tom said, as I helped pack the trestle tables away. 'You've got some pretty innovative ideas for transforming this place. Hookes Bay could do with a few more people like you, don't you think, Dominic?'

'I'm not entirely sure Hookes Bay could cope with more than one Alice,' Dominic replied.

'Fancy coming down the Sir Winnie for a pint?' Tom asked.

Dominic shook his head. 'Sorry, Tom. I'm still barred.'

Tom turned to me. 'Alice, how about you?'

'Oh, I couldn't, but thank you,' I said quickly.

'I'll join you for a quick one,' Whiskers grunted. 'Bunny's at her art class. She won't be home for at least another hour.'

The two men set off together.

Dominic thanked Cyril for hosting.

'Fingers crossed for Thursday,' Cyril replied with his customary wink. 'Alice was a revelation. Never underestimate a Keaton, eh, Dominic?'

'I'm not a Keaton,' I pointed out.

'I meant Kitty, of course,' he said, 'conjuring you up like a white rabbit out of a magician's hat. There's a lot more to Kitty than meets the eye, Alice.'

As I was beginning to learn only too well.

The rain had ceased and the clouds had broken up. It was only just dusk.

'How come you're barred from the Sir Winnie?' I asked, keen to prevent Dominic from zooming off.

'I had a run in with another customer a while back. The landlord hasn't forgiven me.'

'A fight you mean?'

'I prefer to call it an altercation.'

'Did the other customer get a ban too?'

'I doubt it.'

'So where do you go when you want a drink?' I asked, determined not to be put off. I felt quite triumphant after such a successful meeting, and up for the challenge of breaking down Dominic's defences.

He hesitated. 'I buy a beer from the Co-op.'

'Fancy doing that now?'

Another hesitation, followed by a sigh. 'Okay, why not?'

We headed down to the esplanade and settled into one of the concrete beach shelters.

'I feel like a teenager sneaking out behind my parents' back,' Dominic remarked handing me a can. 'You're leading me astray, Alice.'

'Is that a good or bad thing?' I asked. He wasn't exactly smiling but he didn't seem quite as brusque as earlier; an encouraging signal.

'I'm not sure. Just don't suggest we head off to the arcade to play the slot machines. Now what are you looking at?'

'You. Why do you always put up this barrier? I want to help. I want to save that pavilion just as much as you do.'

'So you're still in, then?'

'Of course I'm still in.' I sighed. 'How could you doubt me after that performance? I've got this far, I'm not backing out now.' I placed Maureen's carrier bag across my knee. 'Anyway, I've got some additional research material here, just so I can perfect my Jez Keaton pout. That Maureen woman insisted I look through her scrapbook of old newspaper clippings. Apparently, her nephew used to be in Jez's band.'

'Maureen Batty's got even more marbles missing than Kitty. They're good friends.'

I sensed a softening in Dominic's demeanour. 'That doesn't surprise me. Kitty must have primed her. She told me Kitty always knew Jez had got some girl into trouble. Tom seems a nice guy. That's quite a story he told about the American soldier and the local landowner's daughter.'

'Sometimes you can't make these things up, can you?'

'No. It's very romantic. I take it Whiskers is married to

Bunny Mitchell, the parish council clerk?'

Dominic nodded. 'You've met her?'

'I attended her Zumba class.'

Dominic found this incredibly funny. 'You are joking?'

'No seriously. She takes a Zumba class in fluorescent pink Lycra. And you shouldn't laugh. She managed really well for a woman of her age. I only hope I have that amount of energy when I'm seventy.'

'Oh, I'm sure you will. Anyway, I just hope Mitch realises how important it is to be discreet. We will need the support of the parish council eventually, but I'd like to have the Modernist Preservation Trust on board first. However, I suspect Mitch will go straight home and spill the beans. It's not Bunny I'm worried about, it's Kevin Galliard.'

'That name sounds familiar. I'm pretty sure one of my pupils is a Galliard. The mother has already asked if her daughter can continue to have private lessons with Mari. She doesn't trust me.'

Dominic laughed again. 'I'm not surprised she doesn't trust you. Yes. Galliard is a local man. Hastings is a meticulous planner. He's determined to get this development through, whatever. It's the biggest project his company have undertaken.'

I decided it was time to be bold. 'So if Danni is a Hookes Bay girl, and you're from Ireland, how did you meet?'

Dominic opened his second beer. I'd hardly touched mine. 'We were both working for the same company in London,' he said. 'She was on an internship and I'd taken the job after qualifying in Dublin. To be honest I was beginning to get a bit fed up of living in the city. I'm a country boy at heart. My family own racing stables in County Kildare. Danni and I got talking at work one day and she mentioned she had a couple of horses and why didn't I come down to Hampshire for the weekend and do a bit of riding. It just mushroomed from there. Six months later she was planning a wedding. Hastings provided the cash for us to set up a practice together in Portsmouth. Naturally, I wanted to concentrate on sympathetic restoration projects, because that's my field of expertise, but

Danni was happy to do whatever Daddy wanted, which basically meant working on his new build schemes. Professionally, I felt compromised. The conservation work dried up and Hastings' projects took precedence. Working for Hastings ruined my reputation as a serious player in the restoration sector. I realised too late I'd sold my soul to the devil.

'Danni is just like her father. She has this way of sweeping you up and before you know it you're indebted. I'm assuming that's what happened with Robbie Mayhew. Hastings definitely has some sort of hold over him and I suspect it's something to do with gambling. Grant likes a flutter at the race track and Robbie must have debts, although he doesn't exactly look like a man who's short of cash with that mansion in Broken Lane and his holiday home in the Canaries. I imagine the pavilion is the only asset he can get rid of without arousing the wrath of that dippy wife of his.'

'I suppose gambling, the nightclub scene, it all goes together, doesn't it?' I remarked. 'But like you say, they don't seem like couple desperate for money.'

'Hastings has something on them that's for sure. He's the one exerting the pressure. I know what it's like to be on the wrong side of Grant Hastings and it's not pleasant. I'm currently engaged in a costly legal battle to reclaim my share of the practice. He's basically bankrupting me.' Dominic let out a huge sigh. 'Part of me thinks just walk away, let it go, but then there's the house as well. Danni and I own a converted watermill. It took me five years of blood, sweat and tears to restore and a great deal of money. Unfortunately, several times during the restoration process Hastings helped us out financially. Danni doesn't want to give the mill up and Daddy doesn't see why I should be entitled to a penny because he provided a fair amount of cash for its restoration.'

It certainly seemed as if Grant Hastings had played an influential role in Dominic's marriage, and the subsequent break-up. There wasn't so much as regret in Dominic's voice, as sadness. Fleetingly I wondered if he still had feelings for Danni. I could recall him saying she was the one suing for divorce; did that mean he would be still prepared to give things another go?

I tried to sound sympathetic. 'It does sound like a right mess. Is that why you've escaped to the junk yard?'

He nodded. 'Originally it was just a hobby. I've always collected a few odds and sods as I went along. I'd buy and sell on eBay. The boat shed was cheap storage. Now it's the only income I have until the legal battle is resolved, and I don't think Hastings is going to stop pursuing me through the courts until I've lost every penny.'

'Presumably you heard about the pavilion plans from Danni? This has been going on for some time?'

'Yes. I had to do something. I couldn't let him get away with this.'

'So your motives are not entirely altruistic?'

He finished his second beer. 'That's rich, coming from you, Alice.'

I ignored him. 'I meant every word of what I said this evening, about my plans for the Arts Hub.'

'I'm sure you did. I *know* you did.' The beer had definitely made him mellow. 'I'm not doing this to get my own back on Hastings. I'm doing this for myself. I sold out. I took Hastings' money and designed blocks of faceless apartments when I should have been out there preserving more buildings like the pavilion. I lost my integrity and I'm ashamed of the man I became. If I can do something good here and return the pavilion to its former glory, then I can hold my head up high again.'

It certainly sounded as if he was speaking from the heart. Dominic lacked Kitty's guile to be playing the sympathy card. He put his hand on my knee, a surprising gesture which caught me unawares and sent shivers of pleasure and longing throughout my entire body. 'So, what about you, Alice?' he asked. 'What brings a nice girl like you to Hookes Bay, apart from a spot of intrigue? Are there any skeletons in your closet? What about significant others?'

Skeletons and significant others? If he knew anything of the Tara Wakely fiasco he'd certainly know about skeletons and significant others. So why was he asking? *He didn't know*. The thought hit me like another warm blast of summer sunshine, joyful and liberating. Dominic knew I wasn't a dance teacher called Alice Paige, but he genuinely had no idea who I really was. Kitty hadn't told him and he hadn't sussed. Not everybody was so obsessed with celebrity, not here in sleepy Hookes Bay. *The Sunday Stargazer* was well off the radar of an intelligent man dedicated to preserving old buildings with a passion.

'There are too many skeletons to mention but I certainly don't have a significant other,' I confessed, trying to keep my emotions in check. 'It's just me.'

His fingers tightened on my knee. He gave it a playful squeeze before standing up with a stretch. 'That's good to know.'

'Is it?' I asked, gathering up the carrier bags and jumping up beside him.

'Well yes, I just wondered.' He appeared to have gone quite shy. 'Come on, I'll walk you back to Crabhook Lane.'

He held out his arm and I linked mine through his. All the way back to the bungalow I fantasized about our goodnight kiss, but when it came, in the glare of Kitty's security spotlight, it was little more than an awkward peck on the cheek, but even that seemed to represent a significant shift in our relationship, and a distinct thawing out.

I was far too restless to sleep: *Dominic likes me. He likes me not.* It was like pulling petals off a daisy. Kitty was also tossing and turning in her room. I had become used to her confused nocturnal mutterings and knew better now than to disturb her. Kitty disliked her moments of weakness being witnessed.

I made a cup of tea and sat down at the kitchen table with Maureen's scrapbook. Her nephew Derek Woodford, nickname *'Woody'*, was Jez Keaton's best friend and Urban Rebel's bass guitarist. Besides several photographs of a teenage Woody with Jez, faded news-clippings were pasted into the pages, evidence of the band's increasing popularity.

'Local acts performing on Hookes Bay recreation ground during the carnival festivities include the Jolly Farmers, Griselda Wickton and Urban Rebel.'

'Hookes Bay's very own Urban Revel headlined a concert to raise money for the new youth centre in Gosport.'

'Local band Urban Rebel will be playing a gig at the Joiners Arms in Southampton on December 16th.'

There was a full-page feature from the entertainment section of the South Coast Gazette. *'Urban Rebel set for record deal,'* ran the headline. *'The Hookes Bay band have been signed up for a series of gigs in London. Jez Keaton and fellow band members – 'Woody' Woodford and brothers, Vince and Paulo Bonetti – met at secondary school. The gigs are planned for the new year and Jez hopes a record deal will follow. "This is very exciting news for the band," he told the Gazette. "We're currently in talks with producer Stevie Newman-Smith at Metropolitan Records and we can't wait for the opportunity to perform in front of a London audience." Urban Rebel will play at the Pavilion Club on New Year's Eve but it looks like this could be their last gig on the south coast for some time.*

'For any fans keen to support the group up in London, the tour dates are as follows...'

This was Jez's big tour; the tour that led to the meeting with the significant someone who was going to change his life. My eyes skipped down the list of venues, recognising a familiar nightspot or two. The Piranha Club was still going; it was the scene of my one successful comedy improv session. The Blue Fin, that was another name I recognised from my dim and distant past, just off Soho and more renowned for its open all hours bar service than its live music scene. Then I stopped. *The Roundhouse, Old Edmonton Road.*

I wasn't familiar with The Roundhouse but I knew the Old Edmonton Road. It was a mere mile or so away from the London council estate where I'd grown up. I double-checked the date of the newspaper article and then it hit me like a bullet. Dominic was right. Kitty did have a back-up plan, and it was totally fool-proof.

Nine months after Urban Rebel had played a gig at the Roundhouse in Edmonton, just a stone's throw from where my maternal grandparents still lived, I had been born. Not Alice Paige with her fictional ID, but me, Tara Wakely. The myth that Jez Keaton had a daughter was totally plausible because my father wasn't named on my birth certificate and my mother hadn't considered it something anyone needed to know. For a woman who barely knew how to turn on a computer, Kitty had been meticulous in her research. Theoretically, I really could be her grand-daughter.

Had Jamie Coulter mentioned I'd been raised by a single mother in his article? More than likely. It was another black mark to tarnish my character. Could I recall bemoaning '*I never even knew who my father was*' in that Knightsbridge Hotel room? Quite possibly. The last thing I wanted to do was trail through back-copies of the *Sunday Stargazer* to ascertain exactly what had been printed. Whatever I had said, I had quite literally talked my way into Kitty's hands.

No-one could refute my identity. My mother had been run over by a bus when I was fourteen. Like most people who are killed by buses, my mother's death wasn't an unlucky falling of fate but a successful suicide attempt. It wasn't her first attempt, but it was her first using public transport.

She had always told me my father was someone I didn't need to know about because he was never going to be part of our lives. 'You have the same colour eyes,' she had once conceded when after a science lesson on genes I had attempted to ascertain exactly what family characteristics I might have inherited. 'And his mouth.' My grandparents were equally as tight-lipped, which wasn't surprising as they never met my father from start to finish.

'I wouldn't be surprised if Nicki didn't even know his name,' Granddad Bert had once said in full ear-shot of both myself and my mother. My grandparents were not pleasant people. They'd used my mother's death as an excuse to wash their hands of me. I'd been very fortunate indeed to have been fostered by Viv and Ray, my gratitude to them, and the support they'd given me over the years far surpassed any genetic ties I felt to my mother's family. But as for my father? I'd given him very little thought.

There was no denying that Jez Keaton and I shared certain physical similarities. The more pictures I saw, the more that resemblance became apparent. We both had hazel eyes, naturally nondescript brown hair, a cleft chin and a generous smile which many a director had remarked made it impossible for me to 'do tragedy'. A happy coincidence for Kitty.

The last picture in Maureen's scrapbook was a photograph of Urban Rebel posing on the stump of Hookes Bay pier. The Bonetti brothers were characterised by their curling black hair, one short and wiry, the other a taller, effeminate looking young man. Maureen's nephew Woody lacked the good looks of the others with a hook nose and straggly blond hair. He strummed his guitar, while Jez had his slung across his back as he balanced on one-leg on the very tip of the pier.

He and my mother would have made quite a couple. Boyfriends had come and gone over the years, and Jez, with his predilection for music and illegal substances fitted Nicki Wakely's preferred type. I quite liked the idea of a having a potential rock-star for a father, it would certainly explain that inherent need to perform. I also liked the idea that I did have some hitherto unknown connection to Hookes Bay.

However, there was no point day-dreaming. It was hard to imagine anyone ever referring to my teenage mother as a woman who could change lives, and in any case, if my mother had met a potential rock-star she certainly wouldn't have dismissed him as inconsequential. She'd have clung to him like a limpet.

My tea had gone cold. I yawned and rinsed out my cup. Right on cue, Kitty let out a pitiful wail, the despairing cry of a grieving mother. I took one last look at the picture of the young man clowning about at the very spot where he had later fallen to his death, and closed the scrapbook. It was no wonder Kitty was haunted. If Maureen Batty was to be believed, Phil Kendrick's theory that Jez had thrown himself into the water on a hallucinogenic high was nothing but unsubstantiated guesswork. I could understand why the policeman had clutched at straws. There was no plausible explanation to account for Jez's death. How likely was it that a boy who had spent his entire life hanging around on Hookes Bay Pier and possessed the balancing skills of a professional acrobat, would simply slip and fall?

Chapter Twenty-One

Kitty

She heard the click of the latch. Crabhook Lane was starting to feel like Spaghetti Junction. It was too early for Belinda. They weren't due at the hospital until twelve.

'Hello, Kit, are you home?' How typical of Robbie that he should bother with such a stupid question. Of course she was home. 'Someone been doing your garden?'

She knew she should have stopped Alice. 'It helps me relax,' Alice had said. Kitty could think of far more pleasurable ways to relax than getting your fingers covered in dirt and digging great big holes in the ground. What was that about foster parents, though? A stab of shame. She'd not known about that.

Kitty shifted in her chair. She was feeling really uncomfortable; she'd hardly slept a wink all night, pains in her stomach. A bad sign. She wasn't going to mention it to Dr Birtwhistle. He'd whisk her off onto the ward and wire her up to some drip and that would be it. Best to keep quiet.

Alice had gone off to Pebbles again this morning, looking very pleased with herself. Apparently, the inaugural meeting of the Pavilion Conservation Society had been a great success. Kitty felt piqued. She should have been there, it was her pavilion after all.

'We've got time for a cuppa before your appointment, haven't we?' Robbie said. He brought her a mug. *A mug.* Would he never learn? 'Tell me a bit more about Alice Paige, Kit.'

So he was finally becoming curious.

'What about her?'

'A little bird told me she might be staying here.' Robbie glanced back out into the garden. 'Got green fingers has she?'

'Callum.' Kitty said at once. 'Penny's boy. He was off school again. He came and did the garden.'

'Oh, pull the other one,' Robbie said. 'That boy wouldn't know one end of a pansy from the other.'

'I like her. She needed a place to stay.'

'She could have rented an Airbnb like anyone else. Why take her in?'

'Felt sorry for her.'

'Why didn't you tell me that she was staying here?'

'It's my house. I can do what I like. She's company for me.'

'Is she paying you a good rent?' Kitty stretched out her back. Did Robbie never think of anything else? 'I don't know what sob story she's sold to you, Kit,' he carried on, 'but I don't like to think of someone taking advantage of you.'

I didn't know you cared, Robbie. 'She's not taking advantage of me.'

'Good. So where's she from then?'

'She's worked all over the world according to Mari. That's why she's got such big plans for the dance school. That's why she wants new premises.'

'Oh yes. I hope you haven't said anything more about the pavilion?'

Kitty pouted. 'I don't see why it wouldn't work.'

'You know perfectly well why it wouldn't work. Hastings' solicitors phoned yesterday. They're keen to get this deal sorted out once and for all. There's another twenty grand in the pot.'

She decided to change the subject. 'Are you going to take me to the hospital or is Belinda coming later?'

'Lindy'll be along soon.'

'Is she all right? She looked decidedly peaky the other day.'

Robbie winced. 'She's just a bit anxious, that's all.'

'She's always anxious.'

'I know. She's stressed about you, about this deal with the pavilion.'

'Why she's stressing about that?'

'She just is, you know Lindy.'

'Can't they give her something for her nerves?'

'She doesn't need any more tablets.'

'Therapy then? Take her to see someone. Don't know how you put up with it, Robbie.'

'I love her. That's why I put up with it.'

Kitty glanced up and caught his expression. Pure dejection. She felt the stirrings of sympathy. Robbie wasn't known for his sensitivity.

'Why did you marry her, Robbie?'

His fingers clasped his mug. 'It's a bit late to be asking that, isn't it?' he said.

'You think having children would have made a difference?'

'Of course it would have made a bloody difference.' Robbie slammed his mug down onto the side table. 'What a stupid thing to say. You know it would have made a difference. When we lost the baby… that was the worse time. The worse time ever.'

There were tears in his eyes. She hadn't meant to upset him. She was fond of Robbie, in her own way. What had made her bring up Lindy's miscarriage? It was something they never talked about. Kitty had dealt with her loss with matter-of-fact stoicism because that was what you did in those days, but Lindy… no. Hers was an entirely different situation. Kitty had already had Jez when she lost her little Alice, but Lindy didn't just lose Robbie's baby, all hope of any other children had been dashed. Something wrong with her womb, the doctors told Robbie. They should have been warned after her first miscarriage that she'd never carry a child full-term. But this is her first miscarriage, Robbie had protested. Kitty had remained quiet. Who knew what these young girls got up to at university, or when they were living abroad. Robbie and Lindy had subsequently tried to adopt, but after a lengthy application process, the agency had turned them down, said they weren't suitable. It had been a bitter blow. Robbie said Lindy saw it as a punishment.

Punishment for what? Kitty had always wondered. Getting her father's pills mixed up had been a blessing in disguise. It could have happened to anyone. None of the medical professionals had ever queried it.

Kitty had wanted to deflect Robbie's questions about Alice, yet he was supposed to be thinking about Alice. She wanted him to suspect, to second guess, to doubt, to dither, to delay. She had become too confused, and now she had upset him. She was too old for this. Too weary. In too much pain.

'Kit, are you all right?'

'Yes, of course.'

Robbie got up and began to pace around the conservatory. Now what did he want?

'Just going to take a pee,' he said.

He never used her bathroom, never took a pee in her house, never normally stayed long enough. He was probably snooping, peering into Alice's bedroom, searching for clues. Damn her hearing. She couldn't tell what doors were opening, closing. The toilet flushed.

'So you'll think about the extra twenty then?'

'The extra twenty what?'

'The extra twenty thousand Coastline have offered you?'

'Yes, yes of course.' *As long as you think about Alice. Long and hard.*

He kissed her cheek. 'I'll see myself out. Lindy'll be here in half an hour or so.' He paused. 'Where's Alice now? Is she teaching?'

'No, she's hiding under the bed, didn't you check?'

'Kitty.' Robbie's shoulders drooped.

'She takes herself off to Pebbles. Goes to use the internet.'

'Oh right. Good luck at the clinic.'

'I'm sure Lindy will fill you in with all the gory details.'

She reached for her stick, heaved herself to her feet, shuffled across to the doorway and negotiated the step onto the patio. In the greenhouse, two sturdy tomato plants were sprouting from one grow-bag while something leafy and green was taking over another. She plonked herself down on the bench where Hughie used to sit smoking his pipe. It was as if someone had attacked the garden with a pack of felt-tip pens. Kitty's new flower bed was a riot of colour.

Alice was turning out to be a bit of a dark horse. A chip off the old block, some might say.

Chapter Twenty-Two

Tara

Act two, scene one. Pebbles Café. Enter stage right, Robbie Mayhew.

In the flesh he was far less daunting than the seedy villain I'd pictured in my head. Kitty had given me the impression of an overweight hoodlum. Robbie did have a paunch, but it was no more than any other man in his late fifties, and he was well-groomed, smelling of mints and spicy aftershave. He wore leather jeans, white shirt, and a black waistcoat; the Status Quo look, but without the hair.

'You must be, Alice,' he said, sliding uninvited onto the seat opposite.

There was no point pretending I didn't know who he was. 'Hi, and you must be Robbie.'

'That's right.' He puffed out his chest. 'I hear you're the new owner of Mari Freeborn's dance school?'

'That's right,' I confirmed with a smile. 'I've got big plans for it.' At least that was no lie.

'I just want to make one thing clear before you get any ideas into your head.' The chest puffed out again. 'My stepmother has a very vivid imagination. I don't know what she might have told you, but moving back into Hookes Bay Pavilion is not going to be an option for the dance school. It won't happen, full stop.'

'Thank you for making that so clear, Robbie,' I smiled. 'It does seem such a shame, though, in the circumstances.'

'What circumstances?' His eyes narrowed.

The opportunity was too good to miss. 'Well, I've seen the studio and it is absolutely perfect. It seems almost criminal not to put it to good use. A shame for Kitty too, to know the facility is sat there deteriorating. I know how much the dance school and that building mean to her.'

'The pavilion is in a bad state of disrepair. There is no way I could consider leasing you the studio. It wouldn't be safe.'

'I'm sure it's nothing that couldn't be fixed.' I paused. 'Long term I'm seeking permanent premises. The community centre is totally inadequate. Are you sure I couldn't tempt you? I'd be prepared to pay a premium rent for such a prestigious location.'

'Prestigious?' Robbie spluttered. 'I thought you said you'd seen the pavilion. Are we talking about the same place?'

'Yes. And there is something quite magical about it, don't you think? It sings to me. You know the first time I came to Hookes Bay, it was almost as if something was drawing me here.'

'Really?' Robbie raised an eyebrow.

Pebbles' sour-faced waitress sidled up to our table. She'd been giving me the evil eye since I arrived. No doubt she'd cottoned on to the fact that I could make one cup of coffee and a croissant last a considerable amount of time.

'Don't see you in here very often, Robbie. What can I get you?'

'Nothing for me, Terri.'

'What about your friend? Another coffee?'

I resented her interruption. 'No, thank you. I'm just finishing.'

'Are you local?' she asked. 'Seen you in here a few times now.'

'Alice is staying with Kitty Keaton,' Robbie informed her. 'She's taken over from Mari Freeborn, you know, running Kit's old dance school.'

'Oh really?' Her expression changed. The waitress was about the same age as Robbie. If she'd lived in Hookes Bay all her life she would have known Jez. I shut my lap-top and placed it in my bag.

'I've a dance class at half-one,' I said. 'I don't want to be late.'

The waitress turned her attention back to Robbie. 'Is Lindy back from the Canaries?'

'Yes. And this is a business meeting, Terri. No need for you to go spreading tales.'

'I wouldn't have dreamed of it.' The waitress backed away.

'Gawd, what is this place like,' Robbie said with a hint of humour. 'So, where are you from Alice? You're living with my elderly mother, I'm sure you can understand my concern.'

'Of course.' My face muscles were starting to ache with so much benign smiling. 'I'm originally from London but I've travelled extensively. I spent several years working in the US before heading to the Middle East.'

'And now you plan on settling here in Hookes Bay?'

'Yes. As I said earlier, I feel drawn to this place. It's like I've known Hookes Bay all my life.'

'Really?'

I curled my lip, put on a bit of pout, ran my fingers through my hair. I'm not sure why. Pure mischief, probably. I justified my behaviour with the inherent need to save Hookes Bay Pavilion and secure my future. A frown appeared on his face and I saw the puzzled flicker of déjà vu in his eyes for the first time. Robbie's brain was working overtime.

Sometimes I just don't know when to stop. I leaned closer and put my hand on his arm in what I hoped was a reassuring gesture of friendship, or *family*. 'Oh yes,' I said. 'I think it must be in my blood.'

Ethan Hobart's arrival in class was greeted with a ripple of self-conscious giggles from his fellow pupils. Undeterred, Beth yanked him into the starting position at the end of the line of pink tutus. The little boy grinned at me and then turned to examine his neighbours with a look of fearless curiosity.

My instinct had been right. I was rewarded with a display of clumsy but highly enthusiastic prancing. Ethan was not going to be a ballet dancer, but then it was unlikely that any of the toddlers in this class were going to be prima ballerinas. I wanted my pupils to excel, but to me that meant fulfilling their individual potential, and Ethan did just that. After twenty minutes Beth took him away to the far corner of the room where he played with the percussion instruments I had collected from the pavilion until he created so much distraction that all the other pupils wanted to join in. The class ended in a crazy musical ensemble, a conga chain snaking its way around the community centre. Mari would have had a fit.

'Are you going to come and join us next week?' I asked as the rest of the class filed out to their parents and carers waiting in the vestibule. Ethan responded by hugging my knees. 'I take it that's a yes?' I looked at Beth.

'Could he?' She couldn't keep the hope from her voice. 'He wasn't too annoying? I don't want to stop the others from learning things.'

'They're learning things,' I assured her. 'I will definitely sort out a music class for next term, but for now you are more than welcome to bring him along every Wednesday. It's worth it just to see that cheeky grin.' And his mother's obvious relief.

Beth's gratitude had a profound effect on me. Saving Hookes Bay Pavilion was no longer pie in the sky, it was a necessity.

I spent Thursday morning at the bungalow preparing for the lunchtime meeting at the yacht club. I had to get my hands on that studio and I would do whatever it took. Kitty was not a good influence. I'd already started to work on Robbie. Next step, the Modernist Preservation Trust. Dominic had said Sam MacDonald was flying down from Glasgow. A crusty old Scotsman in a kilt, or a suave Ewan McGregor type? I pinned my hopes on the latter and deliberated for some time on what to wear.

It had to be a skirt because I had good legs, and whilst Dominic was oblivious to my charms, Sam MacDonald might not be. I plumped for what Hal had once disparagingly referred to as my 'Doris Day does hedgerow' outfit, a favourite vintage 1950s wildflower print skirt which I coupled with a bottle green three-quarter sleeved cardigan and matching pumps.

I had totally miscalculated. When I arrived at the yacht club, for one horrible minute, I thought Dominic had actually invited his estranged wife to join us. At first glance the woman seated between Dominic and Tom was a carbon copy of the photograph of Danni Hastings I'd viewed on the Flynn Design Consultancy website – an elegant brunette in a white silk blouse and a navy pencil skirt. Her legs were tanned and bare, and her feet encased in a pair of strappy red Laboutins. As I approached the trio I realised to my relief that the hair lacked a little youthful lustre, the skin on the neck was loose rather than taut. My mean streak immediately surfaced and aged Sam MacDonald at around the fifty mark, although realistically, she was probably mid-forties.

'Hi Alice,' Dominic said, rising from his chair. 'Sam, meet Alice Paige. Alice has some great ideas for utilising the pavilion after its restoration.'

The brunette smiled and held out her hand. 'Hello, Alice. Samantha MacDonald, Field Officer for the Modernist Preservation Trust. I'm very pleased to meet you.'

I wasn't sure I was pleased to meet her at all. Dominic couldn't do enough for her. Even Tom appeared to have fallen under her spell, stuttering painfully through his spiel about the history of Hookes Bay without any of his previous fluency.

When the menus arrived, Dominic insisted on the wine-list, and of course, if Sam wanted starters, we would all love to join her; there was nothing Dominic liked more than a good baked Camembert.

'What do you recommend for mains?' she asked with a girlish flick of her hair. I'd never regretted my pixie cut more.

'The steak is very good,' Tom suggested.

'I like mine very rare,' Sam replied.

Dominic was sure if she specified exactly how many minutes cooking time, the chef would be only too happy to oblige. I ordered a salad and listened with half an ear as Dominic discussed his detailed plans for the building work necessary to restore the pavilion to its original state. My eyes travelled around the marina until I heard Sam direct a question at me.

'Sorry?'

'You have detailed plans on how the pavilion would operate

with financial independence?'

Dominic raised an eyebrow at me questioningly.

'My ideas are very much in their infancy,' I confessed before giving her a brief rundown of my proposals for the Hookes Bay Community Arts Hub.

Sam appeared unimpressed. 'You have the relevant organisations concerned with these activities already on board, I take it?' she asked.

'I'm currently canvassing support.'

The food arrived. Sam prodded her steak. It wasn't so much rare as still alive. 'What research have you carried out?' She asked, her knife poised for the kill. 'You mentioned a café bar. This would be in direct competition with the food outfits already in town. How could you ensure its viability? There is a 500 seater theatre in Fareham less than six miles away, at least another three venues of a similar size in Portsmouth. How would you attract not just acts, but audience participation? I believe there is an existing community centre with function rooms in Hookes Bay. How would you ensure the new centre appeals to customers?'

'Have you seen the existing community centre?' I spluttered. 'There would be no comparison in the quality of facilities available at the pavilion. As for the café bar, that would obviously be offered for tender and we would ensure that whoever was awarded the contract was fully aware of the need to ensure profitability.'

'My executive board will need to see hard evidence that the venue is a financially viable proposition,' Sam pointed out.

I felt indignant that my ideas had been dismissed so readily. I gritted my teeth and tried to keep a pleasant look on my face. 'I think you're missing the point. Saving Hookes Bay Pavilion isn't just about restoring the fabric of the building, it's about honouring and recognising its history. Lionel and Kitty Keaton had a vision of bringing the arts and quality entertainment to this little corner of the south coast. This project shouldn't just be about financial sustainability, it should be about accessing opportunity and fulfilling dreams.'

'Alice is very passionate about the project,' Dominic cut in quickly. 'As I explained this morning, she already runs a dance school in Hookes Bay and would be one of the first community groups to relocate to the pavilion.'

Sam looked up. 'I don't doubt your good intentions, but I'm not sure one dance school is going to impress my board of directors. Do you have any personal experience in co-ordinating a venture of this scale, Miss Paige?'

Blood ran from her steak.

'I've been a professional performer for many years.'

'I take it that's a no then.'

Tom had ordered moules marinière and was struggling to remove a particularly clingy mussel from its shell. The waitress had forgotten to bring the finger bowl. I offered to fetch him one, glad of the chance to get away.

When I returned to the table the conversation had reverted to the aesthetics of the building. Dominic was wooing Sam with an impressive portfolio of his previous renovation projects.

'As you can see,' he finished, 'I have vast experience in the restoration industry.' The closing image on his laptop was a watermill, presumably the family home. It looked idyllic.

'I don't doubt you have the necessary expertise, Dominic,' Sam said, 'but the Trust normally like to appoint their own architect and project manager. We have a very experienced team.'

'Of course. I understand.' His disappointment was obvious.

Sam MacDonald pushed her empty plate to one side. 'Look, I don't doubt that you are all very committed to restoring your pavilion. I'm a great fan of Eric Milner myself, and I'll do all I can to convince the board that this is a building worth saving, but you're a very small band of people without a cohesive business plan or a campaign of public support. Ideally, I should be returning to Glasgow tomorrow with not just the proposed building work schedule, which Dominic has kindly provided, but a list of voluntary and professional organisations committed to the pavilion's restoration together with a comprehensive report on the pavilion's commercial and financial viability. You haven't got that.'

'I can provide you with a business plan,' I interjected. 'I'm working on it already.'

'You are? Well, that's great news.' I ignored the look of scepticism on Dominic's face. 'And you do have a voluntary committee?' Sam continued.

'Yes.' Dominic snapped. 'I've already explained. The Pavilion Conservation Society has had its inaugural meeting.'

'Then I'll need to see minutes.'

'I can write up the minutes,' Tom assured Sam.

'Could I have them by this time tomorrow?' She turned to me. 'And your business plan? Any chance I can have that by first thing Tuesday morning? The Board meets next Wednesday. I'll need something concrete to put to them.'

'Of course.'

'Well that's a start. I'm still unsure how far you can run this campaign without publicity.' She put her hand up to stop Dominic interrupting. 'I know your concerns, but why not strike now, pre-empt the development company and get the public behind you while you can? Exposure in the local media can sometimes work wonders.'

'It's such a tricky situation,' Dominic replied 'Canvassing the local community is obviously important, however, I believe publicising our plans to restore the pavilion could put the building at genuine risk. I know the people behind this company, and they are ruthless. I have genuine concerns for the building's safety. If we knew a counter-offer was on the table from the Modernist Preservation Trust then it would be a totally different scenario.'

Sam sighed. 'It's going to be a hard sell to the board.' She frowned. 'Trust me, I do want to help you. I'm just trying to think what people in these situations have done in the past. Have you thought about seeking patronage from a local celebrity, or even better, a minor royal?'

A celebrity? Just what I needed. Perhaps I could contact Georgie Gold. She seemed to be able to secure publicity by simply getting out of bed.

'I don't think we have any royals in Hookes Bay,' Dominic said with a forced smile.

'I'm not joking, Dominic,' Sam replied. 'Do you want to save this building or not? If I can't secure the funding, you guys are on your own.'

'I'm sorry,' Dominic sighed. 'It's just that everything takes time and time is the one thing we haven't got.'

'How poorly is the pavilion's owner?' Sam queried. 'I'll obviously consider your case a priority but it would be good to know whether we're looking at months or weeks.'

All eyes turned to me. I shook my head. 'I'm sorry I don't know her prognosis.'

'Okay, I understand the sensitivity of the situation.' Sam began to gather up her belongings. 'It's been a pleasure meeting you all. We'll keep in touch. Think hard, though, about what I've said.' She sprung to her feet. 'Right, Dominic, I'm just going to visit the ladies' room and then can you drop me at the station? I've got another couple of properties to view in the area. I thought I might as well make the journey south worthwhile.'

Chapter Twenty-Three

'Well she's a force to be reckoned with, isn't she?' Tom remarked as we watched Dominic escort Sam MacDonald to his van.

'I suppose she's just doing her job,' I replied somewhat begrudgingly. 'She did make our efforts seem somewhat amateur.'

'I think Dominic is being over cautious,' Tom confessed. 'I did all I could to publicise our efforts to save the signal box. The campaign was regularly featured on local radio and in the *South Coast Gazette*. As they say, there's no such thing as bad publicity.'

I didn't contradict him even though my own experiences had taught me otherwise. I was currently skulking around Hookes Bay in an attempt to avoid running into amateur theatre critic, Lindy Mayhew; the last thing I wanted was a genuine local journalist probing too deeply into my background. When I had agreed to help Kitty I had definitely ticked the 'no publicity' box

'As for celebrities,' Tom continued, 'you must have met a few famous names on your travels? Haven't you got any friends of friends you could call up?'

This was just the sort of comment I had been dreading. I gave what I hoped was a nonchalant shrug. 'I'll have a think about it,' I promised, knowing I would do no such thing.

How could I possibly approach any of my theatrical contacts? Tara Wakely was supposedly on retreat in Thailand, and could hardly phone a friend asking for help promoting the cause of a seaside theatre, especially if she added that she was working incognito as a dance teacher called Alice Paige. That was likely to send any potential celebrity patron running a mile.

If the truth of my identity leaked out now, the campaign to save the pavilion would fall at the first hurdle. Grant Hastings and his cronies would have a field day and Dominic would lose all credibility. I couldn't possibly let that happen. I was treading on very shaky ground

'By the way,' Tom said hesitantly, 'I was just wondering if you'd do me a favour. It's my golden wedding anniversary next month and the kids have arranged this big party for us. Jenny's over the moon about it, but personally, I'm not a party person. The thing is, Jenny loves to dance and I've got two left feet. I was just wondering,' he flushed, 'whether perhaps, you'd consider giving me a couple of lessons? I'd like to surprise Jen, whisk her onto the dance floor with a proper anniversary waltz. I'd pay you, of course.'

'Of course I'll give you lessons. Fifty years of marriage is certainly worth celebrating.' I felt my eyes welling up. If I needed any more evidence that I was doing the right thing by staying in Hookes Bay, then this was it. *To provide opportunity*. At seventy, Tom wanted to learn to dance. If only he had made his request when Sam was still here.

'It would have to be kept secret,' Tom stumbled on, 'the lessons, I mean.'

'I totally understand.'

'I'm not quite sure where we could go to practice. I can't do it at home obviously.'

'Maybe after one of my classes in the community centre?'

'Jenny's quite pally with Bunny Mitchell so it would have to be when she's not there.'

'That would be difficult then.' Bunny was ever-present at the community centre office. In addition, finding a suitable timeslot without her knowledge would be impossible. 'I might have to see the vicar's wife about the church hall.'

'Jane's also a good friend. I suppose we could ask Cyril about using the lounge at Wheatsheaf Court?'

I pictured the carpeted floor and all the heavy armchairs that would have to be moved out of the way and shook my head. 'No, Tom, that's not practical.' There really was only one place in Hookes Bay suitable for clandestine dance lessons. 'Leave it with me,' I promised. 'I'll be in touch.'

I had after-school dance classes to keep me occupied for the rest of the afternoon. As I walked back at Crabhook Lane, I called Aaron.

'You remember when I was trying to put together that proposal for Hal, about my stage school idea, and you offered to help me out with a business plan, I don't suppose you've kept a record of it?'

'I might, I might not,' he replied cautiously. I explained briefly what I had in mind. 'Crikey, Tara, you're a quick worker, you've only been in that place a few minutes. It'll take quite a bit of re-jigging. You'd best email me all the details.'

Next I phoned Bea.

'Do we know any celebs who live in this part of the world?' I asked dispensing with any preliminaries.

'How would I know who lives in Thailand?' she replied, her voice barely audible above a cacophony of background noise.

'No, my real part of the world, Hampshire. I need to find a celebrity patron.'

'Look Tara, I'm a bit busy right now. Can I call you back in the morning?'

'It's sort of important.'

'And so are the Foxy FM Music Awards.'

'You're at an award ceremony? Why didn't you say?'

'I just did.'

'But there must be loads of celebs there. Ask them if any of them have holiday homes on the south coast. Just don't mention my name.'

She hung up on me.

Just as I was about to enter the bungalow an unknown number popped up on my phone.

'Hi, it's Dom.'

At last. 'Oh, hi.'

'I just wanted to say thanks, you know, for trying your best at lunch.'

'Don't sound so despondent.'

'Well, our case was a bit of a shambles, wasn't it?'

'No. I think we have a very strong case. I'm working on that business plan as we speak. Your calculations obviously impressed her.'

'I don't know about that,' Dominic mused. 'Anyway, nothing much we can do now is there?'

It was as if Sam MacDonald had sucked the wind out of his sails with her statement about the Trust's preference for using their existing team of architects. Dominic had always assumed he would be the one working on the restoration.

'Hey, keep your chin up,' I said. 'Sam had some good ideas and I think we should go with what she said. I'm teaching full-on for the next couple of days, but I don't suppose you could possibly bring that crate of old programmes round to Kitty's for me? I want to take a better look, see if there are any big names who once performed either at the theatre or the nightclub who might be able to help us out. What do you think?'

'I suspect most of the variety acts mentioned in those old programmes are dead.'

His apathy was starting to grate. 'We've got to do something. You can't just give up,' I argued.

He sighed. 'Sure. I'll drop them round tomorrow.'

'Thank you.'

After a quick supper I called Barbara Kendrick.

'Alice, lovely to hear from you,' she said. 'Have you decided to give the Am-Dram a go?'

'Yes, I'd be very keen,' I replied. 'But first I wanted to put a proposition to you. Is there any chance of meeting up over the weekend?'

'A proposition, that sounds intriguing. Of course. Why don't you come round for coffee on Sunday morning?

'Great, thanks. While I'm on the phone, I don't suppose you know of any celebrities with connections to Hookes Bay?'

'Celebrities? Goodness me. The only person who immediately springs to mind is Frankie Jones. Do you remember him? He was in a sit-com that ran for years, probably before your time, *Yes, Mr Jones*. He started out as a blue coat at Muntings, the holiday camp in that used to be in Broken Lane. He was an entertainer there back in the 1950s.'

The name rang a bell. An elderly comedian wasn't quite the calibre of celebrity I had been hoping for. However, if he had been based at Hookes Bay in his youth he would certainly be familiar with the pavilion. He might even have known Lionel and Kitty.

'Is he still alive?' I wondered.

'As far as I know,' Barbara replied. 'You could always try Googling him.'

'Thanks, I'll give it a go.'

I set out for Pebbles at eight the following morning and, in order to keep the waitress sweet, ordered a full English breakfast and a pot of tea. My Google searches revealed that Frankie Jones, real name Harold Francis Popple, was now in his eighties, married to his fourth wife, Lilly, thirty years his junior, and living out his retirement on the island of Guernsey. He had indeed started out as a blue coat at a holiday camp on the south coast although I couldn't find any specific mention of Muntings.

A recent news article about the comedian was dominated by Lilly's heart-wrenching account of Frankie's increasing battle with dementia. He didn't sound like the ideal candidate for a publicity campaign. However, he had coined a catch-phrase that had become an integral part of the English language, and was an indelible national treasure. Desperate times called for desperate measures. All he would need to do was recount some tale of his time in Hookes Bay. I could offer to write the piece for him, or at least Kitty could, her scriptwriting skills were way more advanced than mine.

I felt quite optimistic by the time I returned to Crabhook Lane to prepare for an afternoon of teaching. Mari was finally heading out with John for an entire weekend of sailing and it was the first time I was going to be solely in charge for the busiest two days of the week.

Kitty had been in bed when I'd left and she was still there when I returned. Penny had been in and out in my absence.

'Is everything okay, Kit?' I asked, gently knocking on her bedroom door.

'Just a bit tired,' she murmured. 'Don't worry, Penny's seen to me. You can come in, I'm decent.'

She was propped up in bed in a yellow fluffy bed-jacket, wig in place and fully made up, a ubiquitous cup of tea on the bedside cabinet beside her. She had a pile of magazines on the bed, including the latest edition of *What's Hot*.

'I'm going to be out teaching until nine tonight,' I told her.

'Don't worry about me, duck. Just needed to rest. Lindy'll pop round later, I'm sure.'

'Do you have a spare set of keys to the pavilion?'

'Of course I do,' she replied.

'Could I borrow them? I want to take another look round.'

Kitty retrieved a bundle of keys from the bedside drawer. 'Look after them, mind.'

I promised I would and warned her to expect Dominic with the box of theatre programmes. 'I don't suppose, back in the 1950s, you ever encountered the actor, Frankie Jones?' I asked. 'You might remember him as Frankie or Harold Popple. He was an entertainer at Muntings.'

'Never heard of him,' she muttered, reaching for her cup of tea. 'I thought you'd already looked through those old programmes. Why do you want them here?' I might have been mistaken but a distinct flush of colour spread across her cheeks.

'I want to see what stars of past and present performed in the pavilion's hey-day,' I replied. 'See if there's anyone who might be able to help us out now.'

'What's the point in digging up old ghosts?' she grumbled.

An ironic comment from someone who had created an entirely phantom granddaughter.

Chapter Twenty-Four

Kitty

Frankie Jones. That was a blast from the past. Where had Alice dragged that name up from?

Frankie was pre-Jez. She'd just turned thirty when he'd started coming into the pavilion for a drink on his evenings off. Normally you couldn't drink in the pavilion bar unless you'd paid to watch a show, but Lionel made an exception for Frankie.

'We're all in this business together,' he said.

Frankie had aspirations. He had a good voice, Kitty had heard him sing, and he could make her laugh. Lionel, for all his sophisticated charm, wasn't known for his sense of humour.

'They've let me out on parole for the night,' was one of Frankie's favourite sayings. Or, 'the escape team managed to cut a hole in the wire.'

She could picture Frankie now, fingers stroking her cheek, the longing in his puppy dog eyes, the yearning in his voice. Kitty knew better than to fall for an act like that. She'd grown up in the theatre, surrounded by lechers and rogues. Her mother was a music hall star who performed alongside Vesta Victoria and Nellie Wallace before getting killed in the Blitz, leaving Kitty with a feckless father who would have sold her off to the highest bidder if Lionel Keaton hadn't fallen for her charms and whisked her off to Hookes Bay. She hadn't sought sanctuary with Lionel to ruin it all for a backstage romp with Frankie Jones. At least not until she caught Lionel with his hand up some young slapper's skirt.

Frankie Jones had a Triumph Thunderbird. He'd bought it when he finished his national service.

'I treated myself, Kit,' he said. 'And now I can treat you.'

He'd ride over from the camp, pick her up and then they'd head to Pepperthorne Point, where they would scramble through the brambles to a sheltered patch of shingle, just yards from the perimeter fence of the depot.

And then he'd gone. Just like that. Spotted by some talent scout, one of the boys at the camp told her. He hadn't even come back to say goodbye. He'd ridden off on his motorbike without her. Just like James Dean. No, not like James Dean. That was Jez.

Frankie Jones. James Dean. Jez. All very similar. Very easy to get people and dates confused.

'A baby, after all this time?' Lionel had been over the moon.

Chapter Twenty-Five

Tara

I phoned Tom Whybrow in a break between classes and arranged to meet him at the pavilion at seven on Saturday evening.

'That's just perfect,' he said. 'Jenny's baby-sitting the grandchildren.'

Kitty was already asleep when I finally made it back to the bungalow. I was disappointed that Dominic hadn't left a message with the crate of programmes. While I tucked into a microwave meal I began to trawl though the contents.

In addition to the variety shows which continued well into the early 1960s, the programmes detailed the performances of classical plays starring the Keatons' own company of professional actors and actresses. When the pavilion transformed to a dance hall and then to a nightclub, the double-spread programmes gave way to one-page flyers. Would the aging members of a notorious 1960s rock band remember playing a gig at the Pavilion Club right at the very start of their career? I doubted it. Although providing an engrossing and valuable history lesson that kept me awake into the small hours, the programmes offered little prospect of finding a celebrity patron.

Saturday passed without incident. Shelbie Solway, one of Mari's older girls acted as my assistant for the day. I saw something of my younger self in Shelbie. She always arrived early for class and lingered at the end. She wasn't the most talented of Mari's pupils, but she was definitely a grafter. It hadn't taken much persuasion to convince her to help me out in exchange for some extra singing lessons.

Straight from the community centre I dashed to the pavilion where Tom was already waiting patiently on the front steps.

'Sorry I'm late,' I panted. There were keys of varying sizes on the ring Kitty had given me and it took several attempts to find the correct one for the stage door. Tom helped me locate the light switches.

'I haven't been in this place for years,' he exclaimed as we entered the foyer. 'I'd forgotten how grand it was.'

'It is quite magnificent, isn't it? Did you come to the club when you were younger?'

He shook his head. 'As I said, I'm not a dancer. When we moved into Hookes Bay we had a young family. We didn't have time or the money for nightclubbing. My kids used to the come to the disco every now in their teens but not regularly and certainly not recently.' He pulled a face. 'Wasn't the sort of place for decent folk.'

'What did you do before you retired?' I asked heading up the stairs.

'I worked at Titan, as a civilian.'

'With the chemical weapons? But you don't glow,' I teased.

Tom laughed. 'There were no chemical weapons at Titan.'

'So what did they keep there then?'

'Afraid I can't tell you, love. Signed the official secrets act when I started work. Anyway, it's all long gone. The bunkers, the storage units, were all filled in thirty years or so ago. I oversaw the job myself. It took over 10,000 tonnes of concrete.'

It was impossible to enter the studio without admiring the view, I saw Tom follow my gaze out of the window.

'At least we'll finally get rid of that pier, whatever happens,' he remarked.

'Do you remember when Kitty's son had his accident?' I asked.

'I remember it well. Commander Cartwright helped to organise the search teams. Navy divers were called in. He was a great chap. It was such a shame.'

'Yes. Kitty still has nightmares,' I said.

'No, I meant about the Commander, although yes, of course, shame about the young man.'

'What happened to the Commander?' I moved away from the window to set up my laptop on the piano. I had downloaded a playlist of waltz music for Tom.

'He suffered a massive stroke,' Tom said. 'It just happened at work one day. Left him paralysed from the chest down, totally dependent on other people. He'd always been such an active man, playing rugby, mountain climbing, canoeing. It was devastating. One of my colleagues went to visit him afterwards. He said he felt so helpless. The Commander was begging him to put him out of his misery. Ken said he couldn't go and see him again after that. Thankfully, he only lasted a couple of years. It was no life.'

'How awful.'

'Oh, it was. Brian Cartwright was a terrific base Commander. The ones that came after were no match. There's always a bit of rivalry with the locals when you have a big military presence in a little town like this. Commander Cartwright did so much to improve community relations. I remember when he had his fiftieth birthday, he threw this big fund-raising ball, invited everyone on the base and half of Hookes Bay. Grand night it was. Kitty's boy was there then, if I remember, with his band. One of the ratings must have booked them for a laugh. It wasn't the Commander's type of music at all. Fortunately he'd ordered a cabaret act for the main event.'

'I understand Robbie Mayhew is married to his daughter.'

'That's right. She had to come back from abroad to look after him. I can't remember where she was, Hong Kong or somewhere like that. She'd gone there straight from university. Now she did glow, not that you'd know it, to see her today. She was vivacious as a youngster, only way to describe her. Her father doted on her.' Tom took off his pullover and folded it neatly on the piano stool. 'Little wonder she's a mere shadow of the girl she once was. I mean, if Brian Cartwright asked Ken to put a pillow over his head, makes you wonder what he asked his daughter, doesn't it? So, where do we start?'

I manoeuvred Tom into position. The story of Commander Cartwright's tragic demise had tainted my enthusiasm. No wonder Lindy liked to retreat to the Canaries to immerse herself in poetry.

Just as Tom appeared to be gaining confidence and picking up the steps, we were interrupted by noises from downstairs, the excited bark of a dog, followed by heavy footsteps on the stairs. Robbie.

'Oi, what's going on up there?'

Tom's shoulders sagged. 'Mayhew?' he whispered.

'Don't worry, I can handle him. It's only me, Robbie,' I called out, 'Alice Paige.'

'Alice?' Robbie appeared red faced in the doorway. He was in baggy denims and a leather jacket, clutching a Chihuahua under his arm.

I switched off the music. 'Sorry, Kitty lent me a key. I needed a place for some extra teaching. Just a one-off.'

The dog was plonked unceremoniously onto the floor. Robbie turned his attention to Tom. 'Who are you?'

'Tom Whybrow. I asked Alice to give me some private lessons.'

I was determined to keep things civil. 'It's Tom's golden wedding in a few weeks. He wants to surprise his wife.'

'I thought I told you the pavilion was out of bounds,' Robbie growled. The dog gave a little yelp of excitement as it found an old ballet shoe.

'I appreciate that, Robbie, but it seemed the perfect place. We had to find somewhere secret. Tom doesn't want his wife to know, you see. It's a surprise. Romantic don't you think?'

Tom gave an embarrassed cough. 'Perhaps I ought to be going. Thanks Alice.' He picked up his pullover and edged towards the doorway. 'Will you be okay?'

I nodded. 'Sure. I'll be in touch about another lesson during the week.'

Robbie waited until Tom was well on his way down the stairs before he took step closer. No mints today. He reeked of nicotine and body odour. 'I don't know who you are, Alice

Paige, and I don't know what story you've spun my stepmother, but I want you out of her house and out of Hookes Bay within the next twenty-four hours. Do you understand?'

I had to keep calm. 'Are you threatening me, Robbie?'

'No. I'm just offering you some advice. What are you after? Money?'

'No, of course I'm not after any money.'

'I mean, if it is money, I can give you some.'

'I don't want your money. How many times do I have to tell you?'

'So what are you doing here then?'

'Trying to run a dance school.'

'Pull the other one. Lindy looked you up on the internet. You've never run a dance school in your life. I suggest you go back to Crabhook Lane, tell my stepmother you've had a change of heart and pack your bag.'

The last thing I wanted was Lindy looking me up on the internet. Could little white lies mask the bigger one? 'Look Robbie, you're right, I haven't ever run a dance school before, but I love to dance, love to sing, I've made an adequate living touring as a performer for years, but you know how it is. You can't live that life forever. I'm just starting out on my teaching career, which is why Hookes Bay is such an attractive proposition for me. A small school, but with big ambitions.'

'Oh yes, I've heard all about your ambitions. So what is it going to take to get you to leave?' He took another step closer. 'My fist in your face?'

I shrank back. He wore knuckle dusters. 'I don't think Kitty will be too pleased when she hears about this,' I stammered, my heart racing. I'd thought Robbie was all bluster, but now I wasn't quite so sure. His body was taut, his shoulders hunched, poised for a fight. Robbie wasn't tall, but he was bulky. One fist could do an awful lot of damage. 'If I leave she'll want to know why. What do I tell her? That you threatened me? Is this how you got rid of Mari Freeborn?'

'Mari Freeborn quit of her own accord.'

I had to use all my powers of resourcefulness. No point being meek and mild Alice now. 'Why don't you want me in your pavilion, Robbie? Oh, I forgot. It's not your pavilion, is it? Not yet. Kitty's still hanging on in there, isn't she? It's like she's had a whole new lease of life since I arrived in Hookes Bay.'

'You little bitch.'

Just as I thought he really was going to swing a punch there was another sound from downstairs. The Chihuahua skipped across to the doorway, shoe in its mouth.

'Now what?' Robbie snarled, backing away.

More voices. Voices I recognised but didn't particularly want to hear, at least not together: one Scots and female, the other Irish and male.

I followed Robbie as he stormed out of the studio. Dominic Flynn and Sam MacDonald stood below us in the foyer.

Dominic was wearing an electric blue suit with an open neck crisp white shirt. He looked as if he had stepped out of the pages of a clothing catalogue, even his unruly hair had been tamed. Sam MacDonald was in a little black dress and a red bolero. The effect was quite dazzling. They looked like a sophisticated professional couple out on a date.

Dominic had lost his air of despair and was in full flow extolling the virtues of the pavilion to Sam.

'What the fuck are you doing here?' Robbie bellowed. 'This is private property.' He took the stairs two at a time. 'How did you get in?' He turned at me. 'Are you in league together? What is this? Some sort of secret dance society?' He was perfectly serious.

'Of course we're not in league together,' Dominic said, coming to his senses. 'Kitty let me have a key. Sam, this is Robbie Mayhew. He's Mrs Barker's stepson. He manages the building for her.'

'Manages?' Robbie spluttered, unhappy at his demotion.

'You have a wonderful building here, Mr Mayhew,' Sam MacDonald said. Too late I realised that Dominic's use of the word 'manages' had given her totally the wrong impression. She had no idea Robbie was the enemy. 'You have a near perfect example of early twentieth century architecture. I'm a big fan of Eric Milner.'

'You've lost me already,' Robbie replied. 'I know who pretty boy here is, but who are you?'

'Samantha MacDonald,' she extended a slender hand. 'I represent the Modernist Preservation Trust.'

I caught Dominic's eye in dismay as Robbie repeated the last two words. 'Preservation Trust?'

'Kitty was keen for the Trust to see the building while it remains intact.' Dominic made a hasty attempt to defuse the situation. 'For prosperity's sake, I offered to arrange a viewing. That's all.'

'I bet you did.' Robbie retorted.

The Chihuahua deposited the ballet shoe at Sam MacDonald's stiletto-clad feet. 'Gorgeous little thing,' she crooned, bending to pet it. 'What's it called?'

'Chico,' Robbie replied momentarily distracted. Over their heads Dominic looked to me for help.

'What are you doing here?' he mouthed.

'Don't ask,' I gestured back. 'Just get her out.'

He nodded. 'Look Sam, we've probably seen enough.'

'Oh, but I was hoping to see upstairs again.'

'The studios are a modern addition,' Dominic said, 'completed during the 1960s I believe?' He pretended to consult Robbie for confirmation.

Robbie shrugged. The building's history didn't resonate with him at all. 'No idea, mate,' he muttered.

'As I pointed out on Thursday, it's the exterior that remains very much in its original state,' Dominic said, placing a guiding hand on Sam MacDonald's back to steer her into reverse mode. 'Perhaps we should complete our tour outside.'

'Oh, don't mind me,' Robbie said, gathering Chico into his arms. 'If Kitty's given you the key just make yourself at home. Be my guest. My stepmother appears to be handing out pavilion keys willy-nilly right now.' He stepped towards the rear corridor. 'I'll leave you to it. See it while you can. After all, it's only a question of time.' He stopped and looked at each of us in turn. 'Be under no illusions, any of you. Once my stepmother's gone, this building will be mine and I'll be selling it to Coastline developments at the first opportunity.'

Chapter Twenty-Six

'What a vile man,' Sam MacDonald said.

'I hope your return to Hookes Bay is indicative of the Trust's interest in preserving the pavilion, Miss MacDonald,' I said, eager to establish that she hadn't just returned for a date with Dominic which from the way they were all over each other wouldn't have surprised me.

'Yes. It seemed silly not to come back for a second look before heading back to Scotland. After completing my other viewings, I do feel that Hookes Bay Pavilion is very worthy of the Trust's consideration. Dom and I are heading out for a spot of dinner when we've finished. Do you want to join us?'

If the invitation had come from Dominic, I might have accepted, despite the fact that three would definitely be a crowd.

'No, I'm sorry, thank you. I've been working all day. I need to head home for a shower and a good night's sleep,' I smiled.

'You'd be very welcome. We'll wait for you,' Dominic said. But it was too late. Nobody wanted to be an afterthought.

'You'll lock up when you've finished?' I asked, picking up the ballet shoe from the floor. It was covered in dust and dog saliva.

'Yes of course.'

When I awoke on Sunday morning it was tempting to hop straight on my bike and head to Craven Farm to stake out the caravan park to ascertain whether Sam had been invited back for a nightcap. I resisted the urge to look up flight times to Glasgow. Surely Dominic would have taken her to a hotel, not a mobile home? In an attempt to banish my irrationally jealous thoughts, I took a run along the seafront. It was a beautiful clear morning and the pavilion gleamed in the sunlight. It really deserved better surroundings than the boarded up Carlisle and the stunted pier. Why couldn't Hastings just build his apartment block and leave the pavilion be?

After a quick shower, I headed over to see Barbara Kendrick. Barbara and Phil lived just a street away from Mari in a similar mock-Tudor detached house. As it was such a glorious morning, Barbara suggested we sit in the garden. I was relieved to hear that Phil was at work.

'Sundays are always busy,' Barbara told me. 'Have you booked your second lesson yet?'

'I've got too much else going on right now,' I said taking a seat on a padded sun-lounger. 'In fact, that's what I wanted to chat to you about.'

'Oh? I thought you were signing yourself up for our next production?'

'Well, yes, that too.'

After stressing the need for discretion, I outlined my ideas for the arts hub.

'I was only saying to Phil I wondered what was going to happen to the pavilion if the new development goes ahead,' Barbara said when I'd finished. 'I suppose I just assumed it would disappear.'

'I think that's what Robbie Mayhew and Grant Hastings want people to think,' I confirmed. 'But it's not what Kitty wants.'

'You've certainly come up with a very interesting alternative.' Barbara sounded impressed. 'You've got my support. It would be great to see live theatre back in Hookes Bay. Historically, Kitty *was* the Am-Dram, as you can imagine. She ran the club for years and always used the studios for rehearsals.'

'Would you mind if I used your name in my report to the Modernist Preservation Trust?'

'Not at all, go ahead,' Barbara said to my relief. 'You can definitely include us in your plans, and I might be able to help you out with another couple of organisations.'

'Really?'

'Oh yes. Did you know we have an *a cappella* singing

group here in Hookes Bay? I'm sure they'd be interested, and there is a drama therapy group who meet in Fareham once a month. The pavilion would be a far more suitable venue for them. I can get you the contact numbers.'

'Brilliant,' I said gratefully.

'Oh, and you should contact Jordan Lockwood. The man's a genius.'

'I'm sorry?'

'I met him at a function last month. He was there with some pupils from St Stephen's, they put on quite a performance. A sort of rap choir, I suppose you'd call it. Never seen or heard anything like it. You could certainly do with someone like him on board. I believe he's the new peripatetic music teacher for our area. I'm sure if you phoned the education authority they could put you in touch.'

'Thanks, I'll try that tomorrow.'

I felt my confidence returning. With Barbara's support and several new leads to investigate, I had every reason to remain positive.

Back at the bungalow, Kitty was spending another Sunday by herself. I had recounted my run-in with Robbie over a dehydrated fishcake the previous evening. Both Kitty and Cyril had been shocked and I was pleased to hear the Mayhews were not expected to call in today.

'Lindy'll be entertaining some of her posh literary friends for lunch,' Kitty said. 'Not quite sure what part Robbie plays in the after-dinner conversations. Lindy probably sends him off to do the washing up.'

'Why don't I take you out somewhere?' I suggested. 'Even if it's just Pebbles.' I was fed up to the back teeth of going to Pebbles but Kitty kept a wheeled walking frame hidden at the back of the pantry. I saw no reason why she couldn't use it to walk that far.

'I don't want to go to Pebbles,' she complained. 'Not while Terri Cawle still works there.'

'Is she the waitress? How do you know her?'

'Used to be a barmaid at the club,' Kitty muttered. 'She and Robbie once had a bit of a thing.'

I could easily picture Terri and Robbie together. 'This was before Belinda came along, I take it?' I asked.

'Yes,' Kitty hesitated, 'this was a long time ago.'

'Tom Whybrow was telling me about Belinda's father. He said he had a stroke or something? It sounded awful.'

'It was very sad,' Kitty agreed. 'Not that I was fond of the Commander myself. The man was a right snob. He'd certainly be turning in his grave if he knew she'd married Robbie. But you wouldn't wish what happened to him on to anybody. He went back to being a baby.'

'So when did Belinda and Robbie get together?' I asked.

'After he died,' Kitty said. 'She had to come back from Singapore to look after him. He had nobody else. His ex had re-married and Lindy was an only child. We'd always known her, of course. She lived with her mother in the West Country but she was always up at the base during the school holidays. She was never the same, not after that.'

'Well, you wouldn't be, would you?' I agreed, making a mental note to look up some of Lindy's poetry. Was it dark, to reflect her tragic past, or light and fluffy escapism?

'Perhaps you could just help me into the garden?' Kitty suggested. 'We could sit on Hughie's bench and have a picnic admiring your new flower bed.'

I dashed to the Co-op for some cheese and cold meat, and also picked up a bottle of Pimms. I'd been almost tea-total since arriving in Hookes Bay, despite Kitty's invitation to help myself to the exotic selection of beverages stashed in her vast cocktail cabinet. I hadn't had the heart to tell her most of the bottles were well past their use-by date, in some cases by well over a decade.

There was a small folding table in Hughie's shed which I set up next to his bench.

Kitty confessed she'd never had a Pimms. 'Is it alcoholic?' she enquired, helping herself to a second glass.

Just as I sat half dozing in the sunshine, my phone rang and Dominic's number popped up.

'Talk of the devil,' I answered. The Pimms had gone straight to my head and I'd been enjoying a very pleasant daydream.

'Alice, is that you?'

'Yes, hello Dom, it's me. How are you? How's Sam?'

'I dropped her off at Southampton Airport first thing this morning. Hopefully she's safely back in Glasgow by now.'

He had dropped her off first thing. Once again I tried to stem the tide of envy. If Dominic's seduction techniques saved the pavilion, shouldn't I be glad?

'Did you have a good evening?' I enquired, taking my phone for a stroll around the garden.

'Yes. We went to the Bistro De Paris in Southsea. The food was excellent. You should have joined us.'

'Not much fun playing gooseberry,' I pointed out.

There was a significant pause. 'Have you been drinking, Alice?'

'No.' I hastily put down my glass on the back door step.

'You sound a bit weird. Never mind, I was just phoning to ask how you were getting on with your business plan?'

'It'll be ready to mail off to Sam tomorrow.'

'And the old programmes. Any luck with them?'

'Not yet, no, but thanks for dropping them around.'

'Look, I'm sorry I doubted you. I realise I'd become so obsessed with the aesthetics of the building I'd forgotten that it's just as important to give it a new lease of life inside as well. I think that what you are doing is just brilliant, Alice.'

'Well thank you, Dominic.' Was he trying to be conciliatory again? Perhaps sex with Sam had put him in good mood. Sex with Dominic would certainly put me in a good mood. I perched on the step beside my glass. 'It sounds quite hopeful if Sam felt interested enough to make a second trip,' I said.

'Yes, it does. I was very surprised when she called to ask if she could pop in before flying back. Obviously, the other properties she had on her agenda didn't capture her imagination as much as ours.'

'That's good news isn't it?'

'I hope so. We'll touch base again in the week some time?'

'Sure.'

'When are you teaching?' Was he actually trying to pin me

down to a specific date. *A date?* I almost felt light-headed. Perhaps a night out with Sam MacDonald had loosened Dominic's inhibitions.

'I'll give you a call when I'm free,' I said with a smile on my face. Two people could play hard to get. *Let's see how he likes it*, I thought, although as soon as I ended the call I regretted it. Behaving like a capricious school-girl was hardly going to appeal to a man of Dominic's intellect and integrity. Without a doubt the Irishman had crawled under my skin in much the same way as the pavilion. Common sense told me we were mismatched, yet the attraction was instinctive and irrefutable.

Chapter Twenty-Seven

Kitty

She rarely made demands on Belinda and Robbie's time. She was genuinely grateful that Lindy was prepared to ferry her to her various medical appointments and sit for lengthy periods in waiting rooms, but, enough was enough. Robbie had overstepped the mark. It was time for him to realise just what he was up against.

He'd made various excuses. No, he couldn't pop around straight away. Lindy was entertaining. He had things to attend to. Kitty didn't even know what he did all day now that he was no longer running the club. Finally, three whole days after Alice had told her about the encounter in the pavilion, he turned up.

Kitty had never been a great disciplinarian. Jez had been left to his own devices for much of his childhood and was used to getting his own way. When Robbie had joined the family he'd had to fit in as best he could. The boys had sorted their own differences out. Kitty had never felt the need to step in and Don had been equally as laissez faire.

Robbie was approaching sixty. It was probably a little late to start administering discipline now but he looked suitably shame-faced as Kitty reminded him, in no uncertain terms, just who owned Hookes Bay Pavilion.

'How dare you treat my houseguest like that,' she hissed, standing in the kitchen and clinging onto the counter-top for support. 'I'll decide who uses that studio space, not you. Alice is breathing new life into that dance school. What's wrong with her using the pavilion while it still stands? Are you worried Grant Hastings will think you're backing out of his deal? Exactly what hold has that man got over you?'

Robbie physically squirmed. As she suspected, she had touched a nerve. Grant Hastings had Robbie dangling by his balls. Well, it was time for Robbie to show some balls. This was the battle Kitty had been relishing. She was going to enjoy watching Robbie's reactions to her drip feed of toxic titbits.

Robbie hopped onto the defensive. 'It's not that at all, Kit,' he said. 'There's no need for you to get on your high horse. I was worried about you, that's all. Alice Paige is taking advantage of you. You've let a complete stranger into your home, you're treating her like she's—'

'Family?' Kitty helped him out. 'Alice doesn't feel like a complete stranger to me, Robbie. I feel like I've known her all my life. Don't tell me you don't feel that too? Alice is staying. You got that, Robbie? Staying. Overstep the mark again and I'll be thinking long and hard about what happens in the future.'

'What do you mean?' Alarm leapt into his voice.

'Doesn't she remind you of anyone, you idiot? Think about it. Give Alice the respect she deserves or I might change my mind about leaving you the pavilion.'

'You are joking?'

'Do I look like a comedian?'

'You're just winding me up.' Robbie began to pace up and down the tiny kitchen.

'You can tell your friend Hastings I've changed my mind,' Kitty said. 'Nothing's happening, not while I'm alive. Not now I've got Alice. If she wants to use that studio, she can. Coastline can wait. In the meantime, you, Robbie boy, had better behave yourself. Blood is always thicker than water.'

He stared at her. She could almost see the cogs turning. Robbie had that kind of face. Very expressive, gave everything away. She almost felt sorry for him, but not quite.

'You wouldn't dare.'

'I wouldn't dare what?' she taunted.

He stepped back into the conservatory, took a seat in her chair. *Her chair*. He was dazed. *Flabbergasted.* That was the word. The great big oaf.

'You can't be serious? You don't think for one minute that Jez... that... that Alice is...'

'You need to watch your weight, Robbie,' she said for no other reason than because she knew Robbie was sensitive to these things.

'What?'

'Your weight. You're getting fat.'

It was a lie because Robbie wasn't actually in such a bad shape for a man of his age. Lindy kept a strict control on his diet. He still smoked though. Kitty could smell it on him, despite the potent aftershave and pungent mouthwash.

Jez wouldn't have let himself go. Jez would still be lean and trim. He'd be doing those iron man challenges like someone Penny had mentioned just the other day, running in triple marathons and then cycling to London and back.

She could see him now, leading the field. She blinked. Old age dulled the imagination; reality clouded the vision. As much as she tried, the image didn't materialise. She couldn't envisage the fifty-seven year old Jez, with greying hair, lines on his face, jowls. All she could see was that young man of twenty-four, the image of his father, slinging on his leather jacket, lighting up a cigarette and heading out of the door

'Bye Ma, see you in the morning. Don't wait up.'

The last words he had said to her. And then this lump of a man had abandoned him at the club at the mercy of the Bonetti brothers just because he wanted to get his leg over with the barmaid. Sometimes she took great pleasure in sticking pins in Robbie.

'You go and apologise to Alice right now,' Kitty hissed. 'Then you man-up to Grant Hastings and tell him I'm not signing anything. You got it?'

Robbie shook his head. 'Oh, Kit,' he said. 'You're making a huge mistake.'

'You think at my time of life, I care?'

Chapter Twenty-Eight

Tara

I'd come across several music teachers in my time with Drama Queens but I'd never met one quite like Jordan Lockwood. Afro-Caribbean, six foot six, tapered dreads, thighs as big as my waist, size fourteen Nike trainers. He looked as if he should have been sprinting around the basketball court as opposed to running recorder club.

The leisure centre seemed an appropriate place to meet. Tracking him down had been very easy. A quick call to the Education Department, an exchange of emails and I caught the bus into Fareham to meet him in his lunch hour the following day. I liked a man who was decisive.

'So how did you get to hear about me?' he asked after I had given him a brief run-down of my proposals for the Hookes Bay Community Arts Hub.

'I heard via the grapevine that you have a brilliant rap choir. That's the sort of activity I'd like to encourage to entice the youth of Hookes Bay into the pavilion.'

'I would be only too happy to help you out,' Jordan replied.

'It's all a bit hypothetical at the moment,' I told him. 'But if you can pledge your support.'

'Of course,' he smiled. 'I hear there's a great pizza restaurant down in Hookes Bay. Fancy trying it out one night? We could discuss things in further detail.'

With his chocolate brown eyes and long dark lashes, it was a shame Jordan Lockwood was only just out of teacher training college. Unlike Dominic Flynn, he was very quick to hand over his mobile phone number. I couldn't think of one good reason to refuse his invitation apart from our obvious age difference. It was flattering to know I wasn't an afterthought.

During our chat I name-dropped Drama Queens several times to make it clear I wasn't some charlatan with no experience of working with young people. As we said our goodbyes he suggested I send my CV into the Head of Drama at St Stephen's.

'St Stephen's is a specialist performing arts school. They would probably welcome someone like you coming in every now and then and running a workshop.'

Caught up in Jordan's enthusiasm, I almost promised to email my CV that afternoon, until I remembered that Alice Paige's CV was work of pure fiction. It was Tara Wakely who was the Drama Queen. At some point I was going to have an awful lot of explaining to do. My web of deceit was growing daily, and it was starting to make me feel very uneasy.

Kitty had been feeling poorly since Sunday. Twice during the night after my meeting with Jordan, I had to go into her room. She complained of pains in her chest and in her stomach. She was hot then she was cold. She refused my offer to call an ambulance.

'If they take me into hospital I'll never come back out,' she protested.

Finally, at about five in the morning, she seemed to settle down although I stayed by her bedside, dozing in a chair. I scrolled through her mobile, which wasn't password protected, and found a number for Belinda. I called at eight-thirty. The phone was answered by Robbie.

His concern seemed touchingly genuine. 'Should we come straight over?' he asked.

'She seems settled now. I don't know Kitty's medical history. I just thought you should be aware.'

'Yes, you did the right thing.' He was gracious, if not exactly apologetic. 'That was very good of you, er... Alice.'

Penny arrived at ten. 'You look dreadful,' she told me. 'Go and get a couple of hours' kip. I'm here now.'

I'd barely slept for more than a few minutes when I was awoken by the sound of a car pulling up onto the drive. Bleary eyed, I peered through the net curtains. An ash blonde in her mid-fifties, dressed in white linen trousers and a sheer silver vest, stepped out of a cream sports Mini Cooper. She made her way around to the back of the house and I heard a brief exchange with Penny. I ran my fingers through my hair and grabbed a kimono over my shorts pyjamas.

'Ah, you must be, Alice.' Lindy Mayhew's greeting held no warmth.

I apologised for my dishevelled appearance. 'I was just trying to catch up on some sleep.'

'I'm sorry I woke you.' Lindy spoke with an effortless air of superiority and a distinct hint of sarcasm. Despite the initial impression of elegance, she verged on the gaunt. Her dove grey eyes appeared too big for her elfin-like face. 'I would have come over earlier but I had some errands to run in Portsmouth,' she said, turning back to Penny. 'The traffic was dreadful.'

'Really there was no need, Kitty is fine now,' Penny assured her. 'Fast asleep. Would you like tea, Lindy?'

'Oh, it's too hot for tea. I'll just have a glass of water.'

'Let me get it,' I said. I ran the tap and added a couple of ice-cubes, then for good measure, sliced a lemon. Rather liking the sophisticated look I made myself a glass too.

'Oh you didn't need to go to that much trouble,' Lindy said, immediately dismissing my efforts. 'It's just a flying visit.'

'Alice likes to look after people,' Penny remarked. 'I'm sure Kitty must have told you what a Godsend she's been.'

'Actually, Kitty has said very little about Alice,' Lindy replied. 'Shall we take a seat in the lounge?'

It sounded like a command rather than a suggestion. I'd always considered myself a non-judgemental type of person, ready to give anyone the benefit of the doubt, but my dislike for Belinda Mayhew was instant. I sensed the feeling was mutual.

She removed a pile of fluffy cushions from the sofa before sitting down.

'I understand you have great plans for Mari Freeborn's dance school,' she said once the offending items were out of the way. 'Some sort of major expansion?'

I nodded. 'Oh yes, I believe the school should encompass all the performing arts, not just dance.'

'That's a lot to take on for someone so young. How old are you, Alice? Thirty, thirty-one, thirty-two?'

I recognised a blatant attempt at fishing for information when I heard one. I suspected Lindy knew exactly how old I was, or at least knew what I was going to tell her. 'I'm thirty-three.'

'And you're originally from London, I understand.'

It was important to remain polite. 'Yes. I grew up on a North London council estate. I won a bursary to study dance in Boston at the age of sixteen. It was a wonderful opportunity. Since then I've been mainly working abroad.'

'So how did you come to hear about Mari Freeborn's dance school? I wouldn't have thought that would have made the international news?'

'Kitty knows a lot of people.'

A smug smile flickered momentarily on her face as she offered up her next words like a challenge. 'I suppose it's a relatively small world, isn't it? There's only a couple of professional dance bodies, aren't there? Not that Mum's ever been affiliated to any of them. And neither have you, Alice. I'm not sure how many of Mari parents you're hoping to fool with your fictional CV.'

I started to reel off the same excuses I'd given to Robbie. 'This is my first teaching post after an extensive career abroad…'

'Save it, Alice, or whoever you really are. I've heard enough lies in my lifetime. Don't waste your breath on me. I don't doubt for one minute that Kitty's put you up to this, but I suggest you get out now with your dignity still intact.'

I decided an air of innocence was the best tactic. 'I don't know what you mean.'

Lindy gave a shrug. 'Have it your way. Just don't say I didn't warn you. Robbie might be a pushover when it comes to his stepmother, but I'm not. I know the game she's playing, and I don't believe you're Jez's daughter for one minute. I knew Jez. I knew Jez better than any of them.'

'I'm very sorry,' I said. 'Now I really don't have any idea what you're talking about.'

'She chose you well, Alice Paige. There's no mistaking the physical similarities, but on the other hand, Jez had a very common face. You're a good actress, though, I'll give you that. You might not be a professional dance teacher but you've certainly got competent theatrical skills. Did Kitty put an ad in *Stage* magazine?'

Dominic had described Lindy as dippy, but the woman sat opposite me in Kitty's lounge definitely had her wits about her. I could quite see why Kitty had been so reluctant that we meet. Her assertion that I was a professional performer of some sort was pretty astute. Although Lindy didn't look like an avid aficionado of the *Sunday Stargazer* or *What's Hot*, the name Tara Wakely would be familiar to anyone who kept abreast of happenings in the West End. If Lindy called Kitty's bluff to prove my parentage, our case was lost. I tried to hide my consternation with a brittle smile.

'Are you going to look in on Kitty now that you're here?' I asked.

She stood up and shook her head. 'There's little point disturbing her when she's asleep.' She flicked imaginary specks of dust from her silver vest. 'She's got a hospital appointment tomorrow anyway. I'll pick her up in the morning at half-nine.'

We appeared to have reached an uneasy stand-off. I didn't doubt hostilities would continue.

Sam MacDonald acknowledged receipt of my business plan. Aaron had done a great job, and I only hoped it was filled with enough relevant information to overlook the missing CV. I'd followed up the other leads Barbara had given me, stressing the need for confidentiality with the promise that a grand press release would follow once maximum support had been achieved. I relayed all this information to Dominic in a text after another joyful, distracting Wednesday afternoon in the company of Ethan Hobart. As I waited for a reply a message from Jordan Lockwood popped up on my phone. He really was a quick worker.

'Don't suppose you're free tonight for that pizza?'

First come, first serve, I thought. Why not?

'You're looking pleased with yourself,' Beth remarked, as she disentangled a tambourine from Ethan's clutches. 'Good news?'

'I suppose so,' I said. 'A date actually.'

Beth grinned. 'Anyone I know?' She looked at me expectantly, raised an eyebrow and mouthed something that looked suspiciously like *Dom Flynn* over Ethan's head. I shook my head, puzzled. She gave a quick shrug. 'Oh well, come on, Ethan. We'll be back next week, say goodbye to Miss Alice.'

Ethan threw his arms around my legs in a hug.

Jordan and I were La Scala's first customers of the evening. The restaurant was open plan, and the chef, wiry and bald, welcomed us from behind his counter with a cheerful 'Buona sera, Signore, Signorina.' This had to be Paulo Bonetti.

A teenage waitress with a distinct family resemblance showed us to a table by the window.

Jordan had a humungous appetite. 'Sorry,' he apologised as he ordered double portions of everything. 'I'm in training for a triathlon.'

'Why are you teaching music if sport is your first love?' I enquired.

'Oh no, music is my first love,' he insisted. 'But I like to keep fit. You look pretty fit yourself, Alice. Have you ever thought about doing a triathlon?'

It had never crossed my mind. 'Performing arts is definitely my thing, not sport,' I told him.

More customers arrived. I found myself relaxing with a large glass of Pinot Grigio, although Jordan stuck to water. He was an enthusiastic talker with a whole series of amusing anecdotes to recount. I wondered what had attracted him into teaching.

'I had a brilliant mentor at my comprehensive,' he said.

'You just want to emulate your heroes sometimes, don't you?'

I didn't like deceiving Jordan Lockwood, just as I hadn't liked lying to the *a cappella* choirmaster or the chairman of the drama therapy group. Jordan was a very likeable young man with a genuine desire to enhance the lives of his pupils. I wanted to be as honest with him as I could. Before I could dwell on my predicament, we were interrupted by a loud rendition of *'Just one calzone'* to the tune of *O Sole Mio* from the kitchen as Paulo loaded more pizzas into the wood oven. He was putting on a good show for his customers.

'Would you like the dessert menu?' the waitress enquired.

'Oh no, not for me thank you,' I shook my head.

'Do you have tiramisu?' Jordan asked. 'Bring us two.'

Over his shoulder I could see some sort of fracas taking place further down the street outside the Taj Mahal Indian Takeaway. With Jordan temporarily distracted by Paulo's singing, I craned my neck to get a better look. Dominic Flynn appeared to wrestling with two thugs who had just stepped out of the Sir Winnie. I recognised one of his assailants by his distinctive orange check fleece as the man who had been propping up the bar on my first visit to Hookes Bay. The second man, who could well have been his companion on that day too, had the more aggressive body language, shoving Dominic's shoulder. Just as I was wondering whether I should rush to Dominic's aid, the owner of the Indian Takeaway emerged onto the street and broke up the argument.

Dominic headed out of sight while the orange check and his mate high-fived each other before swaggering to a parked black BMW. As the second thug hopped into the passenger seat I caught sight of the logo emblazoned across the back of his jacket. *Coastline Property Services.*

'Do you want a slice or not?' Jordan asked as the double dose of tiramisu arrived at the table.

'No, go ahead,' I insisted, still distracted. The Sir Winnie regulars certainly seemed to have it in for Dominic. I needed to find out more about Coastline Developments.

It had been nearly a week since my abortive attempt to

speak to Bea. I'd tried her a couple of times since but she hadn't replied to either of my messages, so it was a pleasant surprise to finally receive a call from her as I walked back to the bungalow. Jordan had promised to keep in touch, but with an intensive period of training coming up he explained he wouldn't be able to see me for at least another week. This wasn't such a bad thing. I had enjoyed his company but the more I inter-acted within the community, the more embroiled my deception became.

'Hi, Tara, how's things?' Bea sounded very upbeat.

'Okay,' I replied, 'have you found me a celebrity patron?'

'Not exactly,' she replied. 'Just thought I'd give you a call to see how things were. Sorry I didn't get back to you earlier. I've been rushed off my feet at work. Anyway, make sure to pick up next week's copy of *What's Hot*.'

'You know how I feel about that sort of magazine.'

'Oh, it's nothing like that, nothing to do with Georgie Gold, for once. No, there's going to be some pictures in there from the Foxy FM Awards.'

'Pictures of you, you mean?'

'Yes. And you'll never guess who I'm with.'

Bea changed her boyfriends with the waning of each new moon.

'I haven't got all day, it's nearly my bedtime, just tell me.'

'Gus Henley.'

'Who?'

'Gus Henley. Lead singer of Exocet.'

I racked my brains to picture Gus Henley. 'Isn't he an overweight, bearded rocker?'

'Not anymore,' Bea enthused. 'He's had a bit of a make-over, hired some sort of personal trainer, looks amazing.'

'Great. I'm very pleased for you, and for him of course. So, are you an item?'

'Not quite,' Bea trilled. 'But we had dinner over the weekend and I've been invited to watch the recording of his new TV show.'

Gus Henley didn't have a particularly high profile in the media. Exocet played loud, heavy metal music and were not particularly easy on the ear, or the eye. 'He's on a show?'

'Yes, he's going to be a judge on this new Battle of the Bands programme.'

'Why is everyone so obsessed with talent shows?' I groaned.

'Because it makes good TV.'

'No, it doesn't. It just thrusts vacuous muppets like Georgie Gold into the public eye.'

'Ooh that's harsh,' Bea laughed. 'Anyway, if it all goes well and we carry on seeing each other, he might be able to help you. He's from the south somewhere, Basingstoke, I think he said.

'Bea, we're miles away from Basingstoke. It's not even on the coast.'

'I'm only trying help.'

'Sorry.' Perhaps Exocet could play a charity gig, if and when the project got off the ground. I shouldn't discount any offers of support. I had reached Kitty's front door. 'Thanks Bea, and good luck with Gus.'

'Keep your fingers crossed,' she ended. 'And don't forget to buy the mag.'

Chapter Twenty-Nine

I'd made a vow never to buy another copy of *What's Hot* or any of its contemporaries in my life. With Kitty already retired to bed, I helped myself to the last dregs of the Pimms and fired up the ancient PC. When the internet limped into life I discovered Coastline Developments consisted of an entire empire of subsidiaries. It made very depressing reading. Grant Hastings had his fingers in an awful lot of Hookes Bay pies.

I resisted the urge to call Dominic to check he hadn't suffered damage at the hands of his attackers, and typed *Belinda Mayhew poetry workshops* into the search engine. At least this business appeared to be Hastings-free. Belinda had her own impressive website: Poesia de Montana, *Poetry from the Mountains*. Lindy didn't just organise her own workshops at the family retreat in Lanzarote, but could be engaged to offer an entire range of 'creative writing' related activities, anything from poetry readings to team-building days.

Lindy didn't appear to have published any books in her own right, but she had an MA from the University of Warwick and was credited with poetic contributions in various anthologies. As Cyril had correctly reported, her impressive CV also included mention of her role as arts reviewer in the *South Coast Gazette*. In any other circumstances, I would probably be canvassing her support for the Arts Hub.

The searches did nothing to boost my morale. Without a doubt, when it came to Grant Hastings and Lindy Mayhew, I needed to tread very carefully.

In order to take my mind off the worst case scenario, I browsed images of Gus Henley. There were some recent photos of the singer with his new look, but no snaps of Bea. One particular picture led to a feature on Exocet's website where I learned the change of image coincided with the release of the band's first album with their new record company, Metropolitan Records.

'Two of the tracks on the new album are a collaboration with veteran record producer, Stevie Newman-Smith.' Gus told his fans. *'Stevie's talents are legendary. She is one of the most innovative producers in the business.'*

Metropolitan Records. Stevie Newman-Smith. I knew those names. What I didn't know, however, was that Stevie Newman-Smith was a 'she'. Was it a typo?

I opened up yet another page.

Stephanie 'Stevie' Newman-Smith was now seventy, although I'd have never guessed it from the numerous photographs available on the internet of the peroxide blonde in her skin-tight leather trousers. I scanned her Wikipedia page. Newman-Smith, originally from New York, set up her own record company, Metropolitan Records over thirty-five years ago, talent spotting several early punk and new wave bands.

Was Stevie Newman-Smith the woman Jez had predicted was going to change his life? It made so much more sense. I'd known, in my heart of hearts, that my mother could not possibly have been the woman of Jez's dreams. So why did I feel so disappointed? It was illogical.

I found myself clutching at straws. Why did I feel such affinity to Hookes Bay? Why was I so attracted by the prospect of having a stake in that pavilion? Was I really just answering the call of my profession, or was it something more? What of Maureen Batty's claim that Kitty had always suspected Jez had 'got a girl into trouble'? Was that nothing but a red-herring to add credibility to my presence in Hookes Bay? Kitty Keaton was a scheming, manipulative woman. I wondered when she had mentioned her suspicions to Maureen; thirty years ago, or thirty days?

First thing the following morning I gave in and called Dominic. After the second attempt I left a message. 'Hi Dom, it's me, Alice, just wondering if you've heard anything yet from the MPT. Maybe you can give me a call back. I'll be in Pebbles this morning, then I'm teaching until seven. After that

I'm at the pavilion with Tom until about eight. Speak soon.'

Surely he couldn't ignore that, could he?

Kitty had rallied around and asked me to help her out of bed and into the conservatory by the time Penny arrived an hour earlier than usual at nine.

'Lindy's increased my hours,' Penny explained. 'I'll be here all day for the next few weeks.'

'Just a few weeks?' Kitty muttered. 'Is that all she thinks I've got left?'

I made a hasty escape to Pebbles. There was little point continuing to work on the pavilion proposal until I heard back from the Trust's executive board. Instead I finally devised a programme for the summer showcase. Mari was returning to take her advanced ballet classes that afternoon and I wanted to have something concrete to show her. I ordered a coffee and took up my usual perch in the window. After about half an hour I saw Paulo Bonetti pull up outside La Scala. I watched him lift a crate of supplies from his van and head into the restaurant, leaving the door wide open.

It would only take one quick question. *When you were on your tour in London with Urban Rebel do you remember if Jez ever got off with a girl called Nicki after the gig at the Edmonton Roundhouse?* If he said no, I could quash those suspicions once and for all and my equilibrium would be restored. I headed across the road.

'Sorry, signorina, we not open yet,' he called as I entered the restaurant.

'I appreciate that, Mr Bonetti. I was just wondering if I could have a quick word.'

'You look familiar.' He frowned. 'Do I know you?'

'I was in here last night.'

'Was there a problem with your meal? Are you here to complain? Because if you are, I'm very sorry, but really you should have said something at the time.'

'No, no,' I assured him. 'The meal was lovely. Great. No, I wanted to talk to you about Jez Keaton.'

Paulo Bonetti's demeanour changed in an instant. The happy Italian was gone, and so was the mock accent. He slammed a cupboard shut under the countertop.

'I'm fed up being hounded like this,' he said. 'I told the police everything I knew thirty odd years ago.'

'I'm not hounding you,' I said hastily. 'I wanted to ask you about the Urban Rebel tour in London, just before Jez disappeared. About a girl…'

'I don't know anything about any girls,' Paulo growled. 'I don't know anything. Has she set you up to this?'

'Nobody's set me up. I don't know what you mean.'

'That old boy of hers, he was like a bloody terrier, he just wouldn't let go. He kept coming in here all the time asking questions. I nearly took out a restraining order. I wasn't there, do you understand? Jez Keaton's death had nothing to do with me. I left the club at eleven and I never went back. The police believed my statement, so why can't his mother?'

He stormed across the restaurant and put his hand on the door. 'Now, as I said, we're closed.'

I had no choice but to leave.

'What have you done to upset him?' Terri Cawle asked. She stood smoking outside Pebbles, one foot pressed against the wall like a petulant teenager. She must have witnessed the whole episode.

'I don't know,' I admitted. 'He seems overly sensitive. I mentioned the name Jez Keaton and he nearly bit my head off.'

'I'm not surprised. No love lost there,' Terri said. 'So, why were you asking Paulo about Jez?'

'I was just curious. I thought they were friends.'

Terri snorted. 'Only while it suited Jez,' she said.

'What do you mean by that?'

'You know the fairy story about the princess who kissed a frog and found her prince charming?' Terri asked. I nodded, puzzled. She stubbed out her cigarette 'Well, when you kissed Jez Keaton you uncovered a toad. Let me get you a latte.'

Since I'd become a regular customer Terri had made no attempt at being sociable, and I wasn't totally sure she could be trusted. There was no love lost between her and Kitty that was for sure. Paulo's reaction had caught me completely off-guard, but there was a chance Terri might be able to cast some light on the reason for his behaviour. In any case, Paulo hadn't answered my original question but he had certainly raised another. Kitty clearly suspected him of having something to do with Jez's disappearance.

'Kitty told me you used to work at the club,' I said, when Terri returned with my latte and a glass of water. 'You knew Jez well?'

'I was at school with him,' Terri said, taking the seat opposite me. 'I knew all the band. Woody, Vince, Paulo. Known them all for years. Intimately.'

For a second I wondered if Terri was about to contest Lindy's claim that nobody knew Jez better than she did. It wasn't that difficult to picture Terri being a notch on Jez's bedpost, but the notion of Lindy being one of his conquests, if that's what she had been intimating, seemed quite far-fetched.

'Did you know Belinda Mayhew when she was younger?' I asked out of curiosity.

Terri gave a shrug. 'She used to hang around in the school holidays.'

'Were she and Jez were quite close?'

Terri shrugged. 'She might have thought so, but Jez just strung her along, like he strung everyone along. Of course he wrote that stupid song for her, *Lou-Lou, you're my dirty little secret,* so I suppose she thought she was something special.'

'He wrote that for her?' Mari would be disappointed.

'Yeh, that's what she used to call herself back then, Lindy-Lou. Loopy-Lou more like, the way she used to drool all over him. To be honest we never saw that much of her after she went off to university. Probably came to her senses, although obviously not, otherwise she wouldn't have married Robbie, would she?' Terri gave a short laugh. 'Jez could be a right bastard. I expect Paulo told you that.'

'Not really, no. Were you working at the club the night Jez disappeared?'

She nodded. 'I was there until about eleven then me and Robbie left. His mother has never forgiven us.'

That made sense. 'So who else was there besides you two and the band? It was some sort of celebration party, wasn't it?'

'Hardly a celebration. There was Cliff, he was one of the bouncers, acted as the band's roadie, he'd come along with a couple of local girls, I can't even remember their names now, girls who used hang around hoping to get off with Jez or Vince, although I could have told them then they were wasting their time.'

'Why was that?' I interrupted.

'Vince was gay. He had the hots for Jez too by the way.'

Terri was being deliberately provocative. I ignored her. 'What do you think happened after you left?' I asked. 'You said it wasn't a celebration? So how was Jez? What sort of mood was he in?'

'He was full of himself as usual,' Terri replied. 'Desperately trying to placate Paulo Bonetti with a load of garbage, about how he'd have him in his backing band when he got famous, blah, blah, blah. Robbie and I had heard enough. We left him to it.'

'What do you mean, he'd have Paulo in his backing band?'

'So you don't know?' Terri raised an eyebrow. She looked like she was sucking on something quite delicious. 'Jez told everyone to come to the club because he was throwing a party. We all thought that meant he'd heard from the record company with an offer of a deal, but he hadn't. There was no record deal, at least not for Urban Rebel. The record company only wanted him. They wanted a solo artist. He'd sold them all down the river. Nice guy, eh?'

I tried to keep my face neutral. 'So how did the others react to his news?'

'How do you think they reacted?' Terri smirked. 'Took him down to the end of the pier and threw him off? Is that what you want me to say? It's what *Mommy Dearest* thinks. She's given us all the third degree over the years. She was convinced that's what happened, and that Vince and Paulo conspired to cover it up.'

'They must have been pretty pissed off,' I remarked.

'Yeh, they were. You would be, wouldn't you, when your

best mate dumps you like that, but the idea of Vince and Paulo being killers is laughable. Kitty didn't give up though. She sent that last husband of hers on a crusade to interrogate us all. The truth is none of us know what happened because none of us were there. There was a security camera above the entrance of the club. Jez accompanied Vince and Paulo to the front door of the club and locked up behind them. He was alive when they left. Kit said somebody must have gone back, but there was no evidence for that.'

'What about drugs?'

'Blame it on the magic mushrooms?' Terri sneered. 'Been talking to Phil Kendrick have you? It was no secret Jez would sneak down the pier for the odd joint when he was working at the club, but there was no need to skulk off by himself when the place was empty. That time of night he could have walked the length of Hookes Bay esplanade snorting cocaine and no-one would have stopped him. He hadn't been drinking excessively, at least not when Robbie and I were still there, and the Bonettis were only ten, fifteen minutes behind us.'

'What about Woody? Where was he in all this?'

'Nowhere. He hadn't showed up. I heard Vince ask Jez what had happened to him and Jez said Woody was probably off on one of his benders, nothing unusual about that.'

'Woody had a drink problem?'

'Woody had all kinds of problems,' Terri finished her glass of water in one gulp. 'To be honest, if any of the guys had chucked Jez off the pier I couldn't say I'd blame them. Jez had one huge big ego. He wanted fame and he was going to get it at any cost. It didn't seem to matter who he trampled on along the way. For what it's worth,' she said, standing up, 'do you want to know what I think?'

I shrugged. I was pretty confident she was going to tell me anyway.

'Aliens,' she said, collecting up her empty glass and my cup in one sweep. 'Jez Keaton was abducted by little green men from outer space. I'd put money on it. Now go home and tell that to his mother. Then she might get off our backs once and for all.'

Chapter Thirty

So much for my attempts at playing amateur sleuth. My interest in Jez stemmed from the remote possibility that he could have impregnated my mother simply by playing a gig within a half-mile radius of her home. Now I had opened up an entirely different can of worms. Jez had announced he was abandoning his fellow band members in favour of a solo recording contract. Minutes later he disappeared off the pier. Coincidence?

I put myself in Jez's shoes. If I'd been offered the lead in a West End musical at the tender age of twenty-three would I have turned it down out of a sense of loyalty? You had to be ruthless, single-minded, and dedicated to succeed in show business. The boys were all performers, presumably with ambitions of their own. Were the Bonetti brothers so incensed they deliberately threw Jez off the pier? Were they larking about? Had there been a fight? Were they all covering up for each other? Robbie and Terri included?

I had lots to think about. At the community centre that afternoon Mari seemed reassured her girls hadn't suffered in her absence. She announced that John was talking of a flotilla holiday in July, which might mean she had to miss the summer show altogether, music to my ears. After I'd handed over the reins for the last ballet class of the day, I headed to the pavilion and my second assignation with Tom.

Tom admitted he'd been practising in his living room every time his wife left him on his own.

'Well it's paid off because I think you've got it,' I told him. 'When's the party?'

'Beginning of August. I'll send you an invitation.'

'Thanks. Have you heard anything from Dominic?'

'Yes, I meant to tell you. He called me just before I left

home. He's going to meet us here at eight.'

I'd been checking my phone like a teenager all day. Why couldn't Dominic have called me? I tried to mask my disappointment. 'Has he had any news?'

'Sounds like it, doesn't it?' Tom grimaced. 'Let's hope it's good.'

'Would the MPT have made a decision that quickly?'

Tom shrugged. 'We'll find out in a few minutes.'

Almost on cue we heard footsteps on the stairs. Dominic didn't appear to have suffered any visible injuries following his encounter outside the Indian. He was wearing chino shorts and a casual polo-shirt. He seemed particularly jovial. 'How's the foxtrot coming on?'

'Tom is an exemplary pupil,' I replied, wondering if there was any way I could convince Dominic that he might need a dance lesson or two.

Tom glanced at his watch. 'Sorry to rush you but Jenny will be home by half past. Have you heard something?'

'Sam's put our case to the board but they've come back with a couple of queries,' Dominic said. 'The main bone of contention appears to be our lack of support from the local council.'

'Do you mean at a borough or parish level?' Tom queried.

'Sam seems to think getting the parish council on board will show the Hookes Bay community supports our plans.'

'Isn't the Conservation Society enough?' I asked.

'Apparently not,' Dominic replied. 'We're going to have to go public.' He must have caught my worried expression. 'Don't worry, Tom and I can handle this. I've already called Mitch. Bunny is going to gather together as many councillors as she can for an ad hoc meeting of the Parish Council as soon as possible next week.'

'I think Alice should be there,' Tom said to Dominic. 'She can put on a pretty impressive performance when she has to.'

'Thank you, Tom. It entirely depends what day it is,' I said quickly. 'I might have lessons or something.' I turned to Dominic. 'What about this spy, the man Galliard? Aren't you worried about him?'

'After our encounter with Robbie last week I've already put Hobo on extra watches,' Dominic replied.

'You don't need to worry about Robbie. Kitty had words. As far as I know he's conversing with Hastings at his peril. She's told him there will be no more negotiations.'

Tom picked up his pullover from the piano and said his goodbyes. Dominic and I followed him at a slower pace down the stairs.

'Right,' he said, as we locked up the stage door. 'I'll say goodnight then.'

Playing hard to get appeared to have completely backfired. I had hoped for an invitation to relocate to the beach shelters with a bottle of beer again at the very least. I was so confused I was back to ripping up daisy petals.

I took a deep breath. 'Dominic, what's going on with you?'

'What do you mean?'

'You know what I mean. I left you a message this morning. You could have called me back. Instead you called Tom. Why do you have such a huge problem with me?'

'I don't have a problem with you. I have two phones. Sorry. I haven't checked all my messages.'

Somehow I didn't quite believe him. 'You can hardly bring yourself to talk to me, yet the other night you were congeniality in itself.' I sighed.

He ran his fingers through his hair. 'I'm sorry, it's just...'

I lost my patience. 'It's just what, Dominic? You've got a split personality or just that you're an ignorant, cold fish?'

I began to head off along the esplanade, biting back tears of humiliation. What was wrong with me? Why had I said that? Dominic had done nothing to encourage my affection. Barely out of one toxic relationship, he was hardly likely to be rushing head long into another. It was my fault I'd fallen in love with the unobtainable. There it was. I'd admitted it to myself. I'd fallen in love, hopelessly, stupidly in love with a man who had done his best to put me off. That was my fault, not his. I'd built my hopes on the flimsiest of signals; I had a history of falling for my leading men or, in Hal's case, my directors. It was a hazard of the job but I wasn't on the stage any more. Bizarre as it was, this was real life.

'Hey,' he caught hold of my arm. 'I've had a bad day, okay. That's all. Things have really kicked off with this legal battle over the practice. Hastings' solicitors are on my back. He's timed it perfectly.'

He looked as dejected as I felt, but for very different reasons. I immediately felt guilty that I was putting additional pressure on him.

'Sorry,' I muttered. 'You should have said.'

'Well, I've said it now.' He put his hand on my shoulder. When he saw my tears his face became a mixture of bewildered concern. 'Come and sit down here for a minute.'

He led me to a small section of sea-wall that had half crumbled onto the beach. It made a sort of natural if somewhat uncomfortable seat.

'Alice, trust me. I'd like to get to know you better, honestly, but...'

There was always a 'but'. 'It's complicated?' I suggested with a sniff. I didn't want to fall out with Dominic. Whatever our personal relationship, we had to fight the pavilion campaign together.

'Very,' he agreed. 'There's an awful lot of things I would rather be doing right now than listening to lawyers dissecting my finances and my marriage. Hastings has really upped the ante and I have to fight my case. I need to get my practice back up and running. That has to be my priority.'

His business was his livelihood. Far more important than me, and in reality, saving the pavilion. He didn't need to say any more. In that moment I hated the entire Hastings family with a vehemence I'd previously reserved for Georgie Gold. Dominic was a passionate and caring man. I'd seen that in him on our first day together at the pavilion; it was part of the attraction. This personal battle with Hastings was consuming all his energy; it was sucking him dry, and leaving nothing but an embittered empty shell.

'Sometimes it's good to have someone to talk to,' I said, hating having to resort to platitudes. I could barely keep the longing out of my voice. Sitting in such close proximity but being unable to offer anything more than clichéd comfort was almost unbearable. 'I was in La Scala last night. I saw you outside the Indian takeaway. Two guys were laying into you. Has this got something to do with Hastings too?'

'What were you doing in La Scala?'

'Eating a pizza.' There was no point trying to make Dominic jealous by mentioning Jordan Lockwood. He would probably encourage me to enjoy a fling.

He looked down at the shingle. 'Danni's seeing this guy. He works for her dad. I always knew she liked a bit of rough, after all she married me, but the thought of Mark Murray lounging about with his feet up on my coffee table. Urgh, it's like...' he shook his head. 'I can't stand it.'

It was some consolation to know that Dominic's prime concern appeared to be the treatment of his furniture rather than his wife. 'Does he have a mate who wears an orange check jacket?' I asked.

'Yeh. That's Darren Hastings, Danni's brother. Anyway, he told me Danni's pregnant.'

I gulped. 'You mean with him?'

'Oh God, yes,' Dominic said quickly. 'He was just gloating about it. I should have ignored him. Danni always told me she didn't want kids. Anyway, with Danni now pregnant, I've pretty much lost the house but I'm determined to get something out of the business, I have to. The junk yard won't sustain me long term, and as Sam MacDonald made perfectly clear, even if the Modernist Trust do go ahead with purchasing the pavilion, they'll bring in their own team of architects and restorers. I need to get myself back out into the field, actively seek new projects.'

'Perhaps you could sweet-talk Sam MacDonald into giving you the job.'

Dominic smiled. 'I wouldn't bank on it. I understand Mr MacDonald is a big hairy Scotsman.'

'I didn't realise there was a Mr MacDonald.' Although I was very pleased to learn that there was.

'Well there is and his name is Graeme and he's something big in the restoration business himself.'

'So you and Sam didn't ...' I'd spoken my thoughts out loud.

'Didn't what?'

'I thought, you know, when I saw you on Saturday you were very cosy together, and then you said you took her back to the airport first thing on Sunday morning, I just wondered…'

Dominic looked amused. 'You thought Sam and I spent the night together?'

'Why not? She's an attractive woman, you're an attractive man.'

'Thank you for the compliment,' he sighed. 'Another time, another place, eh, Alice?'

No, now. Now was just perfect. But it didn't happen. We sat side by side, not even touching each other, the air between us thick with tension. His body was rigid; his face staring across the water to the Isle of Wight which was lit up like a twinkling Christmas tree.

'You could just try letting go and follow your heart,' I said in a hoarse whisper.

A muscle in his cheek flinched. 'I've followed my heart before, Alice.'

But I'm *different*, I wanted to cry. I'm not Danni Hastings with her horses and her money and her Machiavellian father.

He cleared this throat. 'I need to get home. I've got a hectic schedule tomorrow and Hastings' lawyer is as sharp as a knife.'

'Then you must go and fight your case,' I said.

'Shall I walk you back to Kitty's?' It was an empty gesture and we both knew it.

I shook my head. 'No. I'm fine just here for now, thanks.'

Chapter Thirty-One

As much as I wanted to wallow in my misery, I couldn't. I knew from past experiences that the best remedy for a broken heart was to immerse myself in work; a rehearsal for the summer showcase on Saturday and a full day on Sunday toiling in Kitty's garden. With time to kill on Monday morning and feeling certain I wouldn't be welcome back at Bunny Mitchell's Zumba class I headed into Fareham to the leisure centre and signed up for gym membership. Exhausted, but invigorated I returned to Hookes Bay in a determined frame of mind.

I wasn't prepared to give up on Dominic; we were allies if not friends, but mindless pounding on a running machine provided ample opportunity for organising random thoughts into some semblance of a sensible order. With a romantic interlude with Dominic off the cards, at least for the time being, I decided to focus my energy into something else. I was going to solve the mystery of what had happened to Jez Keaton, and the first step was to assess how easy it would be for someone to fall off Hookes Bay Pier.

From the gym I headed down to the seafront and to the rear of the pavilion. The wooden decking looked solid enough although it would be impossible to test it any further without vandalising the chain link fence to gain access. I knew from Dominic's old photographs that the pier had originally extended for a couple of hundred metres into the sea before terminating in a rectangular viewing platform. What was left was an area no more than twenty metres long and three wide, supported by four rusty iron girders. There were iron hand rails on either side and some sort of ledge at the far end, together with twin sets of wooden blocks that had once supported bench seating. Two further girders rose from the water some thirty metres off shore, the only remaining evidence of the original structure.

'Penny for your thoughts,' a voice called out. I hadn't noticed Beth and Ethan Hobart below me on the shingle. Ethan was scooping up handfuls of pebbles at the water's edge. 'Do you want to come and join us?' Beth asked. 'We've got doughnuts.'

Ethan was in shorts and wellies. He gave me one of his toothy grins.

I jumped down onto the beach and squatted beside him. 'How are you, Ethan? You've got some pretty pebbles there.'

He unclenched his fist to show me his treasures.

'Are you on guard duty?' I asked Beth, nodding back towards to the pavilion.

She laughed. 'Paul's in there now, just measuring up. Apparently those people from the Trust are quibbling over some of the costs involved.'

'Oh?'

'They're not happy with the estimates. I don't know the details. Anyway, Paul's going to see if he can re-jig some of the figures to make them more acceptable. It's the last thing Dom needs to be worrying about right now.'

'Oh yes, he told me about this thing with Hastings' lawyers.'

'That wife of his is a right bitch,' Beth said. 'I only met her once, when Paul was working on the mill with Dom. I had to drop something up there and she kept me waiting on the doorstep like I wasn't good enough to cross the threshold. Dom's such a nice guy, I can't understand what he ever saw in her.'

'Oh well, we can all make mistakes when it comes to love,' I sighed. I was naturally curious to know more about Dominic and Danni's relationship. 'How long have you known Dominic?'

'A few years,' Beth replied with a knowing smile. 'Paul's helped him out on a couple of projects now. As soon as he can distance himself from the Hastings family the better, as far I'm concerned. He needs to cut all ties and move on. I keep telling him. He deserves some happiness after everything they've put him through.'

'Do you know the Hastings family very well?'

'Everyone in Hookes Bay knows the Hastings family,' Beth replied, tearing off a chunk of doughnut and handing it to Ethan. 'But I wouldn't say I knew them well. You certainly don't want to get tangled up in them, that's for sure. They do have a bit of a reputation.'

'Has Grant always been in the property business?'

'He's a self-made man,' Beth replied. 'Started out driving taxis and then bought out the company. You've probably seen his cabs around town. I'm not quite sure how he got into property development. It's a bit of a step up.'

'Perhaps he married money or something?'

'I don't think so,' Beth laughed. 'I've bumped into Tina Hastings a few times over the years and as far as I know she grew up on the council estate in Leigh Park. The money definitely came from somewhere else. Maybe he won it on the horses. Oh, Ethan, no, you put the doughnut in your mouth and the pebbles in the water, see, like Mummy.'

I sensed I wasn't going to glean any more information from Beth about Dominic. Beth seemed a loyal friend, and I felt encouraged by her words. 'You said Paul was inside? Has he got any tools with him?'

'I expect so. What do you need?'

'Wire cutters.'

'Can I ask why?'

'I want to get onto the pier.'

'Can't you just ask Kitty for a key to the padlock? There's a gate on the far side.'

There were numerous keys attached to the fob Kitty had already given me. I pulled the collection from my bag. 'Maybe it's one of these,' I said hopefully. 'I'll give it a try. Thanks.'

I was in luck. With Beth and Ethan watching from a safe distance I was able to unlock the gate and make my way onto the pier. It felt a little shaky underfoot but there certainly weren't any missing boards. With the handrails protecting either side it was impossible to see how anyone could fall off. In fact, as I locked the gate behind me, I concluded that Terri Cawle's suggestion of an alien abduction might not be so ridiculous after all.

On my way back to Crabhook Lane I received a call from Dominic informing me that the Parish Council were going to meet the following evening. Bunny had been able to gather together the minimum number required for a quorum and had, miraculously, found a time slot at the church hall. He left it up to me to decide whether I wanted to attend or not.

'I'm not sure anyone on the council would be curious enough to question your authenticity,' he said. 'And Tom's right. You can put on an impressive performance. This might be our only chance to win these people over.'

'Is that your way of saying you want me there?' I asked, delighted that I was needed but also wary of the implications. More deceit equalled bigger repercussions.

'Oh, I'm sure we can manage without you, but some of the old boys on the council might be susceptible to your charms.'

I decided it was a gamble worth taking and spent all morning cobbling together a speech on the importance of the performing arts in society. It was something I re-hashed from the internet. With the diverse and wide range of activities I envisaged for the pavilion, I concluded that the Hookes Bay Hub would not just be a valuable resource, but a highly desirable local asset.

The chairman of the council was a man called Tim Seymour, a sailing type with a ruddy complexion and trim white beard. Besides Bunny who was there to take the minutes, and Kevin Galliard, three of the other four councillors were women, while the remaining elderly gent looked as if he had been wheeled in from a nursing home. I highly doubted any of them would be susceptible to my charms.

'As I am sure you are all aware,' Tim began. 'We are here to debate whether we as a Parish Council are prepared to pledge our support for the preservation and restoration of Hookes Bay Pavilion. As you know, the pavilion is currently empty, and has been for the last twelve months since the manager of the nightclub, Robert Mayhew, had his licence withdrawn following a series of complaints from local residents.

'Let me say first that I have already been approached by Grant Hastings, outlining his proposal for the redevelopment of the seafront. Coastline Developments intend to apply for planning permission for the construction of an apartment block together with retail and commercial units. Mr Hastings has made no secret of the fact that he would like to purchase the pavilion from its current owner, Mrs Katherine Barker. The pavilion would then be demolished in order for the new development to have direct water frontage which would involve some changes to the current road layout. I understand that Mr Flynn here and Tom Whybrow, have now formed a conservation society to save the pavilion from demolition in direct opposition to Coastline's plans. Having listened to Grant Hastings, it's now only fair that we hear the other side of the story.'

'Thank you, Mr Chairman,' Dominic said, rising to his feet. He gave the hard-sell with his very professional PowerPoint presentation, although there was a distinct air of weariness about him. I wasn't entirely sure he had captivated his audience's imagination. Tom too, gave a pared down version of the historical significance of the pavilion. The councillors looked bored. No doubt they'd heard it all before.

The first rule of improvisation was to gauge the audience and I gauged the average age of my audience to be seventy, predominantly middle to upper class. I doubted any of them had any appreciation of the type of facility I envisaged for the pavilion. These people would rather have the youths who hung around outside the amusement arcade placed under curfew than encourage them to take part in a pop-up drama club or an MC session.

I didn't have Dominic's carefully crafted illustrations, I only had my vision, and a natural ability to show-off. When Tom finished, I stood up and introduced myself, or rather I introduced Alice Paige, the new proprietor of Hookes Bay Academy of Music and Dance and the instigator of the proposal for the Hookes Bay Community Arts Hub.

'How many of you remember the pavilion ballroom in its heyday?' I asked. I nodded in the direction of one of the elderly ladies. 'How about you, madam? Can you recall attending a variety show at Lionel Keaton's Theatre of Dreams?'

'Certainly not, dear,' she replied with a haughty snort. 'But I can certainly remember that bloody awful nightclub.'

I carried on regardless. Without prompting, Dominic projected a picture of the pavilion from the post-war period onto his laptop.

'Lionel Keaton was an innovator,' I said. 'He wanted to entertain, to educate and facilitate. That philosophy would be my motto for the proposed Arts Hub. My aim is to create a permanent performing arts academy together with facilities for community groups and a live entertainment venue.'

I dappled my speech with quotes from various educational experts and the theatrical elite; everyone from Sir John Gielgud to John Osborne had had something to say about the importance of the performing arts in society. I reeled off the activities I hoped to lure to the pavilion, ensuring I included as many ideas as possible that might appeal to the more genteel folk of Hookes Bay.

'A fully restored pavilion would be unique, outside and in,' I concluded. 'Any seaside town can have an apartment complex with uninterrupted access to the waterfront,' I looked directly at Kevin Galliard before turning to Tim Seymour, 'but not every council has the opportunity to have a unique, innovative, ground-breaking facility in an historic building like this. I believe by creating this arts hub Hookes Bay will become the envy of every town on the south coast. Let's make it happen.'

I took a step back. Had I done enough? Bunny obviously thought so because she clapped her hands and a polite ripple of applause ensued before Tim asked if anyone had any questions. There were a few; mostly about the funding, which

Dominic was able to assure the council would be the responsibility in the first instance of the Modernist Preservation Trust.

'I suggest we take a motion to the vote,' Tim Seymour announced.

'Perhaps we could have a few minutes to debate the matter amongst ourselves?' Kevin Galliard suggested.

'Of course,' Dominic said after a slight hesitation. I followed him outside while Tom headed off to the kitchenette to make himself another cup of tea.

Dominic kicked at a clod of earth, unable to hide his frustration before taking a perch on the brick wall that separated the hall from the adjacent churchyard.

'Galliard shouldn't even get a vote on this,' he said, 'it's a direct conflict of interest. You heard Tim Seymour, Hastings has got to them all already, before he has even submitted his plans.'

'Hastings doesn't own the pavilion.' I reminded him. 'He can't do anything with it right now.'

'He's just waiting for Kitty to die.'

'She isn't dead yet. We have to remain positive. At least we've got this far.'

'The eternal optimist.'

'Well, one of us has to be,' I retorted. Dominic's belligerence was beginning to grate. 'You do realise I want this as much as you, don't you?' I said. 'I've put my heart and soul into this project just like you, and my own money.'

'Your money? Kitty bought the dance school for you.'

'No she didn't. I didn't use Kitty's money, I used my own. I own the Hookes Bay Academy of Music and Dance, and my future hinges on this. Me, Tar …' I stopped myself just in time. This was definitely not the time for the big Tara Wakely reveal.

Dominic looked confused. 'But why? Why did you buy it? She told me she gave you the money.'

'I wanted to do something just for me.'

'And that meant owning a dance school in Hookes Bay?'

'Yes. I mean, to be honest, it's never been my life-long

ambition to own a dance school in an obscure south coast town full of geriatric day-trippers, but I did have plans for the future that involved some sort of stage school idea. That was my retirement plan. I wanted to give something back to society. I was put in care at the age of fourteen and a weekend drama club saved my life and my sanity. It gave me something to focus on when all around me my life was going to pot. I want to give other kids that same opportunity. I appreciate it's not something you would ever understand.'

He shook his head. 'I don't understand you full stop,' he said.

'Since I left stage school at the age of eighteen I've worked consistently. I'm a professional actress, and I am passionate about what I do. Architecture isn't the only profession that cares about our heritage, Dominic.'

Bunny stuck her head out of the doorway. 'Ah, there you are. We've taken our vote. Do you want to step back inside?'

Dominic seemed reluctant to answer. I grabbed his arm and dragged him towards the hall. 'Sure. We're just coming.'

Chapter Thirty-Two

'I'm off to tell Cyril the good news,' Tom said as we headed out of the church hall ten minutes later. 'I promised to let him know how we got on. I can't believe we received the council's unanimous support. It's a pretty resounding result.'

'Only because Galliard wasn't allowed to cast his vote,' Dominic pointed out.

'Don't belittle our girl's performance,' Tom grinned. 'How do you do it, Alice?'

'It's my job, Tom.'

Tom hurried off into the dusk of the churchyard. I turned to Dominic. 'Well, I think that deserves a celebratory drink, don't you? Don't suppose you fancy a no-strings beer from the Co-op?'

He raised an eyebrow. 'Persistence is one of your more admirable qualities. Go on then. One beer.'

I linked my arm through his before he could change his mind. The High Street was deserted. Even La Scala appeared to have closed early.

'Can I run something by you?' I asked as we walked past the empty restaurant.

'Go on.'

'I'm beginning to think Jez Keaton's accident was not an accident.'

'That's a bit random isn't it?'

'Kitty has nightmares. She's been having these nightmares since I arrived in Hookes Bay.'

'I can see the connection.'

'That's not fair. Apparently Kitty believes that one of Jez's bandmates pushed him off the pier.'

'She told you that?'

'No. Terri Cawle, who works in Pebbles, mentioned it. She used to be a barmaid at the club. The thing is everyone thought Jez threw this party to celebrate the band's record contract, but the band didn't get a contract. The record producer wanted Jez as a solo artist. When the band got back to Hookes Bay, with all the boys on a high thinking they'd got this deal, he told them the truth.'

'Nice guy.'

'Exactly. I've looked at that pier. I can't see any way someone could just fall off.'

'I'm not totally sure being dumped by your lead singer is a valid motive for murder. I thought it was all to do with drink and drugs.'

'According to Maureen Batty, Jez wasn't taking drugs.'

'I wouldn't trust anything Maureen Batty tells you.'

'I think the police jumped on the drugs story because it explained the inexplicable. Why would Jez wander off down the pier by himself? He had to be right at the very end when he fell to catch the outgoing tide. The two guys, the Bonetti brothers, were the last people to see Jez alive. That makes them the prime suspects.'

'It sounds like you've been reading too many detective novels.' Dominic said. 'What could these Bonetti brothers possibly hope to gain by pushing Jez off the pier?'

'I don't know. But apparently Vince Bonetti was gay and lusted after Jez. Maybe he felt doubly let down. As for Paulo, well, he could have been a rock star and he ends up rolling out pizza dough for a living.'

'So they push him off in a fit of pique?' Dominic could barely contain his mirth. 'What about the other band members, Miss Marple?'

'The only other member of the band was Maureen's nephew. This is where it gets even more interesting. They were expecting him and he didn't show up. What if he told Jez to wait behind for him because he was going to be late? Woody is furious when he hears about the record deal. They have a fight on the pier and Jez ends up in the water. Sounds quite plausible don't you think?'

'I'm sure the police questioned everyone connected with Jez quite thoroughly at the time.'

I was warming to my theme. 'But what if nobody but Jez was expecting Woody to turn up? Terri said they all thought he was on a bender. Apparently he had a bit of a drink problem. He could have slunk into Hookes Bay without anybody seeing him and slunk straight out again. Hookes Bay is hardly Leicester Square on a Saturday night. Who would have been around to see him?'

'I don't know. Taxi drivers, night shift workers, insomniacs…' Dominic raised his hands in a gesture of exasperation. 'I thought there was a security camera at the club?'

'Only at the front of the building, not at the back.'

'You've thought of everything, haven't you? I'm concerned that you're starting to sound slightly obsessive. Maybe I'll forego the beer before you push me off the pier to test out your theory.'

'Don't tempt me,' I teased, glad that Dominic's mood had lightened. 'Talking of obsessions, what do you know about Lindy Mayhew?'

'Not a lot.'

'We need to be careful of her.'

'Do we?'

'Yes. She told me she knew Jez better than anybody else and he definitely didn't have a daughter.'

'How would she have known what he got up to when he was off touring in London?'

'My thoughts exactly, but they were quite close as youngsters. Apparently it all fizzled out when she went off to university, but they might well have kept in touch.'

'Actually, that might explain Kitty's lock-up.'

'Kitty has a lock-up?'

'Yes, at Secure Storage, that huge yellow building on the Fareham Road. I had to go there to collect the old programmes and photo albums. It's full of Jez's stuff: records, books, clothes, guitars. It felt more like a shrine than a storage unit.'

'You think Lindy could be responsible for it?'

'You've seen the state of the bungalow. Do you think Kitty would meticulously label every box she put into storage? Take a look if you don't believe me. Kitty had no qualms about giving me the key.'

'Oh, I've probably already got the key.' I slipped my fingers into my handbag and retrieved the keyring Kitty had given me. As I suspected, one of the keys bore the yellow plastic fob bearing the Secure Storage logo.

'Yep. That's the one,' Dominic confirmed. 'I think it's unit number ten.'

I made up my mind to take a look next time I went to Fareham.

Dominic seemed quite pensive as we sat down in the nearest beach shelter. It was a mild muggy evening. The sun had just fallen into the sea and orange streaks filtered across the cloudy sky.

'Any progress on the legal battle?' I asked. I wasn't particularly keen to embark on another conversation about his grievances with Grant Hastings but I wanted Dominic to know that I cared.

'Not yet,' he sighed, 'and all the time I'm arguing with Hastings' bloody lawyers I'm losing even more money because I've had to shut up the yard. Hobo's sitting in whenever he can but he's got other stuff to do as well.'

'If it's just a question of sitting there and answering the phone, I could help you out if you want,' I volunteered. 'I don't teach in the mornings.' My offer didn't emit the positive response I hoped. To fill the void I continued. 'I bumped into Beth and Ethan on the beach the other day. Beth said Paul was recalculating some of the figures for the MPT.'

'Oh, it's nothing,' Dominic said, opening his beer can. 'They were just nit-picking. I'll email Sam in the morning and tell her about the parish council and send her the revised financial schedule.'

I tried again. 'I meant what I said about the yard. I think reclamation and salvage could be another very handy string to my bow.'

'You're never going to give up, are you?' he said.

'Not when I believe something is worth fighting for,' I replied.

He turned to face me. There was something in his expression I hadn't seen before? Gratitude, or something deeper and unfathomable? It was the beer. It had made him mellow again. All I had to do was get Dominic drunk and his defences slipped.

'I've really misjudged you, haven't I, Alice?'

'Oh I wouldn't beat yourself up about it,' I replied. 'I've made plenty of bad judgements in my time.'

'Come along to the yard tomorrow at ten. Hobo can show you what to do.'

'Great.' I smiled.

He didn't turn away. In fact, he continued to study my face, almost as if he was seeing me for the first time. Something had shifted between us, as if the air was charged with an expectant under-current.

'Who are you really, Alice?'

'You don't want to know.'

'But I do. How can we... how can I...?'

I put a finger to his lips to silence him. I wasn't going to let the truth spoil the moment I had been waiting for. Our eyes were locked.

He put his hand over mine, turned it over and brushed his lips across my palm before taking his time to kiss the base of each finger. It was a totally unexpected, incredibly tender gesture. I closed my eyes. The touch of his tongue on my skin sent tingles of anticipation soaring through my entire body. I let out an involuntary gasp of pleasure.

Just as I sensed our mouths were about to meet, a car came careering along the esplanade with the screech of burning rubber. As both Dominic and I jumped to our feet, it slammed straight into the front of the amusement arcade.

Chapter Thirty-Three

Kitty

'I see there was a bit of trouble down on the prom the other night,' Robbie said, taking a large bite out of a ginger nut. 'Those joy riders were at it again.'

Kitty watched in despair as the biscuit crumbs spilled onto the bedcovers. 'Yes, Penny told me.'

'Wasn't her boy, was it?'

'I heard that,' Penny called from the doorway. Kitty liked to keep her close when Robbie was around. Penny was cleaning the bathroom with all doors open. 'Sorry to disappointment you but Callum is always safely tucked up in bed by ten o'clock. He is only fourteen, Robbie.'

Robbie grunted unconvinced.

'How's Lindy?' Kitty asked, changing the subject. Lindy hadn't made an appearance for days. Kitty felt peeved.

'Her nerves are bad again.'

Kitty had had enough of hearing about Lindy's nerves.

'Is Alice not here?' Robbie enquired, glancing around the bedroom as if he expected her to spring out of the wardrobe.

'She's working.'

'I didn't know she worked mornings.'

'She's got a new job.'

'Where's she working then?' Robbie asked.

Did he think she was stupid? If he knew where Alice was he'd probably be round there like a shot threatening her with violence again. 'Somewhere in Fareham,' she lied.

It appeared to satisfy him. Robbie picked up the copy of *Let's Chat* Penny had left on the bedside table. 'Don't know why you read this rubbish. You don't even watch half these soaps.'

'I like to do the crossword. Keeps my brain ticking over.'

'You've never done a crossword in your life,' Robbie snorted.

'Robbie, that wretched dog of yours is peeing in Alice's new flowerbed,' Penny shrieked.

'Coming,' Robbie called, not exactly jumping to his feet. He handed her back the magazine. 'There you go. Shall I just leave it here on the top?'

'No, tuck it in the drawer.' Kitty said. 'I'll look at it later.' She didn't want that particular edition left lying around.

Kitty wasn't entirely happy about Alice's blossoming relationship with Dominic Flynn. A little pin-prick of jealousy. Kitty had always had an eye for a handsome young man. Kitty had hardly seen Dominic since Alice had arrived on the scene. When he'd first heard of Coastline's plans he'd been a regular visitor to Crabhook Lane. Perhaps he was just keeping his distance as damage limitation in case everything went pear-shaped. Not that it was going pear-shaped. According to Alice now that the parish council were on board it was just going to be a matter of time before the Modernist Preservation Trust made their bid for the pavilion.

Time. Kitty couldn't help but feel it was running out. Not that Alice seemed perturbed. She had acquired an added spring in her step for the last few mornings. She was getting a suntan too, her face browning up. Who'd have thought: freckles? She must have inherited those from her mother.

Alice never spoke about her mother. Kitty's conscience was pickled in guilt. If only she had found Alice sooner. The girl had a heart of gold. She was rapidly making friends in Hookes Bay. Cyril seemed devoted to her, and Maureen Batty too. Alice had sat by the bed and shown Kitty the scrapbook that Maureen had given her. Kitty had no idea Maureen had been such an avid fan of Urban Rebel.

'That's Jez teaching Derek the guitar,' Kitty had said, halting the flow of pages with a shaking hand, pleased to be able to make some sort of constructive comment on the pictures. Kitty hadn't kept much track of Urban Rebel's humble beginnings; she'd just been glad Jez had found something to keep him occupied. Don had been a very demanding husband. 'Derek used to come to the pavilion on a Saturday morning when I was doing my dance classes,' she told Alice. 'Jez gave lessons to quite a few of his school friends. Look, here's another picture of him with Lindy.' At least Kitty thought it was Lindy. Young, blonde, denim shorts. Yes, definitely Lindy. How could Kitty forget the shorts? Even Don had been captivated by those legs and he'd been bedridden.

'So after what happened to Jez,' Alice had said, when every page of Maureen's scrapbook had been devoured, 'did you ever hear from Woody again?'

Kitty tried to remember. There had been so many comings and goings in those first few days it was hard to recall who she had seen and who she hadn't. Robbie had fended off most enquiries. Kitty had talked to the police, although not the press, she'd left that to Robbie too. Surely Derek had called round to express his condolences?

'Did Hughie ever manage to track Woody down?' Alice asked.

Dear, kind, gentle Alice. How did she know about Hughie's investigations? 'I don't know,' Kitty replied in a rare moment of candour. 'I really don't know.'

It's time to move on, Kit, Hughie had said when he had returned from a day out in Portsmouth, his face grim, his whole manner deflated. *You have to accept it was an accident. Let it go.*

But how could she let it go? Jez was her son; her only child. You just couldn't abandon them, lose faith. Jez could have walked the length and breadth of Hookes Bay Pier in a blindfold and he wouldn't have fallen off. *A mother knows.*

Chapter Thirty-Four

Tara

As soon as I arrived in Dominic's office I could see that babysitting Hookes Bay Architectural Reclamation and Salvage wasn't going to be a particularly taxing task. Hobo ran through the very basic ledger system which listed all the prices paid and the projected sales value of all the goods in the yard. My duties were basically to answer telephone enquiries and take messages. Physical customers were rare.

'We don't get that much passing trade tucked away down here,' Hobo said. 'To be honest, Dom doesn't get much trade at all. Most people know what they want in this business so they phone first to check. Of course, if you do see anyone browsing, head outside like a shot and entice them in.'

On my first morning we didn't receive a single visitor, although the phone rang a couple of times. I hated inertia and was not used to having time on my hands. However, there were two good reasons for persevering. The first, I wanted to strengthen my connection to Dominic by becoming indispensable, and secondly the junkyard had Wi-Fi. No need to face the mocking scorn of Terri Cawle as I continued my investigations into Jez's disappearance.

What should have been a triumphant evening celebrating our success at the parish council had been ruined by a pair of teenage joyriders. The driver and his passenger had emerged from the wrecked car looking stunned but in one piece. The amusement arcade manager and his assistant had both boys in arm locks before the police even arrived. Dominic had suggested we slip away before we were asked for witness statements. The promised kiss had never materialised, not even on Kitty's doorstep. Dominic had seemed agitated by the incident on the esplanade, and hadn't been in touch since. I had no idea where I stood. Sitting in his leather chair at least gave me some sense of affinity.

With business quiet I turned my attention to tracking down the remaining members of Urban Rebel. Vincent Bonetti was very easy to find. *Naughtie Nettie*, as he now liked to be known, had his own website, a prolific public Facebook page and a very vocal presence on Twitter.

'Best night's cabaret ever' one reviewer recalled after seeing him perform.

'Laughed until I wet myself,' another observed.

Vince Bonetti was a very successful drag artist with a regular Friday night set at a club in Brighton. His blog chronicled his rise to fame, and even included a brief paragraph about his misspent youth with Urban Rebel.

'Even then I knew that wasn't the life I wanted to lead,' he wrote. *'The tragic death of my best friend and band mate, Jez Keaton, was the turning point that made me re-evaluate my life. Jez had been encouraging me to 'come out'. We'd been mates since school and didn't have any secrets from each other. Jez had stood up for me and protected me. I owed it to him to be true to myself. I moved to Brighton and have never looked back.'*

I decided I could eliminate Vince from my murder enquiries although it might be worth contacting him later to discuss Jez's 'secrets' in more detail. Derek Woodford, on the other hand, had no online presence.

At the end of my first week Dominic finally made an appearance in the junkyard.

'You look very much at home in my chair,' he remarked with uncharacteristic cheerfulness. 'Have you sold anything?' I felt very much at home, although I had sold very little.

'This man Aidan Chapman has called a couple of times about some stove he said you were sourcing for him for his boat,' I told him. The two calls had been the highlight of my day. 'Who needs a stove on a boat?'

'He's after a specific wood burner for his barge,' Dominic

replied. 'Yes I have found him one, but I'll have to go all the way to Shoreham to collect it and right now, that's not one of my priorities. Have you got his number? I'll call him with the details and he can go and fetch it himself. I'll sacrifice my profit margin. Aidan's a good customer. I don't want to keep pissing him off.'

It was easy to see why Dominic was so keen to reclaim his professional practice. He would make no money in the junkyard if he kept directing what few customers he had elsewhere.

'Are you happy to carry on?' he asked. 'I've been putting feelers out on a couple of private restoration jobs and I'd really like to follow them up. It means I need to be out a fair bit.'

'Sure,' I replied. 'I told you, I'm free every morning.'

He hesitated. 'What about evenings? I really should take you out for a meal.'

'I'd love that,' I said at once. I'd played hard to get before and it hadn't worked. I smiled, seductively. 'We never did get the chance to finish our celebrations the other evening did we?'

Finishing our celebrations appeared to be the last thing he had in mind. 'It would be my way of saying thank you for minding shop,' he said, deliberately avoiding my eye and retrieving some paperwork from his filing cabinet. 'You've probably realised I can't afford to pay you. How about next Saturday?'

That was a whole week away. 'Saturday is normally fish and chip night with Kitty and Cyril,' I pointed out.

'I'm sure they can spare you,' he winked.

I was surprised to see Mari arrive at the community centre at the start of my Wednesday afternoon class. Ethan was already tearing around the hall in anticipation, shaking a pair of maracas. Mari couldn't keep the look of disapproval off her face.

'I wasn't expecting you,' I said. The weekend away sailing had done Mari the world of good. I'd hardly seen her since, apart from when she came to take the advanced ballet classes.

Even her interference in my plans for the summer showcase had waned now she knew she might have to miss it altogether.

'Mrs Galliard is worried about the forthcoming exams,' Mari said. 'Claudia's got the afternoon off school so I said I'd give her an extra lesson. I hope you don't mind but I thought we could just requisition a quiet corner.'

With Ethan on the premises there was no chance of a quiet corner. And I did mind. This was my time, my class. Mari was undermining my authority. I bit my tongue. *When I had my own premises…*

'Sure. Help yourself.'

Beth did her best to curb Ethan's enthusiasm but he was fascinated by Claudia. Needless to say my lesson ended early and in chaos. Beth dragged a screaming Ethan from the building while the other parents gathered up their offspring in the vestibule. Bunny Mitchell glared at me from the parish office.

I waved off the last of my parents in the carpark. Just as I was about to return to the hall to clear up after Ethan's trail of destruction, Mrs Galliard pulled up in her convertible. At the same time a man in his late fifties in a tight-fitting suit, emerged from a large sleek coupé occupying the disabled parking bay. He was accompanied by a gangly youth of sixteen or seventeen.

Mrs Galliard gave a girlish giggle as she greeted the newcomers. The trio made their way into the building together.

'Ah, here she is,' Mrs Galliard said. 'Alice, do you know Grant Hastings?'

'I don't believe we've met,' Hastings said before I could answer. He wasn't an unattractive man but there was something distinctly disingenuous about the smile he gave me. 'I've heard all about you, of course.'

Bunny jumped up from her desk in the office and flung open the door. 'Mr Hastings. To what do we owe this pleasure?'

'It's really Miss Paige I've come to see,' Hastings said to my disconcertion. 'But as you are here as well, it's actually rather fortuitous. Have you got a minute?'

'I'm a very busy woman, Mr Hastings,' Bunny grumbled.

We entered the hall en masse as Claudia scrambled into a pair of leggings. 'What's going on, Mum?'

'I bumped into Mr Hastings and Darius in the carpark,' Mrs Galliard said. 'Thanks, Mari. If you don't mind, we'll settle up next week.'

'No problems, Mrs Galliard.'

Darius idly kicked at Mari's kit-bag which she'd left by the door.

'Hey, don't do that,' Claudia hissed. 'What are you doing here anyway? Have you come for some ballet tips?'

The boy reddened.

'Best you run along now,' Hastings said to Claudia, his benign smile fixed on his face.

'Claudia does have a point. What are you doing here, Mr Hastings?' I asked. 'I'm more than happy to sign up your son for some dance or singing lessons if that's what he wants.'

'No need to be facetious,' he replied, the smile slipping in an instant. 'I'm here because I've got a proposition to put to you and Ginger Spice.'

'Excuse me?' Mari said. 'What did you call me?'

'Mr Hastings,' Bunny huffed, 'I really don't think that is appropriate…'

Mrs Galliard edged Claudia towards the doorway. 'Claudie, let's go,'

'I'm not going anywhere,' Claudia retorted, shaking her mother off. 'I want to hear what Mr Hastings has to say.'

Mrs Galliard gritted her teeth. 'I'm sure that whatever Mr Hastings has to say is none of our business. In any case, we're due at the nail bar.'

'I don't want my nails done now,' Claudia replied.

'I suppose what I've got to say might affect Claudia,' Hastings said. 'After all, it is something to everyone's advantage.'

'I'm all ears,' I said, pulling the kit-bag out of Darius' reach. The poor boy had terrible acne, his embarrassed flush highlighted his inflamed skin.

'Bunny, that cubby hole of yours back there isn't really a

suitable working space, is it?' Hastings said, the sinister smile back in place. 'You deserve something better. How would you like a brand new, spacious, purposely-designed parish office?'

'Well, obviously I'd be delighted,' Bunny replied, 'but—'

'No buts,' Hastings said, putting up his hand to silence her. 'I'm going to build an entirely new parish centre for Hookes Bay. I intend to completely refurbish and extend this existing building to create a purpose-built home for the pre-school. It can't be good for the little ones of Hookes Bay to have their lessons here, unpacking and packing up after every session, and then we'd create a second hall, which would be ideal for meetings of the parish council and private hire. I've already spoken to Jim at the Taekwondo club and Mel at short mat bowls. They're desperate for better facilities. And of course, these dancing girls would have a permanent home here too.'

Before anyone could speak, he continued. 'I am committed to supporting local community projects. All the work will be carried out by my experienced team with no cost to the parish council, or the parishioners whatsoever.'

'Mr Hastings, I don't know what to say.' In the short time I'd known Bunny I'd never known her to be lost for words, and despite her professed speechlessness, she wasn't now. 'Obviously, this is good news,' she gushed, 'excellent news in fact. I was only complaining to Tim the other day about the damp in this building. I had to throw out an entire box of ruined allotment permits from the back cupboard. And I should have a counter, for visitors, with a buzzer and proper sliding window. It would be so much more professional.'

'Naturally the finer details of the design would need to be discussed with the council, although we would try and accommodate individual requirements,' Hastings replied.

'Does Tim know your plans?' Bunny could barely contain her excitement.

'We've only spoken briefly,' Hastings confirmed. 'When we submit our plans to the Borough Council we will add on a rider outlining the proposed refurbishment of the existing community centre facilities. So, if Anna Pavlova and Ginger Rogers want a new performing arts centre in Hookes Bay, they can have it. Here. No need to waste money restoring that pavilion.'

He was like a hyena, stalking his prey and Bunny was easy game, devoured in his first attack.

'This is so unexpected,' Bunny continued to flap. 'And so generous of you, Mr Hastings. What can I say but thank you?'

'I like to think of myself as something of a philanthropist,' he smirked.

'You're nothing of the sort,' I snapped. 'You're only making this offer because you're desperate to get the pavilion site.'

'To be fair, Alice, this has moved the goalposts considerably with regard to the pavilion,' Bunny said.

'You can't make a pledge of support one week and then withdraw it the next,' I cried.

'Oh, it's hardly as black and white as that,' Bunny protested.

Hastings took a bow. 'I'll leave you ladies to fight it out. Personally I think that common sense will prevail. The restoration and refurbishment of Hookes Bay Pavilion will be nothing but a continuous drain on this council's resources for many years to come. I'm offering a simple, cost-neutral alternative.'

I could hardly contain my anger. 'Nobody is asking Hookes Bay Council for a penny towards the restoration of the pavilion.'

'Oh, come on,' Hastings sneered. 'That type of poncey arts facility always needs local government support. It's unsustainable in a place like this. And it's not just that, is it? I take it you've seen the damage to the amusement arcade, Bunny? What a ruckus that was the other night. With the pavilion gone we can change that seafront road entirely. There'll be no more joyriders along the prom.'

Now I understood Dominic's agitation. The incident couldn't have come at a worse time. If I hadn't personally witnessed the two teenagers emerge from the wreckage of the mangled Mercedes, I might have thought Grant Hastings was behind the wheel himself. It still wasn't beyond the realms of possibility to imagine Hastings orchestrating the entire accident. Darius might well know a joyrider or two. He wasn't so much flushing now as glowing like a beacon.

'We will definitely have to take that into consideration,' Bunny agreed. 'I think Mr Hastings has made a perfectly sensible offer, ladies. I need to go and speak to Tim.'

'The community centre and the pavilion should be two completely separate issues,' I called after her as she hurried back to her office. 'Tell Tim that.'

Hastings turned to me his voice little more than a hiss. 'So now it's just you I've got to deal with – the little Keaton protégé.' It was almost as if he had forgotten Claudia and her mother were still in the room. His face was so close I could see his nostril hair and feel his spittle on my skin. 'Lindy's right. There is a physical resemblance, but you're playing a dangerous game, young lady. I'll tell you now, you're wasting your time if you hope to do anything with that pavilion. I've got the full support of the Borough and the County Council for my plans for Hookes Bay. Those men know which side their bread is buttered on. Unlike you. Come on board with the new parish community centre, and I'd see you very generously rewarded, maybe with some nice new equipment. Think about it. And think about the consequences if you don't.'

It was impossible not to feel intimidated. First Robbie, and now Hastings. 'Are you threatening me?' I asked, hoping I sounded more assertive than I felt.

Hastings bared his fangs. 'I'm just pointing out the benefits of us all being on the same side,' he said.

I shook my head. 'I'll never be on the same side as you.'

'I think you should leave, Mr Hastings,' Mari interrupted. She struck a defiant pose, arms folded across her chest.

Hastings gave a shrug and stepped aside. 'As you wish. Come on, Darius. Our business is done here.'

Darius slunk off after his father. A sigh of relief resonated around the room.

'I don't know how Dad puts up with that man,' Claudia muttered.

'He puts up with him because it's his job.' Mrs Galliard snapped. 'Mr Hastings is a very good employer, and we all reap the benefits, you too young lady, before you get on your high-horse. I think the fact that he is prepared to make this offer for the benefit of the entire community is very magnanimous of him.'

Mari was indignant. 'You should be ashamed of yourself, Mrs Galliard, defending that man.' I'd never seen her so angry. 'He called me Ginger. Nobody calls me Ginger. And he threatened Alice, you heard him.'

'Well, I don't think it was a threat as such.'

'Yes it was, Mum.' Claudia shared Mari's outrage.

'I haven't been called names like that since I was at school,' Mari fumed. 'Some people have no respect. I thought Rob Mayhew was bad enough but he's a positive teddy bear compared to that bully.'

'Bully he may be,' Mrs Galliard said, 'but Grant Hastings is used to getting his way.' She lowered her voice, even though he was well out of earshot. 'Seriously, Mari, you don't want to get on the wrong side of that man.' She gave an involuntary shudder. 'Trust me.'

I'd seen the icy glare in Hastings' eyes and I tended to agree with Mrs Galliard. An unmistakeable aura of menace lingered in the room, even after his departure. Not for the first time since my arrival in Hookes Bay I felt out of my depth. False bravado was all well and good, but outwitting Hastings was going to require a theatrical performance of Oscar-winning proportions.

Chapter Thirty-Five

'I should have guessed Hastings would pull a trick like that,' Dominic said when I phoned him that evening. 'Let's just keep this to ourselves for now. I'm certainly not going to mention anything to the MPT. We have it on the record that the parish council pledged their support. Let's keep it that way.'

I'd already decided to say nothing to Kitty. 'Poor Mari was quite traumatised by Hastings' visit,' I told him. 'Is his daughter that terrifying?'

'Ten times worse,' Dominic replied. 'Seriously, Alice, you need to be on your guard. I've booked us a table by the way, for Saturday. There's a new place just opened up in Gosport called the Quay House. I'll pick you up at eight?'

'Great.' I was glad of the distraction. My encounter with Grant Hastings had affected me far more than I was prepared to admit. The truth was, Hastings did have Mari and me quaking in our ballet shoes. I had been very quick to accuse Bunny of a cowardly surrender, but she'd lived in Hookes Bay a long time and was probably fully aware of Hastings' dubious reputation. Better to succumb to the first bite, than prolong the chase and be torn apart limb by limb. Hastings was happily turning the screws on Dominic, albeit through the courts. It was easy to picture him resorting to less subtle tactics.

The Quay House sounded quaint and romantic. Did I need to buy new clothes to wear? Something slinky and sophisticated? I could easily pop into Fareham on the bus after my last class. Just as I was contemplating a delicious seduction scenario a message from Jordan Lockwood popped up on my phone.

'Hi Alice, it's the big race on Sunday. Fancy coming along to support me? We start at the leisure centre at 7.00 am.'

At 7.00 am on Sunday morning I planned to be snuggling up to Dominic in his caravan.

'Really sorry,' I typed back. *'Can't make Sunday. I'll be thinking of you.'* With any luck I wouldn't be thinking about him at all, but I needed Jordan on my team. *'Have a great race. Perhaps we can catch up some time next week?'*

Jordan's reply was instant. *'Sure no probs.'*

Before heading to the shopping centre, I decided to pay a visit to Secure Storage. Despite the company's name, there appeared to be very little security on the site and a young receptionist happily directed me to Kitty's unit.

The minute I stepped into the room I knew Dominic was right. It wasn't Kitty who was responsible for this orderly collection of memorabilia. I couldn't open a cupboard in the bungalow without something falling out and hitting me.

On bookshelves, childhood TV annuals stood like soldiers alongside music- related hardbacks, together with folders and notebooks of sheet music. Boxes stacked on the floor were all labelled; Jez's entire record collection was catalogued and stored in alphabetic order.

None of the boxes were sealed. In one, labelled *Ornaments,* I found the typical paraphernalia of a teenage boy's bedroom. Jez was a former Hampshire U14 long jump champion with a silver cup to prove it; there were medals from school sports days, commemorative beer mugs to celebrate 18th and 21st birthdays, and a collection of seaside trinkets typical of holiday souvenirs.

Did Jez take holidays? Kitty had mentioned her cruises with Hughie but I'd seen no evidence or photographs of family trips with Don Mayhew. A gaudy chipped ashtray bore the inscription *Greetings from Plymouth Hoe.* A gift perhaps? I flipped over a dog-eared postcard of Warwick Castle. *Dear Jez, went to see a band at the SU bar last night, nowhere near as good as UR. Visiting Dad weekend of the 1st. Meet up Friday? Usual place, usual time? Lou-Lou X*

So Lindy had remained in touch with Jez when she'd headed off to university. Was that significant? The postmark was too faded to decipher a date. She could have been in her first term, or her last. Surely if Lindy was still involved with Jez at the time of his disappearance, Terri Cawle would have relished the opportunity to mention it?

I returned the postcard to its home at the bottom of the box, sensing its displacement might be noticed.

I looked around the storeroom in despair. Besides the boxes and crates there were three guitar cases, together with amps, microphone stands, two filing cabinets and four large suitcases. My morbid curiosity got the better of me. I gingerly opened one of the suitcases to be hit by the overpowering aroma of old leather. I lifted out a jacket, a waistcoat and trousers. I'd seen photographs of Jez wearing something similar. *She'd even kept his boots. And cleaned them.*

Surely in the natural course of events, this mausoleum of a teenager's infatuation would have been cleared by now? Lindy's assertion that nobody knew Jez better than she did was starting to bear an alarmingly ghoulish ring of truth.

I couldn't wait to get out of the room and back into the fresh air.

I persuaded the manageress of a vintage second-hand shop to stay open just long enough so that I could take a better look at a burnt orange strappy maxi dress hanging in the window. She refused to allow me to try it on but I decided the uniqueness was worth the risk. Back in the bungalow the rashness of my decision became apparent. The dress was certainly striking; it showed off my newly acquired suntan and it clung in all the right places, but a little too well. I would have to hold my stomach in for the entire evening. Hopefully the Quay House would offer a choice of salads.

I decided to get up extra early on Friday morning and head out for a run. Hobo was due to take care of the junkyard which at least would give me time to complete a routine of waxing, nail polish and re-application of hair colour before the afternoon's classes. There would be no time on Saturday for pampering. A shampoo-in application of *Toffee Fudge* hastily purchased in Boots the previous evening promised 'elements of summer' and was lighter than my previous shade. I was aiming for a more fun, casual look, with the ulterior motive of eventually returning to being an unnatural, sun-kissed blonde.

I knew Hookes Bay well enough now to know the most strenuous jogging routes. A full workout would involve a circuit of the nature reserve. I paced along the perimeter fence of the old airfield and headed towards the wetlands. Perhaps a triathlon was an obtainable ambition after all.

A couple of dog walkers were on the track ahead. I immediately reduced my pace. I'd never have put Lindy Mayhew down as an early riser but it wasn't so much Lindy I wished to avoid, as her companion. I recognised the second dog as the Staffie who'd nearly bitten my ankles off once before, and unless I was much mistaken, the dog's owner was Grant Hastings.

Thankfully there was a split in the path and Lindy and Hastings disappeared out of my view. I took the more overgrown track through scrubland and yellow gorse towards Craven Farm. As I ran past the observation point I threw a casual glance over my shoulder. Lindy and Grant were still on the path below. He had his arms around her and she was sobbing against his chest.

An allegiance between Lindy Mayhew and Grant Hastings was an unexpected and additional menace. Lindy had contacts on the local newspaper. Hastings just had contacts. How much digging would they have to do to uncover my true identity? One word from either of them and the whole strategy for saving the pavilion could come crumbling down. I could almost see the headlines now in the *Sunday Stargazer*: '*Tarty Tara Does It Again...*'

Friday afternoons were always hectic, leaving no time to dwell on the risk of an untimely exposé. I wanted to ask Kitty more about Lindy, but I didn't know where to begin. Kitty didn't like talking about Jez, which had become apparent when I'd tried to tackle her about Derek Woodford. Her past revolved around the pavilion, around her life in 'the business' as she called it. I could hardly confess to snooping around the storage unit.

She was looking decidedly grey when I arrived home after classes on Friday evening and even greyer on Saturday morning, refusing my offer of help to get out of bed. She assured me Robbie would call in later.

My date with Dominic couldn't come soon enough. I arrived back at Crabhook Lane at seven so full of excited anticipation that it didn't even register that Cyril's scooter was not parked in its regular Saturday evening spot on the drive.

It was only when I tried the handle and discovered the conservatory door locked that I realised something was wrong. No Cyril. No fish and chips. No Kitty.

I hurried back around to the front door. Once inside the bungalow it was quite apparent what had happened. The 'emergency hospital bag' that Kitty kept by her bed was gone. I tried Robbie's number. It went straight to voicemail which immediately made me even more anxious.

I phoned Dominic. It seemed rather callous to go out for a romantic meal if Kitty was on her last legs, but on the other hand, she'd rallied round before. My dilemma was compounded when Dominic didn't pick up either.

I called Penny. She hadn't heard from Lindy or Robbie but suggested contacting local hospitals to see if Kitty had been admitted.

'Which one would they take her to?' I asked.

'Probably St Mary's. I'll get you the number. Oh and Alice, don't panic. She's a tough old bird.'

My fingers were shaking so much I could hardly hold my phone. Kitty couldn't die yet. She couldn't die until we'd heard back from Sam MacDonald, she couldn't die until the deal with the MPT was signed and sealed.

After several minutes, the switchboard operator finally confirmed that Mrs Katherine Barker had been admitted that morning.

'Can you tell me how she is?' I asked.

'Are you a relative?'

'Yes,' I said with relief. 'I'm her granddaughter.' The words came tumbling out despite the evidence to the contrary.

To my relief the sister in charge of Kitty's ward assured me that Mrs Barker was comfortable and as well as could be expected for an eighty-eight year old woman *'in her condition.'* Alone in the empty bungalow I felt bereft. Kitty had been ever-present since I'd moved in. I wandered out into the garden. The grass was turning brown. My flowers were limp and parched, my tomatoes wilted.

I ran the outside tap, filled a couple of watering cans, and rang Dominic again. Still no reply.

There was no response from another attempt at Robbie and Lindy. My grief turned to anger that they hadn't the decency to return my calls. If anything did happen to Kitty the first thing Robbie would do would be to give me my marching orders out of the bungalow. I had to concoct Plan B and it wouldn't come from pacing the back garden like a caged lion.

8.15 pm. The speediest date preparation ever was all in vain because there was still no sign of Dominic. The burnt orange maxi dress seemed far too garish for my sombre mood.

8.30 pm. No reply from Dominic. No calls from the Mayhews.

I decided to set off for the junkyard. Maybe Dominic had got caught up in something and forgotten the time. If not, and he was driving down from the caravan park, I could flag him down. The red van was parked on the marina. My first instinct was correct. Typical.

The warehouse was in darkness. I hesitated.

'Dominic?' Nothing. I continued into the depths of the boatshed. 'Dom? Are you here?'

A small noise, like a shuffle, from the office.

'Dominic, is that you?'

Another grunt.

'Jesus!' I flicked on the office light. Dominic was curled up on the floor in the foetal position, blood all over his face, his white T-shirt covered in filthy footprints. 'Christ, Dominic, what happened? I grabbed the rag by the sink that served as a tea-towel. 'You need an ambulance.'

'No.' At last he could speak, spitting out blood.

'Dominic, you can't move.'

'Yus I can. Help me up.'

I manoeuvred him into a sitting position, propped up against the filing cabinet. 'That's better,' he groaned. I didn't like the way he was holding his right arm.

I looked for his phone then saw it, smashed and kicked out of reach. 'Who did this?' Instantly I thought of the thugs outside the Indian takeaway. A shove in the street was different. This was a thorough beating. 'What would have happened if I hadn't come along?'

'Someone would have missed me eventually,' he grunted.

'How long ago did this happen?'

'I dunno... couple of hours maybe. I was about to leave to go and get ready. Nice dress.'

A nice dress now covered in blood and totally impractical for crawling around on all fours. I had to hitch it up onto my thighs in a very unladylike fashion.

'I really think that cut needs stitches,' I said, looking at the wound above his eye, 'and your arm doesn't look quite right.'

He winced as I touched it. 'Nurse Alice can make it better,' he muttered.

'No. Nurse Alice is going to call an ambulance.' I had to take control. 'This is a criminal offence which needs to be reported. Who was it? Danni's boyfriend?'

'Hastings offered me my house back.' Dominic said as my fingers poised over the keypad on my phone. 'And my business.'

'He what?'

'If I withdraw all negotiations with the MPT I can keep The Mill House and the whole practice.'

'You are joking?'

Dominic shook his head. He seemed to be finding it easier to talk. 'He came to see me this afternoon.'

'And then did this to you?' I was appalled.

'No, this was a couple of his friends. They called by a bit later.'

'You mean his thugs?'

'It wasn't anyone I recognised but undoubtedly it's Hastings' idea of aiding the decision making process.'

I stared at him. 'But what about the legal proceedings?'

'He'll refund all my costs.'

'I take it you turned down his offer?'

'Of course I did. We're this close to securing the pavilion's future. I'm not going to pull out now.'

I liked a man with principles and pride. My admiration for Dominic was growing by the minute. Unfortunately, it might all be irrelevant. I dabbed at his eye again. 'Kitty's gone into hospital,' I told him.

'That's not good news. Still, it's probably the safest place for her right now.'

'Why?'

'Because it will save Robbie Mayhew from having to put a pillow over her head.'

'Robbie? It's Lindy we ought to be worrying about. I've seen her and Hastings together a couple of times up at the nature reserve, walking their dogs. They seem pretty close.'

Now didn't seem the time to say anything more.

'Lindy Mayhew and Grant Hastings?' He considered the idea. 'I suppose it might explain a few things.' He winced as he tried to move into a more comfortable position. 'Christ that hurts.' He clutched at his right shoulder.

'Come on, you really do need to get to A&E,' I said.

'Can't you drive me? I don't want a fuss.'

'I can't drive, remember.'

'How does anyone not drive these days?'

'I grew up in London, I work in London. I've never needed a car.'

'Shit.' Dominic moved again. 'Okay, but I don't want an ambulance.'

I had no choice but to call a Coastline Cab.

Chapter Thirty-Six

Four hours later, Dominic was patched up after being diagnosed with a broken collar bone and fractured ribs. He had six stitches above his eye.

'You can't go back to the caravan and be by yourself,' I said as we waited for yet another Coastline Cab to take us back to Hookes Bay. 'Not tonight.'

'Nurse Alice, are you propositioning me?' He gave me a weak smile.

I offered him my arm to lean on. 'Tara. My real name is Tara Wakely.'

I don't know what made me say it. Perhaps I just wanted Dominic to have a chance to get to know the real me, or at least, a pared-down version of the real me, before everything imploded on us.

'Tara.' He rolled the word around his tongue. 'I like it. Tara. The Seat of Irish Kings.'

It was almost as if he hadn't fully heard. I held my breath and waited but he said no more. With an enormous sense of relief, I realised that the reference to an ancient myth from his homeland was the only connection that came to his mind.

Back at Crabhook Lane I insisted he have my room for the night.

'Shouldn't you stay with me? I might have concussion.'

I helped him out of his blood stained T-shirt and shorts. He slipped under the sheet in his boxers, embarrassed, but grateful. For once I knew when to keep silent. I stayed on top of the sheet. We sat side by side, propped up against the fussy, floral pillows.

This was how I had always wanted us to be, together with no lies between us, but not with Kitty about to die and the pavilion about to fall into Robbie's hands. What if the MPT came up with an offer on Monday? Could the paperwork be prepared in time? Would anything signed on a deathbed be legal? Surely Robbie would contest it? We were already flogging a dead horse.

Instinctively I rested my head on Dominic's good shoulder. He didn't shrug me off, although in fairness that was probably because he couldn't. He smelt of disinfectant.

'Sing something.'

'I'm sorry?'

'When we first met, that day I showed you the pavilion, you said you were a singer.'

'You remember?'

'Of course I remember.'

I was filled with a warm sense of vindication. I had been right all along. The chemistry had been there from day one.

'What would you like me to sing?'

'I dunno.' His voice was slurred and woozy, the effects of the high-dose painkillers. 'Something soothing.'

I had an extensive repertoire of songs, musical classics I knew word for word, but there was one song that had been written specifically for me, a ballad, to be sung unaccompanied. Hal had commissioned a solo for *Rockabilly Rose*; something, he said, which suited my 'husky, dusky, slightly off-key' voice perfectly. *You'll have the audience in tears*, Hal had insisted. I'd never had the chance.

'I'll sing *Who Needs Nashville When There's Cornbread to be Baked*,' I said.

'I'm sorry I don't know that one.'

'It's from a new musical, a sort of Cinderella story, set in small town mid-west, 1950s. A girl and her two brothers enter a talent contest with the prize of a trip to Nashville. The boys head off without her, saying Rose has to stay home to look after the farm because their daddy is ill. Then while she's at home, baking cornbreads, this stranger turns up, his van's broken down outside the farm, and he hears Rose singing. Turns out he's a Colonel Tom Parker-type character, something big in the music industry so he signs her up and she goes to Nashville anyway.'

Dominic's eyelids were drooping.

'I'll just get on and sing it, shall I?' I said.

'Yes, please.'

It was weeks since I'd used my voice for anything other than shouting directions in class, but after a faltering start, I completed the first two verses.

'That was beautiful,' Dominic slurred.

'I didn't think you were still awake.'

'I'm not.' His voice was tender. 'Thank you, Tara.'

'What for?' I murmured. 'Messing up your life?'

'No,' he replied, 'for coming into it.'

His good hand gently stroked my hair. I felt his lips softly brush against the top of my head.

'Night Tara.'

'Night Dom.'

When I awoke in the morning light was streaming in through curtains. Dominic was sleeping, his breathing regular and sound, slumped slightly to one side. I slipped off the bed and plumped up the pillows. Keeping upright was imperative, they had been very insistent at the hospital. His right eye was swelling nicely and his cheek was a lovely shade of purple. I had a quick shower and returned to the bedroom just as he was stirring.

'You need to take these,' I said, placing a couple of painkillers and glass of water on the bedside cabinet. 'If you give me your key I'll head over to the caravan park and pick up some clean clothes for you.'

'I don't know where the key is. It was in my shorts pocket.'

'Well, there's no sign of it now,' I replied, shaking out his shorts. 'It probably fell out when they knocked you to the ground. I'll go via the yard. See if I can find it.'

I had locked the gates to the yard behind us when we left and had those keys safely in my handbag.

'Thanks. My other mobile's up at the caravan. Can you fetch that too? And my laptop, is that at the yard? I'll need that.'

'No you won't. There's no Wi-Fi here,' I reminded him. 'I'll look for your mobile. Do you know where it is?'

'Bedside drawers. And no rummaging around. I know what you women are like.'

'Rummaging around in your drawers is the last thing on my mind right now,' I assured him. His painful look of mock disappointment cheered me up no end.

I found Dominic's door key after a quick scramble around on the floor of his office. From the marina I cycled straight to Craven Farm. There were about twenty very permanent-looking mobile homes on the site, some with wooden verandas complete with patio sets and flower boxes although Dominic's possessed only the minimal of personal touches. I resisted the urge to rummage and grabbed underwear, a pair of clean shorts and a couple of loose-fitting tank-tops and front buttoning shirts.

As I cut back into town through the nature reserve I spotted Lindy Mayhew's familiar cream mini in the car park. There was no sign of Lindy, or the dog, but I recognised the car she was parked next to. She and Grant Hastings obviously couldn't keep their hands off each other. It seemed obscene with Kitty at death's door.

When I returned to the bungalow, Dominic was fast asleep again. As I unpacked new supplies of pain relief and lemon barley water my phone rang. It was Robbie. I headed out into the garden to answer the call.

'We should have let you know last night but I'm assuming you realised Kit was admitted to hospital. Anyway, thank you for concern. We were at the hospital all day.'

'Actually, I rung around last night, found out where she was.'

'Oh good. Lindy's already gone in again this morning, but it's nothing to worry about. Kit just had a bit of a turn. Gave us all a bit of a fright I think.'

I could hardly contradict him about Lindy's whereabouts. 'Would you mind if I visited?' I asked.

'Um... no of course not. She'd probably like that very much. Maybe wait until tomorrow?'

'Sure. Perhaps I could bring something in for her?' I was revelling in my nursing role.

'Lindy said she'd drop by to collect some clean night clothes.'

'Oh. Okay.'

I needed to be on high alert. The minute I had ended the call from Robbie the front doorbell rang, making me jump out of my skin. It couldn't be Lindy as she would let herself in around the back. Dominic would definitely have to remain confined to my room at the front. This thought, and its implications brought an involuntarily smile to my face. As I was already outside I skipped around to the front garden.

Kitty's neighbour, Mrs Deacon, stood on the doorstep.

'I wasn't sure anyone was home,' she said. 'Just wanted to check if there was any news? We saw the ambulance yesterday.'

I had gathered quite early on that the Deacons, a quiet retired couple, tended to keep themselves to themselves, or at least keep themselves out of Kitty's way.

'Kitty's fine,' I assured her. 'Thank you. I'm not sure when she'll be home but apparently it's nothing too serious.'

'That's good,' Mrs Deacon gave a knowing nod. 'I'll leave you be. You'll let the old solicitor chappie know? I managed to head him off at the pass yesterday when he turned up with his fish and chips, bless him. He seemed quite upset.'

'Solicitor?' Then it dawned on me. 'Cyril, of course. I'll pop round and tell him later. Thank you.'

The doorbell woke Dominic up. 'Did you know Cyril used to be a solicitor?' I asked as I perched on the bed laying out the clothes I had retrieved from the caravan.

'Yes, of course. He's been a great help keeping Robbie on his toes.'

I handed him more painkillers. 'Cyril, a help?'

He struggled to mimic Cyril's habitual wink. 'When you might need a last minute change to your will, it's very handy to have your personal solicitor on call. Kitty's a crafty old witch.'

I told Dominic I'd seen Lindy and Hastings up at the nature

reserve again. 'Whatever she is doing with Grant Hastings she's keeping it a secret from Robbie.'

'If they are having an affair, it wouldn't be his first that's for sure,' Dominic replied. 'I need to stretch my legs.'

'Shall I wait outside while you get dressed?'

'Embarrassing though this is going to be, I might need you to help me.'

I held up a pair of clean boxers and smiled. 'With these?'

'No,' he grinned, 'with my shirt. I need the bathroom first.' He snatched at his boxers with his good hand and swung his legs out of bed. I helped him to his feet. He staggered off to the bathroom clutching his underwear and shorts. More cuts and bruising were visible on his back. Hastings' thugs had really laid into him.

With Dominic occupied I went into Kitty's bedroom to pre-empt Lindy's visit. For some reason I didn't want Lindy snooping around Kitty's room, although I was now doing exactly that.

'Georgie's new love interest?' ran the headline on the copy of *Let's Chat* magazine I found shoved into the bedside drawer. *'Is it all over with Hal Claydon?'*

I no longer cared. Events on the south coast had taken precedent, and London didn't just seem physically miles away, it belonged to a different lifetime. With no intention other than a quick, satisfying gloat, I flicked to the relevant pages in the magazine.

'Georgie Gold (22) was spotted canoodling with male model Josh Yates (26) at a recent party at Gigi's Nightclub in Soho, fuelling speculation that her engagement to theatre director, Hal Claydon (43) may be off. Ticket sales for Georgie's West End debut, Rockabilly Rose, *have slumped following a series of bad reviews. Known as a hard task master Claydon dumped his long-term live in lover, actress Tara Wakely, in favour of Georgie following her appearance on the talent show* Make Me A Star. *If Georgie has already moved on to Josh, does this mean that Claydon may be ready to forgive his ex in order to save his failing show? Tara Wakely*

hasn't been seen since supposedly fleeing to Thailand on retreat, following her vehement attack on Georgie's acting ability.'

Although there appeared to be no further evidence that Georgie's relationship with Hal was over apart from the night club sighting, the article left me perturbed. A minuscule and thankfully murky picture of Hal and me, taken at the very start of our relationship, accompanied the feature. Returning my hair to some semblance of its natural colour no longer seemed such a good idea. Unfortunately I now looked far more like the Tara Wakely in this picture, than I did in the infamous shot that had graced the *Sunday Stargazer*.

Just as I was about to shove the magazine back into the drawer, I heard the scrunch of tyres on the gravel. No wonder security experts always recommended gravel as a burglary deterrent. It was an excellent early warning system.

I just managed to help Dominic back to my bedroom before Lindy made her entrance through the conservatory.

'How's Kitty?' I enquired at once.

'Determined to defy medical science,' Lindy replied without a trace of humour in her voice. 'I'm just here to pick up a few bits.'

'I've just started sorting out some clothes,' I said, following her into Kitty's bedroom.

'There was no need. I'm more than capable.' To my horror Lindy's eyes immediately fell onto the copy of *Let's Chat* which in my haste to hide Dominic had only made it halfway back into the bedside drawer. She picked it up without a second glance. 'I'll take this. It'll give her something to read.'

'Oh, I think she's probably already seen that one,' I said, making a grab for the magazine. As I lurched forward she swept *Let's Chat* out of my reach so that I was left clutching nothing more than the front cover.

'Now look what you've done,' she glared.

'I'm sorry,' I muttered, willing her to discard what was left of the magazine into the nearest bin. Instead she made a point of placing the tattered remains firmly into her bag, together with the clean nightdress and underwear I had already sorted out.

'Even if Kitty has seen this edition, it will give me something to read. You've no idea how tedious sickbed duty can be. Trust me, I've years of experience. Even the most downmarket reading material can suddenly seem illuminating.'

Let's Chat could prove more than illuminating. Lindy was an intelligent woman. How long before she put two and two together?

Like Kitty, I too could be living on borrowed time.

Chapter Thirty-Seven

On Monday Dominic had an emergency dental appointment which he insisted he could manage without me. As Hobo offered to pick him up and drop him back I cadged a lift into Fareham to catch the train into Portsmouth to visit Kitty.

The hospital was a maze of outbuildings but I eventually tracked Kitty down. Her eyes were closed when I arrived but I sat by the bed and talked regardless of her inability to respond. There was no point telling her about Dominic, about Hastings' threats or attempts to bribe the parish council. Instead I rambled on about the plans for the summer showcase and recounted the tale of my first professional job – a stint in a theme park production of *Aladdin*, which had resulted in hospitalisation following a fall from the flying carpet.

One eye opened. 'Clumsy girl,' she muttered. 'I wouldn't have given you a role in one of my shows.'

I squeezed her hand and her fingers clasped around mine.

'Any news from that trust fund?' she asked hoarsely.

I shook my head. 'Not yet.'

What time did we have left? Days, weeks? It certainly wasn't months anymore.

'You will come again, won't you?' she asked as I kissed her goodbye.

'Of course.'

I followed the signs for the exit and ended up in a totally different part of the hospital complex, leading out into a narrow one way street. I set off in search of the bus to take me back to the central station. An old church stood at the end of the street and on the pavement, even closer than I had hoped, was a bus stop. The bus timetable revealed that buses called at St Nicholas' Church every half an hour and I had just missed one.

The church was no longer a place of worship. A discreet sign in the old porch welcomed visitors to the St Nicholas Homeless Shelter. According to Maureen Batty, St Nick's was the last known abode of her nephew Woody. I was probably wasting my time, but I had half an hour to kill and nothing to lose. I took a deep breath and pushed open the door.

The small shabby reception area was unmanned. I rang the bell by the Perspex window and a man in his mid-to-late thirties with dirty blonde dreadlocks emerged from a rear office.

'Hi, how can I help?'

'I know I'm clutching at straws,' I began, 'but I was just wondering if you have any record of a man named Derek Woodford? I believe he may have stayed at this shelter many years ago. He might have called himself Woody back then.'

'Derek Woodford?'

I felt a glimmer of hope in the way the man repeated Derek's name. 'You know him?'

'Oh yes,' he confirmed, 'we know Derek Woodford very well.'

'You do? That's fantastic. Do you know where I could find him? I'd really like to get in touch.'

'Are you a relative? A friend?'

'I'm a friend, of a friend. My dad,' the little white lie slipped out so easily, 'used to play in the same band as Derek, back in the 1980s.'

'Well, you're in luck. Father Derek is with us this morning. He's down the corridor in the billiard room. I'll take you on through.'

Father Derek? Had Woody been using the facilities for so long he could claim the status of patriarch of the shelter? How could I possibly confront a man who'd been homeless for years with wild accusations about Jez's disappearance? In any case, Derek had a drink problem. Would he even remember pushing his best friend off the pier?

Derek Woodford stood beside the pool table surrounded by a group of young men. I recognised him immediately from the photographs in his aunt's scrapbook. He wore baggy jeans, a checked shirt, and a very visible dog-collar. Not an elderly down-and-out, but a man of God.

'You've got a visitor, Father,' the receptionist announced.

All heads turned. Derek looked up and smiled. He had broken yellowing teeth and his thin grey hair was tied behind his back in a long straggly plait. A very modern priest. Perhaps he had found God later in life. Perhaps he had needed to salve his conscience?

'How can I help?' he enquired.

'This is going to sound so stupid,' I said. 'But I was wondering if I could talk to you about Jez Keaton.'

He frowned. 'Do I know you?'

I shook my head. 'I am a friend of Kitty's. My name is Alice Paige.' The white lie I had told the receptionist was not so readily forthcoming this time round, although the second one slipped off my tongue like second nature.

'Okay, I can spare a few minutes.' He handed his cue to one of the young men. 'Here Billy, take my place. Shall we go somewhere private?'

I followed him out of the billiard room and into a kitchen off a communal dining area. He made two coffees and we sat at one end of a large Formica table, cups in hand.

'How is Kitty?' he asked.

'She's not well.' I was at a loss to know in what direction to steer the conversation. 'She's in hospital and is currently on borrowed time. I've just been visiting her.'

'In St Mary's, is she?'

'Yes.'

'I might pop in and see her then.' He gave me another gap-toothed smile. His face was a mass of lines, crow's feet that almost stretched to his ears. 'We go back a long way, as you must know if you want to talk about Jez.' He gave me a puzzled look. 'You do look familiar.'

'I've just got one of those faces.' I returned his smile. 'Look, the thing is, Kitty hasn't got long left, and I just thought, you know, she's never had closure about Jez, about what happened that night. I've heard all the rumours, and the suppositions, and I know Kit doesn't believe it was an accident. I've been trying to ask around, hoping that somebody might know, or remember, something that maybe they didn't confess at the time, that might help her, to put her mind finally at rest.'

'So that's why you've come to see me? You think I have some vital piece of information I've been withholding for the last thirty years? I wasn't even there.'

'I know that. But I also know about Stevie Newman-Smith and the solo record deal.'

Derek raised a sparse grey eyebrow. 'Stevie Newman-Smith? That's a name I haven't heard for a few years. You have done your research, young lady. What would they call Stevie now? There's a term they use, isn't there, for the older woman.'

'The older woman? You mean a cougar?'

'Yes, that's it. Poor Jez didn't know what had hit him.'

'Jez had a relationship with Stevie Newman-Smith?'

Derek nodded. 'She was all over him like a rash. I wasn't convinced the feelings were reciprocated but Stevie wasn't used to people saying no to her, and naturally Jez wanted that record deal. You look a bit surprised.'

'I'm beyond surprises,' I lied. I couldn't see how this revelation could be significant to what happened in Hookes Bay, but it almost certainly put the final nail in the coffin with regard to my parentage.

'I'd just really like to know what happened the night Jez went missing,' I reiterated. 'Why didn't you turn up for the party?'

'A lot of what happened in my past is lost in the fog,' Derek confessed. 'I had an alcohol problem for many years, and before you get any ideas, it had started long before Jez Keaton told me he was quitting Urban Rebel to pursue a solo career. We met in Pebbles that afternoon. He wanted to tell me about Stevie's offer before he told the others because he knew how much the band meant to me. Vince was a talented musician with a great personality but his heart wasn't in it anymore. That had become apparent when we were in London. We all knew he was gay. Jez told me Vince was about to 'come out', a pretty bold move back in those days, and apparently he'd already talked about going off to pursue other ventures. We were a rock band and Vince was getting more into electro pop. Paulo had always been happiest when he was working in the restaurant. He'd only stuck with the band so long to keep an eye on Vince, but me and Jez, well, we'd been together since we were thirteen, fourteen.' Derek locked his forefingers together. 'I thought we were like that.

'I'll admit, I was devastated when he broke the news. I called him every name under the sun, even took a swing at him, and missed, incidentally, then I took the train into Pompey and drunk myself stupid. I ended up in the police cells overnight. They told me I'd smashed in a window in a record store. I had no knowledge of what I'd done. Mickey's Records used to be my favourite shop, it's where Jez and I used to hang out on a Saturday afternoon when we were teenagers. I couldn't ever imagine being that violent, but that's what it does to you, drink, you see. It destroys you, and it makes you destroy the things you love.'

'So the night Jez went missing you were in police custody?'

Derek nodded. 'Now you look disappointed. Did you think his going off that pier had something to do with me?'

I hastily shook my head. 'No, of course not.'

'I don't blame Jez for wanting stardom,' Derek continued, before I had a chance to compose my thoughts. 'We were both chasing the same dream. Would I have done the same if Stevie Newman-Smith had singled me out from the others? I expect so. Without a doubt, Jez would have been a huge star. But it didn't happen. I lost a good friend and we parted on bad terms. I've had to live with that.'

'Is that why you turned to God?'

'I've done time, love. Prison. Let's just say over the years I've had ample opportunity to reflect and contemplate the meaning of life.'

'So what do you think happened? I've seen pictures of Jez balancing on the end of that pier on one leg. What happened to make him fall?'

'Sometimes we just have to accept there's no one to blame,

no-one responsible,' Derek replied with a placid smile. 'As much as we look for answers, there aren't any.' He glanced up at the kitchen clock on the wall. 'Now, I really should be getting back to my game of pool.'

'You really think he just tripped up?' I could barely hide my frustration. I had gone around in a complete circle and eliminated all of my chief suspects in one go. I should never have listened to Terri Cawle and her salacious rumours.

Father Derek stood up. 'I'm very sorry if I haven't told you what you wanted to hear.' He picked up the empty coffee cups. 'Let me just pop these into the kitchen and I'll walk you back to reception.'

I couldn't leave St Nick's empty handed. 'Before you go,' I said, following him into the kitchenette, 'could you just answer one more question?'

'I'll try.'

'Lindy Cartwright, Robbie Mayhew's wife. She and Jez were close when they were younger, weren't they? I just wondered when it all fizzled out.' I thought about the contents of Kitty's lock-up. '*If* it fizzled out. I mean they'd been friends for a long time. Just because she went off to university it didn't mean they stopped seeing each other, did it? She must have come back to Hookes Bay pretty regularly to visit her father. Did she ever come to the club? Where was she the night he went missing?'

The coffee cups clattered to the floor.

'So sorry,' Father Derek said, clutching hold of the sink. 'I've been dry for ten years and I still get the shakes every once in a while. Being born clumsy doesn't help.'

I bent to the floor and picked up the cups. 'No damage done,' I said.

'Thank goodness for the wonders of melamine,' Derek murmured. 'This place wouldn't have any crockery left otherwise. Did you drive here or use public transport?'

'I was asking you about Lindy?' I reminded him.

Derek's composure had returned. 'Oh, we hardly saw Lou in Hookes Bay once she'd gone off to university. It was all over between her and Jez. All over long ago.'

Chapter Thirty-Eight

Derek Woodford was a man of God. Surely I had more reason to believe his version of events than Terri's Cawle's spurious tale, so why did I leave St Nick's with the distinct impression he hadn't been entirely honest with me? Something about my mention of Lindy Mayhew had ruffled him. I had lots to think about on the return journey to Hookes Bay. I hopped off the bus outside Wheatsheaf Court and called in on Cyril to update him on Kitty's situation.

He was entertaining Maureen Batty.

'Come and join us, my dear,' he insisted. 'The pot has just brewed.'

I knew from experience that Cyril liked his tea dark and sweet. Maureen was in charge of the catering arrangements and presented us both with cups slopping with an insipid milky liquid.

'How was Kitty?' she fussed as I sat down with great care.

'Quite chirpy,' I replied. I wasn't sure whether it was wise to mention my encounter with her nephew at St Nick's.

'Cyril and I were just talking about you, weren't we?' Maureen continued. 'Were your ears burning?'

I shook my head. 'What were you saying?'

'That it must be a source of great comfort for Kitty to have you here, my dear,' Cyril said, reaching across and patting my knee.

'I've found something else for you of young Jez's,' Maureen said. 'Don't let me forget to go and fetch it before you leave.'

'Perhaps it would be wise to go and fetch it now?' Cyril suggested with a patient smile.

Maureen hopped to her feet, totally oblivious to the tea spilling onto Cyril's carpet from the cup in her hand. 'Yes, of course. Good idea. You know I have a memory like one of those big tea strainer things.'

'You mean a sieve, Mo, dear.'

'Yes. That's right,' she giggled like a school girl. 'I'll be two ticks.'

Whilst she was out of the room I hastily relieved Cyril of his tea cup and deposited the contents in the sink.

'She means well,' Cyril commented gratefully, 'but there are limits.'

In Maureen's absence I filled Cyril in on the events of the last couple of days. He was appalled at the attack on Dominic.

'Hastings has openly overstepped the mark this time,' he grunted. 'Young Flynn needs to press charges.'

'That's what I told him,' I agreed. 'Unfortunately the problem will be proving that Hastings had anything to do with the gorillas who set on Dominic.'

'Sadly I suspect you're right,' Cyril sighed. He took off his spectacles and rubbed at his left eye. 'A lot of the dubious goings on in Hookes Bay have tenuous links to Hastings, but somehow he just manages to keep himself above the law. He seems very good at coercing people into doing his dirty work for him.'

'Do you think Robbie Mayhew owes him money? Is that why he is so keen to let Hastings have the pavilion?'

Cyril shook his head. 'For all his faults, Robbie is not a gambler, and I can't think why he would have needed to borrow money from Hastings. Lindy is a wealthy woman in her own right; her father left her everything so money has never been an issue.'

'Unless Robbie needed money for something he didn't want Lindy to know about?'

'Lindy seems just as keen to be rid of the pavilion as Robbie,' Cyril mused, 'if not keener.'

'Do you think Lindy and Hastings could be having an affair?' I asked just as Maureen Batty returned to the room. She handed me a tatty cassette case.

'There you go, dear. It's a recording of Urban Rebel. Thought you might like a listen. What are you two gossiping about now?'

'The Mayhews,' Cyril volunteered. 'Alice wonders if Lindy and Grant Hastings are having an affair?'

'I wouldn't put anything past that one,' Maureen huffed. 'Back in the old days she was always sneaking around behind her father's back, hanging out on the pier and at the club with the boys. She might be all sophisticated now but that wasn't always the case. A zebra never changes its stripes, isn't that what they tell you?'

'It's a leopard and its spots, Maureen,' Cyril corrected.

'Whatever. I see you've finished your tea. Would you like another cup?'

When I returned to Crabhook Lane Dominic was slumped in Kitty's chair in the conservatory, his face puffed up like a hamster.

'What was the verdict?' I asked.

'An extraction,' he muttered. 'I'll have to have an implant.' He could barely muster a smile to show me the damage. 'How was Kitty?'

'Tired, but worrying about the pavilion.'

'I'll chase Sam MacDonald as soon as I can talk,' he promised, waving a pharmacy bag at me. 'Meanwhile it's more painkillers.'

'I think you're more doped up than Kitty,' I remarked.

Dominic was determined the yard should continue with business as usual and I agreed to cover the office for the next couple of days. Tuesday was quiet, Hobo pottered in and out making a few deliveries and Aidan Chapman, a reticent young man hiding behind an abundance of unnecessary facial hair, called by hoping to thank Dominic personally for the tip-off regarding his stove.

Just as I was saying goodbye to Aidan my phone rang. Only a very few people possessed my number, and fearing the worse regarding news of Kitty, I answered with a hasty 'hello' without even thinking to check the caller ID.

A male voice responded. 'Hello, Tara.' I froze. Why had I thought for one minute that I could escape my past? The last time I'd heard those smooth dulcet tones I'd been in a hotel bedroom in Knightsbridge. How the hell had James Coulter tracked me down? 'That is you, isn't it, Tara? A little bird told me this was your new number.'

Ending the call without speaking would only confirm all James needed to know. I had to think on my feet.

'I'm so very sorry,' I said in my best impression of Samantha MacDonald. 'You must have the wrong number. I don't know anyone called Tara.'

'Are you sure about that?'

'I think I know who I am, young man.'

Aidan Chapman raised an eyebrow. He had no idea of my name but he certainly knew that less than two minutes previously I'd been speaking to him without any trace of a Scottish accent. I smiled as I pressed the end call button. 'Sorry about that,' I said. 'PPI. It's the only way to get rid of them.'

I returned the phone to the desk as if it were contaminated. I told myself it was just an opportunist phone call. I trusted my friends and my family implicitly. The only way James Coulter could have got hold of my number was from someone who wished me harm. It had never occurred to me not to leave Lindy my mobile number as I rang around frantically on Saturday evening seeking news of Kitty. If Lindy had made the connection from reading the incriminating edition of *Let's Chat*, was it too much to hope that she had simply passed my number onto James to confirm her hunch? I could only pray my Samantha MacDonald impersonation had been enough to put him off the scent.

Chapter Thirty-Nine

I stopped at the Co-op on my way back to Crabhook Lane and purchased yet another new SIM card. I had little choice if I wanted to keep James Coulter at bay. I dreaded the thought of having to resort to more furtive scurrying from Kitty's bungalow to the junkyard or community centre and back, continuingly looking over my shoulder for a hiding journalist. Surely nobody was interested in the Georgie Gold versus Tara Wakely affair anymore? Georgie had moved on by all accounts, so why couldn't I?

Dominic was still zonked out, although he was talking of heading back to his mobile home within the next few days.

'You're in no fit state to look after yourself,' I pouted. 'Don't you like being here with me?'

'Have you seen the film *Misery*?' he joked. 'I think you're starting to enjoy my incapacity just a little too much.'

There was an element of truth in what he said. I did like having him at the bungalow, although any thoughts of a seduction scene were currently completely off the cards.

I kept my phone on silent and my laptop and Kitty's PC quite firmly switched off. I'd promised Kitty I'd visit her again and after my Wednesday afternoon class I set off for Portsmouth. Kitty seemed quite revived, although apparently there were no plans for her to return home.

'They want to run some further tests,' she told me rather proudly. 'Seems I'm a medical phenomenon. We Keatons are a special breed.' As Kitty was only a Keaton by marriage, and I wasn't a Keaton at all, I wasn't sure we had any claim to a miraculous hereditary gene-pool. She was enjoying the attention of the nurses, and Dominic was right, the hospital was probably the safest place for her. If everything blew up in Hookes Bay, it was best she was out of the way.

Her talk of her Keaton heritage reminded me I had yet to play the tape Maureen Batty had passed on to me. Kitty kept an old cassette radio in her kitchen, and as Dominic had seemed in better spirits when I'd left to take my class, I planned to cook him something special for dinner, especially as the effects of his visit to the dentist appeared to be wearing off. Urban Rebel could provide the musical accompaniment. On my way home from the hospital I stopped at Sainsbury's to pick up the ingredients for a risotto.

The murmur of male voices stopped me in my tracks even before I reached the side gate. Dominic had a visitor. There was no sign of Robbie's car in the street, or Hobo's truck. A growing sense of dread took hold in the pit of my stomach. I edged along the side wall of the bungalow, hardly daring to breathe.

'So,' I heard Dominic say, quite cheerfully in his thickest Irish accent, 'your next project is definitely going to be this musical set on a futuristic space station? You really think that would work?'

'I'd like to think audiences are ready to embrace the space age,' his companion replied.

I placed my carrier bags onto the gravel of the drive and slipped off the latch on the gate without making a sound. Creeping like a cat burglar I craned my neck to try and make out the shapes behind the frosted glass of the conservatory side panel.

It couldn't be. Not here. Not now. James Coulter had been bad enough, but he'd been safely tucked away in London at the end of a phone line and I would continue to refute his claim that I was Tara Wakely until he could prove otherwise. But this was different. This was a total intrusion into my privacy, an invasion of calamitous proportions. What an earth was Hal doing here in Hookes Bay?

'Right.' Dominic sounded unconvinced. I could hardly blame him. I'd told Hal a couple of years back that his idea for a sci-fi musical was a non-starter. Dominic was in Kitty's chair where I'd left him. Hal sat opposite, facing the window. The French doors to the garden were wide open. 'So what makes you think that this friend of yours would be ideal for the starring role?'

'Because I owe her a starring role,' Hal replied. He had to be drunk. 'I've messed up big time, mate, and I would do anything to get her back. She'd have been bloody brilliant in *Rockabilly Rose*. Now the show's going to close. I've been a complete fool.'

Why was Dominic engaging Hal in conversation about musicals? Why hadn't he just told him to get the first train back up to London?

'You have no idea what a prick I've been,' Hal continued.

'Oh, try me,' Dominic suggested.

'I've been the archetypical middle-aged man in a crisis,' Hal groaned. 'Some young girl, young enough to be my daughter, flutters her false eyelashes at me, sticks her tits in my face, and tells me I'm the man of her dreams. Sugar daddy of her dreams more like. There's no fool like an old fool. And all this time, Tara is faithfully hanging on in there, refusing to believe I could be so stupid. I treated her like shit, more or less chucked her out on the street when I knew she had nowhere to go. And then, I'm stuck with this child, out clubbing until four or five in the morning when all I want to do is go home and sit on my comfortable sofa and watch TV.'

'With Tara.'

'Yes, with Tara. I know Tara can talk, and sometimes she used to drive me nuts talking, but at least she can hold her own in a conversation. She's an intelligent woman. Georgie chirps like a little bird; tweets – yes, constantly on Twitter and Instagram, Pinterest or whatever… mindless drivel about celebrities and soap stars I've never heard of. And there's no warmth to her, no compassion. It's all about *her, her, her*, whereas I realise now, Tara was completely selfless. You know she had this totally tragic childhood, her mother committed suicide, she never knew her father, her grandparents disowned her, but she has this huge heart of gold. She gave up her free time to work with this drama group, you know, for under-privileged kids and running workshops in schools. She had this dream of running her own performing arts academy so that everybody could have the same opportunities that she had. I was going to help with the financing and she'd already started looking for premises, and then Georgie came on the scene and I let her down.

'The worse thing is, the press got hold of a story about Tara afterwards, and made her out to be this crazy, demented, jealous creature with no morals, and that isn't Tara at all. I could have defended her but I didn't. You probably saw it yourself on the internet. She supposedly stole some money intended for Somalian refugees and I knew it couldn't possibly be true. Tara's the sweetest, most considerate woman I know.'

I hoped he'd finished but with Dominic silent, he continued his woeful lament.

'What you see is what you get with Tara. There's no duplicity, she isn't capable of it. She just gets on and does things, whereas with Georgie, every move is carefully calculated for maximum publicity. I was carefully calculated. Oh yes, she wins this TV show, the production company want her in a musical, and wham bam, suddenly she hasn't just won the talent show, she's on all the front pages and in all the gossip columns.

'And the girl doesn't eat. Lettuce, a stick of celery, an occasional avocado. That's not a meal. I know Tara was very conscious about what she ate, it's a hazard of the business, I suppose, but she never expected me to follow the same bloody diet. And Tara can cook, I mean not in any great way, but Georgie can barely use a tin-opener.'

'Your Tara sounds like a great girl.'

'She is. Look, are you sure you haven't seen her?'

'No, I already told you, it's just me and my nan living here and, as I said, we had this car accident, which is why I look like this, and why my nan is currently in hospital. There's nobody else here.'

'But I was given this address on good authority. I've come all the way from London.'

'Sounds like someone has fixed you up. Sorry you had a wasted journey. Let me call you a cab to take you back to the station.' Finally Dominic had said something sensible.

'Maybe I've got the house number wrong. I should try the neighbours.'

'Oh, I wouldn't do that. I know most of the neighbours. I'd have known if she was here.'

Hal got up. I shrank back against the wall of the house. 'Shall I show you another picture? She's pretty stunning, isn't she?'

'She sure is,' Dominic conceded.

'Look at this one. We'd gone to London Zoo. Tara adopted a pair of fruit bats.'

'Good for her. Now, why don't you let me call that cab?' There was a pause before I heard Dominic again. 'Hello, can I order a taxi please, 35 Crabhook Lane, back to Fareham train station. Soon as you can. Thanks.'

Hal was now pacing the floor. 'Look, if you do see her, you know, if I leave you my number, you could let me know? I'd really appreciate it. I feel she must be in this town somewhere. I knew all that stuff about Thailand was just a ruse. Nobody, not even Tara, needs to detox for more than a couple of weeks. I need to see her, to talk to her, tell her what an idiot I've been. I'll buy her a stage school if that's what it takes, if that's what she wants. I'll set her up in business or she can go back to performing. Do you have a woman in your life... er, sorry, I've sat here rambling on and I don't even know your name.'

'It's Dominic.'

'Dominic, do you have a woman in your life?'

'Not right now, no, I don't think I do.'

'Well, when you do find the woman of your dreams, don't fuck it all up like I did. If you find your Tara, hold onto her tight and don't let her go.'

Hal's wallowing self-pity was unbearable but Dominic's denial hurt more. I turned, picked up my shopping and sprinted down to the seafront.

Chapter Forty

'Jesus, you've been gone for hours.' Dominic shuffled out from the bedroom. He was barefoot in boxer shorts and one of the vests I'd bought from the caravan. The stubble which had hardly been visible that morning was now quite prominent. His hair was greasy and matted. Goodness knows what impression he had created with Hal. 'How was Kitty?' He hardly looked at me as he spoke.

'Surprisingly cheerful actually.'

'I stink. I need a shower. I've decided to go back to the caravan tomorrow. I need some time to re-evaluate my future, and I can't do that here.'

'What do you mean, re-evaluate your future?'

'Well, I'm basically finished, aren't I? In case you haven't noticed I can't use my right arm. What hope have I got of winning those jobs I've been quoting for? I'll have enough trouble controlling a computer mouse let alone picking up a fucking pencil. Right now, taking up Hastings' offer of half my house and all of my practice doesn't seem like such a bad offer after all.'

'You've got to be joking? But what about the pavilion?'

'You know the score. Even if the MPT do come up with the funding at this late stage, they'll appoint their own project manager. I don't need to be part of the team any more. I've set up the Conservation Society and Tom is perfectly capable of running that, just as you are perfectly capable of running your arts hub. I'm seriously thinking about going back to Ireland.'

'What?'

'I could take Hastings' money in lieu of the practice and the mill and head home. Start up afresh.'

I stared at him. How could Dominic possibly think about

deserting Hookes Bay now? 'Have you heard from Hastings again? Has he offered you that option?'

'No. But he would, if I asked. If he thought that getting rid of me would pave the way for him to get his hands on the pavilion. He's not to know it's all out of my hands.'

He began to shuffle towards the bathroom.

'Do you need any help?' I muttered.

'No. I'm sure I can manage.'

I emptied the contents of my shopping bags onto the counter top. Dominic obviously wasn't going to tell me about Hal's visit. Did I mention that I'd overheard his entire conversation? I didn't believe any of his excuses about needing time to re-evaluate. The simple truth was that he now knew exactly who I was. The curse of Tara Wakely had reared its ugly head and he was bailing out while he could.

It had gone very quiet in the bathroom. The water had stopped running. What if he had had an accident? Slipped or something?

'Dom,' I gently tapped on the door. No reply. 'Dom. Is everything all right? Have you managed to have your shower?'

I tried the handle. He had locked the door.

'Dom, can you hear me. Are you okay in there?'

'Yes, of course I'm fucking okay.' He flung open the door. 'Stop fussing will you?'

He had tried a one-handed shave with one of my lady razors. Blood seeped from a nick on his chin.

'You should have kept the stubble,' I said, stepping into the bathroom to inspect the cut a little closer. 'I quite liked it.' I tore off a piece of toilet tissue. 'Here let me,'

'I'll do it,' he snapped. As he dabbed at his chin with his one good hand, the towel he had wrapped around his waist slid to the floor.

Averting my gaze I bent to pick up the towel.

'Jesus! Will you just get out and leave me alone?'

Dominic's bad mood pervaded over the evening meal. We poked grains of undercooked rice around our plates. If Hal thought I was great shakes at cooking, Georgie had to be really bad. Eventually, Dominic pushed his plate to one side.

'Have you seriously thought about what you're going to do if this plan for the pavilion doesn't work out?' he asked.

'No. I don't want to think about it.'

'Well, you should. Seriously.'

'Seriously, I'll think about it when it happens. Not now. It's not over until the fat lady sings, remember?'

'Talking of singing, what is this racket on the radio?'

'Urban Rebel. Maureen Batty gave me a cassette.'

'And they got a record deal based on this?'

As much as I wanted to disagree, I couldn't. Jez was never going to win any awards for his song-writing skills. I'd only been listening with half an ear as one tune merged into another. As yet I'd heard no mention of the enchanting *Lou-Lou*, although one track had featured a very repetitive refrain of '*Let's go backstage baby*'. I got up and switched the tape off.

'Thank Christ for that,' Dominic said. 'You have to face the fact that Kitty will die and Robbie will inherit the pavilion. Your job here is done.'

'No. My job is staying with Hookes Bay Academy of Music and Dance. That's my business. I own it. If I can't have the pavilion, I'll have a brand new community centre to run my classes in.'

'You know you won't be happy doing that.'

'How do you know what will make me happy?'

'You've hardly got any pupils,' he mumbled. 'Your client base is always going to be kids who want to come after school and at weekends. It's not going to be practical or profitable.'

'I don't tell you how to run your business so don't start going on at me about mine.'

'You'd have more opportunities if you went back to London.'

Here it comes. I speared the final piece of soggy, overcooked asparagus and poised my fork above my plate. 'What makes you think that?'

'It's where you're from isn't it? You must know people? Go back and renew some of your contacts. Who knows what could happen.' He finally met my eye. 'You'll be stunted here in Hookes Bay, Tara.' He said my name awkwardly. 'It's not big enough for you. Your talent will be wasted. Go back to London. Go back to your old life. This time it will happen for you. I'm sure it will. You'd have far more success with a performing arts academy in the capital than you ever would here. It's where it's all at. You should go back.'

'But that's the whole point, isn't it?' I said. 'I want to do something here in Hookes Bay. Why should Londoners have all the opportunities?'

Dominic sighed. 'There's nothing for you here.'

'Yes there is,' I retorted, placing my fork back on the plate. *There's you,* I wanted to scream, but that wouldn't work, not with Dominic in this mood, but there were other people in Hookes Bay who relied on me. 'There's Ethan Hobart,' I pointed out. 'There's Penny's Callum, and Shelbie Solway, all those kids who have the potential to achieve something with the right teaching, the kids who are never going to write an essay, or be mathematicians, scientists or architects. They'll never leave school with ten GCSEs or go to university, but they can rap like a poet and street dance like a gymnast. The creative arts give kids confidence and credibility. That's why I'm going to stay here, Dominic. Everybody is good at something. Everybody deserves the chance to shine, and I'm going to ensure they have that opportunity whether you like it or not.'

Chapter Forty-One

Dominic had already packed by the time I woke up the next morning. I'd spent the night in Kitty's bed and we hadn't spoken since he had 'retired' to my room straight after our evening meal.

'I've called a taxi,' he announced.

'But it's only eight. You've not had any breakfast.' Was he really that desperate to be gone?

'I'll pick something up later.' Almost as an afterthought he appeared to remember his manners. 'Thanks for everything, but I really do need to start managing on my own now.'

I tried to sound light-hearted. 'Sure, *Mr Independent*.'

'Yep, that's me. Give my regards to Kitty when you next see her.'

We stood facing each other. 'You could always visit her yourself,' I suggested.

A muscle flinched in his cheek. 'And say what, that I've failed her?'

'You haven't.'

A car pulled up outside.

'That must be my taxi. I've got to go.' Dominic leaned forward and brushed his lips across my cheek. 'Bye, Tara.'

As he stepped out of the front door I realised it wasn't his taxi. It was Robbie Mayhew. Had something happened to Kitty? Grief hit me like a physical pain.

Robbie caught sight of Dominic. 'What are you doing here? You're a sight for sore eyes. What happened to you? Walked into a door did you?'

'Grant Hastings happened to me,' Dominic replied.

'Hastings?'

'Oh, don't pretend you don't know.'

'But I don't know.' Robbie looked genuinely puzzled.

'Never mind that,' I interrupted. 'How's Kitty?'

Robbie rubbed at something in his eye. 'They're moving her into Madeleine House, the hospice. That's why I've dropped by. I need to collect some stuff from here to go in her room. Personal stuff, make it a bit homely for her. Ambulance is taking her at ten this morning.'

'Oh, right,' I gulped. 'So she isn't going to come back here?'

'No.' He gave the bungalow a disparaging glance. 'She's not sentimental about being in her own home at the end, like some people are. The hospice is the best place for her now.' He turned back to Dominic. 'You didn't answer my question. Why are you here?'

'I told you. Hastings set a couple of thugs on me.'

'Oh, come on. Pull the other one. Is that what he told you, Alice? Some sob story to get you into bed?'

I stared at Robbie. 'He didn't get me into bed, and even if he did, what is it to you?'

'Because it's an abuse of my mother's hospitality. It's bad enough that she took you in, let alone this con merchant.'

'You're a fine one to be calling me a conman, Rob Mayhew.' Dominic was seething. I could see the anger bubbling beneath the surface.

'Look mate, piss off, or I'll give you another shiner to match the one you already have.'

'For Christ's sake, Kitty is dying and you're acting like a couple of schoolboys.' I stepped between them. Robbie didn't scare me anymore. 'Go and fetch what you need, Robbie. Kitty's room is a bit of a mess because I've been sleeping in there whilst Dominic recovers from being beaten up by your friend's henchmen.'

As Robbie stepped over the threshold he waved a fist at Dominic. 'Get off my mother's property, Flynn.'

'What hold has he got over you, Robbie?' Dominic persisted. To my relief I could now see the taxi approaching. 'What debt do you owe Hastings? Is it the horses, the blackjack table?'

'I don't owe anybody any debts,' Robbie snarled.

'So what is it then? Why are you so keen to sell him the pavilion? He doesn't need it. He can build his flats without it. You know how much that building means to your stepmother.'

Robbie took a step forwards. I put a hand out to stop him.

'Maybe it's not you who's so keen to suck up to Grant Hastings,' Dominic sneered as the taxi pulled up. 'Maybe it's your wife. Maybe it's Belinda who is doing all the sucking.'

The colour drained from Robbie's face. 'What the fuck did you say?' He pushed me to one side and I stumbled. I felt a sharp pain as my head hit the door jamb.

The taxi door slammed. Dominic was gone.

I heard footsteps on gravel from next door.

'What's going on here?' Mr Deacon peered over the fence. 'Is everything all right. We heard shouting?'

'Yes,' Robbie snapped. 'Sorry.'

'It's not bad news is it?'

'No, well, we're moving Kit to Madeleine House. That's all, I've just come to collect some things for her. Sorry to have disturbed you.'

'Rightio. Give Mrs Barker our regards, won't you? If there is anything we can do.' Mr Deacon leaned further over the fence. 'Are you all right, dear?'

I slumped on the doorstep. I could feel blood on my scalp.

'Oh God, Alice, I'm so sorry,' Robbie said, helping me to my feet. 'I didn't mean to hurt you.'

'No, I know you didn't mean to, Robbie, but you did.'

'That toe-rag Irishman. Why, why, why?'

'Why what?' I asked, keeping hold of Robbie's hand to steady myself. My ear was ringing.

'It's just a scratch,' Robbie consoled.

'Oh, that's good then. I won't report you for GBH.'

'That man Flynn has wound me up from day one.' Robbie muttered. 'You do know he's Hastings' ex-son-in-law, don't you?'

'Yes, of course I do. And do you know that Hastings deliberately ruined Dominic's reputation as an architect and effectively bankrupted a decent, honest man?'

'You think that's what Flynn is? A decent, honest man?'

'Yes I do. And that's not all. As I am sure you are probably already aware, Hastings is bribing local councillors to get this Carlisle development through planning, which is actually illegal. And he threatened me.'

'Huh. I don't believe you.'

'I have witnesses.'

I headed inside to examine my wound. Robbie followed me. 'I thought some pictures would be nice to brighten up her room at Madeleine House,' he said as if nothing had just happened. 'One of Hughie, her favourite. Jez, of course. Maybe one of me and Lindy, if I can find one.'

'Look on the mantelpiece.'

When I returned from the living room, clutching a towel and a bag of frozen peas to the side of my head, Robbie was sat on the sofa studying the photo as if it was the first time he had ever seen it.

'I always thought Lindy was out of my league,' he said somewhat wistfully. 'Our wedding day was the happiest day of my life, but it was very low key, what with her dad just gone. I took her to Barbados for our twenty-fifth and we renewed our vows on the beach.'

He seemed to be in a reflective mood. I decided to be brave.

'Robbie, Dominic's right. Why are you so desperate to get rid of the pavilion? You know Kitty wants to see it resurrected. You know how much that building means to her. It plays a significant part in your family's history, in this town's history.'

'It's not really any of your business, is it?' he said, putting the photo to one side.

'Well, actually, I think it is.'

'Oh yes, of course. I'd temporarily forgotten. You've managed to convince Kitty you're Jez's daughter, haven't you? Or is it the other way round, she's convinced you? Is that it? To be honest Alice, you might well be Jez's daughter for all I know, because he wasn't particularly fussy about who or what he slept with.'

'You didn't like your stepbrother very much, did you?'

'What's that supposed to mean?' Robbie sighed.

Why had I never suspected Robbie before? I knew he could fly off the handle at the drop of a hat. My current injuries were testament to that. 'Were you jealous of him?' I asked.

'Now what are you getting at? No, I wasn't jealous of him. Jez was an arrogant, selfish bastard who treated everyone like a piece of shit, including his mother, incidentally. Why would I be jealous of him?'

Surely he didn't need me to spell it out? 'Because he always got the girls. And he was about to hit the big time.'

'Is that what you think?

'I don't know what to think because none of what is happening makes sense. You are about to inherit a beautiful old building full of history and heritage, and you are going to sell it off to make way for a faceless block of flats. Why? What are you trying to eradicate Robbie? Is it your guilt?'

'Guilt?'

'You knew Jez was on his own that night at the club. Did you go back and push him off the pier?'

'Of course I didn't bloody go back. How can you even think that?' Robbie looked genuinely appalled. 'Yes, I do feel guilty, guilty because I left him there. Don't you think I've regretted that every single day of my life? Jez wasn't always the most likeable of guys but he was my stepbrother. He said he had some business to see to and I wanted to go and have a quick fuck with the barmaid. Does that satisfy you? He seemed okay when we left. He wasn't exactly sober but he seemed quite buoyant.'

Buoyant hardly seemed an appropriate adjective for someone who had subsequently drowned.

'What business would he have to attend to at that time of night?' I demanded.

Robbie sighed. 'I don't know. Perhaps he wanted to check the bloody accounts. Look, let me make it clear. That pavilion has been a millstone around my neck for the last thirty odd years, and I can't wait to see the back of it. Lindy and I have both had enough. The place is nothing but a drain on our time, our energy and our pockets.'

'Lindy and Jez were quite close once, weren't they?

Teenage sweethearts?'

'So?'

'Where was she when Jez had his accident?'

'How should I know? She lived in the West Country with her mother, or she might even have been in Singapore by then. I can't remember.'

'And this thing she had with Jez, it was definitely all over?'

'Of course it was.'

'But she must have been upset when she heard the news?'

'I'm sure she was. Everyone who knew Jez was upset. Why are you dragging all this up? Lindy had a teenage crush. That's all it ever was. Ask her if you like. She'll happily tell you.'

I was quite sure Lindy wouldn't happily tell me anything. I lifted the towel away from my head.

'How does it feel?' he asked.

'I'll live. You're in the clear.'

'I need to get back to the hospital,' he said, standing up with a stretch. 'You do realise the minute Kit's gone, I'm chucking you out of this bungalow, don't you?'

I nodded but couldn't resist a final jibe. 'Unless she's left it to me in her will, of course.'

Chapter Forty-Two

Dominic had been gone for three days and I hadn't heard a word. It wasn't just inconsiderate it was downright rude after the care and attention I had given him. As always in times of despair, I immersed myself in work, but Sunday was lesson-free. My desire to see him again overrode my sensibility. I got on my bicycle and headed over to Craven Farm.

The hedgerows were alive with insects flitting from the sweeping heads of cow parsley to beaming buttercups. Cotton tufts of willow-herb floated on the breeze, filling me with inspiration to plan a wild flower garden in another corner of Kitty's barren plot. I pictured an informal patchwork of purples and pinks, surrounding a romantic arbour, but then I remembered the bungalow wouldn't be my home for much longer. It would soon be time to find a new one.

A trailer was parked across the gateway to the Quaker chapel. It was the first time I'd seen any sign of life at the property. A man in green overalls was clearing the waist-high grass with a strimmer, sending a mini tornado of dust whirring into the air. I continued cycling, blinking furiously. By the time I reached the caravan park my left eye was sore and streaming.

The door to Dominic's mobile home was open. At least he hadn't left for Ireland already. I rapped on the side of the van.

'Dom, are you there?'

He was sat at the small table with his laptop. The sling lay on the seat beside him. He looked handsome again. The bruising was minimal, his damaged eye normal size. He was bare-chested, not even having bothered to dress, nor had he shaved. Takeaway cartons littered the kitchenette's countertop.

'I wanted to make sure you were okay.' I said, entering

uninvited.

'Everything is hunky dory here,' he replied. 'You needn't have worried.'

He was impenetrable to the last, despite the black eye, missing teeth and the broken collar bone.

'Have you had time to re-evaluate?' I asked.

'It's all been sorted. Hastings' lawyers suddenly can't do enough for me.'

'Oh, right. That's good then.'

'As I said,' he looked up, 'all hunky dory, here. And you? Kitty?'

'Moved to the hospice. I'm going to see her tomorrow.'

His face softened slightly. 'How is she, really?'

'Very poorly.' I rubbed my eye. It was so sore now I had trouble keeping it open. 'I have to face the fact that each time I go and see her, it might be the last. Despite everything, I'm very fond of Kitty. I know she isn't related to me or anything, but living with her these last couple of months, and getting to know her, it's going to be really hard to say goodbye.'

'Hey,' – he was suddenly up on his feet – 'don't cry, Tara, please.'

'I'm not crying,' – although I was. 'I've got something in my eye. They were strimming the grass at the old chapel.'

'Let me look. Come into the light, here.'

I cocked my head on one side and very gently with his good hand he prised open my eye.

'Look to left, to the right. Oh yes, I think can see something. Blink…' I blinked. 'There was someone doing maintenance at the chapel, you said? That's a good sign.'

'Is it?' The foreign object was now out. The relief was enormous. For a few seconds, Dominic lingered, his fingers on my face, his bare chest temptingly close.

'Is that better?' he enquired.

'One hundred per-cent,' I gulped.

He removed his hand, stepped back.

'I don't suppose you've heard anything from Sam MacDonald?' I asked desperate to recapture that moment of intimacy.

'No, but I've been having some glitches with my Wi-Fi up here. There'll be nothing now until Monday anyway. I'll get Hobo to run me down to the yard tomorrow.'

'Okay. Not booked your flights to Ireland yet?'

He tapped his cheek. 'Can't go until I've been measured up for my dental implants.'

'Oh, I see.'

'Haven't you got classes this afternoon?' It sounded like a very polite way of telling me to be on my way. He sat back down at the table.

'No, it's Sunday. But you're right, I should be getting on my way. I'm going to start work on my back-up plan. I'm going to contact local schools with a drama workshop proposal. Jordan has offered to put in a good word for me.' Jordan Lockwood had promised no such thing but the need to provoke a reaction was unstoppable. The effect was instant.

'Jordan?'

'Jordan Lockwood, the music teacher with the rap choir who was keen to help out with the arts hub. He thinks St Stephen's would be interested in my ideas.'

'Oh yes, you used to do something similar in London, didn't you?'

'I don't recall ever mentioning it.'

'I'm sure you said something.'

'No, I definitely wouldn't have mentioned it because drama workshops are not something Alice Paige had ever done in her extensive dancing career. I've never told you anything about me, the real me.'

He didn't even have the good grace to look guilty. 'Well, you best get going, because I'm also working, as you can see.'

'Would you like me to clear these takeaway boxes for you? Take them to the bin on my way out?'

'No, I can manage, thank you.'

Dominic was being incorrigibly obtuse. I picked up my bicycle and headed down the track to the nature reserve. The seagulls were better company.

Chapter Forty-Three

The next few days were some of the most miserable of my adult life, on a par with the fall-out from the *Sunday Stargazer* debacle. When Hal had first dumped me, I'd been enraged. I wasn't angry with Dominic; I was sad, sad to the core. In addition, the threat of exposure now hung over me like a thunder cloud.

I visited Kitty as promised. Madeleine House was even more of a trek than the hospital, being situated in a purpose-built building on the outskirts of Fareham. Kitty had her own suite overlooking the hospice's well-tended gardens.

She didn't look like a woman about to die anytime soon. When I arrived she was sitting up in bed, smiling and alert. Although she had lost weight and her features seemed even more bird-like than usual, someone had done her hair and what few curls she had left, framed her face like a white halo.

'You'll never guess who came to see me before I left St Mary's,' she said as soon as I sat down beside her. 'Derek. Derek Woodford. Can you believe it? After all these years. It was lovely to see him. He's a priest. Fancy that! Maureen's never said.'

She soon tired. As I loitered in the tea bar to wait for the minibus to take me back into town, I noticed a plaque dedicated to the memory of Commander Brian Cartwright, whose extensive fund-raising exploits had contributed to the hospice's inauguration. Presumably that was why Kitty had been allocated such a grand room.

Besides the plaque was a framed photograph from the charity ball Brian Cartwright had organised for his 50th birthday party. The Commander was resplendent in his uniform, and beside him, equally as resplendent in a plunging full length evening gown was his daughter, Belinda. The couple were surrounded by smiling guests, many in full naval and military attire. Jez Keaton, in dark drainpipe trousers, black shirt and waistcoat, looked slightly incongruous amongst the dignitaries, but every inch a would-be rock star. He had pride of place on the other arm of the beaming Belinda. The date of the photograph was engraved on the frame. The Commander's charity bash had been held just three months before Jez Keaton disappeared off the pier. I could understand why Robbie might wish to protect his wife's virtue and dismiss her relationship with Jez as nothing but a teenage crush, but as I studied the photograph in detail, it did raise the question of why would Father Derek lie?

The one highlight of the week, as always, was my Wednesday toddler class. It was impossible to come home in a bad mood after a session with Ethan. I hadn't gone online for a couple of days, and feeling in a more positive frame of mind I sat down at the computer to check my emails. One good thing about adopting an assumed name was that I didn't receive the usual catalogue of junk messages that filled up an inbox. Since the weekend I'd received no more than a handful of emails, including one from Barbara Kendrick, enclosing details of the Am-Dram's rehearsal schedule for the autumn production of *The Ghost Train*, and one from Tom, requesting one more dance lesson before his imminent party.

The bungalow was starting to look a bit of a mess. Lassitude and housework didn't mix, so with emails sorted and the computer switched off before anything more contentious arrived, I decided to give the kitchen a good scrub down. As I dusted around the radio cassette player I flipped over Maureen's tape to listen to the remaining songs in Urban Rebel's repertoire. The songs on the second side of the tape were definitely more up-tempo. I soon found myself humming along, even momentarily stopping mid-dust to give *Dirty Little Secrets* a second play. Mari was right. It was easy to see how the catchy tune had become so popular.

I was an actress; a veteran of musical theatre. I was trained to pick up words, to remember lyrics. Two days ago I'd seen a picture of Jez Keaton and Lindy Mayhew which quite clearly proved they were still 'together' when both Derek and Robbie had told me that they weren't. By the end of the second rendition of Jez's signature tune, I had a sneaking suspicion I knew exactly what he was doing hanging around Hookes Bay pier by himself at midnight on the night he disappeared. Or at least, who he was waiting for.

That evening I gave Tom a quick call to let him know that I could meet him at the pavilion on Friday evening.

'Have you been having phone trouble?' he asked. 'I did try ringing you a couple of times.'

'Yes, sorry, I had to change my SIM card.'

'Bad news about the MPT, eh,' Tom said.

'I'm sorry?'

'I had an email from Sam MacDonald a couple of hours or so ago. I assume you did too?'

'I'm not online.'

'Oh, I'm sorry. I assume she would have sent you a copy. I thought Dominic might have spoken to you?'

'I haven't seen Dominic since the weekend,' I said, trying to keep the disappointment out of my voice.

'Oh, well, basically Sam says they just can't justify the initial outlay to purchase the building, but they are prepared to lend their support to a restoration programme. So I suppose it's not entirely bad news.'

How was that not entirely bad news? 'Oh right, well thanks, Tom. I'll see you tomorrow. We might as well make the most of that studio while we still can.'

'That's the spirit, Alice. Who knows, we might be able to convince the Mayhews to see sense yet.'

That I highly doubted, but I kept quiet. I felt physically and mentally drained. I'd already lost Dominic. I was about to lose Kitty, and now Hookes Bay Pavilion and all my dreams for it were dead.

Or maybe not. I returned to the cassette player in the kitchen and pressed the rewind button one more time. Thanks to Jez Keaton's schoolboy song-writing skills, I had one more card left up my sleeve. Hastings wasn't the only one who could play dirty. I wasn't going down without a fight.

Chapter Forty-Four

It didn't even occur to me to not answer the ring at the door. I suppose I secretly hoped against all probability for Dominic, seeking consolation over the injustice of the MPT's decision, but of course it wasn't. However, Hal Claydon was the very last person I expected to see, a slim, trim, '*Georgified*' Hal Claydon.

He stepped forward with outstretched arms. 'Oh my God, Tara, it is you! What's happened? I knew there was something suspicious about that Irishman.'

It was tempting to slam the door in his face. 'What are you going on about?'

'Has he been keeping you here against your will? He said he'd been in a car crash but I knew he was covering up for something. That's why I came back. You look a total mess. What's he done to you?' Hal encircled me in his arms. 'Oh, Tara, you don't know how good this feels.'

It didn't feel good to me. It felt decidedly awkward. I wriggled free. 'Hal, what are you doing here?'

'Can I come in? Is it safe?'

'Yes, of course it's safe. I'm on my own. The old lady I've been staying with is in hospital.'

'Where's Patrick or whatever his name was?'

'You've nothing to worry about, *Dominic*'s not here.' *Nor was he ever likely to be.* That thought almost brought on another bout of tears.

Hal followed me through to the kitchen. 'Oh Tara, I've been such a fool, will you ever forgive me?'

I almost said no on the spot. 'Can I get you a drink?' I held up a jar of instant coffee granules.

'Is there an alternative?'

'Only tea.' Hal hated tea. 'It's surprising what depravations you can get used to after a while,' I told him.

'So you are here against your will? It seems such an odd place to hide out.'

'I am definitely here of my own volition,' I assured him. 'However misguided that might now seem.'

'But what are you doing here?' He regarded the mug of coffee with a look of disdain.

'Shall we go and sit in the garden?' I suggested. I took him to Hughie's bench. 'I designed this flower bed, do you like it?'

He hardly gave my efforts a second glance. 'I didn't know you liked gardening.'

'Yes you did. I made the terrace in your loft apartment into an urban jungle, remember?'

'A few pot plants doesn't make an urban jungle, Tara.'

Hal had lost at least two stone in weight since I'd last seen him. He had also, quite possibly, discovered the age-defying properties of hair-dye. It was a shame the physical improvements hadn't extended to his manners. I didn't have to put up with put downs. Perhaps our relationship had gone sour long before Georgie Gold appeared on the scene.

'I've got a financial backer for a new musical,' he announced, placing his untouched cup of coffee on the bench beside him. 'I thought I'd give you first refusal.'

'That's very generous of you,' I said. 'No plans to revive *Rockabilly Rose*?'

'*Rockabilly Rose* is dead in the water,' he replied. 'I thought we'd do a tour of the provinces first, try it out in Newcastle, Manchester, Southampton and then head up to London for an initial six week run. What do you think?'

'I think you've got a bloody cheek.'

'Oh, come on, Tara. I want you back.' He took my hand. 'Come to London with me. You don't belong in this OAP bungalow, doing gardening and whatever else it is you do here.'

I retracted my hand. 'I run my own dance school, actually. I'm going to turn it into a full-scale performing arts academy. I've got premises sorted out. I've got an existing client base.'

Hal looked taken back. 'How have you done that so

quickly?'

'I just put my mind to it. I didn't exactly have a lot of options open to me but this opportunity came up and I took it. I grabbed it, in fact. I'm very happy here in Hookes Bay.'

'So why do you look like someone's roughed you up?'

'Because I had an accident with a door post.'

'Oh Tara, what has happened to you?'

'Nothing. No, that's not true. Something has happened to me. I found myself.' Or rather I found Kitty Keaton and Alice Paige. I didn't want Hal here polluting my new life. I wanted him gone. I picked up his coffee cup and threw the contents onto my shiny new compost heap. 'I'm sorry you've had a wasted journey,' I told him. 'But I'm not coming back to you or the stage. I'm done with it.'

'Oh Tara,' Hal said, rising heavily to his feet. 'I know I was a fool. I know I treated you badly. Please give me another chance. *Battlestar* is going to be big, I know it is. Dirk Forster – he's my business partner; South-African guy, great guy – has these huge ideas. It's going to be fantastic production with lasers, pyrotechnics, we'll have flying—'

'You know I don't do flying, not after the magic carpet fiasco.'

'We can get some of the younger cast members to do the flying.'

'It's a no. A great big, all round, no.'

'Okay, I get it. So what about this academy then? Sounds like you're investing in something here when you could be investing in something far more profitable in London. After *Battlestar* we could do it. You and me, our own stage school, like we always talked about.' *Oh Hal. Too little. Too late.* 'Is there anywhere round here we could at least go for dinner tonight? At least discuss some ideas? I've come all this way, Tara.'

'Hookes Bay is not quite up to Soho standards,' I pointed out.

'Well, neither are you right now,' he replied. 'There must be somewhere half decent we can go. You can show me what's captivated you about this place.'

The initial attraction of Hookes Bay had been because Hal wasn't in it. However, I was hungry. I hadn't cooked a proper meal since the pathetic risotto a week ago. Perhaps if I smartened myself up Paulo Bonetti wouldn't recognise me and we could get a La Scala pizza. It was the best Hookes Bay had to offer.

I took a quick shower and opted for the Doris Day does hedgerow outfit again, knowing Hal hated it. I suggested a stroll along the esplanade. The seafront was always at its best in the early evening. Families were just packing up from their day on the beach; the smell of barbecues wafted into the air, mixed with candyfloss and sticky sweet ice-cream.

Hal took in the view. 'I take it that's the Isle of Wight?' he asked. 'And that must be Portsmouth, I suppose, in the distance? And what's that funny little building there?' He pointed along the prom.

'That's Hookes Bay Pavilion. That's why I'm here.'

'Can I take a better look?'

'Sure.' There was no harm.

'What is it, exactly?'

'It's the Theatre of Dreams,' I replied.

I began with the story of Conrad Carlisle and the Pepperthornes. I told him about Eric Milner, of everything Lionel and Kitty had achieved during their years in Hookes Bay, and I ended with the fiasco of Robbie Mayhew. The only parts of the tale I omitted were the parts about Jez Keaton and Alice Paige.

'So this is where you are planning your academy,' he said. 'Looks like it needs a bit of a refurb first.'

'Oh, it does that,' I agreed. 'Trouble is finding someone to fund the refurb.'

'You mean you haven't got a financial backer?'

I shook my head. 'We were hoping to get a preservation trust on board but they've just pulled out. It would have to be a community project.' I pointed across the road to the Carlisle site. 'That is going to be a block of new apartments. The developer wants this part of the esplanade included in his plans. When Kitty Keaton dies the pavilion passes to Robbie and he will sell it straight away.'

'Could he sell it to me?'

I stopped in my tracks. 'You?'

Hal shrugged. 'Why not? If it's just the money he's after he doesn't have to sell to the developer does he?'

'Why would you want to buy the pavilion, Hal?' *Please don't say just for me.* The sense of obligation would be huge. Horrendous. Not worth contemplating.

'How much does he want for it?'

'I've no idea. Hal, why would you?'

'I like the look of it. I've spent my entire career in the theatre. There's something quite special about this place. Do you realise the unique contribution seaside theatres have played in our cultural heritage?'

'Yes, I do actually.'

'See. We have that affinity. Maybe I'm not such a monster.' Hal smiled, his old Hal smile. 'I wouldn't be buying it for you, Tara. I'd be buying it for me, but I would be prepared to lease it back to you. I don't think my funds could run to a full restoration project, which is obviously what this place needs, but if you think…'

I'd still be beholden to Hal. He'd still be pulling the strings but I'd be able to stay in Hookes Bay, and I'd have my academy. The MPT would be able to come back on board, and because their financial obligation would be less, I might be able to persuade them to use a local a project manager…

'I'll find out how much Robbie wants for it.' I said without hesitation. 'Let me talk to him.'

Thanks to Hal's impromptu visit, I didn't just have any old card left up my sleeve, I now had an ace.

Chapter Forty-Five

La Scala was busy. The waitress found us a table beside a noisy family which thankfully meant we blended into the background. Paulo barely glanced up from his pizza oven. At nine o'clock I put Hal safely back into a taxi with a promise to be in touch. As I walked home, I called Dominic. After he failed to pick up twice, I left a voicemail.

'There's no point you refusing to answer my call. I know the Trust has pulled the plug. It would have been nice if you'd told me yourself but we need to talk. Something has come up.'

Just as I reached the bungalow, Dominic called back.

'I've only just found out,' he said. 'I told you I was having computer glitches.'

I didn't believe his story for one minute but I didn't want to waste time arguing. 'The thing is there's a possible alternative solution,' I said. 'Hal Claydon's offered to buy the pavilion.'

'Sorry? Who?'

'Hal Claydon, the theatre director. He came to see you in Hookes Bay last week. You pretended you didn't know me. I was there by the way, I nearly barged in on you. I heard every word of your conversation.'

'Oh. So you're going back to him?'

I refused to be drawn into a debate. 'He hasn't the funds to carry out a restoration; that would still be up to a preservation trust or a charitable fund, but he can afford to buy the building to save it from demolition.'

'Well, sounds like all your problems are solved,' Dominic said. 'I hope you'll be very happy together.'

'You really are the most infuriating man I think I have ever met.'

'I think my wife once said something very similar,'

Dominic replied. 'Look, I'm sorry if I'm not jumping up and down with excitement but your friend still has to purchase the pavilion. It's a bit of a big ask.'

'I didn't ask him. He suggested it. Hal says he'll match whatever the current offer is.'

'Well, that's very good of him. I imagine the current offer is huge. Hastings has a lot to lose if the Mayhews do pull out. He won't be happy, I'll just warn you. At least with the preservation trust we had a legitimate body of people behind us. You're on your own here, Tara. You could be playing with fire. In any case, don't forget, the bonds between the Mayhews and Hastings are pretty tight. There's every likelihood Robbie will turn your friend Hal's offer down point blank.'

'I'm not going to talk to Robbie. It's Lindy who's the key player in all this.'

'Are you sure?'

I wasn't sure at all but I had my hunches. I didn't want to have to resort to underhand tactics, but I would, when the push came to the shove. Derek Woodford had been a loyal friend to Lindy, I could see that now, but his loyalty had aroused my suspicions. Lindy had a secret, and people with secrets were always vulnerable. I knew that better than anyone else.

I called Lindy first thing in the morning and to my surprise she readily agreed to my request for a meeting. I assumed she was expecting a full Tara Wakely confession. At seven on Friday evening I headed straight to the pavilion where Tom was waiting for his final lesson. We commiserated with each other on the MPT's decision.

'I've still got another couple of avenues to pursue,' I told him. 'I'm not giving up yet.'

'I'm glad to hear it,' he agreed. 'Technically we have still got the backing of the MPT.'

'But not their money,' I pointed out.

Tom was step-perfect. I reassured him he would be able to lead his wife onto the dance floor with faultless precision.

'You are going to come along, aren't you?' he insisted. 'Dominic's promised to be there.'

I had no faith in Dominic's promises. He'd be back in Ireland long before Tom's party, complete with his new teeth.

After Tom had gone, I took my time making my way down the magnificent staircase. I wanted to linger, soak up the ambience. If my gamble with Lindy didn't pay off, realistically there was every chance this could be my last time in the pavilion. Ever since I had first arrived in Hookes Bay I had pinned all my hopes on saving this building. Dominic had done the same. He had been in a bad place, just like me. He'd lost his job, and his home. We had been drawn together to fight for a common aim. It had been his panacea, just as it had been mine, and now Dominic was cured. He had other projects to pursue. I only had this. As much as I wanted to kid myself, a full-scale performing arts hub would never work in the community centre. Was I really going to be happy teaching children's ballet, fitness classes to the sixty-plus age group and running educational drama workshops for the rest of my life? The answer had to be yes although the prospect didn't fill me with any great sense of joy. I couldn't go back. I wasn't going to give the likes of James Coulter the satisfaction.

I slipped out of the stage door and saw the solitary figure perched on one of the wooden blocks at the end of the pier. Lindy had obviously been entrusted with a key to the pier, just like she had been entrusted with a key to the storage unit. She was wearing a strappy sundress similar to the one she wore in her wedding anniversary photograph. She was smoking a cigarette.

The wind had picked up. Black clouds shrouded the Isle of Wight. A storm was on its way.

'It's good of you to come,' I said.

'No point both Robbie and me sitting by Kitty's bedside for hours on end. I've done enough of that in my time.' She flicked ash into the water. 'You said you had a proposition to put to me. I'm all ears.'

I came straight to the point. 'I know someone who might be interested in buying the pavilion,' I said. 'He's a theatre director in London. You just have to name your price.'

'I assume you're talking about your friend, Hal Claydon?

He tracked you down then?'

'Yes, he did. It was very kind of you to send him my way. He's very keen to invest in a new venture. Whatever Hastings has offered Robbie, he'll match it. And more.'

Lindy gave a vague smile. 'We've already agreed a sale with Grant Hastings.'

'Maybe I need to talk to Robbie. I'm sure he'd jump at the chance at making a few extra thousand pounds. Hal's a rich man. He could be just what Hookes Bay needs. You should at least consider his offer.'

'Take it from me, it's not going to happen.'

'You know Kitty wants to keep the pavilion a going concern. Don't you have any sense of loyalty to your mother-in-law?'

Lindy gave a small shrug. 'When she's gone, what'll she care?'

'Don't you owe it to her?'

Lindy stubbed out her cigarette with a jewelled flip-flop. 'Your business in Hookes Bay is finished, Alice.' She said my name with a deliberate sneer. 'Maybe you should run along now. Start packing or something.'

Only two words sprang to my mind to describe the woman sat before me, her passive face betraying no emotion whatsoever. *Callous bitch.* I leaned back against the iron railings. It was time to lay my ace on the table. 'I've no intention of running anywhere,' I said. 'Tell me, Lindy, where were you the night Jez fell off this pier?'

'I beg your pardon?'

'You heard me. Where were you the night Jez fell off this pier?'

She took another cigarette from a packet in her clutch bag and struggled against the increasing breeze to light it. A sudden wave crashed against the girders and the pier shuddered. It was high tide, the only time of day it was possible to fall to a watery grave.

'Lindy, I know you and Jez were still seeing each other at the time of his disappearance. There's a picture of the two of you, together, at the hospice, at your father's fundraising ball. I know you used to meet here. He wrote a song about it. *Meet me on the pier, we have nothing to fear, Lou-Lou my love, my dirty little secret.* Jez had just got a record contract. He'd have wanted you here for the celebrations. I bet that's what he was doing on the pier, on his own. He was expecting you to turn up, wasn't he? So why did you never come forward, Lindy? You never spoke to the police, told them he was waiting for you. Why not?'

'There was nothing to tell.' Just for a moment her confidence faltered. She sucked on her cigarette, as if taking strength from the shot of nicotine. 'So what if he was waiting for me? Not my problem he was off his face on drink and drugs. Jez and I were over long before he fell off the pier.'

'Really? Is that why you've made Kitty's storage unit into a shrine? Is that why you lovingly catalogued his record collection and even cleaned his boots?'

At last I was getting somewhere. For the first time she looked agitated. 'How do you know about the storage unit?'

'Kitty asked me to go and fetch something from it,' I lied.

The cigarette was stamped out. Another lit. Lindy was playing for time. 'Okay, I'll tell you, because you obviously think you've worked out something wonderful. The truth is, yes, I was coming up to meet him. He was waiting for me. He'd told me about the record contract and I was on a train, coming up to join the party. It takes four trains from Plymouth to Fareham. I missed my connection at Exeter so I turned round and went home. I knew I'd never get here in time. Next morning Woody calls me and tells me Jez has had an accident. Happy now?'

No, I wasn't happy. Lindy's explanation was perfectly plausible apart from one thing. 'Derek Woodford wasn't at the club, and there was no way he could have phoned to tell you about Jez because he was in police custody.'

'Well if it wasn't Derek it was Vince. Or Paulo…'

'Stop lying, Lindy. What are you trying to hide? Something happened that night, didn't it? What was it? An argument? A lover's tiff? What did Jez tell you? Did he tell you the record deal was just for him, not the others? Did he tell you it was all over? Did he tell you about his affair with Stevie Newman-Smith? If my boyfriend told me he'd got off with a woman nearly old enough to be his mother, I'd be bloody furious with him too. I'd probably want to push him off the pier.'

'I did not push Jez off the pier.' Lindy jumped off her perch, waving her cigarette at me. 'You have got absolutely no idea what you are talking about.' In her long dress and flaying arms she looked pathetic and ridiculous, like an inflatable air dancer. 'How dare you come here making these accusations.'

Victory was within my grasp. 'Don't you think Kitty has a right to the truth after all these years?' I demanded. I was thirty years younger than Lindy and far more nimble. I darted out of reach of her flying handbag. 'Don't you think she has a right to die in peace? You know how much this pavilion means to her. Isn't the very least you can do after everything that has happened grant her that wish, to see this building restored? Now I suggest you go and tell your lover that he's not getting his filthy little hands on this pavilion, and then you go and accept Hal Claydon's offer. And then, just maybe, I might keep your secret safe.'

'What did you say?' She clutched hold of the handrail to steady herself. A look of shock was etched on her face.

'I said I'm prepared to keep your secret safe—'

'No, about my lover. You seriously think Grant Hastings is my lover?'

'Isn't he? I've seen the two of you up at the nature reserve looking very cosy together.'

'Oh, you have got this so wrong,' Lindy said, with a shake of her head. 'Do you know what, Alice, or can I call you Tara now? You know what, Tara? You're no better than him. You're no better than Hastings. You'll keep my secret safe. Well, that's very noble of you. And funnily enough, that's just what he said too. He'll keep my secret safe. The thing is he says he'll keep my secret safe if Robbie sells the pavilion to him, and you say you'll keep my secret safe, if I don't. Decisions, decisions. What's a girl to do?'

'I don't understand.'

'The thing is, if you go shouting from the roof tops that I

pushed Jez Keaton off Hookes Bay Pier, nobody will believe you. So I'm pretty safe there. An actress whose reputation is already in tatters, someone who has already deceived half the parents of Hookes Bay with a fictitious CV and false claims about being a professional dance teacher, someone who has already lied to the local council about who she is and what she does. No, I don't think I've got an awful lot to worry about in that department. But Grant Hastings. No. I don't want to be on the wrong side of him. Sorry, Tara. No deal.'

'Are you saying Grant Hastings is blackmailing you?'

She smiled. 'He got there first. Sorry, Tara, dear. Now you really should get back to the bungalow and start packing.'

'So... about Jez?' I stared at her. She was a cool as a cucumber once again.

She smiled, retrieved another cigarette from her bag and reclaimed her perch. 'You were almost right. Ninety per cent right, probably. You want to hear the truth about Kitty's golden boy? Then I'll tell you.'

Chapter Forty-Six

Lindy Mayhew fell in love with Jez Keaton when she was fifteen.

'You never forget your first love, do you?' she said. 'My parents divorced when I was twelve. Dad transferred up here to Titan. I came up every school holiday. There were plenty of other kids my age on the estate. I got to meet their friends, got to know Jez, Woody, and the others. The summer after my O' Levels I came up here for three months. Three whole months of total bliss in the company of Jez Keaton. But after that, I had to go back to Plymouth. I asked Dad if I could live with him, go to sixth form here but Dad didn't approve of Jez. I didn't return again until Christmas. I think it was a conspiracy between my parents to keep me away. By the time I came back the following summer, Jez was into punk, he'd pierced his ears and spiked his hair, while I was still wearing floral frocks and singing Abba songs.

'I went off to university, did a bit of growing up myself. I would see him when I visited Hookes Bay but gradually those visits got less and less. Uni kept me busy. When I finished my degree I settled back in Plymouth near my mum, got a job in a travel company. I told myself I'd grown out of Jez Keaton. I hadn't seen him for nearly two years before Dad's fiftieth birthday party. This is the bit you got wrong, you see. We weren't together. Some of the boys on the base had booked Urban Rebel to play a set. Dad was furious. Jez probably only agreed to the booking because he knew it would wind the old man up. Dad hated him, always had.'

'But the photograph at the hospice? You look like a couple.'

'Jez knew how to turn on the charm,' Lindy smiled. 'Come back to the club afterwards, he said, just for old time's sake. I couldn't believe I fell for it again. One quick fuck in Don Mayhew's office and six weeks later I find out I'm pregnant.'

Now I was the one reeling in shock. '*You're* the girl he got into trouble?' So Kitty had told Maureen Batty the truth. 'Kitty said she knew he'd got someone pregnant.'

Lindy shook her head. 'Well, it wasn't me because Kitty didn't know, that's for sure.' She gave an ironic laugh. 'Perhaps it was some other little slut after all.'

I stared at her, trying to process the implications of what she had just said. 'But what happened to your baby?'

'I should have been old enough to know better, I was twenty-two. I could have managed on my own. I had a good job. My mum would have been supportive if I'd have been brave enough to tell her. I suppose I half hoped if Jez knew about the baby, he'd get down on one knee and propose, marry me and we'd live happily ever after. I had friends in Plymouth who were settling down, already having kids, so I thought, why not me? I decided to come up to Hookes Bay to see him.'

Now that Lindy had started her confession, her words tumbled out like falling dominoes. 'I knew he'd gone to London on tour because he'd done nothing but brag about it at Dad's party, and I knew roughly when he was due back. I phoned Woody first, to check. It was perfect timing. Woody said he was just off to see Jez in Pebbles. He told me Jez was planning some sort of party at the club that night, so I said I'd get the train straight up but wouldn't be there until late. I asked him to tell Jez to wait for me, but not to tell any of the others I was coming. I didn't want a whole barrage of questions. The trains were all up the creek and in the end I didn't get to Fareham until gone eleven, so I jumped into a taxi and came straight to the club. I thought I'd missed him. I could see it was all locked up, so I came round the back, to the pier. And there he was, just here, waiting for me.'

A gust of biting wind whipped Lindy's blonde hair across her face. I felt the first few drops of rain, mingling with the salty sea spray from the foaming swell below.

'He was so excited,' she continued, 'so full of what had happened in London, about his record deal, about this Stevie woman, he didn't even ask me why I'd travelled all the way up from Plymouth to see him. So I told him. I burst his bubble and told him about the baby. For a few seconds he was completely stunned, and then, from stunned he went into denial. How did I know it was his? How did *he* know it was his? Why the hell wasn't I on the pill like every other girl he slept with?

'And because I was so angry, and so upset, I lashed out. He must have taken a step back, one step too far, because the next thing I know is he's gone into the water. I heard the splash, but it was dark and I couldn't see anything. I never meant it to happen. It really was an accident.'

I tried to remain impassive. 'So then what did you do?'

'I called his name, scrambled down on the beach, and waded into the water looking for him. There were no lights, I couldn't see a thing. I ran back onto the esplanade. In those days we didn't have mobiles, the nearest phone box was by the Carlisle, but it had been vandalised. The next nearest was at the sentry point, on the base. So I went there. And of course when I reached the base, the guards recognised me and called Dad.

'I told Dad everything, blurted it all out, about why I'd come up to Hookes Bay, the baby, about Jez, and what had happened on the pier, and he told me not to worry. He said he would go down onto the beach and look for him. He took his car and told me to make myself a hot drink and to go bed. He came home a couple of hours later, said there was no sign of Jez. He said we should wait before calling the police. He said Jez might have swam along the beach. *We all know what's he like*, he said, *he might be playing a prank*. He could be back at Balmoral with Kitty and Don already and we'd be panicking over nothing.

'I did what I was told. I stayed on the base, stayed indoors. When Dad told me Jez had officially been reported missing the following day, he said the best thing I could do would be to get myself back down to Plymouth and pretend I'd never come up to Hookes Bay. He insisted there was no point me coming forward. What good would it do? I know it was wrong. By the time I arrived in Plymouth I was already bleeding. I lost the baby. It was all for nothing.'

There were no tears as she spoke; only a chilling resignation. 'Dad kept me informed of the search for Jez's body. I almost wanted to be found out. I was fully prepared to be questioned, to accept the repercussions, but it never happened. The police didn't even contact me. Woody couldn't have told anyone about our phone call. Dad said even if Jez had mentioned to the others that he was expecting me, I was just to say I missed one of my connections and headed back to Plymouth. Nobody knew I'd been in Hookes Bay apart the two guards on gate duty and the taxi driver who picked me up at Fareham train station. Dad told me he'd pay the taxi driver off, give him some money, and the guards were young ratings, on their first posting. Dad knew they'd keep quiet. He found me a job with some people he knew in Singapore and I left the country a month later. As far as Dad was concerned, that was it. He told me I was lucky. *We got away with it*, he said. That was the level he functioned at. We'd got away with it, but my life was ruined.'

'So where does Grant Hastings fit into all this?' I asked, although I thought I already knew.

She gave a disconsolate shrug. 'He was the taxi driver who picked me up at Fareham train station.'

Of course. It all fitted into place. 'And he's been blackmailing you ever since?'

She shook her head. 'Oh no. Only since he wanted to get his hands on the pavilion.'

'Wouldn't it help you now, to come clean?' I asked.

She shook her head. 'Cleanse my soul or whatever? How can I? It's not just about me, is it? People remember my Dad as a good man. He led the search parties, helped the police with their enquiries, all the time knowing exactly what had happened. And Hastings knew that. After Dad had his stroke, when I was going through his bank accounts, I saw he'd been regularly drawing out large sums of cash. Dad hadn't just paid Grant off the once, he'd paid him off several times. He probably funded his whole bloody property business.'

'And Robbie? Have you explained this all to him, convinced him to do this deal with Hastings?'

'You know Robbie, anything for the money.'

The nightclub had been running at a loss for years and it was only Kitty who insisted on keeping it going. Robbie's sick of being her whipping boy. I want us to spend more time in Lanzarote. I feel safe there. I don't have to pretend or hide.'

'And you've never thought Kitty had the right to know the truth?' I asked. 'The right to closure?'

'I've looked after her, haven't I? Years and years of looking after her. And it didn't matter in the end, did it? Whatever Robbie did would never match anything Jez could have done. The sun still shines out of his backside, thirty-three years later.'

I wanted to ask how she lived with herself, but no doubt she would have some clever answer. Lindy had worked her sob story out over the years. Her words hadn't conveyed any sense of guilt or remorse, almost as if her marriage to Robbie was enough to absolve her crime. Being the dutiful daughter-in-law had exonerated her.

'Are you going to tell her?' she asked, looking up.

Another wave crashed against the pier. Even Lindy reached for the handrail to steady herself on her precarious perch.

'It's not my responsibility to tell the truth,' I replied, although I think my answer was lost in the noise of the turbulence below. 'You have to live with your conscience. I don't.'

I didn't want to waste any more time. As I walked away I fleetingly wondered if I should stay in case she did anything stupid, but Lindy didn't look like a woman about to throw herself off the pier. She was too much of a coward.

I could picture the scene she had described on that night all those years ago. Jez, with his arrogant swagger, scared into panic mode at the thought of fatherhood. I could, at a stretch, sympathise with her predicament, pregnant and on her own. No wonder Jez's disappearance had remained such a mystery. The man who was supposed to be leading the search was the one person who wanted the whole affair covered up. How convenient Jez's body had never been found. If it had, a toxicological report would have made very interesting reading, not a magic mushroom in sight. A forensic examination might have picked up a scratched cheek, or bruising associated with a light push or a hard shove, whatever it had taken for Lindy to send Jez flying into the water.

Jez was no hero but he hadn't deserved any of this, and neither had Kitty. I doubted Lindy would make a confession, but there were two players in this grisly game. Grant Hastings was a cruel and calculating man who had taken advantage of her mistake. He was about to get his comeuppance.

Chapter Forty-Seven

I wasn't sure where the Hastings family lived but Dominic would know. It was a crazy idea, but perhaps like Lindy on that night thirty-three years ago, I was desperate. The pavilion was my baby.

'Dom, please pick up. It's really important.'

'Hey, what's up?'

Kind, amenable Dominic was back. Perhaps he felt he could be generous now, knowing that we weren't going to be seeing an awful lot of each other anymore.

'Where does Grant Hastings live?'

'Meadowsweet Manor, overlooking the creek. Why do you want to know?'

'I'm going to pay him a visit.'

'What now?'

'No time like the present.'

'I'm not sure that would be very wise. You want to tell me what this is all about?'

'Not really.' Dom would advise against any sort of confrontation. On the other hand, I could do with a witness. 'Are you doing anything right now?'

'Um no. I was just about to order a curry.'

'Hold off on the curry. I'm calling a taxi. I'll be with you in fifteen minutes.'

In the five-minute taxi ride from the caravan park to Meadowsweet Manor I gave Dominic a very condensed version of events. Naturally Dominic tried to talk me out of it. Naturally I ignored him.

He was clean shaven, courtesy of Beth.

'She has a very steady hand,' he informed me, then in the same breath, 'how's your friend, Hal?'

'I don't know. I haven't spoken to him. Hal and I were over

long ago, Dominic.'

'Yes, but he's much more your type, isn't he?'

'What's my type?'

'Well you know, theatrical.'

We pulled up at the entrance to a large sprawling house sat at the end of a curving gravel drive. Metal gates had been wedged open, as if guests were expected.

'That's very handy,' Dom said, 'saves us having to bypass the security system.'

A black Range Rover was parked on the drive outside a triple garage. I pressed the doorbell and heard the familiar unwelcoming bark of the Staffie. Heels clacked across a flagstone floor. Tina Hastings' face fell when she saw us.

'Oh. You're not the Galliards.'

'Sorry to disappoint you,' I said with a smile. 'Is Grant home?'

She turned to Dominic. 'Is Danni expecting you?'

'What is it, Mum?' I recognised Danni Hastings as she joined her mother at the door. She was a stunningly attractive young woman, with a neat, compact baby bump just visible beneath a flowing white cotton frock. Her luscious dark hair was scooped into a loose ponytail. She was one of those women who glowed in pregnancy, where I was quite sure if and whenever I became pregnant, I was going to waddle along like a beached whale from day one.

'Dom? What are you doing here?' To my dismay she looked quite pleased to see him. I didn't dare glance at his face in case the feeling was reciprocated.

'Actually,' I said, stepping forward, 'he's just here to accompany me.'

'Who are you?' Tina Hastings asked.

'My name is Tara Wakely. I have a business proposal to put to your husband.'

'In that case you should make an appointment to see him at his office first thing on Monday morning,' Tina replied.

'I think he might want to see me now,' I said. 'It's about Hookes Bay Pavilion.'

Danni sighed. 'You're not still banging on about that bloody pavilion are you, Dom?'

'This has got nothing to do with him, this is about me,' I snapped.

Tina Hastings hesitated. She obviously knew the importance of the pavilion. 'It's really not convenient,' she said. 'We're entertaining. Captain Seymour and his wife are already here, and we're expecting the Galliards at any moment.'

'Tim Seymour?' I asked. 'That's even better. I'm sure the chairman of the parish council would be very interested in my proposal too. Is Darius home?'

'He's skulking in his room,' Danni replied with a smirk at her mother. 'He's not allowed at the dinner table.'

'I'm not going anywhere,' I said, 'until I've seen Grant.'

'Fine,' Tina glared. 'Danni, take Dominic and his friend into the Orangery. I'm just going to check on the poussins.'

'What happened to your arm?' Danni asked as we followed her through a birch wood panelled hallway.

'Some friends of your dad's broke my collar bone,' Dominic replied. 'That's what happened to my arm.'

Danni winced. 'Does it hurt?'

'Of course it bloody hurts. What are you doing here anyway? I thought you were staying up at the mill until it's sold.'

'I was, but it wasn't really working out with Mark.'

Grant Hastings and his guests were reclining on oversized leather sofas in a large conservatory which ran the full width of the back of the house. Hastings was in casual chinos and a short-sleeved check shirt while Tim Seymour had opted for the nautical look with a navy polo shirt and white trousers. His wife could have been his clone, apart from the absence of a beard.

'What is this intrusion?' Hastings demanded, jumping to his feet. 'I thought you were the Galliards. Where's Tina?'

'She's checking the poussins,' I replied. 'Don't worry. We haven't abducted her.'

'Should I get you some drinks or something?' Danni asked. She fluttered her eyelashes at Dom, very long, pretty eyelashes.

'No, I'm fine thank you,' he said.

'I wouldn't mind a glass of water,' I told her, pleased that Dom seemed immune to his ex's charms. Did this woman really think she could worm her way back into his heart?

'Don't get them anything, Danni,' Grant growled. Mrs Seymour exchanged a nervous, questioning glance at her husband who shrugged and shook his head.

'I don't think we've met,' I said, in an attempt to put her at ease. 'My name is Tara Wakely.'

'But I thought you were called Alice?' Tim looked puzzled.

'I'm Gwen,' Mrs Seymour replied warily.

'This won't take five minutes,' I assured her. I smiled at Tim. 'It's quite convenient that you're here, Mr Seymour.'

Tim looked very uncomfortable. He glanced at Hastings. 'If you'd rather we just left you alone for a few minutes, Grant.'

'Oh no,' I said at once. 'Stay, please. Sorry, I'll get straight to the point.' I turned to Hastings. 'I've just had a little chat with Lindy Mayhew. Actually, it was a very long detailed chat, about events that happened in Hookes Bay thirty-three years ago.'

Hastings picked up a glass of what looked like whisky from a side table and took a quick swig. 'Oh?'

'Lindy Mayhew is a complete basket case,' Danni volunteered, hopping onto the arm of the sofa.

I liked Danni less by the minute. 'I agree Lindy has her issues,' I said, 'but she made a major misjudgement in her youth when something happened, which maybe she should have come clean about at the time, but she didn't. Everybody makes mistakes, but not everybody is still paying for them thirty-three years later. Isn't that right, Mr Hastings?'

'You're talking in riddles,' Hastings huffed.

'Okay, I'll make it clearer. Lindy told me a story about a taxi driver who received a large sum of money to keep quiet about something he had witnessed, not just once, but several times over.'

'You used to be a taxi driver didn't you, Dad?' Danni continued, unable to keep the excitement out of her voice.

'This is getting very interesting. Go on, Tara, tell us more.'

'Well, how much more I tell you, really depends on your father, and how much of it he would like revealed. Basically, Mr Hastings, I'm here to suggest that you might wish to rethink your plans for redeveloping Hookes Bay seafront.'

Tim Seymour cleared his throat. 'I'm sorry, Alice... Tara, or whoever you are, but I'm with Grant on this. You're not really talking a lot of sense. If this is about your plans for the pavilion then I thought we had reached an agreement that the existing community centre would be an adequate location for your art club following its refurbishment?'

I turned to Danni. 'Can you go and fetch Darius for me?'

She pouted. 'But I don't want to miss anything.'

'Then be quick.'

Gwen Seymour seized the opportunity to escape and dashed after Danni, mumbling something about helping Tina in the kitchen.

Once they had gone I turned back to Hastings. 'Do you want me to spell it out? Because I can. I think perverting the course of justice is a crime in itself, as is, extorting money with menaces. Lindy Mayhew's father paid you a lot of money over the years. He trusted you, and now you've threatened to expose her, and him, haven't you, in order to get your hands on the pavilion?'

'Lindy can't wait to be shot of that pavilion,' Hastings growled. 'You're barking up the wrong tree.'

'No, I'm not.' I replied. 'You don't care how many people you ruin do you? You could have gone to the police at any time with the information you had, and you didn't. You chose to keep it to yourself and to use it to your advantage. That's what Mr Hastings, does you see, Mr Seymour. Is that really the sort of person you want your parish council to be associated with? Someone totally dishonest, conniving and without a single scruple?'

'Well, I'm still in the dark, I'm afraid,' Tim said.

Grant Hastings' knuckles were white as he clutched his whisky glass. There was a commotion outside in the hallway. When Danni returned with her brother, she was accompanied by Kevin and Sue Galliard. Tina Hastings and Gwen Seymour were in hot pursuit.

'What's going on?' Tina demanded.

'The perfect audience,' I smiled. Dominic attempted to make himself as inconspicuous as possible on the corner sofa.

Darius' mouth dropped when he saw me. 'Oh, it's you.'

I smiled at the boy. 'Darius, how much did your father pay those friends of yours to crash their car into the amusement arcade the other week?'

A steady flush spread across his cheeks as he kept his eyes on the floor.

Hastings took another quick gulp of his whisky. 'Really, this is just ludicrous,' he growled. 'I didn't pay anybody. It's time you left, young lady. Flynn, you're welcome to join us for the evening if you want?'

'No, thank you,' Dominic said, struggling to rise from the squidgy sofa.

'Oh Dom, go on, stay,' Danni pouted, fluttering her eyelashes again.

'I take it you do know who this woman really is, don't you?' Hastings continued to address Dominic. 'She's a liar and a fraud, a fake, paid to play a part. She's deceived the entire population of Hookes Bay, the Council—'

'Yes, I do know exactly who she is, and also know that she has more integrity in her little finger than any member of this family has in their entire body,' Dominic replied.

Hastings was stone-faced. 'You're an ungrateful bastard, Flynn. Darius, head back to your room.'

'Darius?' I had pinned all my hopes on this boy. He couldn't let me down. 'About the joyriders?'

'Dad's right,' Darius mumbled, 'he didn't pay them.'

Grant let out a long sigh. He ruffled his son's hair and smirked at me. 'Satisfied?' He turned to the Galliards. 'Sue, Kevin, I apologise about this. Bonnie and Clyde are just leaving.'

'He set them up.'

My whole body sagged with relief.

'Speak up, Darius,' Danni said with a gloat. 'They can't all hear you.'

'He didn't pay them,' Darius repeated, staring straight at his father. 'He threatened to grass them to the police about their drug dealing if they didn't do what he asked.' The colour drained from Grant Hastings' face.

'Ah.' Tim Seymour let a long whistle of breath. 'Now I see.'

Chapter Forty-Eight

'I've told you before, your talents truly are wasted in Hookes Bay,' Dominic said as we squelched through the puddles in Meadowsweet Lane. The storm clouds had cleared and the moon was shining through the branches of the overhanging trees.

'No, I think Hookes Bay is the perfect showcase for my talents,' I replied.

'How did you know about the joyriders?'

'I didn't. It was a guess.'

'So, what happens now?' he asked.

'I call a taxi to take us home?'

'No, I meant what happens now about the pavilion? We both heard Hastings agree to withdraw from negotiations. He's certainly lost his credibility with the parish council. Are you going to go back to your friend, Hal, to make Robbie another offer?'

'I don't know. That depends on Robbie and Lindy really. I thought for one awful moment I was going to have to spell it all out, about Jez. Thank goodness Hastings didn't let me get that far.'

'No. That wouldn't have been ideal,' Dominic agreed. 'You said you believed her? It was an accident?'

I nodded. 'Yes. Lindy's certainly volatile but I highly doubt it was premeditated murder. If she'd have gone straight to the police, confessed, told Kitty back then, I think she would have been forgiven. It was the cover-up that was wrong, her father and Grant, what they did.'

'I suppose her dad just thought he was making it better.'

'But he made it worse. The thing is, Dom, there was no love lost between Jez Keaton and Lindy's father. I've been thinking, what if he did find Jez's body? Lindy said her dad went off in his car and was gone for a couple of hours. In theory, Jez's body should have washed up somewhere eventually. Would spring tides really have made that much difference? The Commander had the means, the motive and plenty of opportunity to dispose of a body. '

'Don't be ridiculous.'

'Lindy's dad had access to all those chemicals at the depot. Tom Whybrow told me those bunkers were subsequently filled in with thousands of tonnes of concrete. The perfect hiding place. As long as Jez's body was never found, nobody could ever question the accident theory. It would have been very hard to prove Lindy's guilt, even if she had been caught. Even worse, what if Jez wasn't even dead? It hardly bears thinking about but just suppose Lindy's dad found him on the beach, or whatever, still alive and finished him off? Jez had just got his precious daughter pregnant, the family name would be in disgrace. If this guy was as honourable as everybody says he was, surely he would have urged Lindy to confess and not colluded in a cover up?'

'You have absolutely no evidence for any of this.'

'It would explain why he wanted the body hidden, and why he sent Lindy off to Singapore straight afterwards. He wanted her right out of the way. She's an intelligent woman. I bet the idea that her father was implicated in some way occurred to her at some point. It's no wonder she's drugged up to the eyeballs all the time. I bet Hastings sussed it out too. Why else did he keep on blackmailing the Commander? Seriously I never thought I'd say it, but I hope Jez did drown, and instantly.'

Dominic sighed. 'Have you ever thought about writing fiction?'

I gave him a playful punch.

'Ow!'

'Don't whinge. That was your good arm.'

'Are you going to go to the police with your theories?' he asked.

I shrugged. 'I can't see the point in saying anything now.

Poor Jez. I suppose if we save the pavilion, it's some kind of justice for him, and for Kitty.'

'You've grown very attached to young Jez, haven't you?' Dominic said.

'Yes,' I admitted. 'I have. I know it sounds daft but I can't help but wish we were related.'

'Who knows? Maybe Kitty did have some ulterior motive for bringing you to Hookes Bay?'

I shook my head. 'I don't think so. The woman Jez met in London was a femme fatale record producer, not a teenage groupie.'

'Well, what was that dreadful song? *Come backstage baby*? Jez was living the rock star lifestyle wasn't he? A girl at every gig or whatever. The record producer might well have been the woman who was going to change his life, but it didn't mean she had him on a leash, did it?'

'I think she probably did by all accounts. Anyway, it's not something I'm ever going to be able to prove now, is it?'

Dominic came to a halt beside a gap in the hedgerow. Through the moonlight I could see a stile. 'If we cut across this field we can be at the caravan park in five minutes,' he said. He sounded very mellow again. I didn't want to jump to the wrong conclusion.

'I still need a cab to get back into town,' I pointed out.

'Or you could just stay the night and keep me company.'

Was he teasing me? I stared at him through the darkness. 'Do you want me to sing you to sleep again?' I asked. If I kept the conversation flippant, I couldn't get hurt by any misinterpretations.

His expression gave nothing away. 'Not if the only song you can sing is about baking cornbread.'

'I do know other stuff. I have songs for nearly every occasion.'

'Oh yeh? What occasion is this then?' He was very close to me. I couldn't smell any alcohol on his breath. My back was against the stile. His hand was on the back of my neck, his fingers slipping under the collar of my T-shirt, sending electric currents across my skin. Not teasing, but torturing me…

'What sort of situation are we in here, Tara?' He was deadly serious. He really *was* going to kiss me. 'I've wasted a lot of time denying how I feel about you.' His voice was raw with emotion. 'Your friend Hal, when he came to Hookes Bay, most of the time he was talking a load of rubbish, but something he said made sense. He was looking for this woman. He described her to me and he said, if I ever met anybody like her, I should hold onto her, and not let her go, not to mess it all up like he did. Well, you see, I have met someone just like her, although she's even more talented and beautiful, intelligent and witty, compassionate, courageous and loyal than he described, and I nearly did let her go. I'm only hoping she forgives me.'

And then he kissed me. Greedily, passionately, urgently, and totally sober, Dominic Flynn kissed me.

Since that first day at the pavilion, when I'd been captivated by those blue eyes and fine chiselled features, enchanted by that hypnotic Irish voice, and enthralled by his passion and knowledge, Dominic had stolen my heart. I felt I already knew him intimately. I'd seen him at his most vulnerable, I'd nursed him better and I'd long fantasised about making love to him. I'd pictured his long artistic fingers running through my hair – in my make-believe world I had long hair again. I'd imagined his tongue deliciously tantalising my body, caressing me, sending ripples of excitement into my very core. I'd pictured us together, his toned muscular chest rhythmically moving above me, endearments whispered in my ear, our bodies together, united.

I'd waited a long time. It wasn't going to happen quite like it happened in my dreams, but I was determined to make it just as enjoyable. I wanted to show him what he'd been missing, but I had to be realistic. He had a broken collar bone. He was basically incapacitated. He could barely take off his own clothes, let alone undress me, especially as I was wearing Lycra sportswear.

His eyes gleamed with desire in the darkness of the caravan bedroom as I squirmed out of my sports bra as seductively as I could.

'I'm not quite sure how we're going to manage the next bit,' he said when we were finally both naked on his bed. 'It might be a bit awkward.'

'Oh, I don't think so,' I murmured. 'Improvisation has always been one of my specialities.'

I trusted my instincts. There was nothing awkward about making love to Dominic. Despite his broken collar bone, he didn't hold back. He was a generous lover, tender and passionate. And although I caught the occasional wince, or a groan more from pain than ecstasy, he seemed determined to give as much pleasure as he took. I wanted to offer myself to him completely, lose myself, holding onto every tumultuous tremor and savouring every delicious aftershock. When our bodies were exhausted, we lay together, hearts racing, limbs entwined, bathed in a sticky, sweaty afterglow.

'We must do that again sometime soon, *Nurse Alice*,' he whispered.

'Are you sure it didn't hurt?'

'It actually hurt my shoulder like hell, but the rest of me feels an awful lot better.'

I knew then, even if I hadn't known it before, that I loved him. Totally, completely, irrevocably. And I had a sneaking suspicion, following his noble, self-sacrificing demonstration of how to keep a girl happy, that it was finally time to stop ripping up daisy petals. He loved me too.

Chapter Forty-Nine

Kitty

Through half-closed eyelids Kitty watched Lindy take a seat by the bed.

'Changing of the guard,' Robbie announced. He must have been sat there for hours. 'I'll go and stretch my legs for a bit.'

'Don't go, Rob.' There was something different about Lindy. She had some colour in her cheeks for once. On the other hand, Robbie looked worn out. 'There's something I need to tell you.' Lindy's hand closed over hers. 'Kitty, I've got a bit of a confession to make.'

Kitty shook her head, eeking out enough strength to squeeze Lindy's fingers. 'No, Lindy,' her voice was little more than a croak. 'No confessions. Not now. No need.'

'But Mum, I want you to know—'

'No.' Kitty clasped those fingers tighter. 'There's nothing I need to know now.'

It had been such a comfort to see Derek Woodford. He'd always been a quiet boy, a buffer to Jez's exuberance. He'd stayed with her for half an hour, talking about that last day, that last day with Jez.

They'd talked about Lindy too. How the sophisticated woman who had come back from Singapore bore no resemblance to the bubbly young girl who'd hung around Balmoral during that long hot summer, following Jez around like a devoted puppy. Kitty could picture her now in those skimpy denim shorts and a cheesecloth blouse, pencil clutched between her teeth, humming tunes and scribbling away in Jez's notebooks. There wasn't even a trace of the vivacious, confident university student who'd occasionally called in at weekends, captivating Jez with her intellectual conversations, text books in her bags.

Kitty and Robbie had done their best to bring that girl back, but it had never happened. The scars had been too deep. Lindy had looked after Kitty with the same dispassionate sense of duty she had shown towards her father. Without a doubt she loved Robbie. Who wouldn't love a man who was prepared to put up with all those faults for so long?

'Mum, about the pavilion.'

Kitty knew all about the pavilion. And Hastings. She'd worked it out.

'We're not going to do a deal with Coastline,' Lindy announced. 'We've changed our mind.'

Kitty knew only too well it was very easy to promise the world to someone on their deathbed.

'We're not going to let anybody knock it down,' Lindy continued. 'It's going to be safe, isn't it Robbie?'

Robbie's voice was choked. He seemed just as surprised as Kitty by the news.

'Lindy's right, Kit,' he said after what seemed like an eternity. 'We'll keep hold of it. We'll resurrect it for you.'

Resurrect. That was a big word for Robbie. Talking was such an effort. 'Do you really mean that?' Kitty asked.

Lindy clutched her hand. 'Yes, we do. We have to do it, I realise that now. We made a huge mistake, I'm sorry. I think we both just got carried away.'

They'd had a change of heart. Serendipity did exist after all. Beauty, Art and Culture would return to Hookes Bay. What had Derek called it? Karma. It was like some great weight had lifted from her body. *Another great weight*. Lindy withdrew her hand and put her face close to Kitty's.

'I'm so sorry,' she whispered as she kissed Kitty's cheek, 'so very sorry.'

'It happens,' Kitty murmured, half to herself, half to Lindy. 'Sometimes these things just happen. No-one's fault. No-one to blame.'

'I'll phone Grant,' Robbie said, with a decisive grunt, 'tell him Hookes Bay Pavilion is not for sale, and then we'll talk to Alice. Or whoever she really is. And that man, Flynn, about what we can do about a proper restoration.'

'Tara,' Kitty croaked. *Her name is Tara.*

She could think of the girl as Tara now. She had done her job well, exceeded. Give her an Oscar, or a Bafta, a Tony, an *Evening Standard* Theatre Award.

Tara Wakely. You hear a name like that and you don't forget it.

The first letter had arrived just weeks after Jez had disappeared. Jez didn't get much post. A handwritten letter, post-marked London, delivered direct to the club. No surname: *JEZ, Urban Rebels, Hookes Bay Pavilion, Hookes Bay, Hampshire.*

Kitty wasn't in the habit of opening Jez's post, at least not when he'd been alive but now there was all sorts of unpleasant tasks Robbie said she had to do. Thank goodness Robbie had never seen the letter from Nicki Wakely.

Dear Jez

I don't know if you remember me but my name is Nicki and we met after the gig at The Edmonton Roundhouse...

Kitty had read no more and consigned the letter straight to the bin. Two further letters had arrived over the next couple of months, each bearing the same childlike handwriting. Kitty had destroyed those without even opening the envelopes. The fourth letter had arrived some seven months after Jez's disappearance, a bulkier brown envelope Kitty just about managed to snatch from Robbie's grasp.

This time the girl had sent photographs. A baby with a snub nose and a shock of dark hair. She could have belonged to anyone.

I have called the baby Tara, Nicki Wakely wrote.

Kitty had torn the photographs into two and sent the girl a cheque for £500, a lot of money in those days. It had done the trick. Nicki Wakely hadn't written again and Kitty had cast all thoughts of baby Tara aside until thirty-three years later she had seen the name splashed across the front page of the *Let's Chat* magazine Penny had left on the bedside table.

Penny was subsequently dispatched on an erroneous trip to the chemist, with Callum instructed to conduct some covert research on the internet. Within twenty minutes he had told her all she needed to know.

Redemption. She had done what she could.

Kitty had never been religious. Funny how it always came to you at the end. Had she bought her place in heaven? Not that she could go just yet. First she had to speak to Cyril.

Chapter Fifty

Tara

We stand together in a huddle on the end of Hookes Bay pier. It's a very simple casket. Kitty would have chosen something far more ornate.

'Well, here goes,' Robbie says. Lindy grimaces at his choice of words.

In the end it was all over very quickly. Robbie phoned on the Sunday to say Kitty had taken a turn for the worse. He and Lindy were staying by her bedside. He told me that they'd decided not to sell the pavilion, but he said it didn't matter anyway, as Grant Hastings had already contacted him and announced Coastline were pulling out of the deal.

'Who'd have thought?' he said. 'Don't know what brought that on. Perhaps he just got fed up of hanging around.'

'Perhaps he did,' I agreed.

It was all irrelevant anyway. As I'd snuggled up beside Dominic on Friday night, luxuriating in post-coital bliss, he'd told me he'd received an email from Historic England.

'I told you I was having computer problems,' he said. 'I only found the message late this afternoon when Hobo took me down to the yard.'

No wonder he'd been in such a good mood. The Secretary of State had approved his application for listed building status. My Theatre of Dreams was saved, not just once, but three times over.

'Why didn't you tell me earlier?' I cried.

'What? And spoil your fun with Hastings?'

On Monday afternoon Dominic had accompanied me to the hospice and we had sat beside Kitty's bed and told her about all our plans for the pavilion. Her eyelids had barely flickered opened, but her grasp around my hand tightened every now and again, as if she understood, and approved of our plans.

'Jez would be so proud,' she whispered as I said my last goodbye, brushing my lips across her cheek with a false promise of seeing her again very soon. 'So proud of you, Tara, dear, so proud.'

Half of Hookes Bay turned out for Kitty's formal cremation, with one or two notable exceptions. Kitty had made no specific requests regarding the ceremony, her wild scheme for saving the pavilion supplanting all thoughts of funeral planning. Robbie inherited the pavilion, as expected, but in addition to 35 Crabhook Lane and all its contents, Kitty left me a vial of blood in her will, which seemed quite bizarre until Cyril explained about Kitty's request for a DNA test.

'I've had plenty of deathbed conversations in my time,' he said, 'but the one I had with Kitty takes the biscuit. If it's positive she says you're to contact Frankie Jones, the old TV comic. Remember him? Apparently he might be your grandfather.'

So Jez Keaton really had met my mother after his gig at the Roundhouse. How Kitty knew, I've no idea. In truth, I'd felt part of Kitty's family since I first set eyes on Hookes Bay Pavilion. Although I'm grateful for the opportunity to confirm the connection, I'm definitely not going to contact Frankie Jones. Aaron couldn't stop laughing when I told him. 'I always knew you were a natural born comedian,' he said.

With Historic England on board, Dominic is staying on in Hookes Bay. The Modernist Preservation Trust have agreed to part fund the restoration work and are happy with Dominic's self-appointed role of project manager. Robbie has already said he wants to take a backseat. He and Lindy are selling their house in Broken Lane and moving to the Canaries full time. Dominic has suggested applying for additional funding from the National Lottery and the Arts Council, as well as recruiting private stakeholders. Hal Claydon has volunteered, although I haven't yet replied to his request to host the premiere of *Battlestar the Musical*. The pavilion won't be ready to put on a full-scale West End production for some time.

As Robbie lifts the lid on the urn, I reach for Dominic's hand. Fate in the guise of Kitty Keaton brought us together and saving the pavilion saved us, although I am going to have to teach him to dance. Dominic kept his promise and attended Tom Whybrow's Golden Wedding party. If Tom thought he had two left feet, then Dominic has three. Still, I can work on that.

In the end there was no big Tara Wakely reveal. I was out of disgrace, and doing good never made as many headlines as being bad. As the truth filtered through to the residents of Hookes Bay, it was more a question of *Tara who?* than anything else. The Principal of St Stephen's is over the moon at the prospect of a genuine West End star coaching his pupils, so are Mari's parents. As for the MPT, all Sam MacDonald had to say on the matter was, 'Oh, so you have found a celebrity patron, well done you.'

'Get on with it, Robbie,' John Freeborn shouts. He's here under sufferance. 'Let the old witch loose.'

I could never have coped over the last few weeks without Mari. She cancelled her flotilla holiday, completely took over the summer showcase and has become a driving force in the arts hub campaign. The Hookes Bay Academy of Music and Dance will remain in the community centre until the pavilion is fully restored. The community centre will be refurbished at Coastline Developments' expense. Bunny Mitchell is holding Grant Hastings to his promise.

'Oh yes,' she told me, 'I'm having a new office and a side extension. It's the very least that man Hastings can do, after all the mischief he's caused.'

I think mischief is putting it very mildly. The redevelopment of the Carlisle Hotel site will still go ahead, but on a reduced scale with fewer sea views and no direct waterfront access, and we're definitely going to demolish the pier. Hookes Bay will look very different this time next year.

'Goodbye Kit,' Robbie murmurs. I see him wipe a tear from his eye. He shakes the urn and the ashes stream into the air, catching on a sudden gust of wind so that instead of dropping into the sea they fly back into our faces. Lindy flaps her arms wildly, while Maureen Batty claps her hands and shrieks with glee. Cyril has to restrain her. Dominic takes an involuntary step back, determined to avoid contamination, while I don't mind at all if some of Kitty's magic lands on me.

Robbie hands the urn over to Derek Woodford. 'Here,' he says, 'you do it. You'll be better at this than me.'

Derek crouches down and tips the remaining ashes directly into the water. 'We're not just here today to say goodbye to Kitty,' he announces. 'This ceremony is for Jez too. May the Hookes Bay Community Arts Hub be a fitting tribute to you both. Goodnight mate, and rest in peace, Kitty, dear.'

'There's no chance of that,' Robbie mutters under his breath. 'If we don't get this bloody restoration job just right, she'll be back to haunt us all.'

Personally I think she'll be back to haunt us all whatever. Dominic agrees. He is designing a memorial plaque for the grand foyer, dedicated to the entire Keaton family; to Jez, to Lionel and to Kitty. Hopefully it will go some way to appeasing her.

'Do you want to skip the sandwiches at the Sir Winnie?' Dominic whispers as we join the procession leaving the pier. His lips brush against my ear.

'What's the alternative?' I ask.

He hands me a piece of paper from his pocket. 'The Quaker chapel has just come on the market, complete with planning permission for conversion into a residential dwelling. Oh, and a third of an acre garden. We can view it this afternoon. It will be perfect for us.'

I glance at the estate agent flyer and stare at him, not quite daring to believe what he's just said. *Perfect for us.*

There's a glint in his eye. 'Or we could just go back to your bungalow and have lots of sex,' he says.

Since he received the medical all-clear Dominic has been having an awful lot of sex. 'I like that idea,' I say. 'But I think we should see the chapel first.'

'I thought you might say that,' he grins.

'Do you think Kitty will mind if I sell the bungalow?' I

whisper.

'You saved her theatre,' he replies. 'The bungalow is her way of saying thank-you. I don't honestly think she'll care.'

Kitty Keaton was a remarkable woman. It was a privilege to have known her, even for such a short time. She gave me back my confidence and self-respect. I should be the one thanking her.

I glance over my shoulder as we walk along the prom. The atrium sparkles in the sunlight, as it will continue to sparkle for many years to come thanks to Dominic's dedication and some devious Keaton ingenuity. A reflection of a passing cloud momentarily blots the glare, mimicking Cyril's wink. Dominic's right. I don't think she'll mind at all.

THE END

Fantastic Books
Great Authors

CROOKED CAT

Meet our authors and discover
our exciting range:

- Gripping Thrillers
- Cosy Mysteries
- Romantic Chick-Lit
- Fascinating Historicals
- Exciting Fantasy
- Young Adult and Children's Adventures
- Non-Fiction

Visit us at:
www.crookedcatbooks.com

Join us on facebook:
www.facebook.com/crookedcatbooks

Printed in Great Britain
by Amazon